TREASURE OF THE CLAN

The Book of Jasher Part 3

BILL W. SANFORD

ISBN: 1973742977
ISBN 13: 9781973742975
Library of Congress Control Number: 2017911388
CreateSpace Independent Publishing Platform
North Charleston, South Carolina

TABLE OF CONTENTS

For Debra ... always there

Prologue, Somewhere Over Crete, 2025

Franklin Pierce, Senior Reporter for Thomas-Reuters News Agency, was busy taking notes aboard an Airbus A320 flying from Greece. Before leaving London, his editor-in-chief had approached him and had delicately requested he not cover the unfolding story on Cyprus. Only in the last few days had the media become aware that Benjamin Jasher had gone to ground there and that the Cyprus government had proved to be slow to comply with extradition requests. In light of so much international interest in the destruction in Austin and the subsequent abduction of the two American citizens by an Israeli antiquities dealer, it was the first time in his memory that his editor had made such a request. Pierce did not mention the urgency of his last discussion with Jasher that had led to the conference they were all about to attend. Not knowing Jasher the way he had, Franklin doubted his chief would have understood.

He recalled that Jasher's voice was tense with anxiety as he announced, "Look, Franklin, the time has come to put into motion our plan to reveal the discovery and translation of my records. The public has a right to know the truth before it is too late to act."

"I see," replied Pierce. His tone was tentative, yet probing. "So that business a week ago in Austin was intended to accomplish what purpose?"

"Franklin, the impromptu press release I had planned in Austin would have served our purposes. Unfortunately, our opposition in high places had acquired more information over the contents than I had expected, thus he attempted to stop the release. The result was the devastation that followed."

"Was the document or its contents damaged in any way during the escape?"

"Fortunately, no."

"And the translation you have mentioned, where were you in that process when you had to flee the United States?"

"There were still a few matters left to complete on the first half of the manuscript, but essentially it was far enough along to corroborate the translation and reveal the message it contained."

"What did you hope to gain by releasing it then instead of now? As you have pointed out, the manuscript had not been ready for publication."

"I used the proposed announcement in Austin as a gambit to see if anyone was listening and to what extent they suspected about our project. Fortunately, we were ready and survived the attack. Those who opposed us will know that we have not given up; we have merely postponed the inevitable."

The newsman was surprised to hear the previously planned press conference was little more than a ruse to measure the resolve of the opposition. Jasher was playing a dangerous game.

"And now, how far along are you in the translation?"

"We have nearly a full manuscript of the entire abridgment translated and we are close enough to publication to deliver a press statement."

A pause was evident at the other end of the phone. He needed more, of course; ever insistent, the true newsman. "And now, you are prepared to move forward regardless of the danger?"

"Franklin, I have every reason to believe that it is now or never."

"Can you be more specific?"

"The forces that Walker Cain represents are formidable and he is dangerously near to setting events in motion that will change the history of our planet forever. If the future is any reflection of the past, and I believe it is, there is likely to be destruction and death the likes of which our world has not known for millennia."

"Benjamin, I am going out on a limb for you on this because, since I have known you, you have never been wrong, but I assure you that if you are wrong on this one, the press will crucify you and there will be no way that I can protect your reputation nor that of Professors Bedford and Levinson."

"Franklin, the only serious regret at this point is if I am blocked from revealing what has been translated."

"Your records will have to indict Walker Cain conclusively for master-minding a world movement to take complete control." It was a warning as a friend.

"They will do that and much more, and for that reason I know he will make another attempt to move on us as he did in Austin."

"What do you mean?"

"He will be desperate to stop the announcement and publication of the records because he is fearful that the truth will expose him for what he is and cause him to lose the credibility he has worked so hard to establish."

On the other end of the line, Pierce was carefully ripping up a page from a notepad. It seemed oddly eccentric, but a needed distraction when he was nervous or anxious. "Surely, he has people who could spin this press release in his favor. Violence to you and your cohorts would seem an unnecessary risk."

"What we have to reveal is so damning he will consider any consequences unacceptable and he will not permit any more delays to his timetable. This fear will embolden him to take desperate steps to prevent us from uncovering his true identity."

"Just who is he, anyway?" Finally, the question he had always intended to ask.

A pause. Shaking his head in frustration, Jasher said, "I prefer to announce that at the press conference here on Cyprus." Jasher hoped that what he had already said was enough to solicit the support and interest of the press, but these matters had to be settled in their proper order.

Pierce, the newsman, thought it over while he continued stripping the notepad. "All right, fair enough," replied Franklin. It was obvious he was disappointed and concerned that he was putting his own reputation on the line. However, he did venture a follow up-question. "What desperate steps is he likely to take?"

"He intends to prevent the press release from happening. If he can't do that, he will destroy us and anyone remotely connected with our efforts to go public with our discoveries."

"Not being too melodramatic are you, Benjamin?" he replied reproachfully with a light banter to his voice. He had never heard Jasher express himself in that way. Usually the man was quietly confident in all he did.

"Just keep your eyes open, Franklin. We need to have this press conference much sooner than later, possibly tomorrow afternoon?"

"Give me until the following day. Otherwise, I can't guarantee the full coverage you will want." Looking down, he noticed the page was nearly used up, but then so was the interview.

Jasher was disappointed, but replied, "Agreed. Get back to me when you have it set up. I owe you a big one for this, Franklin."

"Just make sure you have all your facts together, old boy." He then rang off. He closed the pad and tossed it to one side. Now thoughtful, he began to phone his colleagues.

And that had been the last word before Pierce had agreed to schedule the conference. It wasn't so much what was said, but the intensity of Jasher's voice that had hooked him. The newsman knew he was sticking his neck way out on this one, but his instincts told him that he had the biggest story of his life and to pass on it was simply beyond what he was willing to do. When he had insisted on pursuing the abduction angle, his chief had agreed reluctantly, but it was obvious he was unhappy with the decision to follow up on the story. There was a hesitance in his voice that had told him there was something deeper that his chief was not revealing. Glancing out the window of the plane, he decided it was probably nothing. After a moment, Pierce shrugged and let it go.

Across the aisles in front and behind of him sat his colleagues from all points of Europe and North America. Jennifer Davis was beside him, and glancing around the plane, she commented, "Looks like we have a full house today, Franklin. Any chance I can get more information on this Jasher fellow before our landing?"

Franklin had always liked Jennie. She was perceptive as well as dogged in her search for the truth. Actually, thought Pierce, she was old school smart and when she wrote something, it was damn good reading. He smiled and teased her a bit.

"Jennie Girl, you are about to meet the one man that knows absolutely something about everything. His memory is photographic as though he had lived as a personal witness through history." Nodding his head enthusiastically, he said, "He has helped me on numerous occasions to get at the source of many international and political issues. Benjamin Jasher is Mr. History."

Jennifer's half-smile and set jaw told Pierce she was about to become stubborn. "According to my sources, he is a fugitive criminal wanted by several countries, including the United States, for breaking international laws. I hear he was known to have made quite a mess in Austin a few weeks back. He and his private army stormed thorough Austin, abducted two university professors and he is now holding them as hostages on Cyprus. Franklin, darling, those are the facts."

Pierce had to concede her points. "Yes, he has stirred up quite a controversy, but according to Jasher, the two professors came along willingly. Also, he declares to have uncovered something historically unique that will shed light on international politics for the past two hundred years, or so he maintains."

"Do you believe him?"

Franklin thought long and hard on that. Finally, he responded, "Yes, I do. He knows things that no one should know, and every time he points me in a direction, everything he says is verifiable. I am a persistent man, but I freely admit that at times I have hit a wall. Most people just don't know where to look, but he does."

"Do tell, Franklin dear," she teased. Jennie, too, was persistent. She just went about it in a different way.

Pierce leaned back in his seat and reflected a moment then finally commented, "A few years ago, I was at a Greenpeace Conference in Durban, South Africa, and I ran into him there at one of the symposiums on global warming. One thing led to the next as it usually does at such gatherings and we found a semi-quiet corner to talk history. I told him of a piece I was writing regarding an unpublished manuscript that had led Eric Blair, aka George Orwell, to write his novel *1984*. Presumably, according to Orwell, he never had that manuscript published because he was warned explicitly not to pursue it. Apparently, the concepts and ideas expressed in this prequel manuscript were not for publication, but for his private edification. Though my original source had assured me that it existed, I was having trouble locating it. Moreover, I admitted to Jasher that I was having difficulty with the background to this heretofore unknown work of non-fiction and what it may have contained and who may have given Orwell the ideas. Jasher nodded his head in sympathy then declared quite boldly, "It was Edward House."

"Who?" Her eyes sickled upwards in honest confusion.

Franklin chuckled and replied, "That was my response as well. According to Jasher, House was on the personal staff of President Woodrow Wilson and wrote all of the international policy papers for him, including many domestic ones. He gave Wilson the needed impetus to be the leading figure for the League of Nations as well as many internationally progressive concepts that we still have today. House was active politically behind the scenes until his death in 1937, but apparently sometime in the early 1930s, he met with Orwell and over a period of years a friendship of sorts developed between the two men. During that time House disclosed bits and pieces of things that only he would know about international geopolitics."

"Surely this had to be a little more than idle talk between two gentlemen drinking brandy and sitting around a fire at the Savile Club."

"Actually, it was. Just before his death, House presented Orwell with a hand written manuscript that exposed and described the workings of an international brotherhood or society of which he had been a part. He told Orwell that if he ever disclosed the specifics of this manuscript, Orwell's life would be in danger. Nevertheless, House encouraged him to write a purely fictional book on the workings and influence of this society with an allegorical slant. Apparently, Orwell took his warning to heart, as clearly manifested in his novels, *Animal Farm* and *1984*. The two of which, according to Jasher, were allegorical versions of this manuscript."

Jenny was both amazed and slightly incredulous of the story. "And this fellow Jasher told you all this? Clearly, he is far too young to have known either House or Orwell, so he is getting the details second-hand. Might his information be more opinion than fact?"

"At first, I, too felt the same way, but when pressed he told me exactly where to find the manuscript." Pierce became quiet, almost reluctant to proceed.

Jenny persisted, "Ok, so you found it?"

Even after over ten years, he was still amazed at what had followed after the conference. He continued, "I was skeptical, of course. Who wouldn't be? But, I followed Jasher's directions and found the manuscript in an old book store in south Liverpool and guess whose name was on the front cover? It said: "Written by Edward House." Franklin paused to recollect the conversation then proceeded. "A few months later, during a layover at Heathrow Airport, I ran into Jasher again and he asked me whether I had found House's manuscript. I hesitated somewhat and said that I had; then a peculiar look came over his face and he asked me whether I had followed up or not on my story. I said I was still working on it, but being curious I asked him how he had known where the manuscript was located. He responded by saying that history was all around us, we just needed the right person to point us in the right direction. And now, I suppose when I run into a wall, he continues to be my guide."

"Did you ever finish the story about Orwell?"

Franklin glanced out the window for a moment, almost ashamed to remember. *Odd to behave that way*, he thought. Then, he smiled ruefully and admitted, "No. And it wasn't like me to do that, but something about the warning House gave to Orwell bothered me just enough to lay the manuscript aside until there was a better time to reveal it. During that chance meeting at Heathrow, Jasher didn't seem surprised that I had not yet written the story. He even commented, *'There are some things about history that can bite.'* He warned me that I should be careful when getting too close. Perhaps after our conference today I will pick up the story again and finish it this time."

Franklin turned to a stewardess and ordered a gin and tonic. Out of the corner of his eye he spied a fast-moving object that appeared to be in the shape of a projectile tracking the plane. Suddenly the missile seemed to receive a go-ahead signal and vaulted forward, slamming into the fuselage. The explosion over the Mediterranean could be seen five miles away from the coast of Crete.

THE TRANSLATION, CYPRUS, 2025

Jasher silently walked through the downstairs hallway into the study. He was feeling tired, but fulfilled as another day had come to an end. The two professors, Bedford and Levinson, were already there poring over the latest translation pertaining to Abraham. Both were deep in conversation, but paused as Jasher entered.

Levinson's expression, now quizzical, reflected his recent discussion with Bedford. He asked, "Jasher, we are perplexed over the phrase, *oath and covenant,* as it appears in the translated manuscript. Obviously, we know in general terms the dictionary definition of the two words, but used together they seem to imply a process or ritual. And if so, how do they apply to the involvement of the Brotherhood? The records make mention of how the Clan extended such rites to its followers."

It was a moment to teach, but an explanation of this topic he knew would lead to more questions. "Gentlemen, the first thing you should understand about the Brotherhood, as they call it, is that this society is an aberration and its precepts are contrary to eternal truths. And, according to the translation of the words of Abraham, the precepts of this society should never exist as they are an offense to all things holy."

Isaac pointed out, "According to my studies of ancient Hebrew texts, the oaths and covenants that God taught to Abraham then later to Moses were considered sacred and carried an eternal bond and everlasting significance.

How could a creature such as Cain offer anything of that nature to his followers?"

"In reality, he can't." This, too, had always bothered Jasher, that men could fall for such blatant lies. "The oath and covenant process that Cain has extended to the members of his Brotherhood signify their allegiance to a false being who has no power to give any legitimate validity to their oaths nor is he in any position to bind any covenant, no matter how much they honor him. These rituals they administer are as false as their cause."

Professor Bedford interjected a personal observation. "In short, what Cain has been offering is a lie."

"Precisely. He traffics in control over the agency of man and wraps his justification for this action up in a false flag of authority while his members call themselves the Brotherhood or Clan of the Scar. According to Cain, his cause is just and he has created his society to relieve mankind of a responsibility we have never been able to fully appreciate or use properly."

Levinson commented, "It almost sounds like he is stepping in to protect us from ourselves."

"As he sees it, he is doing us a favor." Shaking his head in disgust, he added, "It is a pity that so many kingdoms have been set up over a foundation of such lies."

Isaac said, "Speaking of which, our translation indicates the later influence of this Brotherhood upon many kingdoms and empires, notably the Byzantine, the Frankish Empire under Charlemagne and, of course The Ottoman Empire of the middle ages. From our known history of these empires, it would appear that Cain was not always successful at maintaining them. Does this indicate he had a chink in his armor somewhere?"

"Not really. It just means that our written and accepted historical accounts of those periods do not represent the entire truth. Remember that Cain is as committed to have his version of history recorded as I am to have a true and accurate record of his influence."

"But, invariably there was not only an actual decline, but a disappearance of his sphere of influence."

"Those empires only appear to have experienced a period of decline and defeat, when in reality it was just Cain's way of moving on and setting up a new kingdom over the ashes of the old ones. The power and control of emperors and kings rose and fell, but the man behind each simply moved on or formed alliances and consolidated his spheres of influence."

Bedford, the historian, was still puzzled. He pondered over the power of this society and quietly asked, "Jasher, you have alluded many times to the influence of this society on history, but how far-reaching is this brotherhood upon our lives today?"

Jasher paused for a moment, closing his eyes as though trying to remember an experience from which he could draw a conclusive answer. Finally, he stated, "It has been my observation that Cain has used his society to sift through government at all levels, usually from the top down, for sincere, public-driven reform. Under a cloak of well-meaning, concerned intervention, he has subverted the original intent by placing these same laws in lock-step with the overall agenda of the Brotherhood."

Being with Jasher these past few weeks had given Isaac a deeper sense of history. He could almost hear the hoof beats of time gaining on them all. "How is this even possible?" he asked. "I mean, presumably there must be more transparency today than has ever existed before, yet we know little or nothing of this man's influence."

"The dominance of this society over the social legislation of laws has been slow, but effective so as not to alert the general public of the loss of personal control over their lives. Remember, Cain is long-lived and can afford to be patient. He has not made the mistakes of other powerful men who had to move in haste to carry out their changes."

Bedford exclaimed, "Jasher, you are describing a society that is not only just secretive, it is invisible."

"Gentlemen, it is the exact opposite of public and its influence has been insinuated at all levels of government down through history up until the current era."

Levinson brooded, his brow furrowed. "You have mentioned and we have translated the records which imply that Cain and his Brotherhood have occasionally either been thwarted or were forced to halt their progress. Has he ever had to actually disband his society entirely?"

"Aside from the era of Great Flood, the answer is "no." Professors, this society has always existed, though admittedly down through the centuries it may have gone underground for a short period of time, only to experience a renewed resurgence of strength later. Since the middle of the thirteenth century, beginning with the ascendance of the Ottoman Empire and later the Spanish conquests of the New World, it has grown ever stronger and its prominence can be felt at every level of government in every nation of the world today."

"Surely there must be a way to intervene and check its progress?" Isaac's hand came down hard on the arm chair. He still vividly recalled their brush with death as they were forced to make their escape from Austin.

Jasher leaned back and pondered the question. "Remember, Cain's ways are subtle and his power is far-reaching. Most would not even recognize his affects as detrimental to progress because it takes so long for those changes to take hold. Only complete recognition of its design and influence can truly halt Cain's work. Unfortunately, we are not yet at the point where this is feasible, though the translation and publication of our records will go a long way to help us achieve that."

Bedford commented, "But, surely there have been a few notable attempts to stand up to him and push him back into his strongholds, though I must admit that if this was true, then history has been extremely quiet on the subject."

"As you are both aware, the writing of history belongs to the victors and Cain has lost few battles." He paused and added, "I can think of only two historical occasions in ancient times in which a group knew exactly who they were dealing with and did push back. I have already mentioned the people of Zion whose leader was Enoch, but if they had not been taken up and removed from the earth, surely they would have come under fire again. Cain is implacable when it comes to winning; he will never accept defeat."

"And the second account," asked Isaac?

Jasher smiled and commented, "Well, that does deserve a special story, but the historical record I made is not yet ready to be translated. I can assure you, however, that a record was made and will one day come forward."

Isaac smiled and said, "Well now you that you have our attention, at the very least it must be discussed. The knowledge that his plans can be frustrated may serve as a reminder that tyranny can be repulsed, even if our recorded history is mute."

Bedford asked, "Even if the details cannot be yet revealed, what is the historical backdrop of the second example to which you refer?"

Jasher glanced at his watch, realizing the evening was upon them. They had not yet dined, but he suddenly felt he needed to reassure these fine men that hope should never be abandoned, even if the odds were stacked heavily against them. He began with the question, "What do you two know of the lost Tribes of Israel?"

PART 1

THEY WHO WERE LOST

*T*he Jewish diaspora *or exile refers to the dispersion of Israelites, Judahites, and later Jews out of their ancestral homeland, the Land of Israel, and their subsequent settlement in other parts of the globe.*

The Babylonian captivity or Babylonian exile is the period in Jewish history during which a number of Judahites of the ancient Kingdom of Judah were taken captives to Babylonia. After the Battle of Carchemish in 605 BCE, Nebuchadnezzar, the king of Babylon, besieged Jerusalem, resulting in tribute being paid by King Jehoiakim. In Nebuchadnezzar's fourth year of rule over Israel, Jehoiakim refused to pay tribute which led to another siege in Nebuchadnezzar's seventh year, culminating with the death of Jehoiakim and the exile of King Jeconiah, his court and many others. Jeconiah's successor, Zedekiah, and others were exiled in Nebuchadnezzar's eighteenth year; a later deportation occurred in Nebuchadnezzar's twenty-third year. The dates, numbers of deportations, and numbers of deportees given in the biblical accounts vary. These deportations are dated to 597 BCE for the first, with others dated at 587 BCE, and 582 BCE.

Later, during the Roman assault on Israel, after the Bar Kochba Revolt of 132-135 CE, the Romans engaged in mass executions, expulsions, and enslavement. This resulted in the destruction of large numbers of Judean towns and moreover forbade Jews from settling in Jerusalem or its environs (Dio Cassius, Roman History 69.12-14). From this point forward, there was no further Jewish government or overarching legal system thereafter in Judaea. After this failed Jewish uprising in 135 CE, the majority of Jews in Israel were sold as slaves, killed or forced to seek refuge outside Palestine. This effectively turned the expatriate Jews of the Diaspora into a permanently exiled people, deprived of their homeland.

Although some Jews maintained their presence in the Syria-Palestine region, their lack of a governing body made them a disposed and dispersed people. Memory of the last Jewish exile (in 70 or 135 CE) was made common knowledge in medieval Jewish discourse, and also made its way into Christian and Islamic thought and discussion. Nevertheless, some scholars argue against the idea that the diaspora, taken as a whole, is entirely the result of a sudden mass expulsion of Jews from Judea/Syria (Palestine). Some scholars likewise propose that the concept of a sudden, all-encompassing exile is unimportant to serious Jewish historical discussions. Instead, they argue that the diaspora was a gradual process that occurred over the centuries, starting with the Assyrian destruction of Israel, the Babylonian destruction of Judah, the Roman destruction of Judea, and the subsequent rule of Christians and Muslims. (https://en.wikipedia.org/wiki/Jewish_diaspora)

CHAPTER 1

ON THE ROAD TO JERICHO, 163 BCE

The Maccabean Revolt was a Jewish rebellion, lasting from 167 to 160 BCE, led by the Maccabees against the Seleucid Empire and the Hellenistic influence on Jewish life.

The term Maccabees as used to describe the Jewish army of rebellion is taken from the Hebrew word for "hammer". In the narrative of I Maccabees, after Antiochus issued his decrees forbidding Jewish religious practice, a rural Jewish priest from Modiin, Mattathias the Hasmonean, sparked the revolt against the Seleucid Empire by refusing to worship the Greek gods. Mattathias killed a Hellenistic Jew who stepped forward to offer a sacrifice to an idol in Mattathias' home village. Subsequently, he and his five sons fled to the wilderness of Judah to escape justice. After Mattathias' death about one year later in 166 BCE, his son Judea Modiin adopted the nom de guerre of Judah Maccabee, and led an army of Jewish dissidents to victory over the Seleucid dynasty in guerrilla warfare, which at first was directed against Hellenized Jews, of whom there were many at the time in Israel. The Maccabees destroyed pagan altars in the villages, circumcised boys and forced Hellenized Jews into outlawry.

The revolt itself involved many battles in which the Maccabean forces used guerilla tactics consisting of light, quick and mobile assault strikes that were well suited to confront the slow and bulky Seleucid army. After a few surprising victories, the Maccabees entered Jerusalem in triumph and ritually cleansed the Temple, reestablishing traditional Jewish worship there and installing Jonathan Maccabee as high priest and in nominal control. A large Seleucid army was sent to quash the revolt, but returned to Syria on the death of Antiochus IV. Its commander Lysias, preoccupied with internal Seleucid affairs, agreed to a political compromise with Israel that restored religious freedom, at least until governmental affairs in Syria could be resolved. (https://en.wikipedia.org/wiki/Maccabees)

Jasher slowly pulled his donkey across the stark landscape of the western desert of Jordan, a few days travel east of the Dead Sea. Looking up at a metal blue sky and trying to avoid the brightness of the sun, he was reminded of why he seldom ever passed through this part of the world. He shook his head in disgust and said aloud, "Aside from the heat, it is just downright ugly."

With each passing day, his intuition grew stronger that the detour through Israel had been necessary. It was almost as if his journey across this wasteland was expected, but the question that now beset him was the why of it all. He crested a small hill and in the distance he spied a small oasis, and feeling some fatigue, he was reminded that he and the animal were in need of water and a longer rest. Since the evening was coming on, he decided that the stopover would probably linger on into the night and he would leave early the next morning. As he approached the oasis it was not long before he finally discovered the why of the detour: there under a palm stood his long-time friend and mentor, Joseph.

As he drew near the comforting coolness of the palms, Jasher heard a light-hearted voice call out, "Jasher, I see you are fatigued from the long walk across the desert. Please enter the shade of the oasis and rest yourself. It appears your donkey has more stamina than you have. Fortunately, your intellect is slightly higher."

"Joseph, I see your humor remains intact even after so many years."

"To me, my friend, it was only yesterday."

"You must tell me one day how you manage that."

"When you are prepared to ask the right question, the answer will not be far behind. Such is the acquisition of knowledge, my old friend."

"And how will I know the question is right?"

"I suppose, when you are prepared to apply the answer." A smile played across Joseph's face. "Come, let us talk."

After tying up the donkey, Jasher pulled out bread and dried dates from his pack. Water was nearby, so he took the opportunity to fill his *bota* bag and splash a little water across his face to remove some of the desert sand and grime. He was about to ask Joseph whether he would dine with him, but he remembered the messenger had always refrained from taking nourishment. "Still not eating, I see. Not hungry?"

"Thank you, no. There are certain boundaries that I cannot yet cross. I look forward to that day if for no other reason than to acknowledge your courtesy in a more satisfying manner."

"Boundaries? Sorry, I don't follow." It was a slight, probing question, but probably not enough to receive some answers. *Am I really ready to apply them?*

"It appears you are not quite ready for the answers. But, you already know that. It is written on your face."

Jasher nodded then asked, "Well, it is gratifying to have a visit, but I suspect there is more to it than just a reunion of old friends." After he stretched out under the shade, he popped a date into his mouth and began to chew then washed it down with a sip of water from the leather bag. He watched as the messenger settled comfortably under the palm.

Joseph gazed westward as the sun began to melt over the horizon. He had always looked forward to the night sky. "Yes, each trip has a purpose and this one is no different in importance than to any of the others." He was permitted to tarry a little longer than was usual this visit, so perhaps he would take some time to teach Jasher about celestial movements. He smiled at the prospect.

"It has something to do with my detour through Israel, correct?"

"Yes, I am sure you have been feeling that a new mission was long overdue. The impressions you have received lately to turn south were an indication of the importance of that task."

"Yes, it seemed the farther into the desert I walked, my mind seemed to sharpen and the more certain I became that you would appear. I suppose I was not surprised to see you."

"The desert has that effect on certain men." He smiled as he added a slight rebuke, "You might want to remember that the next time you refer to it as ugly."

Jasher was eating a piece of bread when he stopped in mid-chew. With a frown, he responded, "I should be more careful about what I say. It would appear that even the desert has ears to hear."

Joseph laughed at the observation. "Indeed it does. And, I am afraid that you are going to see more of it for the next few months."

"Where am I going?"

"Eventually to Jericho."

"What or who is in Jericho?"

"Someone who you have not seen for many years; Samuel is there."

Abruptly he stopped eating, and having one last drink from his *bota* bag, he put away everything back in his travel pack. "Samuel? By now he should have acquired a family and a son; at least that was the last counsel I gave him before we separated."

"He now has a son, but your primary mission is with the father. At the moment, he lives among the Israelites of Jericho and they have accepted him as their leader and some actually refer to him as a prophet."

Jasher's response was guarded. "How does he respond to that?"

"Just as you have taught him, which is to record history and keep an open mind."

Jasher ventured a personal observation. "Perhaps his mind has been a little too open. Has he crossed a line?"

"I would say no. His mission has been slightly altered even as yours has."

"So, our coming together is no accident. Please explain."

"Samuel is to lead this group from the Samaria region west of Jericho northward to a location south of the Caucasus Mountains on the eastern side of the Black Sea."

"You mean Armenia?"

"I do."

Jasher leaned back against the palm tree and closed his eyes for a moment. "Yes, I see the significance, at least for now. It is a more protected territory and the people are by and large accepting of outsiders. I take it that things in Israel are about to become much worse politically."

"And militarily. The Seleucids will eventually give way to the Romans who will attempt to occupy the whole of the world."

"I suspect my old relative Cain is behind their movement. The Romans have been slowly making alliances and strategic conquests throughout the region, all hallmarks of his influence."

"You are quite right. And, as a result of these political shifts, the tribes of Israel, especially those of Judah, will experience a mass exodus. But they will be permitted to return to their homeland eventually. As you are already aware and have seen and recorded first-hand, most of Israel has already been dispersed, especially those tribes of Manasseh and Ephraim, who having felt the effects of political pressure hundreds of years earlier have already been relocated. But, the remainder will need especial assistance if they are to survive. One of such groups exists near Jericho and Samuel is their leader."

"Very well, but how do I fit into all this?"

"You are to make contact with Samuel in Jericho and inform him of the destination he is to take his group. As you are familiar with that region, you will accompany him and show them all the way."

"I see." He pondered another matter and informed Joseph, "While in Jordan, I heard that there was an Israeli uprising against the Greek Seleucids. It is led by a man by the name of Judah Maccabee who has gained a strong following throughout the land. So far, he has had some success enlisting the citizens of many regions throughout Israel and I do not think he will take it kindly that some Samarian Israelites would choose to leave before he has retaken control of the country for his homeland."

"That is where you come in. You must convince him that the people of the Samaria region and east to Jericho have a different destiny."

"How shall I do that?"

"You will say that his cause is just and so the Creator is prepared to help him against his enemies. Moreover, you will be on hand to record his victory as a testament to the people of Israel that in their time of need, Judah Maccabee was their deliverer."

Jasher smiled and said, "You mean I am to appeal to his ego?"

"Jasher, everyone has a weakness. Judah has a need to have his actions vindicated and remembered. You will be there to make sure that occurs. He will respond favorably, of course, if you approach him the right way." He went on to explain details of the next attack on the Seleucids as well as a possible outcome should Judah decide to cooperate.

"And you think I can convince him to allow the people of Samaria to leave in peace?"

Joseph's smile was quick, his response almost sardonic. "Of course, why else were you assigned this mission?"

Jasher may have lacked Joseph's confidence, but he was prepared to try. He discussed possible stratagems with his friend and pointed out, "You realize, of course, that in spite of anything I do or say, Judah may still object to their leaving."

"Then it would be wise to have the people around Samaria begin preparations for their departure as soon as you arrive in their midst. In any event, the will of the Creator must be obeyed in this matter and His works will not be frustrated by Judah the Maccabee or anyone else."

"As always, a comforting thought," he commented wryly. "I will, of course, do as you ask."

"I thought you might." Joseph smiled and glanced up at the evening sky and noted the first stars had begun to appear. Rubbing his hands together in anticipation of a teaching opportunity, he asked, "Well, let us talk of other interests. Are you ready for a lesson in astronomy?"

Jasher was not sure what that meant, but as Joseph kept glancing up at the night sky he assumed his friend referred to the heavenly lights on display. He leaned back and listened.

It was morning a week later near the old wall and as Samuel gazed out easterly across a vast desert, he spied a lone figure approaching Jericho. A dream the night before had revealed he would soon have a reunion with an old relative he had not seen for over fifty years. To have a better look, he climbed the stone tower of the city and the sight verified what he had suspected. It was Jasher walking along the main road from Amman followed closely by a donkey, and knowing Jasher, the animal would be heavily-laden with writing materials.

Samuel, now eager to see the man with whom he had travelled so many years of his youth, walked out to greet him. As he drew closer, he realized, as so many before him, that Jasher had not aged, but had survived the ravages of time. Samuel rubbed a hand slowly across his short beard that could no longer cover all the wrinkles he had begun to acquire on his face. Smiling, he realized that though he appeared much younger than did others his own age, time was beginning to catch him as it did eventually for everyone; all except for one man. Or the other.

Jasher, as he neared the awaiting Samuel, could see the rooftops of Jericho hovering in the distance, poised in the sun-soaked land like a crumbling, mud-stained benediction to man's earliest efforts at civilization. The village had never been much of a way station and very soon it was about to become deserted.

"Jasher, welcome to Jericho." Both men embraced and Samuel said, "I was hoping to see you once more before I died."

"I told you I would one day return. It was later than I had expected, but I am here."

"And so you are. Come, you must meet my children and wife, Rebecca." Samuel, followed by Jasher, began to walk back to the center of the city.

"I was told you had a son and Samuel, I presume, is his name."

"Of course. That is our custom and I was never one to break with tradition. I suspect your arrival is no accident; doubtless, you have come to record an event."

With a smile, Jasher commented, "That, too, is our custom and I was never one to break with tradition."

Nodding, Samuel responded, "I have had the feeling for some time that a change was coming and that I was to be a part of it, but I do not yet know the specifics, only that my destiny is to be elsewhere away from Israel. It has been unsettling."

"That answer is part of the reason why I am here."

"Was it Joseph?"

"It was."

Samuel sighed, knowing that the choices ahead would be difficult, but necessary. "It helps to know that I have another witness of what I am to do."

Jasher's hand went to his shoulder and offered an encouraging squeeze. "That is how our Creator works in such matters."

Samuel drew quiet, reluctant to mention what must be said. "I suppose you have heard the people here now call me a prophet."

"Is it deserving?"

Samuel was a little defensive. "I did not seek it, if that is what you were thinking."

Jasher found a linen cloth and tamped his brow then his neck. He commented tersely, "If you had sought it, you would not have been called." Looking sideways at Samuel, he asked, "What do you know so far?"

"In my dream, I not only saw you, but I was left with the impression that I was to lead my people somewhere, but I still have no idea where. I presume that is why you have arrived."

"Yes, north to Armenia and from there I have no idea, but eventually that answer will be made known also."

"Armenia? Did we not pass through there once many years ago?"

"We did and as I recall, we were both impressed with what we saw. Joseph explained to me the exact location of our final destination. It would be at the foothills of a large mountain chain. As I recall, the land looks ideal for settlements but it will take months to arrive there."

It was slow in coming, but Samuel pointedly declared, "We have a much bigger problem here in Israel, you know."

Jasher nodded his understanding. "I have heard. It is the uprising of the Maccabees and we must tread lightly to avoid any reprisals once our departure is made public."

"Judah Maccabee will not willingly watch us leave, I can assure you, Jasher. He is not your average docile Israeli content with farming or tending his flocks. The man wants something else and he will not rest until he has achieved it."

"I have heard he is a brave warrior, willing to give his life for this land."

Samuel's brow creased with concern. "He is that and much more. He is willing to give our lives for this land as well."

A few minutes later and they arrived at Samuel's home. Within, Jasher met his wife Rebekah and his children. In the corner standing by the window was his eldest, Samuel. In his late teens, the young man was nearly ready for marriage. He walked up to Jasher and bowing said, "You are as father has described you. He said you travelled together for many years and that when you returned, you would still be young, but how was I to believe that without seeing for myself?"

Jasher turned to the young man's father and remarked lightly with a grin, "I hope you also mentioned that I taught you a few things along the way, Samuel."

Samuel nodded knowingly. "Jasher, he has been prepared for you. It will be his turn soon enough, I suspect."

"Yes, following our journey north, but I will return him to you."

The torrid blaze of the sun had wrung pops of sweat from the man's brow. Judah Maccabee glanced over his shoulder as he entered the coolness of the cave; it felt good to be finally out of the sun. It was mid-day and the heat in this part of Israel was relentless. As if to confirm his sentiment, a drop of sweat dripped into his left eye. Blinking it away he used his robe to wipe the remaining sweat from his brow. He turned from the view and spat, expending nearly the last of the spittle in his mouth. He murmured, "Good riddance." He had born a premonition all day that something was amiss. It clung to his back as chill wet leaves of autumn in Galilee. Cursing, he wished it were autumn.

He had been on the road all day between Shechem and the cave preparing his men for a new strike on the Seleucid Army. He smiled as he thought of how he and his men had bested Viceroy Lysias at Beth Zechariah a few years earlier. The Viceroy had been sent scurrying back to Antioch like a whipped dog to report the failure to his king. Rumor had it that he charged that his army had been treacherously ambushed by cowards who refused to fight in the open as real men. *How else were we supposed to fight,* he wondered? A stand-up fight against a larger, well-armed force would have been suicide and he did not have the men or the time to waste in such a fashion. He intended to ambush and to harry the Seleucid Greeks out of his land once and for all along with their seemingly endless gods of stone. Finding the moisture, he again spat on the ground. *Yes, good riddance.*

He was met at the cave entrance by his commander in Jericho, Thaddeus, an old friend and comrade of several years. He handed Commander Judah a water bag and he drank in great drafts. Judah reflected, it would be this warrior who would take the fight to the invaders in Samaria and he could think of no better man for the job. The two embraced.

Thaddeus remarked, "Judah, it has been far too long, two years, as I recall, since our last victory."

Judah smiled, "But, then it has been two years since we were last invaded."

"Well said, Brother. It appears the Seleucids have not yet learned their lesson."

"Perhaps they need a refresher course in tactics from Eretz Yisrael, our home."

The banter now over, Thaddeus asked seriously, "What have you heard of this new invasion? Can we expect more of the same or will they change their tactics?"

"It matters little, my friend. We must fight as we have always fought. They are a slave to their ways even as we are to ours. They will conquer or die on the merits of their stratagems even as we. But, I prefer our ways. They have never failed us."

Thaddeus nodded his agreement. As he led his commander farther into the cave, he began to report on their state of readiness. "You should know, Judah that our forces in Jericho and most of Samaria have diminished."

Unable to hide the surprise on his face, he blurted, "I don't understand. In the past we have been able to count on them for their help. Our overall strategy to attack the Seleucids from their left flank will be jeopardized without that help. The Greeks have always invaded directly south through the Samarian plains between the Great Sea and the Jordan River, a natural and time-tested route for all invasions. Key to stopping them is our strike forces between Joppa and Jericho."

"I realize that and in the past we were able to call upon them to do their duty and always they responded."

"What has changed?"

"There is a new prophet in the land."

Judah cursed and spat upon the ground. "You mean another old beard has arisen to lead our people out of bondage," he scoffed. "That is our job and we are doing a damn fine one at that and we do not need the help of some ragged old man showing up and stirring up the people for some false hope of salvation that will remove them from our land. Pray tell. Just who is this new Jeremiah?"

"His name is Samuel, but he is unlike any before him. The Tribes are beginning to coalesce around him in Samaria with Jericho at the center."

"What makes him so special?"

"For one thing he is neither old nor ragged; for another he does not speak in riddles and vague promises. He says oppression is coming to Israel and from a source much greater than that of the Assyrians, Babylonians and even the Seleucids. We will not be able to defeat them, or so he maintains."

"And who is this great enemy we cannot defeat?"

"The Romans."

Judah rubbed his beard, hoping to remove the itch and sand. "I have heard of them, of course, but they seem content to remain westward of the Seleucid Empire."

"According to Samuel, they plan to increase their domain partly through conquest, but largely by forming alliances."

"He seems to be well informed politically for a prophet. Where is he getting this information?"

"From another man."

"Another prophet, you mean?" he responded doubtfully.

"No, he is a well-travelled historian by the name of Jasher."

"What is an historian doing in Jericho?"

"Actually, Judah, he is not in Jericho. He is here with us."

Judah stopped in mid-stride then looking about the cave for an intruder, he hissed, "Here? How did you find him?"

"Actually, he found us."

"I told you people to cover your tracks before entering the cave! If he can find our location, then anyone can."

"Calm down, Judah. Of course, we covered our trail, but he seemed to know just where we were located. He just arrived at the entrance and walked through it."

"Well, what are his intentions? Has he come here to stir up our leadership as he has our people in Samaria?"

"I think you should talk with him."

"Talk with him? I am more likely to jab a knife in his throat."

A few minutes later, the two men arrived at the main conclave of field commanders who had assembled to hear Judah give them the details of their next mission. They were all seated around a fire prepared to drive out some of the chill of the cave. There in the midst of the group sat a man with whom he was unfamiliar. Clearly, he was the stranger Thaddeus had called Jasher the Historian.

The Maccabee's tone was abrupt, commanding. "I am Judah. What news have you brought us from Jericho? I presume that is why you are here. Speak up."

Jasher was not offended by the peremptory tone of his voice. He had expected as much. "I am Jasher and have come from much farther than Jericho." He added more firewood to the fire and watched as it hissed and popped from the heat.

There was a hush among the group. Judah reserved his current bantering tone for those he intended to do violence. It had happened before. Obadiah, the commander at Joppa spoke for them all. "Judah, he has brought us a proposition that I think you should think about."

His tone was challenging, defiant. "Now what could he possibly have to say that would make any difference to me?"

Jasher gazed calmly at the Israeli commander and said, "Your next attack will be at Beth Zur. The Seleucids intend to throw a much greater army at you than you have seen in the past. You may have a slight advantage of knowing the terrain, but their sheer numbers will overrun you. They will not leave the land until you are crushed; their king has so decreed it."

Judah remained unimpressed. "How do you know of such things?"

Jasher realized that Judah would only respect candor, not matter how hard it might be to accept. "An angel informed me."

Shaking his head in disdain, Judah responded, "Unlikely."

The location of the next attack against the Seleucids only Judah would know, so Jasher's declaration was news to all within the circle. Glancing toward Judah, Obadiah asked, "Is the attack to be at Beth Zur?"

A challenging smile played across his Judah's face. He stared at Jasher while ignoring the question and mocked, "And I suppose you have the ear of angels? Well, did he tell you how we are to defeat this great army?"

"Actually, he did mention that with the help of the Creator, you would be able to defeat your enemies in the field. There is one proviso, however."

The nerve of this fellow, Judah thought. "And what would that be?"

"You must allow the people of Samaria to depart in peace."

"Impossible. They will attack from the east and west as the Seleucids press towards Jerusalem. Without them, our enemies will roll over Judea leaving us exposed. They will fight or I will see to it their homes are burned to the ground. I swear it."

"Judah, listen to the man," pleaded Thaddeus.

"I suppose he has convinced you all of this madness."

Jasher spoke up and said, "Judah, may we speak privately? I have a message for your ears only."

The others were subdued, all thinking and wondering what all this portended for their revolt. Thaddeus was slow to meet his eyes, preferring instead to stare at the fire, but said, "Listen to the man, Judah."

"Very well, Jasher, you will talk and I will listen." He turned on his heels and headed back to the entrance of the cave, closely followed by Jasher.

At the opening, Judah crossed his arms and his eyes bore unflinchingly into him. He demanded, "All right, Jasher, it is now just the two of us, so speak."

Jasher was equally frank. "You need a victory at the next battle. It will be decisive and without it, the city of Jerusalem and all of Judea will be forfeit. I have been tasked to record that confrontation with the Seleucids and in that history it will show how the great General of Israel Judah the Maccabee defeated an overwhelming host of Greek idol-worshippers with the help of the Creator. Once this is spread far and wide throughout the land, you will have the support of all the people and you will no longer have to coerce anyone into your army. They will come willingly to fight for Israel and stand with you against anyone who would dare invade your nation again."

"And why will they do that?"

"Because I will ensure your exploits will be spread throughout the land and that you have the ear of the Creator who watches over those in Eretz Yisrael."

Judah knew the invading army would be larger and more determined than the last one that had appeared. He had avoided informing his commanders for fear they would desert him. He looked tired, weary from worry that they could lose it all. "Jasher, how can we win with only our beliefs? That is how we were defeated in the past and now too many of our people have been scattered across the land because of our inaction. If I permit the people of Samaria to desert us, we will send a signal to others that our cause is questionable. How do we deserve to hold onto this land if our people are allowed to leave it without a fight?"

"Perhaps you can make a difference, Judah. But you must inspire them, not coerce them. You can have this victory and all others you will need, but you must allow the people of Samaria to leave if that is their wish."

Judah looked out over the distant valley to the northwest and beyond to the Sea of Galilee. "Very well, but I will hold the Creator to his promise. If this is His chosen land, then He must help us preserve it."

Jasher, too, looked out over the valley in the distance. It had been many years since he had last seen Galilee. "This is His land and He will preserve it and I will record your efforts."

A Seleucid Greek army led by Viceroy Lysias in 164 BCE attempted to retake Jerusalem at the site of Beth Zur. But, again, the Greeks were routed by the Maccabees who used their unconventional war style to thwart the Seleucid invasion of Israel. According to 1 Enoch chapters 83-90 (the Animal Apocalypse), the battle was joined on the side of the Maccabees by an angel who had been recording the event. (https://en.wikipedia.org/wiki/Maccabees)

Seven months later, on the fifth day of the sixth month in 164 BCE, the Seleucid Army of Greece was marching through Samaria on their way to Jerusalem. The Viceroy Lysias was at the head of a large army along with his three captains. They had expected more resistance, but were happy for the respite. Suddenly, from the east could be seen a large dark cloud appearing from the desert near Jericho. As it got nearer it seemed as though the land had been sucked up and thrown about inside as in a cyclone. The men of the Greek Army panicked, broke ranks and ran, but the storm quickly overtook them. The grit was everywhere, pushed into eyes and into every pore and orifice. The men stumbled about, choking and retching and many died from the suffocating thickness of the dust storm; others were simply sucked up and tossed miles away. Finally, a few remaining soldiers stumbled out of the storm only to be cut down by the swords and arrows of the Maccabees awaiting them near Beth Zur. It was a complete rout. Upon a nearby hill sat a man, making notes of the overwhelming Israeli victory as the tattered remnants of the Seleucid Army was chopped down and defeated.

CHAPTER 2

THE LAND OF AMAZIAH, 851 CE

"If men were angels, no government
would be necessary."

----- James Madison

In the days of Samuel the Prophet of Amaziah, the Byzantine Empire spread from the Iberian Peninsula in modern-day Spain across the Mediterranean, including Turkey, and well into Egypt along the shores of the Nile River. The boundaries of the empire, because of its vast size, were in a constant state of flux through constant warfare with the neighboring Frankish Empire to the north ruled by Charlemagne. This conflict continued until Cain was finally able to usurp the Frankish throne and gain access to the Emperor and the ear of the Frankish leaders who followed him.

As to the Byzantines, in 867, the imperial throne was eventually supplanted by Basil I, an Armenian protégé of Cain. Despite his humble origins, Basil showed great promise in running the affairs of state, leading to a revival of Imperial power and a renaissance of Byzantine art. He was perceived by the Byzantines as one of their greatest emperors, and the Macedonian dynasty that he founded, ruled over what is regarded as the most glorious and prosperous era of the Byzantine Empire.

On the outward edge of the Byzantine region previously ruled by the Macedonians, was a small country known from antiquity as Armenia by the Greeks. It was here that a small conclave of travelers from the region of Israel had settled some one thousand years previously and had called their city/ state Amaziah, a Hebrew word meaning "Strengthened by God or Strength of the Lord." Owing to their isolated location and peaceful co-existence with neighboring regions, they were allowed to live unmolested until their numbers and peculiar philosophy of living had finally reached the ears of their new masters, the Byzantines.

Among the group, and those of the region, they were known simply as The Tribes. In spite of the growth of so many religions in the region, including Christianity, The Tribes had maintained a belief in the Creator, but unlike their Jewish cousins, had not given way to rabbinism to codify the law of the Torah. They had always been led by a prophet or his descendants who all carried the same name of Samuel. The prophet had been he who would interpret the law and guide the people in spiritual matters and each had done so faithfully for nearly ten centuries. As they had listened and adhered to the word of their leaders, The Tribes had grown strong and had created a near-perfect social existence. Moreover, because of their isolation, they had remained free of outside interference and the ravages of war and expansion from the west.

The first thing one noticed about the city of Amaziah was its orderly, immaculate streets, shops and public buildings. All structures, including residences, having been constructed from the limestone and marble of the local quarries, all appeared a stunning white. All roads and thoroughfares were immaculate and free of unsightly, rotting rubbish, night soils or animal droppings which quite naturally assailed the senses of the weary traveler upon entering every other city of the realm. This was no accident. There existed an unspoken unanimity of purpose among the citizenry that precluded any possibility of offense. At the root of this purpose was a concerted effort on the part of each citizen to take personal responsibility for his collective, as well as individual stewardships.

Assuming the visitors abided by the public law and supported a sober, non-violent behavior while inside the city, all people everywhere within the realm were welcome to travel, visit or even live among the people of Amaziah. Though adopting laws that supported free speech and public assemblies, public contention was strictly avoided. When the inevitable disagreement arose, the city had provided for a means of free legal service for conflict resolution. All men and women were judged fairly according to the law which was interpreted by five civic judges and one chief judge all of which were elected officials with years of public service before they assumed their roles. When there were those who contested the interpretations of the judges, each claimant was entitled to the right of appeal to the chief judge. There were no prisons and no public punishments. The offender, when proved guilty, was asked to provide civil service to the community until his punishment was fulfilled. There were no repeat offenders of the public peace. The contentious citizen was simply asked to leave the region and not return.

In all cities of the realm, save in the patriarchy of The Tribes, children were either educated at home or received no formal education at all. The city of Amaziah, on the other hand, provided free, public education at all age levels, including higher education for older adolescents and all adults. As children grew into adulthood, their intelligence was assessed and they assumed positions in the society which reflected not only their talents but interests and passions as well. There were no idle young people hanging about the streets, roaming free without adult supervision. During the day, youth were either being educated or were expected to assist in maintenance of public buildings and parks. At night, they spent time with their families. Each child, regardless of his status, had at least one responsible parent to provide guidance and discipline. There were no homeless children; all were provided parents if no birth parent could be found.

As the land of The Tribes had no aggressive tendencies towards their neighboring kingdoms, there was no army to maintain. The local police force was purely defensive and required young unmarried men to dedicate a year of their lives to the service and defense of their region as well as the safety and security of the citizenry.

There were no taxes to speak of and no burgeoning governmental bureaucracy to maintain. All men, women and children who could or were able to provide a service to the community were expected to donate of their time and talents and all willingly did so without compulsion. The disabled were all provided with a community service commensurate with their limited abilities so that even the most handicapped and aged could carry a sense of personal pride and civic worth. All the sick and elderly were cared for with the best medications and attention that could be provided. There was no poverty, no helpless indigence, no wanting of any kind. All citizens had everything in common. Each gave freely and all needs were provided.

The patriarchy of The Tribes and the city of Amaziah had existed for over a thousand years. Their innovations and advances in science, mathematics and medicine were freely shared with all the kingdoms of the realm. This had so greatly raised the standard of living of the surrounding regions of Armenia that the people were in awe of the power and intelligence of those in the patriarchy. Thus, peace existed throughout their region and the contiguous lands near Amaziah.

The key to their contentment was that they had all things in common. The notion, not a new one, but one nearly impossible to live unless all were willing to abide by the principle, had been taught them by their first prophet in their diaspora to Armenia. Once they had settled, it was the only way The Tribes had been able to maintain their beliefs and social harmony when so many other societies of the region had failed. This was especially true when compared to those under the control of the Brotherhood of Cain and it was this disparity which eventually brought them under the scrutiny of the Clan of the Scar.

The patriarchy, and especially the city of Amaziah, was an affront to Cain and his society. So, it was into this atmosphere of bliss that the Brotherhood had attempted to place operatives to undermine the peace and tranquility of its citizenry and, if possible, to destroy the near-perfect application of agency that existed only in the region of Amaziah. Despite the ease of entering Amaziah and mingling among the citizenry, there was no way for such an individual to blend in and easily insinuate himself into the government because no bureaucracy was permitted to persist. Invariably, each attempt to insert an agent was met with frustration. Bribery and extortion were also impossible because there was no sense of privilege or class entitlement. To Cain's utter dismay each member of his Society of the Clan that was sent into Amaziah to undermine its social fabric, was himself converted to its precepts of peace and eventually each renounced his membership to their brotherhood.

Cain's usual method of subjugation of the kingdoms within his reach usually came in the form of subterfuge. It was cleaner and left the means of food production of the target kingdom intact, though the people were left just as oppressed. Limited open warfare between kingdoms and its consequential atrocities were permitted in the realm under his control only as a means to an end. The more the people were frightened and occupied with day-to-day survival the more they were willing to give up their needs for self-rule until finally they acquiesced and accepted the inevitable *status quo* of the Brotherhood. This resulted, of course, in their loss of basic freedoms of choice, but there was relative peace.

Cain was beginning to believe that simply planting the idea of the fear of invasion was sufficient to exploit those under his control. So, the constant pressure of limited open combat permitted the exploitation he needed over the people at large with minimal commitment of his armies. His insertion of advisers to each kingdom insured the Brotherhood stayed in power and maintained their control regardless of what happened to the people of the kingdoms they represented. The Emperor or king, of course, was little more than a figure-head, a puppet to be paraded about or wheeled out on demand when a public display of pomp and ceremony was required. But, always behind the great ones, there was Cain.

He was not, however, above sending out an army to simply take what he wanted by force; case in point was his takeover of the kingdom of the Macedonians or his decades-long war with the Sasanians of Persia. However, on a smaller scale such as Amaziah, it was hardly worth the effort of putting an army into the field to quell a local uprising or taking control of a small and isolated enclave of people. More to the norm, he usually applied conspiracy to undermine the government or controlling faction. It had seldom failed; that is, until now.

Cain gazed out the library window over the vast courtyard of his residence in Constantinople. Quickening shadows fell over the Black Sea. It was now coming on dusk and the orb of the sun was beginning slip below the rim of his world. He had just dismissed an adviser he had sent to investigate the Amaziah affair and this latest report of that tiny enclave in Armenia had deeply vexed him. He was deep in thought, trying to develop a plan of action that would break the resistance of their citizenry.

He knew, of course, the root of the problem. "It's that slow-witted fool, Samuel," he muttered. Cain simply could not understand the man's influence. A self-styled prophet, he was described as a drab creature at best who, when excited, invariably became a stuttering moron.

Suddenly, there was a sudden drop in room temperature as though a shivering breeze had swooped in from the north. From behind him, as though reading his mind, a chilling voice responded, "He must be eliminated, you know." Cain knew whose voice it was without turning. He was growing weary of even the occasional appearance of this being. "Of course," agreed Cain testily. "Please tell me something I don't already know."

Cain turned and faced his old confidant and counselor. He reflected, without much interest, that the scourge of time had not affected Lucifer's appearance any more than it had his own. His shape was ephemeral, as though not quite there, fading slightly in then out. When conniving, as he now appeared, his face was coarse and dark whereas his voice self-serving, mildly fawning as always. To Cain, his counsel had become predictable as well as bordering on useless.

The entity continued to prattle on. "Of course, you realize that should Amaziah and the kingdom of The Tribes prevail, eventually its influence will spread out over the realm and consume everything in its path. Its brand of government and social precepts will nullify our efforts to prove that agency cannot work."

Cain shook his head, now annoyed. "Don't be absurd! The "Tribes" as they call themselves, are but a small enclave of refugees compared to the rest of my empire. I suggest we simply keep them bottled up and if they begin to spread out over the remainder of Armenia, I will send in my army and obliterate them."

"I suggest we use deception rather than brute force. We don't want them scattering to the wind."

No doubt owing to his one-dimensional nature, the problem with his old cohort was that he invariably overplayed his scheming nature. Now impatient, Cain retorted, "Of course, but we both know that this method has had disastrous results, what with our agents invariably converting to their dogma." Cain sensed there was something more afoot here and his old mentor was not sharing. "Lucifer, you are holding out on me. What are you hiding that I should know about?"

"Well, I have been made aware of a slight change in our handling of this affair."

"What?"

"Now don't get excited," he soothed. Trying to downplay the news and appease his head-strung protégé, he replied, "The Creator has decreed that we are not to invade their land militarily. We may infiltrate them and influence them through subterfuge, but you cannot (how did you put it?), obliterate them."

Cain looked over at his mentor and disdainfully replied, "So, it is to be Zion all over again, is it?" He fumed then asked, "What was the excuse given this time for meddling into our affairs?"

"There was mention of a second witness to allow agency to exist. I suppose He considers Zion a success of sorts."

Now an old impatience had set in like a well-worn robe. "What success? There was no victory there because Zion was an aberration of the general rule. If I had been permitted another opportunity, I could have pulled that whole country down around their sanctimonious ears." Cain paced, all the while rubbing his scar. He finally stopped and with an accusing finger pointed in Lucifer's direction. "You could help a little more, you know! Is your influence so impotent that I must do everything?"

The dark visitor ignored Cain's attempt to goad him into an open argument. Finally, with insidious conviction he stated, "We must try something more aggressive and public. A clear message must be sent of our predominance and power over the Prophet Samuel and the Chief Judges of Amaziah. The citizenry must be so appalled and chilled by an egregious public display of terror that they will be eager to turn their powers of personal choice over to an enlightened bureaucracy of our choice. It will, of course, result in the implementation of our brand of government on behalf of a frightened, but concerned community."

Naturally, Cain had come to the same conclusion as Lucifer but what was being contemplated had not been necessary since that debacle in Zion over three millennia ago. After some discussion they came to initial agreements over the scope of the operation. The timing would have to be perfect and the men involved would have to be totally trustworthy and skilled. Further, they must be willing to give their lives, if necessary. At the very least, it would take up to two years to set up and execute, but Cain had reached the limit of his patience watching his usually effective tactics yield one failure after another. The following month, several men were under consideration for the mission of infiltration and subversion. After some debate among Cain and his advisers, two conspirators were deemed to be high on a very short list for the mission ahead.

CHAPTER 3

THE CONSPIRATORS

Twenty-two years earlier, in what is now Central Syria of the kingdom of Levant, Shum was a child of thirteen years living near the city of Palmyra in the midst of a combat zone, the control of which shifted from one side to another dependent upon which field commander had the least to lose on any given day and today was the turn of the citizenry of Palmyra's to feel the helpless horror of their situation. It was just the continuation of the same aggression that had begun with no better reason than it now did to remain, which was to inflict terror and instill obedience upon the population.

Tamar walked over to the open window and called to her eldest son, "Shum, please help your sisters set the table. The dinner hour is upon us and your father has worked hard in the city clearing the debris and removing the bodies of the dead. He will need food." Shum's mother, Tamar, had grown old with the misery and anxiety of living in the midst of a battle zone. Every day was a worry she endured and it was taking its toll on her health and sanity.

Shum turned from the window from which he had been awaiting the arrival of his father, Kittim, who had been part of the forced labor detail assigned to cleaning up the city following the latest battle. The war, if it could be called that, had raged on for months. "All right, mother, but there are still soldiers in the street. Perhaps father has taken a different route home or he has been detained."

"Let us pray that is not the case." Her only thought continued to repeat morbidly in her feverish mind: *I could not bear living without Kittim. I cannot hold it all together alone.*

The table had just been set and the food was ready when Kittim slowly opened the door and entered. Seeing his family around the table, he nearly choked with despair at the sights of the brutality he had witnessed in the civic center of Palmyra that day. His life was a constant fear that he would either lose his family to the roaming savagery of the soldiers or not be there for them. Assuming a false mask of hope and optimism, he affably greeted each child and saved a special embrace for Tamar, who needed his strength more than she could ever express.

His smile was broad, but forced and she could read the fear and concern in his eyes. "Tamar, I see you have set a special table this evening. The food smells delicious." The food was meagre, but nourishing, no doubt acquired as a result of bartering what few possessions they still had remaining in the house.

Roving patrols of soldiers of the Byzantine Empire had made day-to-day living for the citizens of Levant tenuous at best. Thus, when military movements were sighted, all the neighboring families in the region around about Palmyra remained vigilant and wary. Just as Shum and his family had sat down for the evening meal, an apprehensive feeling of dread had invaded their midst. Suddenly the door of their home was roughly kicked open and three large men in full body armor stalked arrogantly into the room.

"It is dinner time," the oldest one remarked with a slow smile. The other two voiced a loud agreement and proceeded to the table. The family, now cowering and defenseless, awaited the soldier's intentions.

Shum's father, Kittim, quietly looked around the table and whispered, "Let us make room for the soldiers. They must be famished from their day of fighting." Food was scarce in the city and the little they had could not be spared, but the soldiers had left little doubt that they were going to have their own way.

The beginning of the horror to come passed nearly unnoticed, but each felt the mood darkening around him. While the soldiers removed their breastplates and sat down heavily on the bench, Kittim motioned his family away from the table. With animal-like grunts of approval they fell upon the meal as though it were their last. Shum's father directed his family toward the anteroom in an effort to escape whatever else the soldiers might have in mind for them later.

The largest of the three men commented jovially, "Don't venture too far away. We haven't had dessert yet!" This sally was met with a roar of approval from the other two.

"Sirs," Kittim began cautiously, not wanting to offend, "we have little to eat. What you see on the table is all we have, but you are welcome to it. Please allow me and my family to retire to a kinsman's home to await your departure."

The youngest of the three soldiers motioned Kittim over to the table as if to deliver to him their reply. The response came in the form of a dagger concealed in his boot. One moment Kittim was leaning over them to discuss their departure and the next moment he fell to his knees with his throat cut. The immediate gush of blood down the front of Kittim's robe had counter-pointed the clean, flickering motion of the blade as it had met with his neck. The soldier pushed him backwards roughly toward the wall then with casual ease he turned back around to finish his meal. "You all will remain here until we have completed our meal."

The movement to kill her husband was so sudden and incomprehensible that his wife, Tamar, had not had a chance to digest the result of the attack when he toppled over Shum who was trying to crawl away from the soldiers. Kittim arose unsteadily then stumbled again over to the nearby wall and leaned against it. Blinking slowly, he managed to right himself, but his knees collapsed causing him to slide slowly to the floor. The smell of his blood, rich and coppery, permeated the room; Kittim's family looked on in shocked horror as his blood and gore now stained his robe a crimson red.

Finally, one of the children could contain her terror no longer and a rich scream of absolute misery came from her mouth; the other siblings were only a heartbeat behind her. Tamar crawled over to her husband and placed her hand over the deep cut to stop the flow of blood, but it was too late. His gaze, now blurry, looked upon her one last time then shifting his glazed eyes around the room with wonder they closed for the last time. He took a last breath then slumped over to his side. Tamar slowly removed her blood-stained hands from his neck and shook her head in utter despair. His passing, though traumatic to his family, was nearly forgotten in the shriek of what followed.

The oldest of the three soldiers finished his wine and walked slowly over to the bellowing children and backhanded a small daughter heavily across the room with his leather arm-plate, breaking her neck. Two soldiers decided it was now time to join in for what they termed *"dessert"*. Both of the youngest sons were roughly pushed one in front of the other against a wall then another soldier fetched one of his spears, took aim at close range, and impaled both children together in one throw.

"Well done!" the other two soldiers chimed in and congratulated their comrade on his strength.

Tamar and her two older daughters were now in a state of numbed shock and looked on as if they had stepped unwittingly into a fiendish nightmare. However, the death of his father and siblings had just the opposite effect on Shum. He quickly scrambled over and past the prone bodies through the back bedroom and out the window before the soldiers could finish the job on him. Before he left his home for good, he spied the soldiers advancing toward his mother and cowering sisters. As he ran down the pathway from his home he could hear the beginning of the screams that would haunt his nights and waking moments for years to come. His dreams would leave him in exhausted terror, but also seething with a bitter anger and an unquenchable thirst for revenge.

For the next few months Shum wandered the countryside fending off hunger and hiding from constant attacks of roving patrols. He pushed ever westward until he arrived weary but determined at the home of a kinsman living in the kingdom of Macedonia. There he rested and awaited the day when he could exact retribution upon those armies which had occupied his land and savagely murdered his family.

His uncle, Nabu, a middle range official in the Macedonian government, was proficient at recognizing physical skills of strength and stamina and his nephew Shum fit that description beyond a doubt. Once it became apparent that Shum's athletic skills were only exceeded by his serious, detached nature, Nabu recommended him to an elite training school which Cain had formed to develop his top assassins. His uncle convinced him that he could live with him while he trained in all aspects of the art of warfare. Shum readily agreed and over the next ten years steadily became the greatest assassin in the land.

Shum was a perfectionist and a quick study and there was no weapon with which he was unaware. Nor was there any of which he did not skillfully use and master, thus he became expert in the use of all weapons: knives, swords, garrote, and the bow. His selection of his weapon of choice was always well considered and equal to the task. He was the ideal operative because his movements were deliberate, exact and well planned, using the least amount of energy for the maximum effect. Perhaps most of all, he was utterly remorseless in his execution of the assignment. His physical strength allowed him to excel at a host of different offensive and defensive combat skills, all of which contributed to his success as an instrument of death. It was unsurprising he had accomplished several successful assassinations by the time he had reached adulthood.

Shum had developed a killer's detachment for his trade, but he was observant and had a near perfect memory. He could remember every assignment and every man from whom he had taken his life. He could even remember the look of surprise then terror on the face of each as the knife dug deeply into the throat or the gaze of astonishment as the arrow penetrated the heart. For many years he would only take assignments that took him into the kingdom of Levant to eliminate officials that were slow to learn the lessons of the Brotherhood. He wanted revenge for his family and he hoped that whoever's life he took had been instrumental in their murder. But, no matter how many lives he ended in the hope he was disposing of someone who might have been responsible, after years of doing violence, he realized that regardless of his intentions, he could never bring back his family.

Over time, he had gradually grown tired of the assignments; the looks of abject horror of his targets and his own thirst for revenge no longer appealed to him. The hunt and the anticipation of the kill ceased to quicken his interest. He was tired of taking lives and wondered whether there was something else that could fill this emptiness. Occasionally, he even wondered if there was a chance that he could have a normal life with a wife and family. *Was it too late,* he asked himself? *Am I beyond hope?* When he accepted the assignment to the city of Amaziah in the realm of Armenia, he knew it would be his last. His heart was no longer in his work.

Simeon, a popular and affable man, was from Lombard, a region of modern-day Italy once controlled by the Frankish Emperor Charlemagne. He was a political creature, and once in government, he had used his considerable managerial skills to accomplish many social programs consistent with the interests of the Brotherhood in the communities of that region. He had been unaware of their ongoing interest in his involvements but when he had reached a high level of political responsibility his career had brought him under the serious scrutiny of the Clan. He had first been approached by an agent of Cain while serving as an adviser to the ruler over Lombard. Once contacted, he was easily compromised and accepted several gratuities along the way including membership into Cain's secret society. Through his artful intervention, many in Lombard and the surrounding region had actually converted to the ways of the Brotherhood of Cain and in due course, he had been highly instrumental in assisting the Clan to subvert the Italian government and to bring it firmly under the control of the Byzantine Empire.

Also, Simeon had a small talent for projecting his will over either the highly gullible or innately insecure among those he met. Sometimes, the talent proved quite indispensable to his career. Between his skillful administration and his subtle art of persuasion, under his management, social programs were subtly altered to suit the agenda of the Clan and lives were taken when an official was a little too slow to accept the bribe for his silence or his cooperation. As was the norm in all parts of the realm under Cain's *de facto* rule, Italia then became the target of limited armed conflict in order to pacify and subdue the masses to accept limited self-control of their lives.

Simeon's influence and success in the subjugation of Italia did not go unnoticed. And, needless to say, Simeon's success there had vaulted his career to serve in other kingdoms that had shown a similar reluctance to be managed.

After further successes over the course of time, he was asked to use his delicate handling to perform the subversion of a lifetime in the overthrow of the government of Amaziah. At the time of the invitation, when he was summoned to appear before Cain, he was a resident of Tarsatica as a First Adviser to the kingdom of Dalmatia.

A few weeks later, Shum and Simeon stood before Cain awaiting orders from the head of the Clan of the Scar. Two men could not have been more dissimilar in character, profession and physical attributes. Shum was large of stature and muscular with a handsome tanned face and finely chiseled nose. Simeon was a little older and lithesome, with an open, trusting face, seemingly always smiling. Shum was silent and reserved in nature. Simeon was gregarious and engaging, with natural charisma. Shum was a deadly assassin, whereas Simeon was a born politician with a glib tongue.

These two men had come highly recommended by a trusted member of the Brotherhood who had used them both successfully for a critical assignment in a distant part of the realm in the kingdom of Cappadocia. Cain looked them over quietly, yet thoroughly. Having been briefed beforehand on their special talents and now noting the outward attributes of each, he tried to picture them in the roles that each would play. After a few moments of private meditation, he nodded, as if satisfied. His eyes rested on first Shum then Simeon and finally on both.

His sharp eyes watched for any tremor of doubt or defiance then bored implacably into each. After a moment, he began speaking. "You both will enter the city of Amaziah in the northern region of Armenia a few weeks apart, and in short order you will declare your intentions to become citizens. You must appear to embrace the customs and assimilate their values and in all ways will you appear to be model inhabitants. Shum, because you are athletic and physically attractive, you will become involved with youth programs and present yourself as a role model of the highest caliber."

Surprise had registered on his face. "Sire, as you known, I am an assassin. My special talents hardly qualify me to be a role model for youth."

"Shum, I will concede your point. Also, I know you have an aloof nature but you have proven to be an excellent actor when you put your mind to it, thus I think you are quite capable of donning the robes of a hero if the role demands it. And in this case it has."

Slightly mollified, Shum responded, "How deeply do you expect me to delve into this role?"

"You will socialize and be engaging, even beguiling. You will encourage all manner of personal connections, including a serious one with a young woman of your choice."

"That will be a new experience, Sire. I have never been taught the finer nuances of developing a relationship."

"That is why you will depend heavily upon Simeon to teach you the social graces involved. Besides, you are attractive enough and no doubt will have your pick of eligible young ladies, but do try to show a little finesse."

Shum glanced over to his partner who smiled engagingly in his direction. Patting him playfully on the shoulder Simeon declared, "Do not worry, Shum, my boy. I have had many affairs of the heart; you are in good hands."

Cain's smile was sardonic, and looking at Simeon replied dryly, "To gain the trust of the community, his actions must appear genuine, not forced. Just see that he stays focused on his role." Cain then began a thorough briefing of what he demanded of both men as well as the scope of the assignment and its expected results.

Focusing his attention back to Shum, Cain continued. "When you have gained the full trust and respect of the community, you will be notified of the time and place then you will execute Samuel the Prophet in full view of the public. Having planned your escape beforehand, you will then report back to me. Do you have any questions?"

"How long do you expect we will have to carry on the charade? What if the community doesn't accept us?"

"Shum, I have no doubt you will gain their acceptance. Had I suspected failure, you would not have been selected for the assignment. You will remain in your role until the deed is done; I will inform you when you are no longer needed, but plan on at least three years."

Shum was stunned. Until this mission he had never been involved with a long-term assignment; all the others had lasted a few months at most. This was something far different and reflected the importance of the mission as well as Cain's commitment to its success.

Turning to Simeon, Cain instructed, "Simeon, as you have been previously briefed, the kingdom of Amaziah prides itself on the care of the sick and needy. As a consequence, you will slowly gain acceptance in the community by serving on many service committees, especially for the poor and physically disadvantaged. I want you to be a crusader and trusted friend before the community, a representative and speaker for the weak and frightened. The community must see you as someone who is trustworthy and just, in other words someone they would want to represent them in government for creating laws and policies in their behalf."

"How far up the ladder of government do you intend that I try to attain? If I am reading you correctly, I will need to reach the pinnacle of power."

"Precisely. Once you have gained their confidence and elected to a position of trust on their judgment council, you will work your magic and attain the Chief Judge Seat."

"That may take a number of years."

"It cannot be avoided. Those citizens will need to trust you to guide them through their darkest hour as they mourn the loss of their spiritual leader." Then there was a slight pause as he recalled the report of the last spy he had debriefed upon his return from Amaziah. "Beware of their Chief Judge; I understand he is highly discerning and very effective at his job. On the positive side, my informants report he only has a few years left before his forced retirement. Perhaps that can play into your overall strategy."

"What can you tell me of their personal military support?"

"Purely defensive, but they are strong and committed to the community. Along the way of gaining the trust of the citizenry, you should include their military commanders as well. You must be observant and look for any weaknesses in character and be prepared to exploit them as the circumstances present themselves to gain their support and trust. Eventually, you will procure a personal guard to stand by on the ready should the need arise.

Nodding his head, Simeon felt he now had the gist and scope of his assignment. He declared, "Once I have the support of the community and a few of their military commanders, I will meet with Shum and plan the execution of their prophet and leader."

"Exactly. Then you will decry the outrage to the public and demand a change of government. You must convince them that it is in their best interest to allow changes along the guidelines of the Brotherhood. Once Samuel is out of the way, you will gradually dissolve the council and begin instituting laws amenable to our Society."

"And, if there is a rebellion against my efforts to make these proposed changes?" asked Simeon.

"You will provide security from your personal guard until I can arrive in full force to support your rule."

Cain paused for a moment to ensure each man clearly understood his role assignment. With total conviction he stated, "Let me stress to each of you the importance of living these roles in appearance only. Too many of my former operatives who I sent into that land were lost because eventually they embraced the values of the people of Amaziah and their missions were compromised by sentimentality. If your mission is to succeed, the charade must be complete and your commitment total."

Cain then proceeded to re-outline the expected outcome of their assignments. He re-emphasized that the standing military of Amaziah would be used to support the new social order until he could arrive in force from Constantinople then later after he had returned. Because of the key role that Simeon would play in the mission, Shum would report directly to Simeon and receive his orders directly from him. As communication between Simeon and Cain would be critical, Simeon was ordered to establish an elaborate system using carrier pigeons to be set up as soon as he arrived and settled into his role in the city.

"These are your roles in broad strokes. Obviously, you will need to adapt as circumstances arise and opportunities present themselves."

Simeon was curious and because it seemed relevant to their mission he asked, "Sire, how did the existence of these people come to your attention?"

"Your question brings me to the second objective of your mission. Our Emperor, Silas, hails from Armenia and after I had placed him upon the throne he now enjoys, he made me aware of an enclave of unusual citizens who had settled in a remote part of his country centuries before."

"Unusual?" A look of confusion crossed Simeon's brow.

"They were known as "The Tribes", though some referred to them as the "Historians.""

"Sorry, Sire, but I still don't follow."

Cain patiently replied, "They have maintained a written history of their sojourn from the land of Palestine to Armenia up until the present day. It was reported that they have a large depository of records and the acquisition of this cache of documents for the Clan represent the second objective of your mission. I want you to verify their existence and if they exist, as I am sure that they do, I want them."

Neither man understood the significance of the second objective, but both realized that if Cain wanted their records, that was the end of it and no further discussion was necessary. Turning the conversation back to the first point, Shum, realizing that it would be up to him to execute their spiritual leader, asked, "Who is this prophet they call Samuel?"

With a contemptuous smile, Cain said, "Supposedly, he is their holy man, but do not allow that to sully your view of the assignment. There have been many from that region of the world that made a similar claim but none have ever been immune to a well-placed arrow or blade to the throat and I should know."

"Do you know this man personally?"

"No. I didn't make the connection at first, but when it became known to me that the people of Amaziah were record-keepers then I realized that I knew of the man. He is a descendent of an old friend and that makes him dangerous to our takeover. The only thing you have to know about him is that he represents the primary obstacle to the completion of your mission. He must be removed before the Clan can move in and assume control of their government." *Yes*, Cain thought, *killing Samuel would be a pleasant revenge indeed. Jasher is the only one of his breed that is considered untouchable, but that special dispensation does not apply to his descendants.*

He looked each over critically and said, "This will be my last effort to use subterfuge on these people. Do not fail me." He did not care what Lucifer had informed him. Amaziah would be his or he would tear it down and force the citizens to accept his government. *And if heads had to roll then so be it; the consequences be damned.*

It was a chilly night, and after dismissing the two men, Cain walked slowly over to the hearth and began adding more logs and stirring them about, creating more heat from the hot embers. This small activity always seemed to lessen his anxiety and cleanse his mind, helping him focus on the problems at hand.

He had nearly completed this routine when he heard a voice behind him smoothly whisper, "Cain, you should relax, the plan will succeed."

Cain did not bother to turn around and acknowledge the words of encouragement. Instead he muttered, "We have won so many battles, yet this one is so reminiscent of our failure with Zion. If we fail, it could tip the scales against us irrevocably." He went back to stirring the coals, his mind still deep in thought.

CHAPTER 4

SEBA'S DILEMMA

T hough reserved by nature, Seba was nonetheless a kindly, attentive man and thus when presented with an opportunity to serve as personal servant to Haner, a Judge of Amaziah, he was honored and grateful for the appointment. His wife, Leah, also served as the house cook and both were provided a comfortable, though modest cottage nearby Haner's home where they could live and concurrently attend closely to the needs of the judge.

One might describe Seba as a family man, yet he and his wife of twenty-three years were childless, which is to say that he was family-minded and had always desired children. He had been thus far unsuccessful at consummating the marriage to include offspring, though not for lack of trying during the earlier years of his marriage. But, alas it was not meant to be; thus, soon they would be asked to think responsibly of adoption as was the custom in the city of Amaziah for those in their circumstance. But, this lack of having natural children when so many others of the city were successful was a serious blow to Seba's self-esteem. Still, he was a careful, considerate man totally devoted to his wife and fulfilling his role as a faithful servant. It was unfortunate that his deep seated issues of inadequacy would eventually lead to a break with his sanity.

From the outset, Seba had always been carefully respectful in his relationship with the judge. Because Amaziah was a city where all were treated of equal value, a truly classless society, there were no servants in the sense of someone in a lower class whose role would be considered less important than any other. Thus, when Seba perceived that Haner had begun to be more peremptory and had assumed an ever increasing condescending tone as master of his home, he had naturally taken offense, especially once the criticisms began to be hurled in the direction of his wife.

This evening, Seba was hoping that Haner had thrown off the funk of the last few days. With a smile, he deferentially entered the sitting room to announce the evening meal. He experimented with an amiable, yet hopeful tone of encouragement. "Judge Haner, Leah has completed the evening meal and has set a fine place for us all at the dining table."

Haner stood brooding near the hearth of the fireplace. His eyes moved restlessly as the flames shifted from one color to the next; the Judge seemed mesmerized, detached, even unplugged from his surroundings. Thinking Judge Haner may have misunderstood him, Seba again informed him the table had been set and the dinner was ready.

The Judge turned, slowly blinking his eyes as if coming out of a stupor of thought. Then his anger erupted. "What are you so pleased about, Seba? I heard you the first time!" he snapped. Haner followed Seba into the dining hall, muttering under his breath; it was obvious the judge was angry over something.

When they were all seated, Leah began serving the two men and finally herself. Seba attempted to deflect the strained mood of the evening and asked, "Judge, how was your day? Please tell us about the new legislation to increase community services."

The Judge had slowly raised his head and a dark, rancorous shadow had crossed his face. From a mask of hate broiled a voice filled with the scorn of elite privilege. "Seba, why should I bother explaining such complex legislation to a servant and a cook?" he shot back. "The very idea of you people understanding such things is an affront to my position. In the future, I expect you two do your job and aspire to nothing else!"

Seba, unassertive by nature, was speechless, but managed a weak defense. "I am sorry, Judge Haner. I was unaware you felt that way."

Haner sniffed disdainfully and gave them both a withering frown of distaste. He ate in silence, refusing to engage in any further discussions; the table conversation was now over. Not wishing to incur further oral abuse, both servants refrained from any more attempts to engage Haner that evening. Both felt humiliated from the experience so they quickly finished their dinner then retired to their home nearby.

Judge Haner had been a highly respected member of the community for nearly thirty-seven years. He had served in varying capacities with success and eventually the voice of the people had desired he serve them on the ruling council. He had modestly accepted the honor and for the past six years he had unfailingly dedicated his life in that capacity. Lately, however, matters of state had begun to oppress him; there was no more joy in his involvement. He was not sure why this was so, only that it was.

During the time of his service on the council, there had occurred many personal changes in his life. All of his children were now adults with families of their own and Rachel, his wife of forty-six years, had died only two years previously. He felt alone and the fear of meeting death without her was slowly grinding him down. If depression had been his only ailment, perhaps he may have eventually found help, but his sickness went much deeper.

For months, his behavior had become more and more erratic. At the outset of his affliction he was energetic and alert on one day, but the next he was aloof and despondent. Lately, his behavior had given way to constant criticism and impatience. It had taken all his powers of concentration to avoid any angry scenes or outbursts of emotion in his service on the ruling council of Amaziah. At home, however, with his guard down his attentiveness slipped and his acerbic emotions had begun to take command of his behavior. The Judge was only dimly aware that his memory was failing and his ability to hang on to reality was now in serious jeopardy. Unfortunately, Haner's sickness was not outwardly physical and so difficult to detect. In fact, the only two persons who might have been aware of his steadily deteriorating mental condition were Seba and Leah.

Seba and Leah walked quietly to their nearby cottage in a state of deep concern. From the beginning of their employ, Leah had grown increasingly fond of the Judge. He had been a considerate, engaging man and had gone out of his way to make them feel comfortable in his home. Now, concern for Haner's health had finally reached a point of serious discussion.

Leah finally whispered, "What is wrong with Judge Haner, Seba? The past few months, his behavior has become erratic, almost childish in his demands and his criticisms."

"There was nothing child-like in his voice tonight," Seba commented.

The mid-spring evening was cool but summer was coming on soon. For him, it was his favorite season of the year, but Haner's anger this evening had put a damper on his usual high spirits. The two walked on, and as they turned toward the path leading to their cottage, Seba finally remarked, "The Judge may be sick or perhaps he just misses his wife. It must be difficult for him to grow old and have no companion by his side."

Leah nodded her head in understanding. "For me, it would be the most difficult challenge to endure. I have grown so dependent of your care and companionship that I am unsure what I would do without you."

Seba smiled and patted her shoulder. "Should I pass on before you, you would adapt even as I." He thought a moment then added, "But, Haner was doing so well with his loss. Perhaps it is something else that bothers him now."

Leah, now determined to help the Judge, came to a decision. "We must make an effort to help the man, Seba. Please make discreet inquiries among our doctors. Perhaps there is an herb that we could recommend to Haner to sooth him and diminish the rough edge to his behavior."

Seba was thoughtful for a moment then replied, "You are right, Leah. I will visit an apothecary tomorrow who might be able to prescribe a tea that would be beneficial for him. We know him best and it is our responsibility."

After the two servants had retired, the Judge had clothed in his night robe to prepare for bed, but had got no farther to his bed chamber than the doorway. If was now fifteen minutes later and Judge Haner still stood in the same location, now uncertain and uneasy. The longer he remained standing, the more he found the idea of sleep deeply repugnant. It had been a particularly long day and the matters of state had been especially demanding. More people were arriving to Amaziah each day and there would be a shortage of housing before long unless he could develop a more efficient manner to deal with the influx. "There is too much to be done," he whispered to no one.

Turning away from the bed chamber, he shambled distractedly through the house, all the while muttering and shaking his head as if to clear his mind from conversations that had begun to assail his mind and senses. It is the voices again, he groaned. His hands arose to his ears in an attempt to shut them out. He cried aloud, "I shall not listen." But, it was no good. The voices of his colleagues on the council then finally those of his servants beat incessantly into his mind and gave him no relief. They all wanted the same thing: his death. He began to cry. "Is there no one who can help me?" He moaned.

An hour later and near exhaustion, his mind now feverish from the constant barrage of insistent voices that could not be ignored nor shut out, Judge Haner entered his bedroom and waited. Finally, the voices began to fade, but instead of crawling into the bed, he leaned against the far wall and slid to the floor. While his eyes darted from side-to-side awaiting their return, his hands began to shake. At length he could do little more than moan and weep for the peace he had lost since Rachel had passed on. Leah found him the next morning curled up on the floor next to his bed. His agitation, if anything, had grown only worse by the next evening.

"You impertinent fool!" cried the Judge. "How dare you insinuate that I am ill? I am simply tired from my long hours of thankless toil on behalf of the community. If you carried the weight of so much responsibility as I, you too, would feel the anxieties. But, just look at you with your menial tasks and mundane life. What do you know of my problems?" The two were in the kitchen while Leah stood to one side with a hand over her mouth to calm her quivering lips. The Judge hovered over Seba like an evil ogre with a mask of unbridled rage.

Seba was appalled at the outburst, but could only summon the courage for a humble defense. "Judge Haner, please excuse my concern over your welfare. Leah and I could not ignore your behavior of late; no doubt it was because of these anxieties of which you speak. I merely felt that a soothing herbal tea would be of benefit to you in the late evenings."

"Well, as usual Seba, you have thought wrongly and you ignore your place. Now, bring me my usual herbal blend with honey and be quick about it!"

Simeon, Cain's agent, had been present at Judge Haner's home that evening on committee business and had overheard the angry outburst coming from the kitchen. A moment later and the Judge returned to the sitting room to welcome his guest and as they were chatting, Seba entered the room attentively with tea for both Haner and Simeon.

Judge Haner took a tentative sip then scowled. Apparently, his herbal tea was not warm enough to his liking and he shouted, "You witless cretin, you have brought me tepid tea! You know how much I abhor tea that has been poorly prepared. Now get back to your station and warm up the tea properly and do not return until you have it right!"

With a baleful look of disdain, he pushed the hot cup of tea back into Seba's hand, burning his fingers as the tea sloshed over the brim. Clearly embarrassed at the outburst, Seba mumbled an apology then turned silently back to the kitchen to fetch another cup. Simeon, ever one to notice an opportunity to gain an advantage, noticed the look of cringing humiliation on the servant's face as he scurried passed him. Since his arrival in Amaziah, Simeon had been relentless in his efforts to discover a way to insinuate his way into the upper chambers of government, but his efforts had born little fruit. Simeon made note of the caustic comments the Judge had reserved for his servant and Seba's mortified reaction. It had given him the beginnings of an idea and a plan of action that would reverse his failed efforts.

It was a brilliant, sunny morning a few days later when Simeon made it his business to casually bump into Seba as he was walking to the market for the daily shopping. With all due kindness, he apologetically greeted him. "I am so sorry Seba, I was not looking. I get so busy sometimes I can scarcely keep up with my own feet." His smile was engaging as he asked Seba if he had a few moments to talk.

"Think nothing of it, Councilman Simeon. I too, was gathering wool and should have been more alert. Yes, I would be delighted to chat with you."

As most everyone in Amaziah, Seba was immediately impressed with Simeon because of his dedication and complete regard and respect for everyone, even those that were the meekest amongst them. Seba reflected, in spite of Simeon's demanding schedule, he made such a wonderful effort at ensuring everyone was comfortable in his presence. Most important men, he had recently learned, had nothing but disdain for those who tirelessly served them

The two men chatted over town gossip and the latest sporting events for some time. Both laughed and critiqued the most recent outcomes. Seba exclaimed excitedly, "Councilman, you have such an astute eye for details. I admire that in a man."

"Seba, please call me Simeon. When we are together in the market or on the street, I insist that you refer to me in the familiar. We should be friends." Simeon decided it was time to delicately turn the subject toward Haner and so began to probe the depth of Seba's bitterness. "After all, we both feel a mutual responsibility toward Judge Haner, do we not?" Seba's buoyant demeanor visibly dropped.

Simeon took Seba by the elbow and gently guided him over to a nearby bench where they could talk in private. "Tell me, Seba, and please be honest, are you enjoying your life as a servant to such an important public figure as Judge Haner?"

Sensing that his new friend, Simeon could be trusted, he began to share with him his growing concern at Haner's recent behavior towards him. "Simeon, you were there the other night when the Judge lashed out at me. I can assure you that his behavior that night was not isolated. Over the past few months, his anger and criticisms of me and Leah have only gotten worse over time."

"Curious you should mention it, Seba. Of late, the Judge has seemed more distant, more prone to confrontation with those on the council. One day he seems ebullient and engaging, then next aloof and short with everyone. I thought I was the only member of the council to notice it, but others, too, have observed and commented discretely, of course, this change. I have not known Haner for as long as other citizens, but I had the impression that he had always been the kindest and most respectful of men, a true leader of the community."

"You are quite correct, Simeon; the Judge Haner of late is not the same man. At his home, my wife and I must tiptoe carefully around him now so as to avoid his wrath. If what you say is true, his private behavior has begun to spill over into his public service." Seba, clearly upset, was unable to meet the councilor's eyes. He bowed his head slightly then admitted reluctantly, "Simeon, to be honest, lately Haner has been condescending and critical towards me and my wife. As you know, such behavior in Amaziah should never occur and is not to be tolerated."

Simeon nodded his head in sympathy. With an encouraging smile, he said firmly, "My Brother, you are quite right. What do you intend to do?"

With anguish, he confessed, "We cannot simply leave him. How will the community respond? Our neighbors might think we were being petty and trying to shirk our responsibilities."

Simeon had a keen ear for those who felt disaffected and this was precisely what he wanted to hear. Smiling inwardly, pretension slid over Simeon as a finely molded mask. He pointed out, "I am sure Haner is a fine man and if you were feeling abused he would be willing to listen to your concerns. Have you approached him on this matter?"

Seba responded apathetically, "I had hoped that I could reach him with kindness or reason, but that too has become impossible; he shuts me off from any discussion. You heard him the other evening." Seba raked a shaky hand through his hair then continued. "The depth of his anger and resentment seems to have no boundaries. Even after an attempt to recommend a curative herb, I was severely chastised."

"Perhaps if both you and your wife could sit him down and talk with him, I am sure he would listen. Another person might make a difference."

"We have tried, but he continues to ignore us. I grow weary of his oral abuse and I abhor his treatment of my wife, but what can be done?" he asked with exasperation.

Simeon looked as though he were deep in thought, trying to come up with a solution. Finally, he said with feigned compassion, "Seba, I cannot bear to watch your misery as this man demeans your dignity." Simeon faced the distraught man and placed his hand firmly on Seba's shoulder. "May I make a suggestion that I think will solve your problem?"

Seba caught Simeon's gaze and slightly flinched then with a glow of gratitude on his face, he eagerly accepted Simeon's show of understanding. "Please, Simeon, if you know of some way we can perform our service to Haner without rancor, I beg of you to help us. Otherwise, Leah and I must terminate our arrangement with the community. On the other hand, we cannot become a burden either. We have been given so much and we do so want to fulfill our obligations. You do see our dilemma?"

"Of course, my dear friend, but you need not worry any further. Please come by my residence this evening and I will discuss with you an idea that has just occurred to me. It will require your absolute faith and trust, but if you can do this, then I can provide the means for you to extricate yourself from this intolerable situation."

Seba blinked twice. "Thank you." He could think of nothing else to say.

Simeon provided him an address not far from the town plaza. "Please come by my home after Haner retires for the evening and we will talk." Squeezing Seba on the shoulder, he reassured him, "This will be a special talk just between the two of us." Simeon made closer eye contact then gently whispered in a carefully modulated tone close to his ear, "You will not need to inform your wife of our meeting. Tell her you are going out for an evening walk. For now, this matter will be our secret."

Now tenderly, Simeon, with a mellow smile of friendship suffused across his face, slowly pulled back from Seba. The servant again blinked his eyes twice then nodded his head in understanding of Simeon's offer as though the thought had come naturally to his mind. With a smile he arose to go and to his surprise and complete joy, Simeon embraced him as an equal and wished him a good afternoon. As the two men parted company, Simeon calculated that if he could use his considerable powers of persuasion to dissemble this fool completely, he would be one step closer to accomplishing his mission.

Simeon's mother was an apothecary and exceptional at what she did. She had collected and concocted nearly two hundred different recipes for various medical symptoms. In addition to her ability to prepare compound herbs with naturally forming metals, such as arsenic for medicinal purposes, she was also highly adept at devising poisons. Before starting this assignment to Amaziah, Simeon had visited the esteemed lady and had acquired several such compounds, which when administered slowly and over time would create chronic, short to long term illnesses. One such compound consisted of arsenic and several herbs and when taken together would produce a potent hallucinogenic effect of euphoria, but cause slow degeneration of the liver and kidneys to the victim that would eventually cause death.

Thus, when Seba arrived eagerly that evening to discuss what could be done with his now strained domestic relationship with Haner, Simeon was prepared to provide the answer he desired. Of course, the answer he had in mind for Haner consisted of a lethal dose of arsenic.

Simeon met Seba at the door and greeted him. "Seba, my friend, welcome to my home and please enter."

"Thank you Simeon." Seba rushed in, nearly breathless from the anticipation of having an answer to his worry over his eroding relationship with Judge Haner. Now with eyes all agog and darting from one corner of the room to another, it was clear Seba was in a distracted stage of anticipation. He nearly panted at the notion of a solution and gibbered, "I have been giving your offer considerable thought all afternoon and I sincerely hope you can help our friend, Judge Haner. Actually, I have been counting the moments all day."

Simeon realized immediately that his suggestion to Seba had created a nervous, agitated state of mind. To reduce his anxiety, he employed a few pacifying methods to reduce his anxious behavior. With a quiet, modulating voice, he managed to catch Seba's eyes with his own and said, "Seba, please get me caught up on your family. I ran into Leah in the market today and by chance she mentioned her father was under the weather."

Seba blinked a few times then with a slower, more casual voice he said, "Under the weather would be an understatement. Of late, he seems on the verge of complete exhaustion, but at his age, he does little manual labor, so we are at a loss as to his actual illness and hope that it is not terminal."

Simeon commiserated. "As you know, Seba, old age and sickness go hand-in-hand. It is the natural process of life to death and moreover a condition to which we all must eventually succumb. My own mother was robust and active then suddenly became afflicted and never recovered."

"Oh, I am so sorry to hear of your loss, Simeon. It must have been hard."

Simeon's mask of deception fell easily into place. "Her sickness was crushing, but I nursed her for as long as possible. Emotionally, we became close and near the end when she was in so much pain, she allowed me to stay by her side until her passing."

What a dolt, he inwardly chortled. *He is buying the whole act.* Now putting on a strong front, a tear of sorrow formed at the corner of each eye and slowly fell, but he smiled bravely and admitted, "Yes, it was hard, but our love prevailed in spite of her suffering." The whole story was, of course, a fabrication, but he intended for the performance to be perfect. An unshrinking look of long suffering flitted across his face. It provided just the right touch, he decided. As if coming out of a sad reverie, he brushed away his tears of false sorrow then he seemed to gain strength. "But, that is enough talk of me." He asked quietly, "What medications have been used to care for your father-in-law?"

Seba began to relate that he had gone to a local apothecary for assistance. Simeon listened attentively then congratulated him on his use of the correct medication. He added, "Though I am far from an expert, my mother was an exceptional apothecary and she shared much of her knowledge with me before her passing. I can assure you that you are using the correct herbal medication to treat your father-in-law."

"So, I am doing all that can be done for him?"

"Seba, he is in good hands," Simeon added with encouragement.

Seba appeared delighted that his choice of remedy had been verified. Simeon realized that his subject was now primed to be guided in the right direction, but this next comment was critical and would have to be stated ever so carefully. "Seba, this discussion of medications is so fortuitous. I have been pondering over your current dilemma with Haner and have what I feel is the solution to your problems." Simeon was watching Seba closely so as to detect any lack of interest on his part. He need not have worried. Seba was leaning slightly forward with dilated eyes and was now highly suggestible.

"As it so happens, I suffer from a similar malady as Haner. The more nervous or anxious I become, the more I tend to be short and peremptory with those around me. As my profession requires I work closely with people for positive change, I must outwardly be congenial and diplomatic. Without help, I would soon begin to offend those to whom I wish to work and serve."

Seba nodded slightly, blinking a few times. He moistened his lips with his tongue and with an earnest voice asked, "Whatever did you do, Simeon?"

"My mother prepared me an herbal powder that moderates my natural mood swings and allows me to function at a highly successful level. I have no doubt that it will work in a similar manner for Haner." Simeon paused to allow what he had said to penetrate Seba's highly suggestible mind.

Seba was enthralled and could not take his eyes away from Simeon's. Again, he murmured, almost drowsily, "May I know what it is?"

Simeon leaned forward, again making eye contact and said, "Seba, my dear friend, you have been worried of late over your relationship with Haner, but I assure you that the remedy will soon be in your hands."

Seba, now slowly blinking his eyes and a little dazed, actually felt quite happy that his problem was soon to be solved. Simeon carefully reached into his robe and pulled out a vial filled with white powder. He beckoned Seba to extend his hand and then he placed the container in his outstretched palm. He now intended to plant a long-term auto-suggestion into Seba's delicate psyche.

Simeon continued in a soft voice, "The powder inside is completely taste-less and dissolves readily in liquid. Simply add a small amount in Haner's tea each evening along with his usual herbal blend and serve it warm. You will immediately begin to see a wonderful change in his mood and attitude towards you and Leah. I assure you that you will be doing him an incredible favor. His job can cause anxiety and this herbal powder will help him main-tain a more balanced attitude and behavior."

Seba had a thoughtful, slightly vacant look on his face then abruptly it changed to a smile of gratitude as it slowly registered in his mind the great gift Simeon had provided him. Seba took both of Simeon's hands in his own and thanked him profusely for the help with his dilemma. Simeon arose and, taking Seba by the arm, accompanied him to the door.

Before passing out of the doorway, with a slight smile of gratitude, Seba again took his friend's hand and gave a reassuring squeeze. He suddenly felt the need to embrace his own resolve and so remarked, "Simeon, I will begin the treatment immediately."

Seba turned to exit, but Simeon clasped both of his hands lightly upon Seba's shoulders and sent him one last suggestion. "Seba, given Haner's current reluctance to be helped, he may not understand the good you are doing him, so let us keep this matter between just the two of us. Your wife need not know either. When the vial is empty, simply break it then dispose of it. You and I shall meet again every few weeks to discuss his condition." Seba nodded his agreement with a somewhat vacant smile then walked slowly away from the residence.

A short time later, almost to Haner's home now, Seba reached into his belt and felt the reassuring contours of the vial. He didn't know why it should feel so pleasing. After all, it was merely a small bottle, but as he approached the door to Haner's residence, he held it firmly in his palm. It occurred to Seba that he was looking forward to seeing the Judge happy once again. A sudden smile appeared on his face.

While Seba walked confidently back to his home, Simeon was happily seated in his parlor; his smile of the gracious host had been replaced with that of the clever beguiler. He decided he had reason for self-congratulation. *The suggestions I have planted in Seba's dim-witted mind have been accepted and from this point forward, I can guide his behavior. Cain will be pleased we are one step closer to our goal.*

CHAPTER 5

SOCIAL VISITS

S hum was always one to chase the morning. An early riser, he climbed from his bed and proceeded to perform his exercise routine, and as he worked out, he began to reflect over his stay in Amaziah. Thus far, the experience had been enjoyable, but sometimes it was difficult to reconcile his mission parameters with his feelings toward his involvement in the city. He had been warned that this would happen, but still it sometimes left him confused.

His athleticism, his vigorous prowess and numerous victories on the track and field had quickly earned him celebrity status. Off the field, his untiring devotion to Amaziah's youth committees had set him apart as a dedicated, caring member of the community. Owing to his influence, he was successful in his efforts to reach out and make positive change to disaffected youth. For the past few years, in every way a man could be a role model for young people, Shum had been an outstanding example.

So as not to cause parents and community elders to question his moral values toward the young people of the community, he immediately saw the need to appear romantically interested in young women nearer his own age. After several months of socializing, he finally saw an opportunity to achieve several of his mission goals at the same time. The older sister of one of the troubled young men with whom he was working became a natural target for his attention. His meeting with her tonight had been scheduled a few days prior, and as usual, he looked forward to their weekly dinner engagements.

His daily calisthenics completed, he walked out into the morning sunshine. On his way to the gymnasium, he met with the young man who he had specifically targeted to be an integral part of the mission. As he greeted him with is most sincere smile, he realized that it was growing harder to deceive him. He was after all, the younger brother of the young woman he was seeing later that evening.

Across town, Simeon was meeting with Jared, the Presiding Chief Judge of Amaziah. If his mission was to succeed, Simeon would first have to curry favor from this man. Simeon had always been an astute scholar of human nature and this ability had served him well during the years prior to arriving among the people of Amaziah. As a young man, he had discovered he had a natural flare for politics and an innate understanding of human nature. He could set a man at ease and pick his brain for any weakness in character at the same time. The problem was Simeon had always been a political creature and dealt directly with politicians and knew exactly how to speak their language. Thus, his manner of thinking tended to be narrow and it was difficult to step out of this comfort zone and deal with someone as altruistic as Judge Jared who was no ordinary politician. Perceptive as well as self-abasing, he too possessed similar traits of discernment and Simeon was well aware of this ability. For Jared there were only two shades of color when it came to judging a man's character, black or white, and he never left you in doubt the shade of color he favored.

The Judge had a natural intuition and seemed to know when he was being manipulated or flattered. Jared lacked guile, but could see it immediately in others. In an effort to deflect Jared's innate understanding of beguilement, Simeon had always gone to great strides to ensure the Chief Judge was at ease in his presence. Nevertheless, unlike himself the judge wore no false mask, thus Simeon realized he would have to assume his most sincere pose when dealing with this man. On one occasion, he had even attempted to use his mind tricks on Jared, but had failed. He dared not reattempt the effort.

Simeon was now seated opposite Jared and leaning slightly forward, with his best somber tone, he said, "Judge Jared, as you are aware, my committee reports directly to your third councilor, Judge Haner, who presides over the welfare of the sick and indigent of the city. I regret to inform you that of late he has taken seriously ill."

A register of deep concern fell over the Judge. "How is my esteemed colleague? I visited his home only this past week and his family had made me aware of his deteriorating condition. I was distraught to see him suffering so."

"I, too, had been aware of his ailment and so had decided to pay a visit this morning. According to his daughter, as well as his doctors, Judge Haner has taken a turn for the worse. He has expressed his wish to step down and allow another to preside in his place, if only temporarily."

"I see. His request is unsurprising, given his current disposition. And now it appears his condition has worsened. Do the doctors have any idea from what he suffers?"

Simeon put on his best sad and grieving face, but added his long suffering look for good measure. He shook his head sadly and, as though pronouncing a funerary speech replied grimly, "I am afraid not, Judge. Moreover, they are not optimistic that a recovery will be forthcoming. According to the doctors, his health began to decline some four months ago, though, according to some he had begun to show signs of an infirmity even earlier, but in the spirit of the great servant he was, he worked through it."

Jared sadly commiserated, and knowing how closely Simeon and Haner had labored over the past year, he nodded regretfully, "I was afraid of that."

Simeon changed his mask slightly and tried one of humble optimism. It seemed to fit, thus he was confident as he quietly remarked, "Judge Jared, we all pray that his condition will improve, but should the health of our beloved colleague continue to decline, I was hoping you might endorse my request to assume his post, at least until a permanent decision could be made."

The Judge seemed to think that over, but his eyes were alight with hope. He had despaired that his old colleague and friend would never return to fill his Judgment Seat. Simeon's suggestion, though somewhat presumptuous, was a godsend, given the wheels of government must continue to turn in spite of any setbacks to health. There really was no one else capable of stepping in on such short notice. Finally, he nodded as if coming to a decision. "Simeon, I can think of no one more qualified to execute the office of our esteemed councilor and judge. You have exceptional managerial skills and your tireless work as chairman of your committee has set yourself apart as a man of the people."

"Thank you, Your Honor. I was only doing my duty in partial payment for all the love and support of the community."

"It is simply amazing how much you have been able to accomplish in the few short years you have been a citizen of our country."

"It is gratifying to know I have your support and respect, sir."

Jared, though outwardly delighted at Simeon's request for further service, had always been reticent to completely accept him. His manner always seemed slightly insincere as though he were playing an elaborate role. He chided himself on being overly hard on the man who, after all, had demonstrated himself not only an unflagging servant of the people but much beloved and respected. He had to give the man credit. He did have a natural charisma about him. "I shall bring your name before the counseling board at our next meeting and heartily support your full endorsement."

"Thank you, sir," replied Simeon and embraced the Chief Judge according to local custom. "It shall be my pleasure to serve you and our city in that capacity." A few minutes later and Simeon walked out of the chamber room. He was thinking about Haner, the man he was so eager to replace, and from all reports and his personal observation, Judge Haner had become permanently bed-ridden. It was just a matter of time before he succumbed to the debilitating effects of the poison administered at Seba's dedicated hands.

Though most people of Amaziah were generous and accepting, Simeon recalled that he still had to be careful that he did not raise any undue suspicions from this point forward. He picked up his pace so as to be at home and prepared when Shum arrived. Tomorrow, he wanted a briefing of Haner's declining condition, but more to the point, he needed to give Seba a reinforcing push to stabilize his emotional distress. In the last meeting a few weeks prior, the servant's mind appeared to be unraveling from the frequent suggestions Simeon had placed in his mind to boost his continual compliance with the mission. Haner's ailment, he now knew from his physicians, was terminal and therefore Seba's services were no longer needed. Eventually, Haner would be out of the way, but in the meantime, he would have to deal with Seba. He had decided that Shum would be part of that task. Looking up into the waning light of the day, he stepped up his pace in anticipation of his meeting with Shum later that evening. The mission was coming to a critical stage now and he wanted to ensure Shum's head was still in the game.

Hana brushed her long, strawberry blond hair in a fashion that she knew set off her finest physical attributes: her deep, green eyes, her fine patrician nose and throat. Around her neck, she wore a beautiful gold necklace with alternating stones of garnet and topaz with matching earrings. Her *stola*, or robe, was modest, of course, but of a shade of green which accentuated and complemented her eyes. She was entertaining Shum tonight and intended to be as fetching as she was capable and the norms of the city would allow. Secretly, she would have preferred something more alluring, but her mother had warned her that if Shum was the right man, he would prefer her to be modest and not wanton. But, oh, she wanted to be wanton with that man.

Her brother, Cainan, now fourteen entered the room in his usual brash manner, but unlike his old self that was impetuous and angry, the new brash was less severe, more controlled. The family had Shum to thank for that and his mother and sister did that at every opportunity. Cainan had developed into a master archer, a latent talent that Shum had helped him to discover and was now a source of personal pride for the boy. Of late, it had become obvious his prowess with a bow now approached that of Shum, his mentor and closest friend. After finding a seat, he picked up a nearby bow, a recurve model in exquisite condition given him by Shum, and to Cainan, it was prized above all things he owned. His mind now on the upcoming tournament, he found a comfortable position and began to tenderly polish the bow.

Cainan had lost his father to a construction accident when he was ten years of age and had never fully recovered from the loss. Then, a year ago, Shum had come into his life and everything about the boy had changed.

Suddenly, he accepted more personal accountability and was developing an interest for increased achievement in his studies. He was much less rebellious and less apt to allow his temper to dictate his emotions and his fists rule his actions. In short, he was no longer looking at life with an angry belligerence, but with more tolerance.

Hana's mother, Rachel, was no less beautiful than her daughter but in a more mature way. She walked gracefully into the room and, seeing her son asked, "Cainan, please stand up. I want to make sure you are presentable. Shum will be arriving soon and your sister wants everything to be perfect."

Cainan glanced up slowly but never missed a delicate stroke as he lovingly continued his care of the bow. "Perfection in the social graces is not a goal to which I aspire, Mother." His response, though flippant, carried none of the previous anger of a year ago; he was simply distracted.

Rachel's smile was affectionate. *At least, he would be open-minded for some change in his attire should it be necessary.* "Let me look you over."

With indulgent reluctance, Cainan arose and presented himself for a cursory inspection. As she looked him over, she found his tunic to be suitably appropriate for someone approaching adulthood, but had not yet acquired the graces necessary to be interested. She adored her son, and up until the last year she despaired that he would ever be civil enough to attract and maintain close friendships.

Looking over to Hana she asked her daughter, "Hana, what do you think?"

"Presentable." She flounced her hair and turned to her mother, "The real question is: how do I look?"

Cainan shot back, "Presentable." A smile played across his face as he had hit the mark. Her scowl was more than enough to let him know that he was ahead in points for the evening. The young man tolerated the inspection from his mother then returned to the bow.

"Ok, that's enough you two," Rachel gently chided. Looking back at her daughter she commented, "Your earrings and necklace complement the color of your *stola* wonderfully. I am sure Shum will notice."

Hana chewed on her lip briefly then replied, "I hope so. I want tonight to be special."

"I am sure that it will dear, but please try to be patient with the man."

"Mother, Shum will be here any moment!" she exclaimed. "How is my hair? You know I want to look especially good for him tonight!" For some time now Hana had been watching Shum with an eye to a proposal for marriage. She strongly felt it would be soon and hoped it would be tonight after the evening meal when they would be alone.

"Hana, you look beautiful!" replied Rachel. With love she carefully reminded her daughter, "Please try to be more gracious and less eager. If the time is right, you both will know it."

Cainan, temporarily halting the maintenance of his bow, slightly raised his head in his sister's direction. "Know what?" he asked with typical male density.

The women exchanged exasperated looks and smiled at Cainan's obtuse understanding of his sister's love interests. Rachel felt he should at least be aware of Hana's intentions, so she quietly explained, "Hana has feelings for Shum and she hopes he feels the same for her."

"Oh." Cainan responded without further interest. He resumed his polishing of the bow as well as his thoughts of the upcoming archery tournament that he hoped to win.

Shum was punctual and arrived at the appointed time of the meal. After Rachel showed him into the foyer, he saw Cainan with the bow and announced, "Well, youngster, are you ready to take on the master yet?"

Cainan's smile was instantaneous. "The master? Careful, you may be addressing him before too long."

Shum rushed the young man and locked him in an arm hold. Their usual playful exuberance then proceeded by trading mock punches to the shoulder and face. This duel always ended with one or the other remonstrating to the other who would truly win such a match, then breaking up with good-natured male laugher.

As the men were playing their boyish roles, both women looked on with unvarnished affection and laughed along with them at their playful protestations of victory. Rachel glanced sideways at her daughter and saw the bright color high in her neck and cheeks. Her eyes were bright, gleaming and fixed on Shum. *Oh my,* thought Rachel. *I may have to send Shum home early tonight.*

When the game between Shum and Cainan had run its course, Shum looked over to Hana and his heart, trying to escape, got caught in his throat. If it was possible to appear stunned and hopelessly adoring at the same time, he knew he had just achieved it. To Shum, Hana had become the epitome of beauty and grace. He smiled and quietly greeted her, oblivious now of everything but Hana.

"Hello, Hana. You look wonderful tonight." His hazel eyes had a glow to them of his own. Unabashed love sprung out that he knew must be obvious to everyone.

Rachel definitely noticed. She nodded her approval that Hana had caught the eye of this man and for once she agreed with her choice. Her daughter had made mistakes before giving her heart away to other younger men in the community who lacked the maturity for an adult relationship. Each one had all ended with Hana having her hopes dashed and her heart broken. Shum was more mature, and she reminded herself, really a perfect age for her daughter; at thirty-three, he was nine years her senior.

Looking around at Hana, her mother and brother, Shum realized that he had never known such feelings of family in his life. When he thought of his first family a sense of helpless anger and despair nearly consumed him. So as to avoid that hurt, he had spent much of his youth and now his adulthood repressing all memory of those terrible days in Levant.

His boyhood in the land of Macedonia had been one of loneliness and despair, being passed around from one relative to another and never grasping love in the truest sense. Eventually, he had found purpose in athletic games and his prowess with the bow had come under the scrutiny of a distant uncle who observed a young man with great potential to help the Brotherhood. That had been the beginning of his career with weaponry and the art of the assassin and that had also been the extent of a loving family life, such as it was.

He knew now this would be his last mission. He had lost no love at the thought of leaving the Brotherhood behind, but he was still emotionally conflicted to do his duty. He had taken the assignment from Cain more out of simple curiosity than any deliberate thought. He had never before been asked to be a deep cover, long term operative and he had wondered if he could play the role convincingly. To his amazement, it had all come so easily and naturally. His problem was that he no longer saw himself as a man with a knife, always ready for the kill. He had given more of himself to this role than he had expected and had received so much in return.

Shum felt completely at ease with Hana and her family. The evening meal, now completed, had been delicious, but he scarcely remembered what he had eaten because he had been so focused on Hana. Occasionally, he would take his eyes off her just long enough to answer a relevant question from Rachel or Cainan. After dining, everyone had retired to the living area and had engaged in a lively conversation about the upcoming archery tournament in one week.

Rachel commented, "I have it on good authority that there will be contestants from many parts of Armenia and some from as far away as Tarsus."

"Bring them on," boasted Cainan. "I will lay waste to them all."

"Oh, please!" retorted Hana, a little embarrassed at her brother's brashness.

"Careful, there, youngster," prodded Shum. "These contestants have come from afar and they haven't come here to lose. Are you practicing that breathing exercise I taught you?"

"I practice it even when I don't have a bow in my hand. I will be ready."

Rachel pointed out, "I understand there are to be different levels of competition."

"Correct. An adult and a junior division."

"With whom will Cainan compete?" asked Hana.

"That's a tough question. I will compete with the adults, of course, but Cainan is almost proficient enough to compete at that level," he commented with a pride.

"Almost? I am there Shum. You know on a good day I am almost your equal and you are the best archer in the land without a doubt."

"Yes, on a good day, but you still lack the arm strength. The competition is all or near at my ability on any given day. Don't worry, you will get there."

Cainan was more than a little disappointed; he was so anxious to grow up. "What do I lack, aside from the arm strength, that is?"

"About four years and little more humility," pointed out his sister.

This produced a groan and a glare. She had caught up in points. He turned back to Shum and asked, "But, seriously, what am I really lacking?"

"Tournament level knowledge. It comes with time and experience. There is no set age; you will know when you get there, but slow down and enjoy the journey."

"Very good counsel," commented Rachel. Shum was so good for her son; he was everything that she hoped Cainan would one day become.

Shum discovered, as the evening had drawn to a close that he had begun to feel withdrawn and distracted. He knew what it was, of course: the meeting. It was an unwelcome reminder that this assignment in Amaziah took priority over his personal life. Also, he had grown so fond of Hana and her family that it was becoming harder to deceive them by acting out this role. He was beginning to wonder if he was acting anymore. With genuine sadness, he excused himself earlier than he would have wanted. He could see the disappointment on their faces, especially on Hana's. After he bade Rachel and Cainan farewell, Hana walked him out to the portico toward the gate.

Each looked at the other, and with obvious longing murmured their mutual friendship and fondness. Shum's unexpected early departure had clearly caused her some distress and she was now close to tears. Not wishing Shum to see her this way, she tried to put on a false exterior of strength which she found difficult to maintain, her disappointment was so great.

"Shum, I wish you didn't have to leave so early," she quietly murmured. Inwardly chiding herself, she realized how she sounded: silly and weepy. Hana had hoped she could put on a convincing show of strength, but feared she was losing the battle.

Shum, equally disappointed, felt her distress and wanting to comfort her put his arms around her and drew her close, whispering in her ear, "Hana, please know my feelings for you are intensely real. An important matter has arisen and I must respond, otherwise, I would stay longer. There are things we must discuss, you and I, but I don't want to talk of them and be distracted by this other concern. Can you understand?"

Hana, clearly pleased by the intensity of his feelings, took courage and replied with a smile, "Of course, Shum. Please go to your meeting and think of me later." With a teasing voice, she asked, "Will we see one another again sooner than later?"

Shum pretended to give serious consideration to her question. He responded with equal levity, "Will tomorrow night be soon enough?"

"No." Trying to smile, needing to smile, she then looked directly into his hazel eyes; her hands found the nape of his neck and now roamed freely through his brownish hair. With desperate longing, she tugged gently on his thick locks, wanting him. Then needing him. On tip-toe she arose and gave him a soft embrace then a light kiss. His response was immediate and equal to her own but far too short for either of them. They parted, but the thought of being together lingered with them both long after she saw him walk away reluctantly down the stone path.

Hana turned around and walked slowly back into the house. Rachel was waiting for her as she closed the door behind her. Turning, she saw her mother and covering her face with her hands, she exclaimed, "Oh, Mother, whatever am I going to do? I can no longer bear to say good-night to him." She sobbed, knowing the tears would now come in earnest.

Realizing her daughter needed simple comfort, not words, Rachel held her silently for a long time. It seemed to help. For a while.

CHAPTER 6

POISON

Seba sat despondently next to the bed of the man he had been faithfully serving for the past four years. Though the word *faithfully* no longer applied, he thought dispiritedly. Haner lay there, in a coma and lifeless. Not dead, but near enough. Seba was not sure how he knew, but he understood on some level that he was responsible for the catatonic state of which Judge Haner was now suffering.

It had been only a short month ago when he had come upon the Judge in his study, muttering and crying. Over the course of the next few hours, Haner had talked with his long dead wife incessantly and well into the night. Worst of all, his constant fatigue and loss of appetite had eventually led to nausea and vomiting. Seba had dispatched a messenger to fetch the doctors at the local clinic and they had responded quickly.

"Seba," asked one of the doctors, "Have you noticed anything out of the ordinary about Haner's behavior over the past few months?"

"Of course," responded Seba immediately, "But, I thought his irritability was caused by anxiety over matters of state. Later, he seemed to move beyond that stage then he had episodes where he talked with his dead wife."

"And as to the physical symptoms, would you have any idea what he might have eaten or drunk that was clearly outside of his normal regimen?"

"I am unaware of any. I am his servant and my wife his cook, so we would know if there had been anything outside of the normal introduced into his usual diet." Seba stated all this as if by rote, but deep inside he began to wonder if these were his own words.

The doctor quietly explained, "Seba, we have determined that Haner has eaten or drank a substance that has caused these visual and physical symptoms. As his doctors, our conclusion is that he has been poisoned." The physician looked grimly from Haner back to Seba. "Whatever he has ingested, it will likely kill him."

Seba closed his eyes as if to ward off the merest vision of such a consideration. But, his ears had heard all that his mind had suspected for the last three months. Opening his eyes slowly, shaking his head in misery, he asked, knowing the answer beforehand, "Is there no hope for a recovery?"

The doctor gave the slightest shake of his head and replied, "The advancement of medicine within our community has progressed greatly over the years, but unless we can determine from whence the problem originated, it will be difficult to determine an antidote. We now suspect that some of Haner's vital organs have ceased to function and it is just a question of time before he has heart failure."

Seba bowed his head, sickened beyond words at the failing condition of the man for whom he had been entrusted to care. Another doctor placed a comforting hand on Seba's shoulder and instructed him to rest. Now completed with their examination, the doctors left Haner's bedside and departed for the night. Their parting comments indicated they could do little to reduce the pain and inflammations caused by the infection. As the month drew out, Haner's condition continued to worsen as Seba's anxiety and feelings of personal guilt steadily climbed.

Now here he was, going out of his mind with worry and remorse. *What is wrong with me?* Seba stared vacantly at the wall, detesting his impotence to change the direction of his master's progress and all the time despising himself for something he must have done or overlooked in Haner's care. He remained in that position for half an hour wishing, almost waiting for someone to relieve him of this burden to his soul.

Leah walked silently into Haner's room and seeing her husband's despondency, gently coaxed him, "Come home to bed, husband. We must now prepare ourselves that Haner may never recover."

"I will be along shortly," he murmured. He simply could not remove the idea from his mind that he was somehow responsible. The obsessive nature of this thought began to bounce around in his head so profoundly that he was unable to relax enough for sleep. It was hours later before he stumbled exhaustedly into the bedroom of their cottage and joined her.

At the same time Seba sat despondently at Haner's side, Shum walked fretfully to Simeon's residence near the market place where their monthly meeting normally took place. A messenger had arrived earlier in the day to deliver the message to him for a clandestine appointment that evening with his partner, but for Shum it could not have come at a worse time. He had intended that same evening to propose marriage to Hana but the message from Simeon was an unwelcome reminder of the mission, and knowing his partner in crime, the mission would have to come first. He and Simeon had been meeting monthly since their arrival and had already met once this month. That could only mean that something of importance had come up that would alter his usual routine, probably for the worse. Realizing this was probably the case, he picked up his pace so as to quickly put this unwanted interruption behind him.

He strode up the walkway and was nearly at the door when it abruptly swung open, revealing his mission partner. Simeon scanned for movements in the night, looked both ways to ensure no one had noticed Shum's arrival then with a sweep of his arm, impatiently beckoned him inside. He silently, but quickly closed the door. They both entered the living area and found seats.

Simeon's voice was agitated, on the brink of anger. "Shum, you were instructed to be here earlier. Please explain why you have kept me waiting."

"Get on with it, partner. We have already had our little chat once this month, so this meeting had better have more meaning than usual." His tone had a bitter edge.

Simeon, now perturbed at Shum's impertinence replied stonily, "Don't let your celebrity status in the community go to your head, Shum. What of Cainan? Is he ready?"

"He's ready. I just have to point him in the right direction. Why do you ask?" His reply sounded more like a growl: low and dangerous.

"Well, he better be as good as you say he is with a bow, because the time has come, partner, to take our little charade to the next level. In one month the yearly conference will be held by our holy friends of Amaziah."

"Who do you expect will be in attendance?" He really didn't care, but felt he should at least pretend interest for the sake of conversation.

"I have it on good authority that Samuel will be in attendance and seated on the stage next to the Chief Judge and the rest of us on the Council. Samuel is, of course, your primary target."

"Of course," he added dryly.

Ignoring the sarcasm, Simeon continued. "Once he has been publicly dispatched, pandemonium will break loose. I, however, will valiantly throw my body over that of the Presiding Chief Judge, Jared, acting as a human shield."

"How brave of you. Will that, too, be an act?"

"Naturally, but the public will, of course, view my selfless act as heroic. That is the important thing." To Simeon, Shum's conduct was distracting, even disturbing given the mission was near completion. Simeon commented, "Shum, please try to stay focused."

"Naturally. What else can be done?" Irritably he asked, "Please explain how the taking of his life will play into our mission success."

Simeon reclined back in his chair and steepled his fingers. As though lecturing an obtuse, lazy student, he said, "Dispatching Samuel has always been the culminating moment and the lodestone of our success. Once he is publicly eliminated in such a brutal fashion, emotions will run high and the public will demand changes for the sake of public safety and state security. Moreover, they will be less resistant to drastic modifications to their so-called open society."

"So you assume their world will disintegrate at the death of their prophet?"

"Let us just say, I strongly feel that they may be more open to adjustments to their life style. Without their holy man to guide them, they will lack the direction of his counsel. They will look to another for guidance to restore their ordered lives."

"And I suppose that is when you step in?"

Ignoring the veiled sarcasm, Simeon continued his briefing. "As you may be aware, the Chief Judge holds his position for ten years or until death, whichever comes first. It is my understanding Judge Jared is stepping down after this term of office in three months. He will see my selfless act of heroism to save his life as a clear message to the citizens of Amaziah that I can be trusted as a man for the people. He will insist that I seek election to assume his office at his departure and I can count on his official endorsement. My election will be practically assured."

"Very well, then what?"

"Then, I will carefully and slowly take control of this government, enacting new laws on behalf of the citizens of Amaziah, but I shall place my own people in key positions to administer them. Then I shall find an excuse to suspend their basic rights of public thought and speech. At that point, the Brotherhood will begin to do its work."

"And if dispatching Samuel does not yield the results you desire, then what? It is possible, you understand."

"Then another leading citizen will have to be sacrificed for the common good or as many as it takes until the people demand drastic action be taken to restore their peace and harmony. By that time, the citizens will care little that the price for their peace will be a sudden loss of their freedoms. The effort required to take control of any government requires a proportionate loss of personal freedoms to the people. It cannot be avoided."

Shum had heard this all before in broad strokes, but had never assumed Simeon would vie for the Presiding Judge Seat and effect changes so quickly and in such a deliberate manner. It occurred to him that the scope of their mission had been altered and moved up, no doubt the result of Cain's impatience at our delay in delivering Amaziah into his hands. "Cainan then is to be the distraction, the ruse to allow me to get away after I let loose the arrow that kills Samuel?"

"Shum, if you want to escape, that is the only way," insisted Simeon.

"How is it that I am to escape detection? Within minutes after cutting down Samuel, many will be scouring the city looking for the assassin. This may be an open, liberal-minded society, but they do take their security seriously. Everyone here has a purpose, remember? I will be noticed as being in the building from which the arrow flew and I am notoriously well known for my prowess with a bow. I assure you, it will not be hard to link me to the murder." This had all been discussed previously, but Shum wanted Simeon to verbalize the plan once more. He, too, wanted Cainan's distraction to be obvious, but he also wanted to ensure his partner would be anticipating it. Shum had an alternate plan he had been contemplating, and to succeed it required Simeon's own reassurance of expected events.

"To avoid any suspicion of you, the boy must be in the building and it must appear he has the murder weapon with him. You will instruct him to bring his bow with him to the event. When the security guards enter the building, make sure that you point them in his direction. As a troubled young man with a well-known skill, he will be their primary suspect. In the confusion that follows, make sure you slip away and leave the city. Can you arrange that or not?"

Shum didn't appreciate the patronizing tone in Simeon's voice. Truth be known, he didn't care for any of this. Holding his temper, he responded, "Yes, I can do that. As I have no desire to be tried for murder, Cainan will be in place at the appointed time."

"Good," Simeon replied sardonically. "One other thing and this must be taken care of by tomorrow night."

"So, there is to be more intrigue. Now what?"

"Seba has outgrown his usefulness. Haner is now on his deathbed and soon I will assume his judge seat position permanently. It has all been arranged."

"Congratulations on behalf of the concerned citizens of Amaziah."

"Never mind that! I shall *bump into* Seba tomorrow afternoon and invite him to my home for that evening. The fool is absolutely despondent over the steadily diminishing health of his dear master and will no doubt need me to give him comfort. I will plant one last suggestion into his feeble little mind."

"Let me guess. He is to kill himself."

He didn't care for Shum's tone of voice this evening. "Yes, he is going to hang himself from the rafter of his own home. Your job will be to make sure he doesn't bungle his own suicide. If he can't bring himself to properly complete the task you must garrote him then hang him yourself."

"Is this really necessary?" retorted Shum. "Can't you just use your little mind trick to make him forget his involvement? Must we leave bodies laid about the whole city?" he asked with exasperation.

Angrily, Simeon retorted, "Of course it is necessary. That loose end must be tied up; no one must link me back with Seba's involvement in the poisoning of Haner. If questioned, he will definitely implicate me. Besides, since when have you cared about a few bodies strewn about?"

Shum was silent. Simeon had reminded him of what he least liked about himself now that he had feelings for Hana.

Slowly, Simeon peered at him with a side-long glance. Then with a knowing wink commented, "Hana, that little piece of tail you have been seeing must have warped your sensibilities, Shum."

Since assuming the role of an assassin, Shum had always been a detached, self-controlled man, rarely given over to emotion, but at this moment he had never known such anger in his whole life. He looked deliberately at Simeon and slowly intoned, "You are never to use Hana's name like that again. Are we clear?"

Ignoring his oblique threat and seeing that he had hit the mark, Simeon reminded him, "Shum, the mission must come first. If we fail to carry out our assignment and displease Cain, he will make us suffer in ways that may seem unimaginable to you."

"Please provide an example for my edification."

Leaning forward in his chair, Simeon confided earnestly, "Have you ever seen a man flayed alive, then hung upside down to die slowly of blood loss? If done properly, a man can linger in that position for a full day and I assure that Cain has executioners who can do it properly. I, for one, do not intend to end up that way. If you are smart, you would do well to remember for whom we work."

Shum said nothing, only arose from his seat. He stared stonily across the room at Simeon. Finally, he said, "I will remember. It will be done, just as you have explained."

Simeon was done briefing his partner. He just wanted him gone. "Thank you. Now please report to me tomorrow night when you have completed your assignment with Seba." He then dismissed Shum with a peremptory gesture of his hand. Shum turned and left without another word.

For several minutes Simeon debated his next move. The mission was at a crucial stage and Shum's commitment seemed questionable. Clearly his judgment had been compromised by that little doxie he has been seeing. At length, he concluded, *I think he will stand up to his mission assignment to assassinate their prophet, but he may well try to formulate a plan to remain in the city for the girl. Eventually, one day Shum may feel an irresistible need to confess his part in this plot and could name me as an accessory.* Having come to a decision, Simeon muttered aloud, "And I cannot allow that to happen, Shum." He coded a message to Cain and walked out to the rear of the residence to the pannier where he kept his pigeons. Within minutes, a pigeon was on its way westward to Constantinople.

CHAPTER 7

A FAREWELL TO SEBA

Seba was leaving the residence of Judge Haner when he noticed Simeon from across the street. He was worried that lately his mind tended to wander down paths he would rather avoid. But, seeing Simeon, he felt an uncontrollable relief wash over him. Not for the first time did he realize his friend had such a calming effect upon him. Curious, he thought, the way Simeon had of offering needed encouragement at the right moment. *Perhaps today he could raise my spirits and put things in their proper perspective?*

Now noticing Seba, Simeon sketched a simple salute then once together, he offered an affectionate embrace by way of greeting. "Seba, my friend! It is wonderful to see you. How is our dear friend and colleague Judge Haner?"

"Simeon, Judge Haner has only gotten worse and I do not know what to do. Somehow, deep within me I feel so responsible."

"I am sure that cannot be. You are his devoted servant."

"The doctors have asked me whether I have observed anything different in his diet. I feel I should know the answer and I need to tell someone but I know not what I should say."

"Come, come, my friend. I am sure you have done all you could to help them with a diagnosis. After all, who would know Haner better than you do?"

Seba wrung his agitated hands in despair then ran his fingers distractedly across his face and through his hair. "Perhaps you could help me see things clearly because I fear I am losing my mind."

"Of course, my old friend," Simeon soothed. He smiled inwardly and thought: *this is going to be easier than I had imagined.* He walked Seba over to a quiet bench and looked him in the eyes. He slowly added in a calming and reassuring tone, "Please come by my home later this evening and let us talk this out. I am sure that before you leave, all will be well and you will be able to make sense of this whole tragedy.

"Bless you, Simeon. Of course there is a solution; there must be."

Simeon laid a comforting hand on his shoulder and slowly intoned, "Before arriving, there is something that I would like you to buy at the market."

After leaving Simeon, Seba had felt the need to visit Haner's home one last time. Upon entering the bed chamber, he sadly recalled that Haner, now comatose, had been receiving special care from his personal physicians around the clock. They had all gravely concluded that nothing more could be done for him. Seba had watched with somber eyes as his family had been summoned to pay their final respects and farewells. He had observed their grief and shared in their pain.

He could not say why, but he was aware that he was responsible in a way that he could not quite grasp, thus his walk was heavy as he left Haner's home amidst the grief and sorrow of distressed relatives. A few minutes later, he arrived at a nearby park where he waited for the day to become darker. As the daylight became dimmer he sat with self-loathing and despair and reflected on the day. Though he was not quite sure why he had purchased it, in his lap lay a hemp rope he had seen at a shop in the market. As he gazed upon it and began to gently rub his hand across its coarse texture, he decided it had been the right thing to do at the time. The light stroking of the rope began to have a calming effect on his mind. *Strange that it should give me so much comfort.* Then he began to wait.

As the evening grew later a relay switch in his mind turned over. At the appointed time he arose from the park bench and walked directly to Simeon's residence. He was so sure that Simeon could help him with his depression that he had actually looked forward in anticipation to discussing his worst fears with him. He had decided that he felt fortunate to have a friend so considerate. *This matter would soon be resolved*, he thought. A smile of relief washed over his face and he hastened to Simeon's home.

The evening gloaming was rapidly approaching darkness when Seba knocked at Simeon's door. He was met at the door way and Simeon whispered, "Come in my friend." He accompanied Seba to the living area and graciously added with a smile of encouragement, "You are always welcome in my home. Please be seated."

Simeon noticed the rope that Seba had purchased and now clutched protectively to his chest. He noted the servant's despair and inwardly gloated. *It had been so easy to persuade this moron into eliminating Judge Haner by poison. It would be even simpler to have him dispatched at his own hands. The fool would hardly need more than a slight push in the right direction.*

Seba, now in the presence of this wonderful man, began to confess his feelings of guilt that he may have caused the serious illness of Haner. "There is an idea, a thought I have so close to my recollection that I can almost feel it trying to escape. It has haunted my days and nights and has left me distraught and sleepless. My wife looks at me as those I have gone mad." His eyes darted here and there about the room, restless and haunted by a nightmare from which he has been helpless to awake.

. Simeon leaned forward and placed his hand upon Seba's shoulder and once he had the man's attention, he locked his eyes directly on those of Seba and paused until he had gotten his full attention. "Seba," began Simeon in a melodic and slowly modulated tone, "I am here to help you. Be now comforted. You will trust my judgment and do exactly as I say."

"Of course, I will do exactly as you say, Simeon." Then he added, as if to reassure himself, "You are my friend." A calm feeling of love and gratitude assailed his senses. He smiled beatifically.

"Yes, Seba, I am your friend," he reassured him soothingly. "Your guilt over the suffering you have caused Haner is destroying your soul and you must now make restitution with a truly penitent act of contrition, but this expiation must be done in secret. Only you can understand the depth of your pain and his, so only you can meet it alone. You will send your wife to visit her father for the evening. Do you understand, my friend?"

Five minutes later Seba walked out the door of Simeon's residence. Though at first uncertain, the more he walked the more he realized that there was something he must do. The fog of uncertainty began to scatter leaving him with the distinct impression that the answer was at home. A blissful smile washed happily over his face then with a more confident gait to his step, he increased his pace down the street, almost as if he was anticipating the answer to a desperate prayer. By the time he reached his home, Seba was nearly running. He felt sure that when he arrived at his home he would fully comprehend exactly what he had to do to make things right. Later, in Simeon's opinion, it was clear Seba had done everything just right.

Seba arrived home nearly out of breath from running, but eager to commence his task. Before he greeted Leah, he stored the rope away in a nearby cabinet. Turning into the kitchen, he noticed his wife preparing the evening meal and since his business this evening was not meant to involve her, he fondly took her by the hand and announced, "Leah, I have seen your father today and he does not look well. He asked me to send you over to him this evening to check on him. I, of course, told him I would."

"Oh my! Was he slow of breath?"

Seba lied, though he was unsure why it was necessary. "Yes, I told him to rest and not exert himself. You would be over right away."

"Thank you, Seba, but what of the work at Judge Haner's home?" Her role had been to keep Haner's home and bed chamber clean so she was concerned to leave before her tasks had been completed. She had intended to look in on him before retiring for the evening.

"I will complete the work for the day with Haner. You run along to your father. Send him my love and affection," he added brightly, but to his own ears his words sounded shallow and flat. As he watched Leah depart, he decided he had not truly felt light-hearted at what he had told her.

Leah gathered a night shawl and threw it about her shoulders. On her way out the doorway, she said, "Thank you my husband. You are so considerate." Before leaving she confided, "I feel so badly for Judge Haner. He was always such a good man."

"Yes he was and tonight I shall see to it that he knows how much we have loved him." At saying this, he did feel a little better, though his wife found this statement as oddly out of place. But, she said no more, concluding that

Seba was as much distraught over the inevitable loss of Haner as she was and his feelings, as well as her own, had brought uncertainty to their usually ordered lives. She began to close the door quietly behind her.

His fists flew to his face in agony. *My life is a lie and a sham,* he screamed. His eyes darted around, knowing that his outburst must have been heard, but Leah's look of concern was only for her father; she never looked back. Yet, he knew he had heard the alarm in his own voice. Gripping his hands tightly, Seba felt his mind was coming apart and he now used all the self-control he still had to remain calm. He had been so certain that the answers to his misery would come to him once he had arrived home.

Seba stood by the door way and watched Leah hurriedly walk away and when she had rounded the corner his torment was so great that he shuddered from within then slowly the distraught man closed the door. He stood silently for a few moments with his back against the door, his eyes closed in mental anguish then a notion seemed to occur to him. He turned and walked woodenly over to the closet in the corner and inside he located the rope he had bought earlier in the day. At the time, he wasn't sure why he had done that, the purchase of the item being so unusual and normally unneeded in the regular routine of the day. But, once purchased and seizing it as he walked home, he felt it had been the right thing to do. Then, after talking with Simeon, he now knew why he had bought it. Suddenly another thought turned over into his mind and he walked into the adjoining room.

He looked just above him and noticed a ceiling rafter. Still gazing above, he stood quietly in the middle of the room waiting for the next relay in his brain to switch over. A few moments later it did and he carefully looped the rope over the rafter directly above him then tied it down. He blinked a few times in confusion; he had forgotten something. Noticing a chair in the corner, a smile flitted across his face as though a complex problem had just been solved.

Shum had been waiting for some time. He watched from the shadows as the small, lithe man quickly made his way in the direction of his home. Trying to stay undetected, he had found a large oak tree under which he could observe the whole street without being seen. He watched as Seba pushed open the door without resistance. A few minutes later his wife exited the doorway and made her way slowly down the street. Seba, seeing her to the door, closed it quietly behind her.

At the beginning of his stay in Amaziah, Shum had found it curious that so few people actually bolted their doors whether day or night. After a few months, he began to observe the same custom and was delighted how easily he now slept. *It must be a trust thing.* His musings now complete, he waited another half hour and slowly made his way down the pathway leading to Haner's cottage. He calmly pushed the door and, of course, the door was unlocked and opened easily.

He let himself inside a darkened house and quietly closed the door behind him. A creaking noise caught his attention toward a room adjoining the entrance way. He walked slowly in the direction of the noise now trying to accustom his eyes to the darkness. The room was in the dark save a single candle that had been lit. As if to provide enough clarity for a task, it had been placed on a nearby table. Also, he noted that a chair had been conveniently pulled over to the middle of the room, but was now canted over to one side, as though it had been kicked over. Shum suspected that was precisely what had occurred.

Suspended from the rafter above the stone floor was the slowly swaying figure of Seba. The man's neck was encircled about with a rope that had been casually looped over and around the rafter a few times then tied down. The noose, as it had tightened, had cut severely into the neck that was now quite raw from the struggle. Shum, knowing exactly what a broken neck looked like, was positive that the rope had not broken it; Seba had slowly choked himself to death. In the latter extremities of his desperation, the man must have realized what he had done, and trying to extricate his neck from the noose had simply pulled it tighter until he had run out of air, leaving his listless tongue protruding to one side. Frightened and near the end, Seba had let go his bladder; a puddle of urine had formed just below the body. Shum watched as the pathetic form slowly swayed to and fro while the rope creaked ever so lightly from the strain of a dead weight. The sound was as a morbid benediction to a wasted death. He reflected that his partner, Simeon, had been highly proficient and had not left much for him to do. Disgusted by the sight, he turned around and walked out the door into the night, silently closing the door behind him.

CHAPTER 8

AT THE TOURNAMENT

Hana saw Shum only once a few weeks before the civic conference. At his insistence, their time together was cut short and she sensed something was amiss; he was withdrawn and distant as though anxious to be somewhere else. By now, she thought she knew his moods and understood when he needed to be alone. But, it hurt, and she told him as much on the last night they were together before that fateful day of the public assembly.

"Shum, I understand your need to be alone. Maybe I have pushed you away with my silly daydreams of romance. But, I can't help the way I feel and it hurts when you are away from me. Don't you know that by now?"

Shum could see Hana was close to tears. He took her by the hands and looked directly into her eyes then a dejection so profound washed over him that he was unsure he would be able to bear her look of hurt. Gathering his strength, he gently confessed, "Hana, my feelings for you are profound, but there are things about me and my past life of which I am ashamed."

"Shum, you can tell me anything, but don't shut me out of your life. I could not bear it."

"I just need some more time to work out what I must do." It was a pleading tone from a heart-sick man. "If you will give me a few weeks, everything will be resolved one way or another."

He had turned morosely and fled from her, leaving Hana at the front gate with a spirit dashed and heart despairing. Unbidden, the tears began to form in her eyes; she miserably realized his parting words had seemed so final. Something was happening to the man she loved and she was left helpless to do anything about it.

Shum had made a promise to attend the archery tournament in which Cainan was to compete. He knew, of course, there was much more to his appearance than merely friendly support; the young man had become an integral part to the completion of his mission. Without his involvement, there could be no outcome that Shum was prepared to accept. He watched Cainan from a safe vantage point and applauded at his overwhelming victory with the bow. Knowing that Hana and her mother would be nearby also to offer their support, he made a point to avoid them by skirting their location. What he had to discuss with Cainan was for his ears only. After the tournament, Cainan separated himself from his sister and mother and Shum saw the opportunity he needed to approach him.

Coming up from behind he noted he would be alone with him for a few minutes. His tone was teasing but proud. "Well done, youngster!"

Cainan, upon hearing the voice of his friend and mentor, turned around and his face glowed with pride. "Who are you calling a youngster? Did you see the way I annihilated them?"

Shum responded, "I did indeed. Your technique is improving and soon you will be almost as proficient as your old teacher." They embraced as brothers. It suddenly occurred to Shum that in every respect that mattered, they were. *Would a true friend treat his brother this way?* Shaking his head with disgust, he knew he had little time, so he proceeded with his plan, but looking at Cainan's trusting face, he hesitated.

"Shum, is something wrong?"

"No, but there is an urgent favor which I should discuss with you and I had hoped you would be agreeable to help me."

"Just name it, Shum."

Shum nodded and said, "I know you are to attend the conference being held this month at the new amphitheater. At the other end of the structure there are two tall buildings. Are you familiar with them?"

"I know where they are located. The amphitheater is not far from the central market place and the two buildings are directly behind it."

"That is correct. I need for you to meet me in front of the buildings at the ninth hour of the morning on the day of the conference. You must tell no one, not even your mother or sister."

Cainan, with all the adoration of a younger brother, would never think of disappointing Shum. But, he was curious and asked, "Yes, of course, Shum, but why?"

Shum didn't enjoy lying to him, but he needed Cainan to play a part naturally and not forced. Also, any involvement of Rachel and Hana in this affair had to be avoided at all costs. For the plan to succeed Cainan had to be completely convincing; moreover, there had to be no objections from his family.

"I have in mind for you to assist me on a special security detail that day and I need this to be a private matter just between the two of us. Your involvement would only require a half-hour of your time. Can you do this for me?"

Ecstatic thoughts of bravery overcame the youth. "All right, Shum. I will be there."

"Please bring your bow and a quiver full of arrows."

His eyes lit up at the thought. "Of course. And thank you Shum for this chance to help."

Shum saw the young man's sister and mother from the corner of his eye approaching, and trying to avoid them quickly said, "Thank you, Cainan. I will see you at that time." He punched the young man playfully and congratulated him again on his victory. Shum hurried away when he noticed Hana approaching; she was quickly closing the distance between them.

A few minutes later, both women converged on the boy. "Cainan," asked Hana, "were you just now talking with Shum?" She knew every contour and mannerism of the man she loved, but she had to ask.

"Yes", replied her brother. "He promised he would attend the tournament so when he ran into me, we talked."

Hana watched the slowly retreating figure of the man who had captured her heart and her life. *Surely he must have noticed our approach. Was he trying to avoid me?*

Rachel noticed the hurt registered on her daughter's face. "Hana, be patient with him. He is a good man, but he cannot be rushed."

Hana wiped the tears from her eyes but made no comment.

CHAPTER 9

A FAMILY REUNION

Samuel the Prophet stared worriedly into the fireplace. Normally, he was not a man prone to nervous agitation. He was careful to avoid anxiety as it tended to make him stammer and trip over his own words. According to his wife, Zeruah, it would take an earthquake and a plague of frogs to produce the beginnings of a concern for him, but something or someone was coming and he was left with the strong impression that it would occur that same afternoon and the uncertainty was taking its toll on his otherwise patient demeanor. Then there was that other matter he could not shake from his mind. With a sigh, Samuel began to pace.

"Husband, what bothers you? Is it Seba?"

"Yes, that is part of it." It was a pity that Haner had died so soon thereafter his servant. Both deaths had severely shaken the community.

"Samuel, it has been nearly a month since he took his own life. You and I have both been over to console and support his widow, along with many other women of Amaziah. The man was distraught over the decline of Haner's health and, according to Leah, Seba held himself expressly responsible."

"Yes, but I knew him as a neighbor. It bothers me that I did not notice his worry and foresee his actions."

"I understand, Husband, but none of us truly knows the thoughts and feelings of our neighbors. It would be unseemly if we did."

He uttered a low sigh then an anxious shake of the head. "But, I should have seen it coming."

"Samuel, you have a gift of discerning events that have not yet occurred, but you cannot foresee what others may think. Do not be so hard on yourself." She thought of an old adage: *guilt is an old disease* of good men.

"It did not take a fortune-teller to see that Seba was in pain. The community looks to me for answers, Zeruah."

She decided to change the subject. "There is something else that bothers you?"

Samuel glanced in her direction with and indulgent smile. His wife was one to talk about others with discernment. He paced with his hands behind his back and glanced out the window. "I am not sure, but it is something I have not felt in many years."

"Can I help?"

"Unless you can convince the sun to speed up its setting, I suppose not."

"No, I have never tried that, perhaps your brother could help?" she asked facetiously.

Zeruah was fond of teasing her husband. She knew Samuel's brother, Abram, tended to exaggerate the speed at which he could sell his livestock. A born salesman, Abram needed little incentive to talk; the very thought of making a quick sale would send him off into incredible lengths of conversation to seal the deal. His mouth was seldom silent.

As if to give her suggestion serious consideration, Samuel paused and thought a moment then with a shake of his head said, "No, Zee, he would not be of much help." His pacing continued.

Their eldest son, Samuel, entered the room. He was quiet and reflective, closer in temperament to his father than to the other children. Actually, whenever they were together, aside from the obvious age differences, Zeruah was hard pressed to tell them apart. The young man noticed his father pacing and knew something was amiss. He was a perceptive young man with a talent for divining a person's general disposition.

Glancing at his mother, she silently motioned to indicate that he should take his father for a walk. Nodding his head in agreement, he turned to

Samuel and said, "Father, I have question. It is a spiritual matter and I was hoping we could talk privately."

Samuel stopped his pacing and became aware that his son had addressed him. "Of course, my son, what is the question?"

"Could we go for a walk? I find it easier to speak frankly when I can express myself without interruptions from others."

Zeruah spoke up. "That is a wonderful idea, son. Your father could use the air to clear his head."

He took a moment to pull himself away from the anxiety he was feeling. "Yes, Samuel that is a good suggestion. I was just thinking that we should walk to the top of the hill and talk, perhaps even to wait."

"Wait for what, Father?"

A slightly puzzled look appeared on his face. "I am not sure, yet, but I am confident that it will come to me in time." He put his hand on his eldest son's shoulder and said, "I think we are to meet someone."

Both father and son walked out into the afternoon sunshine and in a few minutes were on the road that led to the top of the hill a mile from their home. As they began the climb to the top, Samuel looked back over his shoulder and noticed the city of Amaziah spread out across the valley floor behind them; it was a sight he never tired of viewing. Today, however, the scene below gave him the impression he might never see his beloved city again. Shaking his head to rid the premonition, he turned and they proceeded slowly up the hill, but the closer they approached the crest, the more certain Samuel began to feel that his previous impressions were correct and that soon they would be meeting someone.

As the two slowed their climb, his son said, "I worry that I will not be able to fulfill my responsibility as the chief recorder of our people."

Samuel frowned, a trifle concerned. "Why is that?"

"I had a dream recently in which I was asked to leave Amaziah. I was left with the feeling that my training as recorder was to be used elsewhere." He kicked a stone out of the way with his sandal then stooped and picked it up, and this time he tossed the stone casually into a nearby bush. Pheasants scattered to avoid any further threats to their peace.

"I see. Well, whether your training is used for The Tribes or for others, it is still a talent well worth applying. What truly worries you?"

"So much of what we record seems to be redundant. We live in a closed society and there is little that differs from year to year."

"That may be, but occasionally we have others from the outside who join us. Just last year several families arrived from our homeland of Palestine. One of which, the ben Judah family, has two doctors of medicine. We accepted them and in time their descendants will become part of us and enhance the diversity of our society. Their histories and ours will become melded as one. We never really know how it will all unfold in time, but we have been asked to do this, so it is done."

"I can understand the social benefit of knowing our genealogy, Father, but why else is it done? Is our unique history so important to the rest of the world?"

"I only know that the final judgment of how we have lived can only come when the Creator has all the books open for review. Did we live as we covenanted that we would? If so, then our records will reflect that. It is not a difficult thing we are being asked to do."

Samuel had heard this explanation before, but there was the other concern that truly mystified him. "What of the fate of others? Suppose they are slow to keep records or simply refuse."

"A good question. Presumably, they will be judged according to the records they have kept. There will be no exceptions. However, each society will be also judged by their understanding of the truth as they understood it. The less they have understood and recorded, the less accountable they will be."

"If that is true, then we are to be held as highly accountable. Our records not only contain our genealogy and history, but our beliefs, as well."

"That is well said, my son. You are quite correct."

A light breeze kicked up the dust. Samuel the Younger covered his eyes then asked, "Does this accountability not overwhelm you at times?"

Samuel felt he was on confident ground with this point. "As we apply what knowledge we are given, we grow in wisdom and self-assurance. One has only to look around at our country of Amaziah to see what advancements we have been able to achieve. Without our records to document our progress and failures, no such growth would have been possible. Yes, our accountability is great, but where much has been given, much has always been expected. It has always been thus. Our Creator would have it no other way."

His son was quiet for a moment then responded, "Father, I still worry that you may have to find another recorder soon."

Father and son walked on in silence a while longer and having finally attained the top of the mount, they noticed a man was seated on a stone, a boulder really. He seemed to be in the act of waiting, as though he had been expecting them.

As they reached the man, the stranger announced, "I am Jasher and you two must be Samuel and Samuel." As he noted their surprise, he arose then smiled a greeting to set them at ease.

Samuel the Prophet looked at his son and squeezing his shoulder, said, "My son, it looks as if I was right. Someone has arrived. But, do not be too surprised that your dream and your voiced concerns have everything to do with the man you are now meeting."

Jasher's long life and mission had taught him that few encounters were accidental. He was therefore unsurprised that Samuel was aware of who he was. Undoubtedly, their records had been well maintained. "Then you know who I am?"

"We have been waiting a thousand years for your return."

Looking at the elder Samuel, Jasher asked, "How many of you have lived and passed away?"

"I am the seventh since the day of your departure; my son the eighth."

Looking past Samuel and his son, Jasher gazed out over the valley below. As if in contemplation, he then closed his eyes and slightly nodded his head. *If not for my long mission that has given me a reason for living, by now time would have reached the point of inanity.* Meeting the eyes of Samuel the Prophet, he said, "I look forward to examining your records."

"I have been feeling anxious all day and now I know the reason. However, I perceive there is much more to your visit than a simple reunion with family."

"You are correct, there is more. Aside from making an abridgement of your records, I have been asked to escort you and your people to a land to the north where they will not be molested by the corruption of men."

Samuel jerked in astonishment. He replied, "I am surprised at your concern. In fact, we have been living in peace and harmony with our neighbors for many years now."

"Nevertheless, the time has arrived for a choice which only the citizens of Amaziah can make."

"A choice?"

"The people of Amaziah are at a cross-road. The choice ahead will not be easy, but it must be made. Your very survival will depend upon it."

"May I know what it is?"

"The hardest decision anyone can ever make: The Creator or the other."

A look of confusion played across his son's face. "Who does he mean, Father?"

"Cain." With a look of sadness, he turned and began to lead his son and Jasher back down the hill. He said no more by way of explanation or conversation; he was deep in thought at the implications of the news Jasher had brought. His own father had taught him about the ways of Cain. It had been a family rite of passage and he had yet to explain to his son the family's unique relationship to him. Why he had hesitated until now, he was uncertain, except now it appeared the time had finally come around.

Realizing his father was not in the mood to elaborate the meaning of Cain, after a few minutes, Samuel the Younger turned to Jasher and remarked, "I have been responsible for maintaining the recordings the last few years and I have read our records in detail since the beginning. Lately, though, I have longed to know more of the world and how our records fit into it all. Perhaps you can provide the answers."

Jasher was only mildly surprised at the youth's comment. He had seen much and knew that when the student was ready, the teacher would arrive and again it had happened. He glanced over to the young man's father and commented, "You have trained him well."

With a distracted nod, Samuel glanced toward his son and commented, "I suspect our visitor has come to take you away. Your mother will not thank him for his visit, though, I can assure you."

Jasher disliked disturbing the harmony of the family, though it had happened many times before. He turned and looked out across the valley below, hoping to find a way to break the news to the young man's mother. He looked back at Samuel's son and confessed, "I look forward to meeting her, but yes, there is another reason why I am here. As your father has pointed out, soon you will accompany me and your training will be extended."

Samuel the Prophet nodded his understanding. "But, what is to happen to our people?"

A sigh then a shake of the head in disgust conveyed Jasher's recurring sentiment about his oldest living relative. "Cain, our ancient enemy has used his powers of deception and intrigue to invade your country and is already poised to take over. I am here on the Creator's behalf to escort your people out of harm's way."

"I have always taught our people to avoid his ways and be alert for such intrusions. Why have we not been made aware of this? How could this have happened and gone unnoticed."

"He is subtle and his craft is insidious. Even your best efforts of discernment could not have detected his methods. It was inevitable that he would find you and now that he has, he will never stop until he has deprived you of that which is most precious: your freedom to choose your own destinies."

"Is this threat so great that we must abandon our homes and disrupt our lives?"

"The Creator's ways are not for us to question, but his counsel is meant for us to follow for our own good and well-being. His will on this matter is to allow Cain his chance to disrupt your peace, but you, as a people, must decide for yourselves whether you would follow Him or Cain. If your choice is to follow the Creator, then it will be my duty to lead you away."

Samuel was thoughtful for a moment then came to a decision. "In one week, we will have an annual conference of our people to give thanks to the

Creator for his grace and continued assistance. I will want you to address our people."

"Very well, I accept this honor."

"Since this is as much a civic decision as a spiritual one, I feel it necessary to involve our civil leaders so as to ensure the social needs of the citizens of our country are addressed before we depart."

"A prudent decision, Samuel, but we should meet with them immediately, tomorrow if possible."

"Since it is reasonable to assume your concern is well-founded then it appears we have less time than I had imagined. I heartily agree, but beforehand, you must return home with Samuel and me and become acquainted with your family."

"Father, inasmuch as he is family, how should we address him? As Jasher?"

"Well, that is a good question and there will be others who may have the same concern." Samuel glanced in Jasher's direction and both awaited his response.

Jasher was rocked somewhat by the question. It had been many years since he had last been in the midst of so many of his family and this was a question that he had never considered until this moment. "I suppose you should simply call me Benjamin. It is a name that I have used on occasions and I suppose it is time that I began using it more. I can think of no better time to start."

On the morrow, Samuel, along with the Chief Judges and Councilors of Amaziah met with Jasher in the Judgment Center. He was introduced and once his address was completed, the judiciary council of the government was not so much worried of Cain as perplexed at the complex logistics of such a mass exodus.

Jasher had begun, "Gentlemen, as most of you are now aware from your spiritual leader, Samuel, that I am Jasher, the same man who led your ancestors to this remote location in Armenia a millennium ago. Though that may be difficult to comprehend, it is nonetheless the truth and it will be up to you to help Samuel and I convince the citizenry of my identity and the truth of my message."

Chief Judge Jared, a practical man, asked, "How is it we are to know for a certainty that you are who you declare to be?"

"And more to the point, whether you are qualified to lead us anywhere," interjected Simeon. *This man is putting a serious kink in Cain's plan.*

"As to the answer to the first question, you need only check the genealogy of your prophet Samuel that I left with your ancestors."

Samuel stood and declared, "I know he is the same man; he identified every male leader of my family from the beginning, including Father Adam. His name was on the list and he knew each one intimately, including Noah, his great-grandfather and Seth, son of Adam."

There was a stir of astonishment among the council and judges. A murmur of assent and grudging acceptance could be heard among most.

Jasher continued, "As to the answer to the second question: Who would be better qualified to lead you out of Armenia than the man who led you here so many years ago? I am he who has been called to do this and there is no mistake or error. The time has come to go, but it must be your choice. I cannot make it for you nor can I coerce you into accepting my message."

"What is the alternative?" It was Jared again.

Jasher's response was implacably final. "Staying would result in a complete loss of your peace and harmony and the removal of your basic rights of choice."

The council broke up an hour later after discussing the broader points of the departure. Various departments would be responsible to flesh out the finer details then later disseminate the information among the people for their deciding vote. A public conference would be held the following week, and this matter would be presented in its entirety before the citizenry, including the proposed plans for departure.

Simeon had heard enough to know that his designs for Amaziah were about to be thwarted and Cain would have to be made aware of these new developments as soon as possible. Immediately following his arrival home, he wrote a short message and went directly to his panier of pigeons.

Cain was angrier than he had been for many years. His advisers, after delivering the message from Simeon, had sat in stunned disbelief as he had railed and cursed and shouted profanities at all within the sound of his voice. Their leader and master, normally self-controlled and even sanguine by nature, or so he seemed, paced nervously about the flagstone floor, his boot steps a counterpoint to each new outburst. As they were soon to discover, his usual appearances had been deceiving. They would have no idea that only one man upon the earth had the ability to send him into such a terrible tirade. On the table before him was the short message bearing the news: *Assignment compromised. A stranger, Jasher, appeared and says he is to remove the citizens of Amaziah within the month. Also, Shum may be compromised. Advise.*

Cain's chief adviser, Demetrius quietly asked, "Sire, what should we advise your operatives in Amaziah?"

Cain brooded for only a moment. His answer was lethal as well as terse: "Tell them: *Shum must assassinate the prophet Samuel within the week. Stall their departure. I and my army will leave immediately.*"

CHAPTER 10

DAY OF THE ASSASSIN

On the autumn day of the public conference, the dawning was partially overcast, but by mid-morning, the rain had pushed through, leaving the air cool from its passing. Winter was still a way off, but summer was definitely over. Pulling a light shawl closer to his chest, Simeon sat comfortably on a cushion in the raised platform of the amphitheater next to the Presiding Chief Judge, Jared. He smiled as he reflected on the special request for comfortable seating he had presented to one of Amaziah's many women's groups. Apparently, his suggestion had been well received. As a result, cushions had been thoughtfully provided by one of the groups to accommodate the older backsides of those on the platform.

Simeon had asked to make the seating and security arrangements, and Jared, realizing the importance of the event, had readily agreed to his request. He had positioned himself strategically to the left of Jared so as to be nearby at the crucial moment of the assassination. To Jared's right sat Samuel, Amaziah's Holy Man then to his right was seated Benjamin Jasher. All other city councilors and judges had been assigned seats either on one side or on the other. Unsuspecting of matters to come, those on the platform were either shaking hands in greeting or discussing the business of the day.

The excitement at this special event was palpable. As Simeon had busied himself with the many preparations involved with the conference, he had come to realize how special this reunion of Amaziah's citizens was to be. As he made note of the surging crowd, he smiled with anticipation while the good people of Amaziah began to congregate and file in for their last conference as a free and open society. *This will definitely be the last public conference*, he vowed.

To still his nervous anticipation, he began to review his plans. *Even though this latest matter that Jasher has brought to the fore has moved up my timetable considerably, after Samuel has been dispatched, within the week Jared could also be removed. Once the citizens see that their holy man and leading civic officer were no longer there to guide them, this nonsense regarding a mass exodus will fall by the wayside, especially once they realize that their only hope to restore order is to elect me to be their guardian. I will preside at least until Cain can arrive with his army and shore up my rule then set all matters straight. As a result of my considerable knowledge of the city and region, I should undoubtedly be elevated to permanent Chief Judge and ruler over Amaziah. It will be the culminating triumph of my career.* He reveled silently at the thought that his work would soon come to fruition.

It was a shame that Shum would not be around awhile longer. I suppose I could delay his demise until he served no further purpose to the Clan, but his loyalty was now in question. His feelings have been compromised and that makes him a liability. No, it will be better to tie off that loose end now before he complicates matters later. He will be so busy setting up and completing his mission today that he will not suspect he is to be eliminated until it is too late. Besides, once he is out of the way, the other assassin could be used to fill his place and remove any further obstacles to the takeover.

The arrival of Jasher had been the cause of much speculation and rumor. His claim to be over a thousand years of age was, of course, ludicrous, and no doubt Cain would put paid to that business once he arrived. In the meantime, perhaps Jasher, too, will feel the agony of an assassin's well aimed arrow or the sudden jab of a blade. There never seemed to be a shortage of such men and I would know. At the thought, a small knowing smile played across his lips. Simeon nearly laughed aloud.

The Captain of the Guard, Nathan, returned slowly, but vigilantly back to his station at the rear of the amphitheater. He was not worried, but he had been taken a little by surprise by a recent discussion. He had just received his latest security briefing from Simeon, the newest Judge over the Council.

During the conversation he had been instructed to focus his efforts around the buildings at the rear of the amphitheater, meanwhile a smaller team had been positioned to circulate throughout the crowd that would be streaming into the conference center. The Captain, now looking around at the position of his men, had nodded that all appeared correct and ready.

During his briefing, Simeon had said something a little unusual that had piqued the Captain's curiosity enough to question the judge for a more detailed explanation of the security assignments.

"Captain, in addition to your normal coterie of guards, Shum, a close friend of mine will also be joining your team outside but behind the amphitheater."

Nathan knew Shum as a friend; actually, everyone on the security detail did. Shum had offered his services on many occasions to share with him and his men various forms of self-defense and surveillance techniques. But, his personal involvement with an actual assignment was irregular.

"Sir, May I ask why he is being added?"

"He will provide you additional security," Simeon replied in a clipped tone.

Apparently, Simeon did not intend to elaborate, but the Captain pressed. "Yes, sir, but his presence and his role might be confusing to my team. May I pass the word that he is here to simply provide backup in the event of an incident?"

"Captain, you may tell them whatever you wish, but his presence today is needed because I say it is."

Nathan quickly covered his surprise at the peremptory tone of Judge Simeon. He quickly assented and backed away deferentially. That had been an hour before the official start of the ceremonies.

Shum, a local celebrity for his prowess on the field, was recognized by one and all as he stood between the two buildings directly behind the gathering place. He carried his ever present bow in one hand and a full quiver of arrows slung over his left shoulder. Though assailed with smiles and greetings from the crowd, he nonetheless maintained a constant vigilance for the approach of Cainan. At the same time, he had to ensure that he was seen with the Captain of the Guard so that his presence would be reported back to Simeon. A few minutes later, Nathan had walked over to Shum and had announced the security details for the morning. The two embraced as though old comrades and exchanged words of greeting.

"So, Shum, I understand you are to show us the correct meaning of security today," the Captain joked with mock levity.

Shum realized his role might be misinterpreted. "No, Nathan, I am here at the request of an old friend to ensure his peace of mind," he replied casually. "I will try to remain out of your way and let you do your job."

Relief was clearly visible on Nathan's face. To make light conversation, he noted, "I see you have brought your bow, Shum. Are you to perform a demonstration to the crowd today as part of the conference?"

With a laugh, Shum replied, "Hardly, I have brought it to save me time later. I have scheduled a training session on the other side of the city following the conference. I thought it best to save some time by bringing it with me." A slight pause then he added with a smile, "Unless, of course, you wish a demonstration?" The bantering reduced the anxiety of both men.

"Thank you, no, but it does send a frightening message to anyone considering a disruption of the event. Well done!" The Captain parted amiably enough and remained at his station some distance away but still within sight.

Shum turned his attention to Cainan who had just arrived as the Captain was leaving. The two embraced and Shum greeted him, "Cainan, thank you for arriving on time and for being so understanding. I did not mean to be so evasive the other day, but I had a purpose for you in mind during the event and I have just now decided the specifics of what it must be."

"Of course," replied Cainan, "Just tell me what you need."

He walked Cainan over to a location just in front of the taller building then he began to carefully explain. "Because of the importance of today's conference, a large number of people will be coming from all parts of the kingdom. I am on security detail and I need you here to assist me. Your assignment will be to walk up the stairs of this building to the third floor balcony, quietly observe the crowd for any disturbances then wait there until I join you. After I arrive, you can then brief me on all you have witnessed that seemed out of the norm, thus you must pay close attention. Can you do that?"

TREASURE OF THE CLAN

Cainan, now clearly excited with the role he was to play during the conference, quickly assented to Shum's request. "Of course, Shum and thanks for trusting me with this assignment." With that, Cainan jogged toward the entrance of the building and quickly moved up to the third floor.

He detested using Cainan in this manner, but from the moment he had made contact with him, Cainan had become part of the plan, and his life would remain in danger until he had completed the mission. Out of the corner of his eye, he made note that the Chief Security Officer had also noticed Cainan taking to the stairs. Shum knew Simeon was having them both watched and he wanted to ensure that everyone who reported to Simeon would have the same story and that the arrangements would be followed to the letter. He needed for Cainan to be in place at the appointed time or this slight change to Simeon's plan was not going to work. Shum watched Cainan leave and hoped that whoever was observing him will understand that the game was in play and all the players ready.

It was noon-day, bright and clear, cool with no wind: an assassin's daydream. The excited crowd could be seen filing in from the front and side entrances; members of the council and judges were busy finding their seats. Simeon abruptly stood and took a moment to scan the crowd at the other end of the amphitheater. The two larger buildings overlooking this new facility were clearly visible in spite of the crowd milling around about them.

He saw the Security Captain approaching and decided it was time for a final briefing of security matters. He knew all things were in place, but he also knew from personal experience that there was no such thing as a perfect plan unless the execution was also perfect. Nathan walked up respectfully to the platform and Simeon began to question him.

"Captain, please report your final assessment of security before we begin the conference," ordered Simeon.

"Judge Simeon, the security detail is in place. There have been no incidents."

"And Shum, have you talked with him? Does he understand his role within your detail?"

"Yes, Judge, he clearly understands his purpose he is to play. He is to provide backup security and report directly to me of any incident."

"Very well. Did you notice anyone with him for any length of time?"

"Well, Judge Simeon, as you know, Shum is a popular figure and receives considerable attention wherever he appears."

"Yes, yes, of course he is." interrupted Simeon impatiently. I meant anyone he may have known or spent any time with him."

The Captain, a little flustered at Simeon's outburst, proceeded with the briefing. "He was seen in the presence of a young man for a few minutes. They talked then the young man bolted up the stairway of the larger building on the right," the Captain explained, now pointing to the building from the podium."

"Did you recognize him, Captain?"

"Not at first, but I asked a member of my detail if he knew the young man and he said that he recognized him. His name is Cainan and he has a reputation as an excellent archer for his age group. It then occurred to me that I recall hearing he had finished first in a recent tournament."

Simeon nodded, now assured that all was in place. A slow smile crossed his face as he realized his end-game was near to execution. *The plan is coming together,* he exulted.

Nathan stirred him from his reverie as he added, "Sir, if I may point out, would it not be more in line with normal security if I diverted more of my men to the crowd inside the amphitheater rather than to the outside?"

"Your point is noted, Captain, but the security team remains where it is." Simeon then dismissed him and began a slow perusal of the crowd. He muttered to no one in particular, "Captain, this plan will not work without an audience." *And Cainan must be seen by several members of the security team as the primary suspect in order to remove Shum from suspicion.*

As Simeon carefully scanned the crowd he noticed a lone man who had positioned himself just inside the entrance to the amphitheater. He caught his eye and the man carefully rubbed his nose, the predetermined code that everything was ready and the players were all in place. Simeon returned the same sign. The man casually turned around and slowly walked out through the nearest exit. After a while, Simeon nodded to himself that everything was as good as it could be. *The boy had been seen entering the building and Shum should now be ready to proceed.* A few moments later the conference began with an opening address by the Presiding Chief Judge, Jared.

As Jared strode forward to the podium to address the people, a hush fell upon the crowd as their Chief Magistrate prepared to begin the session. The acoustics for the structure were superb and as he began his address, all within the crowd heard every word of the speaker distinctly.

As Jared was addressing the crowd, Simeon glanced quickly over at Samuel sitting quietly and awaiting his turn to speak. To the right of Samuel sat Jasher. *Within a few days, he would wish he had never arrived to disrupt Cain's time schedule by suggesting an exodus.* Simeon quickly scanned the distant building to locate some sign of Shum. Then he saw him. His pulse quickened with anticipation and all the while he was thinking: yes, *there he is on the top of the building, his bow in hand, carefully taking aim. It would not be long now, in fact any moment our objective will be complete and I will eventually attain full control of the government.*

When Jared arose to speak, Shum was back at his position just in front of the entrance way to the building. He quickly ran up the stairs and stopped momentarily at the third floor landing to ensure that Cainan was in place. Verifying that fact, he swiftly went up the next two flights to the roof. As he reached the rooftop, he looked around carefully to find the guard on duty. Shum had ostensibly gone up to the roof to relieve him, but he discovered the man had already departed. Finding himself alone, he looked over the roof ledge and spied Cainan still on the landing two flights below him. He called down to the young man, who, upon hearing a voice from above, looked in that direction.

"Cainan," yelled Shum, "you can leave now. I will meet you below." Unaccountably, Cainan, instead of going below, did the exact opposite.

From his position on the roof, the amphitheater podium was essentially at the same height. Shum pulled out an arrow from the quiver, adjusted his sight slightly, and calmly fit it into the bow.

After slowly exhaling a breath, Shum held the air then a moment later the arrow left the bow. Shum realized that it was a beautiful shot, the best he had ever loosed. The day was still and the arrow's trajectory was minimal. It was a simple, slightly downward shot and it hit the mark superbly in the neck, just above the sternum. The man stood, grasping desperately at the arrow, now strangling on his own blood. He went to his knees, now coughing and finally unable to catch his breath, the man twisted then toppled over, breaking off the arrow head that protruded from the back of his neck. Shortly, there was no movement, only a corpse. Simeon was quite dead.

The crowd saw the entire spectacle that had occurred behind the podium. After Simeon went down, councilors and judges dove in a dozen different directions trying to evade a possible follow up shot that never came. Judge Jared, still standing, turned to see a man now dead at his feet. Samuel arose and calmly went over to Simeon to determine his condition. Meantime, as predicted, pandemonium had erupted in the crowd. People began rushing about trying to escape some unseen danger from the sky.

Samuel arose from the prostrated dead man and trying to forestall a dangerous stampede to the exits by over a thousand frightened people, raised both hands and commanded as if with a voice of thunder. "Everyone, remain calm"

Miraculously, everyone heard and everyone obeyed. The fury and fear of the crowd dissipated. Samuel added, "A man has been injured and we must help him. There is no further danger. In an orderly manner, each of you should file out to the exits and we will reconvene the conference tomorrow." When he saw the crowd had reacted calmly and were headed toward the exits, he looked back at Jasher who had joined him behind the podium.

Samuel asked, "Was it Cain?"

"Not him personally; he seldom does the blood work any longer, but I would not doubt he was somehow behind it. At that distance, it was definitely the work of a professional, though."

Jared, sickened at the scene of so much blood streaming from the body, managed to ask, "But, why Simeon?"

By the time the murmuring crowd had started to exit the amphitheater, Shum had readied himself to exit the roof. From just behind him he heard a gently, purring voice. "Well, Shum that was a beautiful shot, except it hit the wrong target, or did it?" Shum felt the unmistakable point of a knife in the sweet spot to his back.

To Shum, the voice was familiar yet taunting. Though he had not heard it for over five years, he still placed the voice with the man. "Balak," responded Shum, "you know I never miss a target. It is simply a point of pride, you know." Shum was trying to buy some time. Asher was a deadly assassin with sharp objects and Shum knew the only reason he was still alive was because Asher was toying with him. Soon though he would tire of the game and simply finish him off.

"Simeon doubted you could be trusted. I guess he was right."

"Balak, what brings you here to Amaziah? I was not aware that Cain had sent a backup."

Shum may not have been aware of who was to be sent to eliminate him, but he fully expected someone to arrive to ensure not only the assassination was done, but that no one was left alive to talk about it later. He could have killed Simeon at his leisure anytime, but he wanted the backup assassin to be flushed out and in the open. Shum had reasoned that it would be much easier to offer a serious countermove only if the operative was working in the open and not from the dark when he least expected him to arrive. It was not surprising Cain would send the best. Balak was the one man who was usually sent in to do a quick, dirty job; he was ruthless as well as sadistic.

"Cain sent me here to take care of any loose ends from your little charade. You were the primary target and the boy was secondary. So, as soon as I finish with you, your little buddy will also feel my knife."

"Why Cainan? You will have a body; just point the finger in my direction."

"The plot will point to a conspiracy and that requires two bodies be found. That was my idea; do you like it?"

"With Simeon dead, there is no one left alive to take over." He had to keep Balak talking.

"It does not matter. Cain is on the way." He scraped the knife point playfully along the spine. "So relax, it will all be over soon."

Shum was thinking desperately of what he could do to distract him or throw him off balance just enough to gain a slight, even momentary advantage. Just at that moment, when Shum knew the knife was about to slice upward through his back, severing and slicing everything vital, Cainan arrived on the roof.

Being totally surprised and seeing his friend in obvious danger, Cainan yelled, "Shum, be careful, he has a knife."

It wasn't much, but just enough. Balak, momentarily startled, glanced behind toward Cainan, now a running figure and coming in fast. Shum drove his elbow into the stomach of the assassin, causing him to fall back off balance. Shum, ever prepared for a fight after years of training, had a short, stiletto style knife that he always carried in his boot. He was on Balak quickly, but the assassin had made a quick recovery and rolled away from Shum's countermove. Balak, now regaining some of the advantage, was in a temporary position of control and awaited Shum's thrust. Just as Shum made a move to jab the shorter knife forward, Cainan came in running low and at full tilt he hit Balak in the back, pushing him forward toward Shum. With incredible speed and force, Shum drove the stiletto's blade upward through Balak's jaw into his brain. The assassin stood there blinking for a moment as if trying to fathom how things had gone so badly, so quickly. Then his eyes rolled up, showing only the sclera; he was dead before his body hit the roof top.

Unfortunately for Shum, with Cainan's help, Balak's forward momentum had pushed his blade into him, slicing along his forearm near the artery. Holding his bleeding arm, Shum was beginning to lose consciousness and now dizzy he was unable to catch his fall. Falling backward, he rapped his head on the roof ledge as he tumbled down toward the roof.

Now recovering from his entanglement with the prone body of the assassin, Cainan leapt over Balak then rushed over to Shum. With a quick movement, he was able to partially catch him as he completed his downward momentum. By this time the chief security detail led by Nathan had reached the roof top just in time to see the two of them stumble. As Cainan was screaming for the Captain to help, Shum was now bleeding badly because of his arm and head wound. The boy's cries for help were the last thing Shum heard as he drifted down into a cold, gray darkness where he slowly lost all sense of reality.

CHAPTER 11

THE AFTERMATH

S hum gradually came out of the darkness around him; he would never forget the feeling of its palpable and smothering insistence. As he had begun to swim against the bleak current of death, the supreme effort to live had won out until the dark veil had slowly parted. The tunnel was now growing lighter and as he gently became more aware of his surroundings he could see he was in a medical clinic somewhere, but the medication he had been administered had left him groggy and a little disoriented. As his eyes focused on small details, he became aware that the room was absolutely clean, immaculate, everything a bright, comforting white.

He was eager to make some sense of his surroundings; a fleet cogent thought passed through his mind and he latched onto it. He could tell that his wound had been bandaged and the flow of blood had somehow been stanched. *What treatment had they given me to allow me such a rapid recovery?* From his formidable experience with these types of arm wounds, he knew that if the person lived, the arm would eventually become infected then useless and would have to be amputated. Or perhaps worse, the person generally bled out until he died. As to his scalp injury, he moved his good arm slowly to his head and his hand felt a bandage. His eyesight was still a little blurry, but he could discern a figure moving in his direction.

A man dressed in a white robe with a greenish apron was passing the room and had noticed Shum stirring. He walked into the room where he lay and with a reassuring smile, the man said, "Hello, Shum, I am your doctor, Manasseh ben Judah. I see the effects of the medication are beginning to wear off. Do you feel rested enough now for a visit? There are some anxious people here who have been waiting to see you."

Shum knew of drugs, of course, but had never experienced them first-hand. Though he was still weak, there was a tingling euphoria. The drug had caused his responses to slow down, so he simply nodded his head and croaked out a yes.

Soon five persons entered: Hana, Rachel, and Cainan followed by two older men who he recognized vaguely but had never met. With a sob, Hana at once came to his bed side, grasped his hand and firmly held it. Pure love and relief washed over her face. The rest wore smiles of reassuring relief at his recovery. He knew that the drug-induced euphoria had little to do with what he was now experiencing. He had never known such feelings of love as he did at that moment.

"Shum, my love, I was so afraid you would die, leaving me alone," Hana tenderly chided him. "Please tell me you will never hurt yourself like this again!"

Shum lightly mumbled, "Well, the next time I intend to get into a fight, I will definitely take your brother along." His voice seemed muffled to his ears, but his clarity of thought was gradually coming back. He looked over toward Cainan who was smiling with pride from ear to ear. "Thank you, Cainan for that heroic effort you made on the roof. Whatever made you climb the stairway? I do recall giving you explicit orders to meet me at the foot of the building."

Grinning, the boy replied, "Well, you were there and the view would be better than below. I guess I just wanted to walk down with you."

Shaking his head slightly in wonder, Shum said, "Whatever your reasons, your timing was perfect and allowed me just enough advantage to catch Balak off guard. I was fortunate. To my knowledge, he had never made a mistake like that before."

The two men who had accompanied the others into the room had followed the conversation with interest. At Shum's last comment one introduced himself. "I am Samuel, my friend." He smiled engagingly at Shum to loosen some of his reluctance to answer then signaled to the other man with a facetious introduction, "And this young man you see to my right is my great-grandfather Benjamin."

Ignoring the remark, Jasher made a slight bow and commented, "I take it then you knew this man Balak from before you arrived in Amaziah."

Shum was not sure what to make of Samuel's introduction of Jasher, but slowly, with resignation Shum answered, "Yes, I knew him and I have known many like him. I was one myself, though since arriving in Amaziah I have long since lost any taste for that type of work."

Samuel met his eyes and gently prodded, "Would you share with us your story, Shum?"

Looking down at his hands, he could almost see them blood-stained a crimson red. *So much blood,* he cried miserably. With deep sadness Shum began to relate his personal saga beginning with his nightmare childhood then to his dysfunctional adolescence when he was taught the way of the assassin. He spoke of the assignment he had taken with Simeon, knowing it would be his last because his heart was no longer in the life he had been taught. Then, with a sob of self-disgust, he related all incidents leading up to the current events which culminated in the killing of Simeon.

With a nod Jasher concluded, "Then Simeon was to take control of the government until Cain's arrival. The assassin, Balak, was sent to eliminate you and Cainan."

Shum replied slowly, "It was Cain. He was behind it all."

At the conclusion of his confession, Hana tenderly put her arm around him, gazed at him with love and whispered, "Shum all that is over and in the past."

Shum turned to her and with despair asked, "Is it, Hana? I wish it were. Will I ever be rid of the stain I carry for all that I have done?" His anguish was genuine; his remorse none could doubt.

Samuel listened carefully to Shum's confession and his obvious sorrow. He seemed to come to a conclusion and glanced toward Jasher who slightly nodded his head in agreement. Now speaking frankly, Samuel asked, "Shum are you ready to become a full member of our society and fully embrace its principles?"

A glimpse of hope seemed to surge forward and catch his heart where only despair had enshrouded him before. "I am, Samuel."

Samuel smiled, then said with a lighthearted tone, "Well, it may take time for you to fully understand us, but I have a feeling this young lady will be an excellent teacher." He added, now more seriously, "You have arrived as an accepted member of The Tribes at a momentous time. Something extraordinary is about to happen and you will be a part of it." Now with added emphasis and greeting he looked directly at Shum and said, "My son, welcome to our family. You are now a part of us. Wherever we go, you too, will be there."

As he looked around the room, Shum smiled at Samuel and relief shown blissfully on his face at the acceptance and love of his new family. He then frowned momentarily and shaking his head he looked over at Jasher and asked Samuel, "You did say he was your great-grandfather?"

Suddenly the whole room exploded into laughter. Hana rushed into his arms and clung to him as Rachel and Cainan also approached his bed and welcomed him to the family. With eyes glistening, Shum realized he had finally found peace and had awakened from a long nightmare.

Long before Cain could reach them, the exodus from Armenia had begun two weeks later and though the logistics of such an operation would have been daunting even by the expectations of a modern-day army, nonetheless in record time, the people of Amaziah had reached the foothills of what would later become known as the Caucasus Mountains. Few knew of the caves contained within that range and fewer still were aware how to navigate them to the other side, but eventually it was done.

Four men stood outside the entrance of the chief cavern; two would enter and never be seen again on the southern side of Eurasia. The other two had a mission to perform and were anxious to be underway. There was only one last task to perform before saying goodbye to Armenia.

Samuel the Prophet looked back south and in the distance could just make out the valley of Amaziah, his home and the home of his ancestors for the last one thousand years. *A long time, but now things will be different. It is time to move on.* Turning to Jasher he remarked, "Take care of my son, Benjamin. He is not the last of our line, but he will be missed. Zeruah will remind me of that on occasions, I will assure you."

Jasher turned to the prophet and declared, "Yes, I know he will be missed, but his mission is with me now and with those who follow him. Our line, Samuel, will persist well beyond my grave."

"Then this labor will never end?"

"As long as people live on this world, there will be a need to record their history. The Creator has so decreed, thus it must be done."

The other man, Manasseh ben Judah, had been a relative newcomer to Amaziah when Jasher had arrived. Perhaps that had been the key factor in his friendship with Benjamin: they were both new to The Tribes. But, that closeness they felt had been immediate; their kinship seemed to cross blood lines. Jasher had seen enough to realize that few encounters were truly coincidental so had decided to encourage their brotherhood, though he knew their time together would be short.

Jasher shook the hand of ben Judah and asked a special favor. "Manasseh, you are a fine doctor and The Tribes are fortunate to have you. Please look after my family for me."

The doctor was a very engaging man and had done phenomenal surgical work on the young man, Shum, who had completely recovered from his injuries. In fact, Shum had been asked to be one of the company captains that had led the exodus north.

"Benjamin it would be my pleasure to watch over them and you can rest assure of that commitment for the remainder of my life."

"Then I will follow the progress of your sons and grandsons and if I can guide them or assist them in any way, you have my word that I will watch over them."

Samuel the Prophet and the physician Manasseh ben Judah embraced the other two men then turned and entered the cave.

Cain had pushed his army hard for over a month but finally they had entered the region of northern Armenia where the Tribes of Amaziah had settled. He had sent his best riders in advance of the army to scout out the settlements and determine their state of readiness. In the distance, Cain's chief captain could see men riding hard from the north down the mountain pass. It would be the messengers Cain had sent to Amaziah the previous week, now returning. Knowing his master to be anxiously expecting any news, the Captain lost no time escorting the scouts through the ranks of soldiers and into the main tent of their leader. Now standing before him, the messenger awaited Cain's command to proceed.

Cain turned and said only one word: "Report."

With barely contained excitement, one of the messengers blurted, "Sire, the entire city of Amaziah is deserted! We spoke with several persons in the adjoining kingdom, and they all say the same thing, "The Tribes are gone." He added, "I saw for myself and I still find it hard to believe, but where the kingdom was there now exists a huge deserted city surrounded by abandoned farms and villages." Both messengers were trembling with fear because they expected Cain to disbelieve him.

It was almost as if the air was removed from the tent. A gloom settled over Cain that he had not experienced for many years. His optimism over the success of the mission had deflated along with the air he was now having difficulty breathing. He never doubted the news, but he decided to see it for himself. Taking a deep breath, he turned his back on the messengers and announced ruefully, "Captain I am going for a walk; we will leave as soon as I return. For the time being, leave me to myself."

Within a week, Cain and a contingent of one hundred soldiers rode up a trail some ten miles from the patriarchy of Amaziah. There Cain had inquired about the city from local Armenians who had lived nearby, but no one could provide any answers, which only gave rise to more questions. Looking around, he noticed orchards and farm land recently harvested in readiness for a long winter. *Or a long journey*, he thought. Near the once thriving city of Amaziah, the farms were now all deserted; even the livestock was gone.

Finally, they had crossed a large stream flowing through the farmland and up ahead had spied a grassy knoll. Local villagers had instructed them that the knoll would indicate the beginning of the City of Amaziah. So, spurring on the horses, Cain and his contingent of riders ascended the hill.

Having attained the crest, Cain and his guards looked disbelievingly over a vast deserted valley of settlements, farms and a large city. Structures gleamed in the afternoon sun, but there were no people to be seen anywhere. "Sire," the captain of his troops cautiously inquired, "Where are the people?"

Cain, unable to take his eyes off the spectacle before him could only answer, "I don't know, yet, but I will. I swear I will." With mounting anger over his defeat, he and the one hundred men descended into the valley and within a few minutes had entered the city. Strewn about were the scattered debris and deserted rubble of a large host of people who had taken flight in haste and had never looked back. Cain followed the trail out of Amaziah and could see the tracks of thousands as they had trod over grass, shrub and rocks leaving a trail that an idiot could follow, but Cain was no fool. Shouting over to his captain, he said, "Surely we can catch them. Their trail will not be hard to follow."

It was two days later in the late afternoon when Cain and his men reached the foot of a large mountain range in northern Armenia and dismounted their horses for a rest. Two outriders had been sent up ahead to scout out the proposed route of the refugees and what they had found had confounded them more than had the deserted city and countryside of Amaziah. The chief scout had ridden up to Cain and the main body of his retinue near a hill and reported, "Sire, up ahead we found a cave opening into the base of the mountain; you can see it from the rise here. Outside we discovered two men as though they were waiting."

"Two men did you say?"

"Yes, Excellency."

"Where are all the others?"

"We were told they had entered the caves and were now gone."

"These two men told you that?"

"Yes, one was named Samuel."

"Samuel, their prophet?"

"Well, I could not say for sure. He was but a young man and not old enough to be their holy man."

"And the other one? I suppose his name was Jasher."

The scout blinked back his surprise, but slowly responded, "Yes, Sire. He called himself Jasher."

Shaking his head in anger he said, "What was his message?"

The soldier, now shaking his head in confusion, reported, "He said he was willing to talk with you, but you should come alone or, as he put it, it will be another five centuries before you see him again."

He muttered under his breath, "The impertinence of that man knows no boundaries." Fuming, he turned back to the captain and ordered, "Very well, you and the rest of the retinue will return back to the city of Amaziah and await the main body of the army to arrive. Tell them I will be back within a few days."

The captain remonstrated, "But, Sire, should you not have a personal guard to accompany you. How can you trust those two men? They may have weapons."

"Captain, the only weapons those two men will have will be ink and writing materials and there are times that I fear that more than I do the sword." Cain mounted his horse and said, "You have your orders."

Without another word, Cain rode hard in the direction of the mountain and within the hour had reached the gently sloping foot. It was rocky and strewn with boulders as though the mountain had recently collapsed from a landslide. In the distance he could see an opening within the mountain and out front stood two men. Angrily, He lashed his horse and they arose as he galloped toward them.

He reigned in his mare and dismounted. With an arrogance borne of years of self-absorption, he walked up to them, hands on his hips and said, "Well, Jasher I see once again you have been busy meddling into my affairs. It will do you little good to hide these people, you understand. Eventually, they will come under my power; everyone will."

"You overestimate your influence, Cain."

"I think not. Once I tire of the Byzantines, I will move on to consolidate my power with other kingdoms and enlarge my empire. It is inevitable."

"Only if you force them."

"Jasher, this is an old argument we have had before." He spread his hand out over the region behind him and said, "Look out across the valley all the way south to the sea. Those pathetic people, what do they know about choice? They have no idea what they want unless I tell them; otherwise, they would have no idea how to govern themselves. Without me, they are as mules without a whip to encourage them along. If it were not for me, there would be no civilization worth having."

"You are right, Cain, this is an old argument and your litany is older than either of us and that should tell you that this subject has been well debated. Do you honestly think you just dreamed up your plan of forced rule and subjugation? I doubt you even realize you have been used as a puppet from the beginning by your true father. He who will desert you in spite of all you have done for him."

Red anger was so deep he could hardly speak. He sputtered resentfully, "You do not know what you are saying!" He pounded his chest and declared, "There are no strings on me! No one uses me! I use them! I am the puppeteer!"

Jasher was tired of goading this man. It was a hollow victory at best and he just wanted him to go away. "Cain, I am here. I will answer your questions, though, as you have witnessed and have been informed, the people of Amaziah are no more to be seen and are fortunately now out of your grasp."

He asked contemptuously, "Where are they? In that dingy cavern?"

"They are."

"That was foolish. I will just have my men enter the cave and butcher them for sport."

"Not this time, Cain."

"And why not? There are no hallowed guarantees you can summon. This cave is not a holy sanctuary in which they can hide."

"True, but they willingly chose to depart from their city and settlements and follow the will of the Creator, not you. And because their choice was counted righteous before Him, he has sanctified their actions and it will be used as a witness against you one day. It has all been decreed and recorded."

Cain brooded with ill-contained anger. "Ah, yes, I see! The sacred records of their fathers will be added to those of Zion. What a paltry, pathetic number when you examine the vast majority of victories I enjoy. Jasher, Amaziah and Zion were aberrations of the general rule and the normal human condition. Surely, even you must know by now that people are incapable of having the understanding of such powers of personal control."

Jasher shrugged. He would not argue with this man any longer. "In the meantime, Cain, as per my mission, I will continue to do what I have been charged to do since the beginning: To keep and maintain records of your conquests and their debilitating affects upon mankind."

Cain shook his head proudly and proclaimed, "Your efforts are futile. In time, you will come to see the truth of what I speak and the Creator will have to bend His will to that reality. The evidence will be overwhelmingly in my favor. As you know, it is all I live for. Just take care, *dear* Brother, that you record only the truth without exaggerations, speculations, or overblown conjectures."

"It will be honest, Cain, as always. Have no fear."

Cain's grin was more sneer than smile and so his answer dripped of arrogance. "I do not fear you, Jasher. I simply loathe you." Turning to Samuel, he commented, "And now I see you have yet another acolyte to indoctrinate. Warn him well, Jasher."

"Will there be anything else, Cain?"

His anger, always near the surface, had returned. "Yes, there is one more matter to be addressed. I intend to destroy the entire city of Amaziah stone by stone and torch the entire countryside around it. I hope they have packed their records, Jasher, because I intend to leave no evidence that Amaziah ever existed."

"It will not change anything, Cain."

"Perhaps not, but it will amuse me, if nothing else. Also, the existence of the region of Amaziah will never be mentioned again in any history I control. It will be as though The Tribes had never existed."

"Goodbye, Cain."

"Good riddance, Jasher." With that he mounted his horse and rode off swiftly to the south.

Samuel glanced at Benjamin, the man his father had affirmed to be his teacher for much of the remainder of his life. Though knowing of Jasher's life expectancy, he would pass on to the next life long before Jasher ever would. Meanwhile, there was much to learn. "Benjamin, I understand why you permitted Cain to meet us. Now I realize what we are up against."

As Jasher watched his ancient rival ride off to the south, he commented, "It is always best to know your enemies as well as your friends." He turned to Samuel and said, "Take care of the records. As long as they are in the open, Cain will attempt to destroy them. In all likelihood, you may never see him again in your lifetime, but you must pass that impression of him on to those recorders who follow you. That has always been our way."

As both men began walking toward the west, Samuel could be heard to ask, "What was Zion like?"

Jasher replied breezily, "Now that is good story, worthy of a lengthy explanation. Come, my young grandson, let us descend yon hill and speak of weighty matters of past events and great exploits of courage under fire."

Samuel smiled; his new life had begun.

Jasher began, "In the days of Enoch the Prophet..."

Thus, that which had started so long ago had recommenced with Samuel, the son of the last prophet of the Lost Tribes of Israel.

PART 2

THE TRANSLATION, REVISITED

Isaac Levinson sipped his water and reflected upon the story of The Tribes of Amaziah that Jasher had just shared. After a moment, he commented, "Jasher, it seems clear that the only distinct tribe of Israel still in existence today is that of Judah, of which tribe I am a descendant. That story you have related to us about the Lost Tribes of Israel presents an intriguing dilemma for the historians."

William Bedford smiled briefly and commented, "Hear, hear."

Isaac pointed out, "William, perhaps you should be the one entertaining this historical oversight, if it can be described as such. Unarguably, their story deserves to be told, assuming of course that they still exist and enough evidence can be found to support their ties to ancient Israel."

Both men glanced over to Jasher. William asked, "What finally happened to them after you led them into the cavern?"

"That was never for me to know."

Isaac asked, "How then can we know for sure that they even exist today as separate and distinct tribes as we of Judah are?"

"Perhaps it was never their destiny to be a separate and distinct people. I quote from the Book of Genesis Chapter 17, verses 4-5: *"As for me, behold, my covenant is with thee, and thou shalt be a father of many nations. Neither shall thy name any more be called Abram, but thy name shall be Abraham; for a father of many nations have I made thee."*

"One might entertain the notion from that passage that though those of the House of Judah might remain distinct in our day, all the others may be mingled among all the people of the Earth, which would be a direct fulfillment of the covenant that the Creator made with Abraham."

Both men were silent for a long moment then Isaac commented, "I look forward to reading their history one day. The world deserves to know the truth."

"Never fear. There are records of their trials as well as the testimony of men of all the tribes who have been called to be special witnesses. Their words will be heard." Jasher was thinking of an old friend, Ephraim ben Judah, who had been asked to suffer so much to be one of those testifiers.

Bedford could not help marveling at the man who sat across the table from them. He had seen it all, the unfolding of history in all its wonder and drama; the ultimate historian of all time. There had to be much more he was not yet ready to share. "When shall we have it all?"

As if coming out of a personal reverie, Jasher slowly shook his head. "One thing is for certain, we shall never receive the answers to all our questions all at once because truth is simply not digestible in that manner. Usually through much trial and suffering, it is parceled out a little here and a little there, to give us time to use it with wisdom, which is why wisdom is a function of time." With a parting smile, he added, "And gentlemen time is a topic for another day." Jasher arose from the table and said, "Professors, today has been long and tomorrow will prove to be even longer. Good night. Rest well."

Levinson and Bedford both acknowledged his good night and replied their own. When Jasher had departed, Bedford asked, "Isaac, what did you make of all that?"

"If wisdom is indeed a function of experience over time then I think we have just conversed with one of the wisest men who may have ever lived."

"Indeed. But, I am curious what he knows of time itself, though."

Isaac thought on that a moment, then sighed, "I doubt we are ready to hear it."

Both men sat and pondered thoughts of truth and time then quietly left the table for the evening.

The Prisoner of Toledo, 1616

According to some apologist historians, the Inquisition was not born out of a desire to crush diversity or oppress people; rather, it was an attempt to stop unjust executions. Since the sixth century, Roman law in the Code of Justinian had made heresy a crime against the state, a capital offense. By the fifteenth century, European rulers, such as those in Spain, believed their authority came directly from God and over time began using this law as a cover to root out all whose customs and religions might differ from their own and potentially undermine their authority. Such persons who were involved in these differing practices were labeled heretics and enemies of the state, and if found guilty, were punished along the lines of a state-sanctioned inquisition. To this end, under the guise of state security, the Spanish monarchs decided to introduce the Inquisition in Castile (Spain) in the fifteenth century to discover and punish Crypto-Jews. In addition to Jewish citizenry falling under their scrutiny, the Spanish monarchy, ever fearful of a resurgence of Arab dominance of their nation, decided to add Islamic followers to those who fell under this category of heretical behavior. In reality, it was little more than a smoke-screen to rid the monarchy of all threats to their political rule and religious beliefs.

To receive a religious stamp to their intentions, in 1478 King Ferdinand II of Aragon of Castile (Spain) pressured Pope Sixtus IV to agree to an Inquisition controlled by the Spanish monarchy. When the Pope expressed his reservations to allow them permission to conduct their own private inquisition, the King threatened to withdraw military support at a time when the Ottoman Turks were then a threat to Rome. Because of this blatant act of extortion, Pope Sixtus issued a papal bull to stop the practice, but he was pressured into withdrawing it by his advisers which resulted in the exercise of the Spanish Inquisition and its proliferation throughout Europe for the next three centuries. (https:// en.wikipedia.org/wiki/Spanish_Inquisition)

CHAPTER 1

THE LIFE OF A MYSTIC

*A mind that is stretched by a new experience
can never go back to its old dimensions.*

----- *Oliver Wendell Holmes*

Antonio Montezinos was *a descendant of Conversos, those who became
Catholic with Jewish ancestry. After the Reconquista (the return
of Catholic Spain from Moslem Spain in 1492), his great-grand-
parents had been permitted to remain in Spain on condition that
they be converted to Christianity. To avoid the close scrutiny of
the Catholic Church, when the Holy Inquisition began in 1492,
many of the Conversos and later their descendants began to
take upon themselves Christian names. Now over a century had
passed, and though outwardly Christian in every way, inwardly
some Conversos practiced a mystic form of Judaism known as
kabbalism.*

*The family of Antonio Montezinos was ancient and had origi-
nated in Palestine and later had settled in Armenia. His Jewish
name was Ephraim ben Judah, a fact that even his Spanish wife
was unaware. Montezinos may have outwardly been a Converso*

and accepted in Spanish society, but inwardly he was Jewish and secretly practiced stylized rituals that would have put his life and that of his family in jeopardy as Crypto-Jews. Thus, in many ways, he felt as though he possessed a dual-personality and such a life was beginning to become more and more difficult to reconcile.

The night was moonless and the rain clouds, though dissipating, still hovered low in the sky. It was no accident that the leader of the Kabbalah Circle had chosen such a night to meet. One by one, usually two to five minutes apart, each member of the Circle warily gazed at both ends of the street then quickly made his way through the back courtyard of Vicente Torres. As had all members, Torres had built a secret room within his basement large enough to accommodate twelve men. Neither his wife nor those of the other members were fully aware of their husbands' activities which transpired at the monthly meeting of this secret group. Many wives were even unaware of where exactly their husbands met, only that one evening of each month they were absent from their home and family. Many excuses, of course, were offered and their families either chose to accept or reject them outright, but most simply did not want to know. In Spain in the seventeenth century, it was generally accepted not to ask too many questions of things that might be difficult to answer. To the members of the Circle, the truth would be impossible for most to tolerate, whereas a lie could hide a multitude of dangers.

As each member walked through the threshold of the inner room, the host for this month's meeting reverently handed out to each member a white robe, prayer shawl and yarmulke, or skull cap, which each member would wear for the duration of the meeting. Each man then entered a darkened room, devoid of light save a few isolated lit candles. In their midst stood the oldest member and mentor of the Circle in Toledo, Antonio Montezinos. It was to him that all members owed their understanding of the practice of the ancient rituals of the kabbalah. Owing to fear of exposure and given the climate of distrust that now existed in Spain, this was the only outward demonstration of their faith that permitted them some degree of safety. But, they could only worship their God quietly and then only in secret behind a closed door. This practice or even intimate knowledge of these rituals would have been sufficient to earn any one of them a guest room in the basement of the local Office of the Holy Inquisition. But being careful had become second nature to these men of faith.

Antonio embraced his friend Vicente Torres and used his true name. "Jacob Levinson, we thank you for having us in your home this evening."

Levinson used Antonio's true name. "It is my pleasure, Ephraim ben Judah. I only wish it could be done more openly with loud thanks and praises to the Lord God, our Creator."

Others all nodded their agreement, but prudently whispered their thanks. It had become the custom to whisper their praises instead of raising their voices to the rooftops as their ancestors had proudly done in *Eretz Yisrael* so many centuries before. In Spain, what they practiced was all that was left of their traditions and the hurt affected each deeply. The kabbalah had become their sanctuary in the desert.

"Come, my brothers. Let us sit and discuss our successes of the past month." It had become the monthly custom for Antonio to ask the host member within the Circle to report to the others any breakthroughs he had experienced in their private meditations of the rituals of the kabbalah. Looking over to the evening's host, Ephraim directed, "Jacob, please begin."

Levinson placed a candleholder in their midst and lit a candle. It began to burn slightly blue then red then yellow and it repeated the order of those colors; later, it began to lightly sputter and it seemed that these began to blend together and produce all the colors then some that had never before been seen. Save for the sputtering candle, it was the only light in the room.

"Thank you, Ephraim." Looking around the circle of his friends, Jacob proceeded. "As we have been taught, there is a relationship between an unchanging, eternal, and mysterious infinity known as *Ein Sof* and the mortal and finite universe we call God's creation. Our purpose, as I see it, is to fathom this relationship and attain spiritual realization as we reach *pardes*, the foundation of all Kabbalistic thought: peshat, remez, derash, sod." Before him lay the Torah; he picked it up and chanted so all could hear these four levels of the Zohar: *"peshat, remez, derash, sod."*

As the chant was repeated, all quietly joined him and also repeated the *parde*s. Each member of the circle closed his eyes and imagined the letters PRDS, the Hebrew word for orchard or paradise (*pardes*). This chant was repeated until the letters appeared in each mind and began flying about in different orders and in different directions. Then began an abstract, mental exercise in which each began by carefully using his thoughts and trying to reorganize the letters in their original, proper order. As this exercise proceeded all finally attained success at reorganizing the letters in their correct sequence: PRDS. When the last member had achieved success, the letters disappeared, revealing a tree, more beautiful and with fruit more desirable than any tree ever known. A collective sigh emanated from the group as each contemplated the personal significance the vision had revealed. After a while, the tree gradually disappeared into a mist, leaving only the letters PRDS. A moment later and it, too, disappeared. The vision was over and all felt at peace.

Ephraim nodded his head in acceptance of the mental exercise. "That was excellent, Jacob. I can only speak for myself, but I think the ritual is one well worth repeating. Each of us should attempt the same process privately in our own closets." From their collective nods, all seemed in agreement that the rite had been well worth learning. Turning back towards Jacob, Ephraim asked, "During this exercise throughout the month, were you ever able to reach the tree?"

Jacob's tone was one of disappointment. He replied sadly, "Not yet. It is almost as if there is something lacking, that I am leaving out a vital step in the exercise. The process to this point has been enlightening and fulfilling on many levels, but I would like to reach the tree and partake of the fruit."

"Perhaps the tree cannot be reached," added another member, Levi Singer. "It is supposed to be illusive such that we should enjoy the journey to the tree rather than to concern ourselves over the end destination."

Ephraim added, "Levi has a point, but perhaps the secret to reaching this allegorical symbol of *pardes* can only be unlocked using a mathematical sequence of numbers added to the exercise."

Each member of the circle smiled at their mentor's fixation on numbers. Levi replied, "Again with the numbers, Ephraim. Is there no other solution for you?"

"For me, no. And so it must be for each of you to find his way to the tree to attain the fruit. I had the impression from our vision that the fruit of that tree was delicious above all other fruit ever planted by our Creator. That makes it well worth the journey to reach it."

Jacob commented, "I, too, had the impression that the fruit was special and yet it also occurred to me that it was symbolic of something greater. What did you make of the fruit? What was it truly?"

Ephraim looked around the room at each man and pronounced, "It was knowledge."

Levi asked, "But, knowledge of what?"

Ephraim bowed his head slightly and closed his eyes as if pondering the meaning of the fruit. He slowly opened them and replied, "It is the word of the Creator that is limitless and eternal. He has something for us to learn; perhaps that is the gift. May we one day become worthy to receive it, my brothers."

The next afternoon had ended gloriously beautiful; the rains of the day before had cleared and the air tingled with life. As Antonio approached the front door of his home in Toledo, with a smile he waved to nearby neighbors crossing the cobble-stone street. At the doorway, he took a few minutes to chat with a neighbor who had complained of migraines and promised to pass by her home with an herbal remedy he had normally prescribed for such ailments. Antonio practiced a form of medicine borrowed from the Arabic physicians known as *medica materia*, an early form of pharmacology which included, among other things, the use of medicinal herbs.

Once inside, it was his usual evening routine to go directly into the dining area and greet his family, but as he walked through the parlor he happened to glimpse at his reflection in the Venetian glass mirror then abruptly halted. He had purchased the mirror a few years earlier; it had been expensive, he recalled, but the spectacle of his reflection was ever fascinating. Today, however, he noted something about his appearance that seemed oddly out of place. His hand slowly came up to his face and rubbed his right ear then his jaw. Shaking his head in wonder, he pondered the duality of his life; *who was he, the man in the reflection or the man outside of it?* He would never vocalize publicly any such maunderings of his mind. Such musings would have cast doubt on his sanity and would undoubtedly affect his standing in the community. He was, after all, a doctor of medicine, respected for his intellect and renowned for his medical acumen by all; moreover, he was a respecter of Spanish law and customs. With a frown, he thought, *but, they know nothing of the man in the mirror, and if they did, that same law would be used to condemn and ruin me, delivering me to the waiting arms of the Inquisition.* The more he continued to stare, the more the image began to twist then contract and finally take on a different form. Shaking his head in disbelief, Antonio discovered to his horror that the face appeared emaciated and beaten, riddled with sores of malnutrition. It was a face of hopeless dread and infinite misery. He continued to rub his hand shakily across his horrified face until the specter of his image had passed.

Magdalena, his devoted wife of thirteen years, had heard her husband enter the house, but after a few minutes she realized he had been detained in route to the dining room. His usual manner of appearance was affably loud and announced his arrival home for the day; today there was only silence. Now curious at his delay, she walked into the parlor and watched her husband silently from the doorway. At an earlier time in their marriage, her gaze would have melted into an indulgent smile, but of late, when she looked at Antonio during odd moments such as these, a note of concern furrowed her brow. Nowadays, her look was speculative as though she were trying to redefine the man into a new role outside their normal, comfortable surroundings of home. At length, she rested her arms just under her bosom, clasping her arms tightly and trying with difficulty to quiet her rising fears as the vision of this terror began to take shape. *Who is he?* She wondered.

Not desiring he hear the concern in her voice, she cleared her throat before speaking. "So, husband, you are home I see." She experimented with a smile though it never touched her eyes.

He flinched slightly before he turned, realizing of course, that she had noticed a tremor reflected in the mirror before he was able to re-apply the mask he had been wearing so carefully for the past few years. He, too, smiled, but like hers it was forced. As he silently closed the distance between them, he berated himself at his lapse into self-absorption. Holding out his hands he reached for hers, squeezed them and offered a comforting embrace and kiss of greeting. "Magdalena, my love, you look wonderful. You must tell me all about your day."

She gradually pulled away from him and walked toward the dining area. Looking back over her shoulder, she commented, "Darling, you must do something about the gardener. His ineptitude is bordering on tiresome. I suggest you dismiss him."

"Diego? I thought you adored his rose bushes."

"The roses are fine, but the pistachio and almond trees look as though blight had hit them."

"Perhaps he just needs help. He is getting old."

She was irritated of the discussion. "Or perhaps he just needs to be replaced."

"I see." But, he didn't see nor understand. Magdalena usually ran the household with an iron hand and brooked no excuses for failure in the duties of the help. *Why is she bringing this to me?* He asked himself. "I will take care of it. Was there anything else?"

She shook her head then looked away distractedly. "Come to dinner and greet your children."

Antonio Montezinos walked into the dining area and there seated around the table were his three children: two boys, Eduardo and Alberto, and his eldest, the darling of his life, Elena, his daughter. All acknowledged his entrance with a resounding *Papá!* He went around the dining table, kissed each one in turn and took his place at the head. He was so proud of the children, their healthy, robust smiles and intellect. All would no doubt grow to adulthood happy and become pillars of their communities. The boys, he had been informed by the fathers of the Church, were highly intelligent and would no doubt follow Antonio in the field of medicine and Elena would grace the home of a Spanish nobleman. He had high hopes for them all and thus his pride was understandably justified.

His smile was glowing, but glancing at his wife seated across the table, he noticed she was withdrawn, even sullen, so unlike her. *Does she know or even suspect?* He asked himself hardly for the first time. His former glow slipped and he found it difficult to regain it.

A few moments later and the two house maids entered and began serving the evening meal. The eldest, Leticia, remarked, "Don Antonio, how has been your day?"

"Wonderful," he exclaimed. "How are you feeling today, Leticia?"

"As you well know, *Señor*, my feet are recovering or I would not be walking about. Thank you so much for the cure." As a result of constant standing, Leticia had been suffering from a mild case of phlebitis in her legs and Antonio, as her doctor, had prescribed an herb used as a blood thinner.

"It was my pleasure. I still do not know if it is a cure, but the medicinal compound has shown to ease suffering for those with inflamed legs."

The younger servant, Josefina, remarked, "You practice medicine differently than do most other Spanish doctors. You are not afraid to learn from the Arabs who were most wise in such matters."

"They were indeed, Josefina. The truth comes from many directions and the wise are those who recognize the benefits in spite of the source."

With that comment, Magdalena, who had been silently following the conversation, looked up abruptly from her plate and cast a shake of her head at her husband, signaling that he should break off this line of conversation. A few moments later, the servants left the dining area and Magdalena fiercely whispered, "Antonio, you must cease such talk of Arabs and their medicines. You know they are no longer welcome here in Spain. I don't know which is worse, the Arabs or the Jews. Both are nothing but trouble and the sooner the holy fathers rid them all of our land the better."

"But, Magdalena, you must not reject all the good that has been done by both societies in making our nation great since the *Reconquista* over a hundred years ago. Yes, they have been outcast, but they still continue to add and enhance our society."

"Antonio, look around the table. Your talk of appeasement puts me and your children at risk socially. You have no right to be so selfish in this manner!"

"It is not appeasement."

"Then, what would you call it? You would have your innocent children cursed for embracing such nonsense?"

Antonio, now exasperated, threw up his hands in bewilderment. "How will they be cursed? It is the truth and our children can only benefit by hearing it, not just from me but from you as well."

"Husband, they will never hear it from me because only the holy fathers preach the truth and they tell us that only the scourge of the Arabs and Jews from our midst will bring us peace and avert the wrath of God upon us all." Now that her maternal instinct had been rightly aroused, she pointed her finger in his direction and exclaimed, "Our precious children must never feel the pains of damnation that await those who tolerate the presence of this vermin in Spain."

Antonio looked at his children, by this time wide-eyed and more than a little frightened by the argument between their parents. He quietly announced, "Magdalena, we should discuss this at another time."

"No, it must be said now. Do you think I am unaware of who your patients are and with whom you associate? Jews and Arabs that is who! And if I know of it, how long do you think it will be before the Office of the Inquisition hears of it?"

Now it became clear to Antonio why his wife had been behaving so strangely and out of character lately. The fear of his public associations had precipitated her panic and her anxiety had been manifested at the dinner table. She still did not know the real truth and he intended that she never would. "Very well, Magdalena, you are correct. Please forgive me. I will put an end of my dealings with those people at once."

She closed her eyes and nodded her head in thanks. When she re-opened them, tears of relief coursed down her cheeks. Rubbing away the tears, she whispered, "Thank you my husband. Now, let us finish our meal."

Antonio was also relieved, not just because he wanted to allay the concern of his children who had witnessed this shameful scene between their parents, but because his wife had been correct. He had been careless and his greatest fear had nearly been laid open for all to see. The secret life he had been leading had intruded upon his real life and his terror of discovery was a reminder to him that he must fight all the harder to be more circumspect in the future. *Soon, after a day of fasting, I will seek the solace and quiet meditation I need to deal with the prolonged anxiety of this dual life, but in the meantime, I must control my lapses.*

CHAPTER 2

THE VISION

Don Antonio Montezinos sat rigidly quiet in a stark room devoid of any trappings of comfort, style or color. He was a follower of the Jewish mystic Abulafia, and indeed had been initiated into the kabbalah by a devoted acolyte of Abulafia's teachings. Thus, he began the ritual by following the great mystic's steps to enlightenment.

Having fasted, and now quietly entering his basement sanctum, he knelt before a small black lacquered desk. For the solemn occasion, he wore pure white garments denoting clarity and purity of thought upon which rested white phylacteries containing small parchments of the Torah. Save for the objects resting upon the table, the room was dark. A light of a single lit white candle inside a lamp occupied the center of the black table. While focusing on the simple light from the candle, he used a series of breathing techniques and psychic cathartic exercises involving complex numbers and Hebrew letters to achieve a state of solemn lucidity of thought. Slowly, from inside the table, he removed pen and ink and a single parchment of paper then laid all the items before him. After a few minutes of quiet introspection, he began to write out specific Hebrew letter groups and their permutations. Being a mathematician, he also added several algebraic equations then lay the quill down. As he slowly moved his head from side to side to different positions on his neck, he paused then began to chant the written letters and numbers in conjunction with his breathing; his eyes never left the light of the lamp. Finally, peace and purity of thought distilled upon him as the cleansing rain.

In addition to the lamp upon the table before him rested three objects of curious design. Each was of pure white ivory and had been constructed to enhance his focus and permit him to unite with the Agent Intellect, or the Creator, through the recitation of His divine name. Once the cleansing of all mundane matters had been achieved, he gazed upon the objects and began to recite the ancient, unutterable name of the Creator.

He slowly closed his eyes and allowed his mind to reach out and begin to imagine himself without a body, leaving behind all worldly concerns. He then began to form the letters and numbers mentally as he imagined their patterns and, after a while, he began to feel an enhancement of his thoughts. The letters began to rotate and the numbers brightened and a sub aural buzzing could be felt, if not entirely heard; he began to project mentally the symbols of the Creator in their true form. Soon thereafter, a wave-like form shimmered from their midst and gradually the light and the low noise began to merge and find symmetry.

The closer the form approached him, the more the sub-aural tone began to dissipate. From the form, a quiet, serene voice intoned, "Ephraim ben Judah, you have been chosen to be a witness before the Gentiles among whom you live."

Having seen the symbols evolve into a form of light, at first Antonio was frightened, but after hearing the still, quiet voice, his fear gave way to pleasure and delight. The joy he felt helped him break through the brightness and the low buzzing until he could clearly discern a man standing before him. Still in a heightened state of suggestible meditation, his mind reached out and asked, "To what shall I witness?"

"You are to be a silent witness to the collective strength and faith of your people. Though you will suffer, even as your people have suffered, if you remain strong in the face of despair, you will be delivered."

"Then I am not to die?" he asked languidly.

"A friend will deliver you from your tormentors. Go to the garden near the coliseum and collect a journal from a messenger who will speak more of your mission. Once you leave the garden, you must deliver the journal to Levi Singer, but before you deliver it, you must write inside it a formula."

"A formula?" he murmured.

"Prepare to receive it," was the response.

In his highly suggestive state, the form of the man began to disappear and in his place a series of letters and numbers in an algebraic expression began to gradually approach him until they appeared brightly in bold relief before his mind. Antonio nodded his head in understanding, the meaning now etched clearly in his subconscious. A moment later, or was it an hour (perhaps a day?), Ephraim ben Judah gradually awoke from the self-induced dream state, slowly arose from the floor and walked out of the sub-basement into the courtyard, again the Spaniard Antonio Montezinos.

He gazed up at the night sky and noticed the stars, but the moon was gone so several hours must have passed. In the last fleeting moments of his dream, or vision, their stellar movements he could almost comprehend and with enough time, he knew he could master their order. All things were now possible, even to endure the unendurable.

As Antonio watched the night sky, out of sight in the shadows stood his wife. It had been a long, exhausting day and the children had been especially hard to handle, no doubt the result of the conflicts she and Antonio had experienced lately, especially the evening before. The courtyard with its flowers and shrubbery and its scent of roses and jasmine had always been her favorite place of refuge, so after the children were down for the night and she had dismissed her servants for the day, she decided to take a moment and stroll out to her garden.

Suddenly, to her amazement, Antonio had appeared from his study and the more she watched him the more she became alarmed. He had discarded his usual clothing and had donned a white robe and was mumbling something she could not quite discern. He raised his hands up to the night sky and after a moment, dropped them then turned and retreated back to his study. Her eyes narrowed in consternation and a fright began to creep into her thoughts and a horror began to insinuate ever so insidiously within her being. But, being a strong-willed woman, she pushed her fear back then shook her head, as if to clear it of all distractions. Her worst fear regarding her husband had been dumped at her feet with all its noxious odors. With a grimace of scorn, she began to contemplate her next course of action. *So, our dinner discussion of the previous night, he has chosen to ignore. I must watch him much more closely and make note of his movements and any more deviant activities.* Now knowing what she must do, her fear was replaced with a cold, decisive resolve.

The next day, Montezinos carefully moved through the bustling streets of Toledo. So as to appear outwardly calm despite his growing anxiety, he greeted his neighbors along the avenue with waves and greetings. Being a popular and respected citizen of the city, this was not unexpected; indeed, had he not shown such attention, the oversight would have been noted. On this day, everything he did had to give the appearance of normalcy. Nothing could appear out of character or unseemly.

As he entered the garden, he noticed just beyond the manicured hedges the ancient Roman circus built during the Flavian dynasty, a subtle reminder that the Spanish had always been ruled by outsiders. The current monarchs may have been Spanish, but they borrowed their values from Rome. Looking around, he noted immediately that there were few patrons about, a first since the garden had always been a popular, oft-frequented public place. He rounded a walkway lined with shrubbery and found a quiet, secluded corner and a nearby bench upon which he could rest and wait.. Closing his eyes, he began to ponder the events of the previous night and what their portent could mean for his life. Being a mystic, most messages he had received had been symbolic, often allegorical in nature, but never had he been contacted in such a personal, literal manner. *Could I have been wrong about the message?* He asked himself. After a few moments of quiet meditation, he sensed rather than detected a presence and he slowly opened his eyes.

A man (or was he?) was standing in front of him to one side and his back to the walkway. The first thing Antonio noticed was that he was attired in white clothing, including his boots. Being a fastidious dresser himself, he appreciated the cut and tailoring of the clothing that fit him perfectly. As Antonio marveled at the immaculate condition and color of his clothing, he noticed the stranger to have an open, friendly smile and an engaging manner about him. In addition to being of average height, his hair was greying at the temples, the eyes deep blue and penetrating.

The man extended his hand in friendship and stated, "I am Joseph and you must be Antonio Montezinos, or should I say Ephraim ben Judah." The voice was confident yet refined and full as a bountiful harvest.

Given the previous night's events, Antonio should have been unsurprised, but hearing his secret name spoken aloud, he was understandably apprehensive. Moreover, on closer inspection, everything about the man was peculiar as though he were more than there. (*Could that be it*, he asked himself?) Perhaps it was the shadows or the angle of the sun, but Antonio could have sworn that the man simply stood out in greater relief than did the surrounding scenery.

As he solemnly pondered this singular meeting, he recollected that occasionally he had come out of a meditative state unsure of the reality of his surroundings. So as to avoid this understandable confusion, he had always carried a physical totem to ensure he had awoken to the real world and this he had encouraged his acolytes to do likewise. For him, the outward connection to physical reality was an obsidian chess piece, a bishop. He reached into his pocket and felt its reassuring contours and knew the man before him was real and not a psychic projection of his subconscious.

The stranger smiled warmly and asked, "Ephraim, does the chess piece reassure you of my reality?"

Montezinos shakily arose. Taking the man's hand, he replied, "It does, but if you are real then my perception of what is real has been greatly shaken and will need to be re-examined."

With a knowing smile, Joseph quietly proclaimed, "The recognition of that is the first step toward true enlightenment. Never forget that your potential is limitless and eternal." He beckoned Ephraim to be seated then joined him. Looking around and marveling at the beauty of the garden, the messenger seemed to pause as if to embrace pleasure before beginning the business of his message. After they were both comfortable, Joseph began to speak.

"Ephraim, occasionally the Creator deems it necessary to call special testifiers to stand as a witness against those who would oppress and deny mankind of their ordained rights and freedoms of personal choice. Your people have been persecuted and afflicted for centuries at the hands of those who would call themselves Christians, but whose hearts are far from the spirit of truth. They outwardly profess that which inwardly they have no conception and are unwilling to learn."

"Then it is to be the Inquisition." A look of deep resignation had swept over him. There was no need for the question; he had known all along what was ahead.

"Yes, Ephraim. It is a symbol of their brutality and hypocrisy. You must remain a silent witness before your tormentors."

Stunned, he could only stammer, "But, why have I been chosen? There is nothing special about me."

"On the contrary, only you have spent a lifetime preparing yourself sufficiently to undergo the trials that await you from your tormentors. Their condemnation must be sure and swift, but without a credible witness to their depredations, they would escape the full measure of justice."

Ephraim nodded his understanding, but he was still unsure that all this might be too much for him to endure. He sincerely wished the duty had fallen to another, but understood that it would be his cross to carry. "Yes, I understand." In the distance a bell rang the hour, but for him it could have been a death knell. Now weary and knowing what was to come, he murmured, "I was told someone would arrange my escape."

With compassion, Joseph answered, "Yes, never fear. If you remain silent in the face of that evil, you will be delivered." From inside his coat pocket he produced a leather-bound book and giving it to him, he directed, "Provide this journal to your follower, Levi Singer. Explain to him that after you are incarcerated, he is to reach out to an old friend of yours, Benjamin Jasher. He is to give him the journal as payment for his services to extract you in route to your public execution. On the last page of the diary, you are to write an algebraic formula you received in your vision of the previous night complete with the explanations. As you were told, Jasher will understand their meaning and application. Do you understand my message?"

So, Benjamin was to be a part of this. Well, if anyone could manufacture my escape, it would be he. After a moment, he replied, "I do, but there is still so much to understand."

Joseph arose as if to leave, but before parting he said, "Ephraim, most could not endure what you are about to face. But, if you can apply what you already know about submerging within yourself and finding inner peace and calm, you will achieve an understanding of your hidden potential. If you can do this, you will survive your incarceration and live to testify against those who would persecute your people."

With an inner grief and despair, he asked, "When I am jailed, what is to become of my wife and children?"

"No harm will befall them, my friend. The Chief Inquisitor will be more concerned with you and your associates. But, unfortunately, your life here in Spain will be over."

Ephraim choked back a sob of loss and disgust for his responsibility in this affair. He stammered, "Because of my involvement in their lives, surely my friends will come under close scrutiny."

As for added emphasis, Joseph instructed, "During your trials, under no circumstances should you reveal anything about your mission nor divulge the whereabouts and identity of those within your circle of friends. This trial is for you alone to suffer and to act as a silent witness during your trial. Your brethren and your family will be protected only if you can remember this." As he stood he turned and instructed, "Please wait until I have departed out of sight before you leave." After a pause, he waved, then smiling he said, "Ephraim ben Judah, remember that you would not have been chosen if you had not prepared yourself for the ordeals to come. You will find the strength. Goodbye, my friend."

Montezinos watched the man as he strolled casually down the flower-lined pathway and around a corner of the garden, but before he stood up to leave he saw a flash of light appear suddenly behind shrubbery, but straightaway vanished. Now curious, Antonio arose and walked along the same path to the park exit, but rounding the corner, there was no one to be seen. *Had it all been a dream? Was it merely as an errant thought that was caught in the half-dream of a waking moment? No, there was that crystal clarity of truth and reality.*

Shaking his head in near disbelief of the singular experience, he exited the park then walked in the direction of the home of his friend Levi Singer. Now realizing what he must do, he made no effort to play the role of the Spanish courtier. His boot steps upon the cobblestone street clicked and clacked in counterpoint to his quickly beating heart. Never had he felt so alive and at one with himself, but singularly alone. True, there was fear of the unknown, but it was a terror that he had been assured he could control. With unaccountable optimism he approached then knocked on the door of his friend and colleague. With luck, he would be home.

Levi Singer, a friend of Montezinos for eleven years, was also known among his Christian friends as Manuel Diaz Suarez. He had been home, but unhappy that Antonio had come calling unexpectedly. "Antonio, are you insane?" You are putting us both at risk by coming here in the middle of the day. You know that we must not be seen together socially."

"Levi, I understand your reluctance to meet in this manner, but my time is short and we must speak. Something extraordinary has occurred and I must speak with you and deliver to you an item of the utmost importance."

Like Montezinos, Manuel was a *Converso*, a converted Catholic and the problem for persons like him was that there really was no safe place to meet a fellow Jew in Toledo for danger was everywhere. As a New Christian, he was always under close scrutiny, and never more so than at the weekly services of the Holy Mass that he attended with his Christian wife and children. What the good people of the city of Toledo did not know for a certainty was whether he was only pretending to be a true Christian. For many citizens, they were always looking for the Crypto-Jew to show his true face. And of course, they were right to be suspicious. Manuel Suarez was Levi Singer, a practicing kabbalist Jew. The public practice of Judaism was forbidden in Spain and Portugal and would have resulted in an immediate introduction to the darker side of Catholicism, the auto-da-fé. His mentor Ephraim ben Judah, over a period of eleven years, had taught him this mystical side of

Judaism that required no outward show of his faith, but an inward resolve toward self-enlightenment.

When Antonio had arrived at the door to his home, Manuel had been the first to hear the knock and it was fortunate he had, because the servants would have surely seen him. Looking furtively to both sides of the street, he quietly, but insistently signaled to him he was to wait around the corner, out of sight. As Montezinos waited patiently, Manuel was hard pressed to dismiss the servants for the day, but once they were gone, he had beckoned his friend into the back courtyard away from prying eyes and listening ears. Like his colleague Montezinos, Suarez had built a secret sub-basement off his court-yard and now indicated that his friend should follow him inside.

Once Manuel had locked the door, not even his own Christian wife had the key to enter, and it was just as well, as she, too, would have found their meeting not only strange, but highly suspect. *Conversos* knew one an-other of course, but any public or social meetings would have given rise to suspicions of conspiracies and practices of Crypto-Jewish rituals by their Christian neighbors and relatives. Thus, exclusive interactions of a friend-ly, social manner were discouraged among fellow *Conversos* and were to be avoided at all costs. What they were doing now was not only ill-advised, but dangerous.

. Some of his happiest and most fulfilling moments in Levi's life had been in the presence of Antonio Montezinos, but if that was so then it was also true that those same experiences were fraught with danger. As he sat listening to his mentor and friend relate all that had happened in the past twenty-four hours, he was beginning to believe that this moment definitely fell into the latter category of dangerous. Suarez was frankly stunned at what his friend had shared, but all he managed to stammer was, "My friend, what do you intend to do?"

Now together privately, both lapsed into the use of their secret names. "Levi, my days of leading you and the others in our circle are at an end. Moreover, if what I think is coming does show its face, as it must, then my life here in Spain is over."

Levi felt a moment of desperate terror and uneasily rubbed a hand across his face and eyes. After a moment he whispered, "And what would you have me do? If what you say is true and you are to be jailed, what of us."

"You must disband the circle immediately and close all associations with each member from this time forward. Inform those members without families they are to leave Spain immediately." With reluctance, he also pointed out, "If I were you, Levi, I would leave Spain also."

He closed his eyes, shaking his head and declared, "And go where? To Turkey and live among the Ottomans? My Christian wife will never go and she will definitely not leave her family. And for me to abandon her and the children would be unthinkable."

"I know, but such are our choices."

Now angry, he hissed, "Ephraim, there must be something you can do to avert this."

"Levi, it cannot be avoided, but when the time arrives and I am arrested, there is something you must do for me."

By now Levi Singer was anxious to extricate himself from any further involvement, but out of duty he realized that he must do something for his closest friend. Reluctantly he asked, "Ephraim, what can I do?"

"You must meet with an old associate and mentor of mine by the name of Benjamin Jasher and arrange my escape."

"Jasher? You have never mentioned him before. Just who is he?"

"A remarkable man and even after twenty years, I doubt he has aged a day. I was a young man living in Italy when I first met him. It was rumored he had known and influenced Judah ben Samuel the first kabbalist of recent times."

"You mean the Judah ben Samuel of Germany who later introduced his son Samuel Abulafia of Zaragoza into our order? Impossible! That would make this Jasher nearly three hundred years of age."

"I will tell you something even more astonishing. It was rumored and never denied that those two men were actually descendants of Benjamin Jasher. Each carried the name of Samuel as has been the custom of his family line down through the ages."

Singer stared, now disbelieving, but coming from his mentor he reasoned there must exist at least a kernel of truth in the matter. "If that is so then this Jasher must be the supreme master of the kabbalah. That seems difficult to accept."

"That was my first reaction also. Benjamin Jasher neither accepts nor denies his association with the kabbalah, but only remarked once that the original teachings have been taken out of context and were distorted and now the rituals should be practiced with great care."

"How is it he knows so much of our teachings and can he even be trusted?"

"I don't know how he came to understand the kabbalah, but many years ago, he taught me a few points of meditation which I now use to attain my heightened state of awareness. I assure you he can be trusted and his knowledge of things past and present are vast."

"When was the last time you saw him? Perhaps he is dead."

"Benjamin appears on my doorstep from time to time, though it has been at least five years since his last visit. As to whether he is still alive or not, you should not worry about that. I am not sure that he can die."

Levi was not sure how to interpret the last comment, but coming from a mystic like Ephraim, he had learned nearly anything was possible. He let out a sigh of desperation, and though still skeptical, asked, "How am I to meet with him?"

"You must travel north to the kingdom of Andorra to the nearby abbey of Saint Joan de Caselle. Ask for Father Raymond and introduce yourself as a close friend of Benjamin Jasher. Provide your Christian name and inform him you have a message for Benjamin. He will ask for the message and you will reply: "Jailed. Need help. Ephraim.""

"Then what?" Levi had been afraid to ask.

"Then, Levi, we wait and pray he arrives before they can break me on the rack."

CHAPTER 3

BETRAYAL

It had been two days since Antonio had met with Suarez and delivered the journal. For Magdalena last evening had been a nightmare. After dinner and the children had retired for the evening, Antonio had excused himself declaring that he was going to the basement to study medical papers and reference books. Normally, this was his private way of saying that he needed some quiet time away from the evening bustle of dinner and children preparing for bed. Since their marriage, Magdalena had always respected his need for solitude at the end of the day and never interfered or complained when he had stated his intentions. But, since noting his behavior of a few nights earlier when she had seen him from the garden, she intended to see if the incident would be repeated. Thus, after he had remarked he was going downstairs, she decided to follow him to the basement a half-hour after he had descended.

As she began the descent, she noticed straightaway that his study was dark which was unusual since he should have been poring over his books or so he had said. She ascended back up to the kitchen area and found a candle, lit it and again began the descent. This time she walked carefully around the room, trying with difficulty to remain as quiet as possible so as not to disturb him on the chance he may have simply dozed off in one of his chairs. But, looking around, it seemed obvious that, save for herself that no one else was in the room. She had cast her eyes toward the doorway that led directly out to the courtyard, and leaving her candle on a nearby table, she decided to investigate whether he had simply gone out for air. After a thorough walk about the yard and garden, this too, provided no answers to his whereabouts. He was simply nowhere to be found. Her hands now on her hips and with a frown thought, *perhaps he had left the house for a walk.*

On her way back into the basement from the courtyard, she noticed something that had been overlooked the first time she had investigated the study area. She would have missed it again except that from the direction she was coming from the outside, it had become more apparent. A small sliver of light was protruding from what appeared to be beneath the wall. Keeping the exit door open behind her, she snuffed out the candle and moved cautiously toward the light. Her hand trembled as it moved upward against the wall trying to find an entrance that led to the light, but not finding one, she quietly moved back through the room and out into the court yard then began to wait.

The more she waited, the more agitated she became. *What is he up to? It is obvious that Antonio is behind the wall, but what should I say? Should I simply confront him with my suspicions?* There was no denying that he was hiding something. She had seen him in the courtyard only a few nights earlier wearing a white robe of some sort and gazing up at the stars. *Had that only been a one-time occurrence or would he re-emerge tonight wearing the same clothing and behave in the same strange manner?*

As she was contemplating these questions, a slight noise came from the doorway. Instinctively, she backed up farther into the shadows to await his exit from the study. A moment later, he emerged outside wearing a similar white robe as before, only on this occasion, he also wore a yarmulke, a scullcap, of pure white. Draped around his shoulders was a shawl of blue and white with a pattern woven into the material. He began walking purposely to the center of the courtyard and looking up and around he seemed to be deciding upon a location. Then, the decision made, from under his arm, he removed a woven mat which he unfolded and placed on a large flagstone. He knelt on the mat, and looking upward at the stars, he began to chant in a foreign language which she surmised must be Hebrew. She moved out of the darkness to ensure a better view of the scene when she noticed the pattern he was wearing on the shawl bore the blue six-point Star of David. Her right hand trembled as she quickly placed it over her mouth to suppress the noise of choked horror coming from her throat. She closed her eyes to remove the abomination from her sight, but tears continued to course down her cheeks in shame. Choking back the hurt, she turned from the scene and fled back into the house through another entrance. She commented nothing of what she had witnessed in the garden to Antonio that night, but her sleep was restless and fraught with despair.

Antonio left early the next morning to make his usual rounds for the day. At home, Magdalena sat rigidly straight and stared at the nearby wall in her parlor room. The old gardener had just picked a bouquet of her favorite roses and had placed them in a ceramic rose-colored vase on a nearby table. She mumbled a thanks then a dismissal, so unlike her, but she was distracted and found it beyond her current ability to stay focused. Ordinarily, the sight and especially the fragrant scent of roses would have been enough to brighten her disposition, but not on this day. She was in a high state of agitation, and if her suspicions were true, then her husband of thirteen years was a Crypto-Jew and secretly practiced his Jewishness by consorting with fellow Jews in Toledo. She had needed desperately to talk with someone who could help her decide what must be done. Friends and relatives were definitely out of the question, especially her mother who had warned her before her marriage that marrying a *Converso* was the same as marrying a yarmulke-carrying Jew.

But, Antonio had always insisted that he was a fully converted Christian and, in fact, after their marriage he had always accompanied her with the children to mass every week. Each child had been baptized and had been given god-parents. He respected and observed every outward sign of Christianity; he had even attended a weekly confessional. Now she had discovered that it had all been a sham. He had betrayed her worse than if he had been seeing another woman. At length, after a long struggle with her conscience, a look of determination came over her as she came to a personal decision. Her dark brows furrowed and her normally light-skinned face became flushed with anger. Taken together with what she had witnessed tonight, the incident of the previous night was not isolated, but was evidence of a long repeated routine. He had left her no alternative; she had the children to think of.

The next day Magdalena had turned to the one person she knew who would understand that which needed to be done. On the other side of the desk from her sat a sandy-haired man dressed in the holy robes of the Church. Father Alberto de la Fuente was the prelate of the Cathedral of Saint Mary of Toledo and confessor for Magdalena Montezinos. He was a tall man, but realizing his height might be intimidating to some, since receiving his current assignment, he had gone to great lengths to appear humble and servile when necessary and especially when conversing with the leading citizens of the city.

Magdalena shifted uncomfortably in the chair across the desk from Father de la Fuente. She had embraced the anger and now despised her husband and his duplicitous activities. She was agitated, but did not know how to begin. The floral paintings on the wall, as well the freshly cut flowers that adorned the prelate's desk gave her confidence and assurance; the man in front of her could be trusted.

The Father smiled benignly and with a quiet voice said, "Please, Doña Magdalena, be at ease. You are worried, I can tell, but you have come to the right place. Now, how can I help?"

For days she had battled her conflicting emotions of hurt and anger while trying hard to throttle her shame and fear, but she had reached a point where a resolution was needed or the conflict would drive her insane. At length, Magdalena nodded her acceptance at her duty; she could restrain her anger no more and blurted, "Oh, Father de la Fuente, my life has been completely turned upside down and I have no one else to whom I can turn for counsel." A tear of despair coursed down her left cheek, marring the light makeup she had been wearing. She quickly reused the handkerchief to dab the offending tear. It had only made her more miserable.

With compassion, the priest patiently allowed her to expend her feelings until she appeared to have her emotions under control. "Please continue my daughter," he whispered with an encouraging smile.

Shaking her head in misery, Magdalena whispered hoarsely, "Father, my husband, Antonio Montezinos, is a Crypto-Jew." Fresh tears of shame began to flow.

Surprise registered across his brow as though he had misunderstood. Nodding encouragement he softly directed, "Magdalena, please explain." After a moment, he added, "Omit nothing."

Having expended her emotions, Doña Magdalena spent the next hour relating all she had noticed and seen over the past year with particular emphasis on the last week. She spoke with a sure firmness as she testified of all she knew and suspected. When she had spent her tale and her emotions, the only feeling that remained was a sense of betrayal and anger that she had decided to embrace and channel toward her lying, conniving husband.

"Father, I leave this matter in your capable hands. Perhaps he may repent, but I and my children cannot tolerate his betrayal. Do whatever you can, but please make our misery and shame go away." Her feelings for Antonio tasted of ashes, now dry and desolate. She arose and prepared herself to leave, dabbing once again at the corners of her eyes, but this time her emotion was not for Antonio; she was past feeling for him. Now her heart and soul went out to her children who would have to endure the public reproach of having a father who was a relapsed Jew.

Father de la Fuente walked her to the doorway. Before closing the door, he reached out and squeezed her hand in comfort then said, "Magdalena, send the children to your mother's home tomorrow evening and dismiss the servants early. Make sure Antonio is at home alone with you. Leave the rest to me."

Nodding her head, she turned and walked across the stone floor of the prelate's residence. The echoes of the tapping and faltering of her footfalls across the tile signaled her despondency in a way that her tears could never do.

The good father watched her depart and contemplated a plan of action. It had been many months since the Office of the Holy Inquisition in Toledo had netted a person of such social importance as the Doña's husband. This matter warranted the highest degree of effort to extract a confession. The public needed to be aware of such ravening wolves among the lambs and he knew just the person to recommend to His Excellency the Grand Inquisitor to reclaim the lost soul of Antonio Montezinos.

Father Ignacio Castro had been feeling uncomfortable all morning. He kept telling himself that it was something he had eaten the night before, but the idea could not stick; he had only eaten a light dinner of boiled eggs, oatmeal and milk and then had immediately retired. He had been summoned to appear before the archbishop and doubtless the anticipation of the interview that would occur today had naturally made him anxious and thus the unsettling feeling in his stomach. As he entered the office of Archbishop Sandoval of Toledo, the Grand Inquisitor General, the personal secretary had asked him to have a seat and await the prelate's leave to enter his presence.

He had just been seated outside the office when Father Alberto de la Fuente had hurried past him with only a backward nod of his head by way of a greeting. The Archbishop's secretary had nodded his head and the anxious priest was quickly admitted into the inner office of the prelate. Father Castro had concluded that this arrival could not be coincidental; it clearly related to his own scheduled appointment with the archbishop. It had been his experience that such discussions had invariably led to arrests and subsequent actions by the Inquisition. *So, this was the reason for the unexpected interview. The Archbishop would naturally want time to examine de la Fuente's version of events before he was admitted into his presence.*

Still the wait was unnerving. After nearly a half hour, Castro arose and began to pace around the outer office, looking at one wall painting after another until he had come upon an oil of the church of the Cathedral of Toledo by Diego Lopez. The colors were vivid and the likeness of the structure was exquisite, no doubt inspired by Lopez' close ties with Toledo. He was about to ask the secretary's opinion of the artist's rendering when the door to the archbishop's office abruptly opened.

Father Sandoval stuck his head through the office doorway and asked Father Castro to join them.

Once inside and the door closed, Castro moved quickly toward the offered hand of the prelate and kissed his ring in obeisance to the Office of the Archbishop. "Thank you, Your Excellency."

"I hope your wait was not too tiring, but I thought it best that I invite Father de la Fuente to review his story with you present before we take any further action by my office."

"Of course, Eminence, I quite agree." Castro turned to the other priest seated to his right and greeted him, "Father, it is wonderful to see you again."

"Thank you, Father Castro." Father de la Fuente looked earnestly at Castro and related, "It has come to my attention from a parishioner of mine that her husband may be a Crypto-Jew and perhaps a secret practitioner of kabbalism. After hearing the details, I felt it prudent to report my concerns to the Office of Archbishop Sandoval. It may be necessary to have you interrogate him properly, Father Castro."

"Of course, Father De la Fuente, that will be a decision for Archbishop Sandoval, but in the past your expeditious actions have always been extremely helpful."

"Father, I thank you for your confidence." He sighed. "This grave matter weighs heavily upon us all in the archdiocese of Toledo. My responsibilities for the spiritual well-being of my flock are of paramount importance and when anything or anyone threatens my congregation, I feel it my duty to act quickly." He looked back to the archbishop and said, "I notified your secretary and you were gracious to allow me a personal audience to present this case, and for that I thank you. Moreover, now that Father Castro is directly involved I feel confident that this issue can be addressed and the matter fully resolved."

As if in reflection of a serious matter to come, the archbishop quietly steepled his fingers; the inquisition process he had in mind would be an onerous task to perform. "Fathers, thank you both for coming. Our discussion at hand is the delicate but necessary trial of a leading citizen of Toledo, Antonio Montezinos. I say necessary because a person of his stature has the potential to infect many other leading citizens that in time would no doubt lead to civil disorder and chaos. Thus, for the good of the Church and the citizenry of our city, we must move forward cautiously but thoroughly." Turning his attention directly to Father Castro, he stated, "Father, this office is prepared to issue a writ of arrest for Montezinos based upon the word of Father de la Fuente and it might be to our benefit if the Father here could relate to you how he came about this information regarding the accused. Please feel free to ask any question that may occur to you. Father de la Fuente, if you will?"

"Thank you, Your Eminence, it would be my pleasure." The Father looked toward the window and noticed the sunshine as it hit the limbs of an old oak. He heard the twitter of a dove, so prevalent in the surrounding grounds of the archdiocese and smiled at the omen of celestial approval of their meeting. Turning back to the priests he began. "You both may know of the Don and Doña Montezinos of our city, but you may not be aware that I am the Doña's personal confessor. Given the serious nature of the matter before us, I did not feel it a violation of the confessional to bring my concerns before Archbishop Sandoval. Actually, she had insisted to meet with me outside the normal confessional process, thus we met privately in my chambers."

"How long have you been her personal confessor, Father?" asked Castro.

"Since Father Ignacio Velázquez passed away nearly four years ago."

"I see. During the four years that you have known her as her confessor, could her confessions have ever been described as hysterical or exaggerated in nature?"

"Not in the least. If anything, she has always shown a great deal of decorum and control of her emotions. I have discovered through experience, as they bare their souls during the confessional, most women find it taxing to hold back their feelings, but the Doña has always struck me as being highly circumspect in her approach to a confession."

"So, you have found her to be detached during the confessional?"

"No, actually more as though she was being deliberate, almost academic in her approach. She reminds me of a mathematician who sees a straight line as the shortest distance between two points. When she is in need of forgiveness, as we all do, she confesses then receives absolution after proper contrition. There is no hesitation or further deliberation on her part."

"Then she would be unlikely to misinterpret or miss the true nature of events then attempt to embellish the facts?"

"Father Castro, I seriously doubt she misses anything."

Castro was relieved and encouraged at what Father de la Fuente had shared with him. There had been recorded cases in which the accuser had held hysterical tendencies and had simply misinterpreted an idiosyncratic behavior as grounds for Satanism. The assigned inquisitor then had attempted to extract a confession of a behavior that did not actually exist. Valuable time and resources had been wasted and in the end the Church was ultimately blamed for the excesses involved. As the chief inquisitor in charge of this matter, he did not intend for such to occur on his watch. "Father, if you will, could you explain what the Doña observed which led her to seek your counsel in this matter in the first place?"

"According to Magdalena, she noticed that her husband had grown distracted at home and had begun to spend more and more time outside the normal routines of what one might expect from a doctor of the community. Antonio became acquainted with several *Conversos* in Toledo and began to socialize with them, at first strictly in a professional sense as one might expect from doctor-patient relationships. Later, she and her husband began to meet socially with certain families at dining engagements. On more than one occasion, she reports, that not only were most in attendance *Conversos*, but that Antonio seemed intimately involved with them."

Castro was immediately interested in this revelation. Crypto-Jews were likely to meet with others of their kind and organize private conspiracies. "What led her to believe this had occurred, Father?"

"According to the Doña, she observed the way the men looked at one another as intimate friends will do over time; the way they talked and laughed so openly without restraint. There were even signs of private handshaking and whisperings. When they departed from these engagements, there seemed to be an unspoken, yet knowing look which passed between them all, almost as though an unuttered message were being sent. She further pointed out that it was all outwardly circumspect and discreet, of course, but inwardly there seemed to exist an intimate understanding and mutual acknowledgement of the other,

"So, it was her perception of events rather than any hard evidence which led her to suspect a clandestine relationship at those social occasions?"

"So it would appear."

"Has there been any open demonstration of deviant behavior on the part of Antonio of which she could not explain?"

"She said he had taken to leaving in the evenings a few times a month and returning late. He maintained that his absences were because of either an ill patient he was treating or a consultation with fellow doctors. That seemed to satisfy her curiosity, but later, over time he had grown more withdrawn and speculative. Antonio would observe his reflection in the mirror and stare for minutes at a time. She described this behavior as eerie and unsettling."

"Father, all of this, though it describes her feelings, does not indicate actual deviant behavior on the part of Antonio Montezinos. Eerie though it may have appeared it is not substantive enough upon which we can base an arrest and trial."

"I, too, had drawn the same conclusion, but then she proceeded and told me something which, when all other things are considered, paints a damning picture of his behavior. She said that he would also spend many evenings downstairs in his basement office poring over medical documents, at least this was what he told her, and on some occasions that did occur. But, earlier this past week, she followed him downstairs a few minutes after he had descended, but reaching the basement she could not locate him. He was nowhere to be seen."

"Could he have simply left the estate to visit a patient and then had forgotten to tell her?"

"That had been her first thought, she said. She went out on the courtyard to await his return, and as she stood concealed in the corner, he appeared from within the basement and had exited to the courtyard. He was dressed all in white and had a prayer mat and a scroll under his arm. He laid the mat upon the flagstones of the yard, retrieved the scroll then knelt in prayer. He began to read from the scroll, all the while looking up at the stars."

"Could she tell which language he was using?"

"She said it was definitely not Spanish; it had more of an Arabic cadence."

"How would she know that?"

"Her father had taken her to Morocco once, and she had watched as the locals prayed before their heathen god Allah."

Castro was shaken at this new discovery. "Then what had occurred?"

"Later, he went back inside the basement. She followed and discovered a light emanating from beneath the wall. She distinctly heard him from behind the wall mumbling, almost as though he were chanting prayers. This same behavior outside in the courtyard was repeated only a few nights later only this time he was wearing a shawl with the blue Star of David woven into the fabric."

The three priests sat quietly for some time. Each was trying to evaluate and interpret the events as related by the Doña Magdalena then Archbishop Sandoval broke the silence. He quietly intoned, "Father Castro, Father de la Fuente, I have made a prudent judgment in this matter and I feel that an arrest of Antonio Montezinos would be in the best interest of the Church and the community. We must discover his true identity and with whom he is conspiring to endanger the spiritual welfare of our followers."

Antonio and Magdalena sat quietly during the evening meal. Magdalena had averted her eyes to avoid looking directly at her husband and little had been said except occasional murmurs of please and whispers of thank-you. Even the servants noted the coldness between the lady and her husband, so it was not surprising that both maids were asked to leave early. On the way back to their quarters, a quick glance between Leticia and Josefina confirmed what both suspected: marital problems.

"Even the children were missing this evening," remarked the older of the two.

Josefina replied, "The lady, Doña Magdalena, sent them to her mother's home, no doubt."

"Don Antonio is such a kind man and so thoughtful. My legs are so much better since taking the herbs. I can actually get through the day without pain and you know how badly I was hurting."

"Yes, Leticia, but the argument the other night at the dinner table that we were not supposed to hear, but heard. It was very serious."

Shaking her head, Leticia sighed, "I worry for the children. We should visit the church tomorrow and pray for them all. Surely the saints and the blessed virgin will look favorably upon them."

As Antonio walked silently into the sitting room, Magdalena was standing by the window overlooking the courtyard. She pulled the curtains slightly to one side and looked out over the yard, now growing darker as the evening sun began to slide down over the horizon. Her brows went up slightly as she noticed the two servants walking across the patio to their quarters. She could see them chatting (probably gossiping) and she had little doubt the topic of conversation was about her and Antonio. *Well, before the evening is over, they and the entire community will have much more to talk about than simple quarreling between husband and wife.* She gripped the curtain and steadied herself for what had to be done now that she and her husband were alone in the house. She examined her feelings and discovered a coldness she had never known before. It would be enough.

She turned to join Antonio in the sitting room and noticed his detachment. The cool mask he wore could no longer deceive her. Behind it, something scuttled about; she could hear a mechanism within him ticking away like a conscience and she intended to discover its true nature. She sat down quietly opposite him and remained silent, watchful and waiting for his next move.

Noting her speculative side-long look, it suddenly occurred to him that they were both in the midst of an elaborate dance awaiting the outcome of the music to decide how to best proceed. He decided not to postpone the inevitable any longer. His course of action was expected, even necessary to set events in motion. The smile fooled no one, least of all Magdalena, as he quietly said, "Darling, I am going downstairs to my study. I will return later."

"Of course, Husband." Her tone, non-committal, unhurried.

Whatever her tone, Antonio paid it little attention. He had made his decision and now his destiny was set, his direction fixed. On the way through the hallway, by chance he glanced at the mirror and what he saw momentarily shook him to the core of his being. He slowed and stood before a reflection of a man he had never before seen or known. On closer inspection, the likeness of his former self was somewhat evident, but the face of the man he had hidden for so long had finally emerged. It was older and gaunt, the hair thinning and silver around the temples. His face was darker and shadowy with eyes wizened by the trauma of trials no man should endure. Yet, the eyes also bespoke a wisdom that would not have been present except for those experiences. He closed them and shook his head to clear the vision and when he reopened them, in the reflection stood the same man he had always known, the man of now and the present. He had seen the man of the future, and now nodding his understanding, he calmly made his way downstairs to the basement. There was something for which he had to prepare and time, he felt, was beginning to slip away as the morning dew at noon day.

Once she heard his footsteps retreating down the stairway, Magdalena waited twenty minutes then lit a candle and walked quietly to the front doorway. After opening the door, she moved the candle from side to side, signaling the soldiers of the Office of the Inquisition that the time had come for the arrest. Across the street stood a half dozen armed men, along with the Chief Inquisitor of Toledo, Father Ignacio Castro. Upon seeing the lit candle being held by Magdalena, the men moved forward, anxious now to proceed and detain the Crypto-Jew Montezinos.

As Magdalena was performing her act of betrayal, Antonio was deep in meditation but wore none of the vestments of his religion that evening. This was the moment of preparation for his trial to come. If he was to survive this crucible, he would need further enlightenment than he had ever before achieved. His breathing had slowed and he sat in the lotus positon as he had been taught by Jasher so many years earlier. His breathing controlled, his heartbeat slowed to a minimum, he then began to quietly chant the unspeakable Hebrew name of YHWH, THE CREATOR.

He let his mind slip out to the infinite, but on this occasion it was more than just a psychic projection. He noted with a detached curiosity that his astral body floated effortlessly above his physical body that was now levitating a foot above the floor. Though he could move about in the astral, he sensed that he was still tethered to his physical self and looking down, this was confirmed. A thin, plasma-like cord still held him attached with his body, and though such a sight might have caused him reason for concern, it brought no fear or despair, but simple acceptance. In fact, while in the astral, he discovered he was beyond all concerns and worldly terrors. He sensed he could actually move about the house and did, though he was careful not to remove himself too far from the physical body still in his meditation room. His eyes seemed to discern more, his capacity to reason and think were expanded and he sensed, though he could not yet confirm this, that there were others there with him also in the astral. For some unknown time (he was unaware of its passage), he remained in that state until he observed his wife leading armed men through the house in the direction of the basement. Realizing they were coming for him, he decided the exercise was over and so quickly re-entered his body as the soldiers burst through the door.

The armed men all wore swords but a few carried lamps and torches to light the way through the darkened basement. When they reached the secret doorway to his inner sanctum they found the door locked from within. After a brutish kick from their boots, the locked door to the meditation room crashed to the far wall, revealing the levitating body of Antonio Montezinos still in a meditative state. Magdalena was the first through the door and there she saw the most amazing sight of her life, one that she would never forget; it would haunt her dreams until her death many years hence. Instead of silent awe at the spectacle of her husband levitating above the floor, her fists gripped in terror while she released a demented scream in a quavering, shrill voice as though she were literally being chased by the hounds of hell. In her frenzied state of mind, that sight would have produced the same horrific results.

The soldiers, because of the dimness of the room, saw little except a man who had slumped over unconscious. The priest Castro, however, stared with horror and wonder at the sight of a man suspended in air above the floor. Though he would later attribute what he saw to Satanism, the experience was enough to force him to question his sanity. In any event, what was viewed in the room, along with the paraphernalia of the devoted kabbalist, was more than enough to indict Antonio Montezinos in the eyes of the Church.

After re-entering his body, Montezinos dropped abruptly to the floor. The men jerked him up to his feet then roughly pushed Montezinos through the doorway. There was a scuffle and as Antonio fell to the floor, he kicked out, his boot connecting with the chin of one of the soldiers, crashing him heavily upon another who had intended to tie up their prisoner. As the injured soldier sat in the corner holding his ruined face, the remainder fell upon Antonio and trussed him up with ropes. Finally, after beating him nearly senseless, the officer in charge began to pull Antonio roughly along through the house by his feet. All the while the priest chanted a litany of psalms and his wife screamed hysterically.

As the soldiers reached the street, Magdalena cried, nearly insane with fear and loathing, "Where are you taking him?" she asked with shrieking, feverish eyes.

The priest looked back at Magdalena Montezinos and replied, "To the basement of the castle of the Archbishop. Do not fear. He will not be back, Doña."

Pulling at her hair, she screamed, "Burn him!" She cried this over and over until the scene spilled out into the street, causing a public uproar that attracted many to the corner. As the procession passed by, Magdalena was still heard to be screaming, "Kill the witch! Burn him!"

At length, her voice, now strained from the effort, was silent; she had fainted from the emotional trauma. Fortunately, the two servants had heard the commotion and seeing their mistress swoon then tumble to the street they rushed to her side and were last seen helping the Doña back home. After a few hours, Magdalena had regained her wits, but the wailing of grief and anger had begun and would be her constant companion for many months to come. Though she would forever see the horrific blasphemy in her basement, in time, she would find resolution in her faith and frequent prayer.

For Antonio, the horror was only beginning.

CHAPTER 4

THE ENDLESS NIGHT

In our sleep, pain, which cannot forget,
falls drop by drop upon the heart until, in
our own despair, against our will, comes
wisdom through the awful grace of God.

----- *Aeschylus*

In the late 15th century, Tomás de Torquemada was a Castilian Dominican Friar and the first Grand Inquisitor in Spain's movement to homogenize popular established procedures for the Inquisition under his jurisdiction. This practice of religious investigation within the Catholic Church became known as "The Spanish Inquisition." Typically, a new court would be announced with a thirty-day grace period for confessions and the gathering of accusations from neighbors, friends and relatives. As it was a common occurrence when someone of importance was accused, because of the community interest, the incarceration and interrogation process usually took longer. The first auto-da-fé (from the Portuguese "act of faith") was held in Seville on February 6, 1481, which resulted in six persons being burned alive. From there, the Inquisition grew rapidly in the Kingdom of Spain. By 1492, tribunals existed in eight Castilian cities: Ávila, Córdoba, Jaén, Medina del Campo, Segovia, Sigüeza, Valladolid and Toledo.

The prisoner was invariably one who embraced differing religious views from that of the monarchy. Crypto-Jews, known in Spain as Conversos and Marranos in Portugal, were allowed to confess and perform penance, although those who relapsed into their old practices and were later discovered were burned at the stake. Many of the prisoners who simply confessed to being a practicing Jew would be released and expelled from the country, though before they left, they were required to leave all their currency and possessions in Spain. Those who were found uncooperative, that is they who either denied their culpability or refused to cooperate with the court, were judged unrepentant and suffered the same fate as those who had reembraced their old habits, which is to say that they were burned alive.

The autos-da-fé could be private (auto particular) or public (auto publico or auto general). However, there were times when the Office felt the need to have the public more involved, thus if the accused was found guilty, the sentence was condemnatory and the ceremony of the auto-da-fé either solemnized their return to the Church or punished them as unrepentant heretics. Either way, before he left the confines of his imprisonment, he would have to incriminate all those who were accomplices in his heresy. Those who refused were considered uncooperative and were burned. There were no exceptions; everyone accused someone.

Although initially the public autos did not have any special solemnity nor sought a large attendance of spectators, with time they became devout ceremonies, celebrated with large public crowds amidst an almost festive atmosphere. The auto-da-fé eventually became an excessive, gaudy spectacle with staging meticulously calculated to cause the greatest effect of fear and intimidation among the spectators. As a reminder to the masses, this spectacle served to be the outward sign of Christian pre-eminence and sent a harsh message to all who would express differing points of religious belief and customs. In reality, it was little more than a Church-sanctioned pretext for the monarchy to persecute those they considered to be enemies of the state, of which Jews and Arabs were now a part. (https://en.wikipedia. org/wiki/Auto-da-fé)

The prisoner, Antonio Montezinos, had been denounced and accused of being a Crypto-Jew, specifically one who practiced the ancient art of kabbalism. Moreover, he had been detained for nearly three months in a dank dungeon tied up to a wall during which time he had been constantly interrogated. This was his trial. In the meantime, his property had been confiscated to pay the court costs and his maintenance during his incarceration. Montezinos, also known secretly as Ephraim ben Judah, had several persons he could name as accomplices to his heresy, but he was stubborn and so the interrogating priest, Father Ignacio Castro, had become frustrated with his lack of cooperation.

The room used for interrogations was located in the deepest room in the sub-basement of the Archbishop's castle in Toledo. Despite the summer warmth and beauty of the outside world, the dungeon stank of cold fear and misery. In the corner, the slow incessant dripping of water upon stone pavements echoed every time there was a pause in the questioning. Today's session had been only the continuation of the desperate trial of wills that Antonio had experienced at the hands of Father Castro.

"Will you confess, Antonio Montezinos?" the priest asked, now in a pleading tone.

The captive looked at the priest with contempt. Father Castro, who had seen that look on many faces as the interrogation process began, but never at the end when the confession was uttered, redirected a question to himself: "The prisoner refuses to speak. Is he qualified to understand the question?"

He studied the tormented man and concluded: *He is prideful, full of arrogance and self-importance, but unfortunately in good health. This interrogation has continued too long, but what can be done? Justice must be served.*

With regret, he returned to the questioning, knowing that it would likely take more time to break him and extract a full confession. It had come down to a battle of wills and Castro was well aware that a confession depended upon whether Montezinos could be broken. Undaunted, Father Castro dug a little deeper into his own resolve. *Would it be enough to plumb the prisoner's inner strength? I will do what needs to be done.*

The basement was cold and damp. The priest reached for his cloak and threw it around his shoulders hoping to alleviate the discomfort. Shaking his head to push back his own weariness, he turned away from the prisoner and walked to a nearby doctor whose purpose it was to insure humanitarian safeguards were observed in the interrogation room.

The doctor shrugged disbelievingly at the prisoner's non-compliant attitude, but concurred with the priest. "I, too, find the prisoner capable of understanding the questioning. You may proceed."

The Dominican regretfully turned at the nearby workmen whose job it was to perform the tortures. The priest threw a withering glance of contempt in their direction and noted without surprise the abject coarseness of each man. Doubtless their own dismal time spent in the Spanish penal system had produced such creatures now devoid of even a suggestion of sympathy for the prisoners now occupying the basement. Their debased condition was palpable and their eyes furtive, devoid of human kindness. Both wore leering, feral smiles as they eagerly awaited once again the signal to begin the tortures to be administered at their hands. They reeked of filth and the infernal stench of dungeons. They were a necessary evil; no sane man could perform such brutish acts.

The priest turned from their eager faces then nodded to a nearby scribe sitting behind a raised dais whose job it was to record any confessions uttered by the prisoner during the course of the interrogations. Father Castro directed, "Write down that the accused was found competent to understand the questions."

After the scribe made a quick note in his journal, the Dominican priest gave a reluctant nod to the awaiting workmen to begin their labors of the day. With practiced speed and strength, they grabbed Montezinos, pinned back his arms and stripped him naked. With equal quickness they lashed his hands behind his back, fastened twenty pound weights to each ankle, and by means of a block and tackle pulley system they attached ropes to his wrists then they slowly began to haul him up nearly thirty-five feet off the ground, almost to the roof of the dungeon.

From below, the work foreman nodded his head knowingly and shouted with a smugness born out of years of experience, "You will talk Montezinos. You must not think you are any different from the other heretics who have occupied my jail."

As the prisoner's arms were wrenched upward from behind, the effort and his own dead weight slowly pulled his shoulders from the sockets. With a confident smile of eventual victory, the workmen left him in this position hanging aloft for nearly an hour. At length, it was clear the hapless prisoner was in anguish, but the interrogation continued from the priest who resumed his petition that Montezinos confess. Noting the man's obvious agony, the Dominican sensed that a true confession was near at hand and thus motioned the scribe to follow him as he positioned himself directly under the helpless man still hanging from his arms. *Perhaps today would be the day!*

"Antonio, my Son, do you now confess to the charges of practicing Judaism?"

For Montezinos, time had begun to draw out slowly as a finely honed blade. Though misery was etched across his trembling face, he nonetheless bore his pain in silence.

The priest experimented with a reasonable, loving tone. "Antonio Montezinos, I can see you are in pain now, but I can assure you that it will only get worse. Please confess or I must reapply the question."

When no response was forthcoming, the disappointed priest and scribe sadly returned to the dais upon which the confession book was laid. He instructed the scribe that the prisoner had been extended mercy but it had been rejected. The priest turned back reluctantly to the workmen and nodded in their direction. Their eyes alighted at the prospect; they had been all but panting to resume their labors on the hapless prisoner.

Now making terrifying noises, the workmen rushed toward the rope from which Antonio was suspended and allowed it to slip nearly thirty feet in a dead drop ending with a bone shattering abrupt halt which tore each of the major joints apart with maximum pain. His wrists, elbows and shoulders were mutilated; the weights on his legs, now magnified many times by the sudden fall and stop, wrenched his ankles, his knees and hips.

Montezinos allowed himself a terrible scream of misery, but before he could focus on his recent pains the workmen pulled him back up to the ceiling to initiate the most terrifying aspect of the torture. Occasionally, when it suited them, the workmen would shout and drop the rope; other times they simply shouted. Again, without any warning, they might drop it a few inches whereas at other times there would be a stomach-wrenching drop almost to the floor and the hideous pulling apart of the joints.

This process continued over the course of the next few hours, followed intermittently by a petition to confess, but still no confession escaped his dry, parched lips. Finally, following the last drop, Antonio had passed out from the pain. Hours later, he awoke in his cell, now naked on the cold stone floor; his now tattered clothes had been tossed carelessly around him in a heap. At first, he was unable to move his arms and legs and his body now hurt nearly beyond human endurance. Slowly and painfully he began to sit up and after a long moment of exquisite pain he managed to attain the lotus position of the trained meditator. As he closed his eyes, he began the exercise of controlled breathing and after a time his mind reached out and he carefully began to push back the pain, the anxiety and his racing blood pressure. A few minutes later, the pain now dulled, he began the kabbalist exercise of the mind with symbols, letters and numbers, each appearing in his mind in bold relief and each carrying a message of enlightenment.

The priest and scribe suddenly appeared just outside his cell. Father Castro was persistent and wanted only to help the prisoner end his pain and misery by offering him relief through a true and complete confession. After making the sign of the cross, he whispered, "Antonio, we have proof beyond question that you are a practicing Jew. Please, for the sake of your soul and what is left of your tormented body, confess and let us end this nightmare once and for all." As if proffering a remarkable gift, he added, "You can be free within the hour; just tell us the names of the other Jews within your circle."

The prisoner said nothing. As if bewildered at the man's reluctance to confess, the Dominican sadly shook his head then glanced toward the waiting scribe and ordered, "Write: the man, Antonio Montezinos, was offered mercy but again rejected it." The good father, after seeing Antonio's state of meditation, presumed the man was possessed. Shaking his head glumly that the prisoner was now using magic to shut out his efforts to reach him, the priest sadly turned around and signaled to the waiting workmen to return him to the interrogation room. They ecstatically fell upon the meditating man, tied up his wrists with ropes and hauled him from the cell. As he was dragged, Antonio abruptly awakened from his meditative state and became fully aware that he was again to be turned over to his tormentors.

Now back in the dungeon of horrors, he was dumped on a table with his back over a small log in such a position that his back was severely strained and his stomach drawn flat, nearly distended, inducing a position that prevented normal breathing. Now tied down over the log, a funnel was placed in his mouth along with a filthy cloth. Water was applied through the funnel, strangling the prisoner as the water and the rag were breathed into his throat then when it appeared he might simply choke to death; the cloth was wrenched out, tearing away membranes and bringing up blood. Again the priest appeared by his side and begged him to confess, but his pleas were met with stony silence. They repeated the torture a number of times, but the defenseless prisoner still refused to break.

Father Castro, now wanting the torment to end almost as much as Montezinos, positioned himself next to the head of the near-broken man, looked into the tortured eyes and pleaded, "My Son, I know you will not be able to speak, but the mercy of Christ awaits you if you simply nod your head by way of confession." He whispered near his ear, "Do you have confederates in your heresy?"

Antonio prayed silently, *Oh, please, my God. Make an end to it.* Montezinos shed tears of pain, but looked away and denied the saving mercy being offered by the well-intentioned priest.

Father Castro sadly concluded that the prisoner had left him no alternative. After months of sincere persuasion, it had finally come down to a full confession or the worst torture of all. With dismal reluctance, the priest nodded his head and the workmen elatedly dragged him to another table where his legs and arms were strapped to a large table with his feet dangling slightly off the end. As the anguished man remained silent, the soles of his feet were smeared with a mixture of pepper, oil, menthol and clove and after the mix was allowed to soak into the pores, coals from an open fire were brought over and passed back and forth across his feet. Immediately, unimaginable blisters arose and produced such anguish that the prisoner shrieked until he finally passed out. He was awakened with cold water and the torture was reapplied. Again and again.

Montezinos was given a few days of rest to think over his plight and reverse his stubborn resistance to the confession that Father Castro knew to be so close to his lips. But, if the priest had hoped that a confession would be forthcoming, he would be disappointed. After a few days the whole process began again, but the only thing heard were the agonizing shrieks and screams of a condemned, nearly broken man. The prisoner of Toledo, Antonio Montezinos, known to a select few as Ephraim ben Judah, never uttered a single word to reveal that he was a practicing Jew or to incriminate anyone within his circle.

It had been months of unrelenting persuasion but Father Castro had finally had to admit that he had failed; Montezinos could not be broken. It had been his first failure to extract a confession and he was unprepared for his sense of personal defeat. With misery, Castro appeared before the Archbishop of Toledo with his report. "Excellency, it is with sincere sadness that I must declare that the Jew Antonio Montezinos has been found unrepentant. He refuses to confess even though the facts are overwhelming of his practice of Judaism. Moreover, he has refused to name others who were also of his secret society."

Archbishop Sandoval bowed his head slightly and slowly nodded as if he had expected as much. "Did he ever offer a defense?"

"Excellency, I feel so completely ashamed of my efforts. In his four months of interrogation, he never uttered a single word. I am sure, with more time, I will be able to finally break his prideful spirit and reach him."

Hearing Castro's final comment, Archbishop Sandoval appeared relieved. His duty before him was obvious and simpler. Thus determined and now decided, he replied, "Father Castro, you have given your best efforts to reach him. Mercy has been extended to him time and again, but like so many of his kind, he has remained willful and has rejected the merciful love of Christ."

Sadly, Father Castro whispered, "Then, it is to be the *auto-da-fé*?"

With deep regret, the prelate whispered, "Father, I am sorry, but he has left us no alternative. It was his choice to make and he made it."

In time, the execution date by public burning along the guidelines of the *auto-da-fé* had been scheduled for the following month in the city square. Meanwhile, the prisoner languished painfully in the dank darkness and stench of his cell. Though his die was cast, occasionally Father Castro appeared at his cell in the hope Antonio might utter a brief word of confession. Regardless, the accused man had remained mute. Now realizing that the man's meditation might be contributing to his futile efforts, Father Castro gave leave to the workmen to enter his cell and beat Antonio whenever he attempted to practice his heresy or whenever it suited them. Thus, eventually, he was left to deal with his afflictions the best he could and when exhaustion from his pain of his beatings overtook him, he lay and slept fitfully on the cold floor and waited the inevitable burning to come.

CHAPTER 5

WHISPERS IN HIGH PLACES

Manuel Diaz Suarez, also known among his kabbalist colleagues as Levi Singer, felt a pang of fear as he glanced around furtively before entering the garden. He abhorred secret meetings in public places, but realized that it would have been worse had the meeting been scheduled at an inn where the patrons were always scrupulously appraised before an order was taken; such was life in Spain.

As he awaited the arrival of Jasher, he began to review Antonio's fate, the same lot that he could easily experience given the right circumstance, and unless this meeting ended successfully, his own rendezvous with the Inquisition would likely become a reality; unless he departed Spain, it was unavoidable. Regrettably for Montezinos, his wife had discovered him in deep meditation one night, and being a good Catholic, she had immediately denounced him to the priests of the Church. Owing to his celebrity status in the community, he had been detained in a dungeon in Toledo for the past four months. Fear and desperation of being exposed had eventually driven Singer to meet with his colleagues to discuss Antonio's plan to involve Benjamin Jasher, an unknown among the group. *What else could have been done? The alternative would have been to wait until the inevitable confession landed us all in a cell next to Antonio.*

Thus his associates of the kabbalah circle had met privately and decided they had to follow up on Antonio's request to reach out to Benjamin Jasher, though even that effort would be fraught with danger. But, it had taken them two anxiety-riddled months before making that decision. The last time they dared to meet as a group had nearly ended in a bitter and near divisive argument. Some had even insisted to be patient, wait it out and pray for enlightenment. Ordinarily, men caught in this predicament in Spain could do little more than to pray for the best that they would not be incriminated by the confessions of others. All citizens were aware that the tortures would not cease on the prisoner unless the incriminations were also forthcoming; self-confessions were never sufficient. Thus many, when faced with the possibility of being caught in the net, simply fled the country penniless.

It was with some trepidation that Levi had walked through a garden at the foot of the hill located in the shadow of the Alcázar fortification. He reached inside of his overcoat for the comforting feel of the leather-bound diary. The jacket was heavy and not in keeping with the weather, but he could not risk carrying about a journal in full view of the public. This diary was more worry, but only part of the greater concern of Jasher's involvement. His coming had given them a possible alternative to their predicament, but what would be the consequence of that action? More possible exposure? This had also haunted every member of the Circle. Desperation had driven Levi Singer to seek out someone who could help them and the man he was meeting had come highly recommended, but there was danger all about.

With a sigh, he knew he was risking so much by exposing himself and the others by joining Jasher at this public meeting place. Then looking around, he began to absorb the quiet, peaceful surroundings of the venue that had been chosen. It was late summer in Toledo and a myriad of flowers were in bloom and the fragrance and beauty seemed to bolster his waning optimism.

Jasher had concluded that in all likelihood, Singer and his cohorts were being watched and any strangers or visitors to their homes would cast suspicion on such meetings. Therefore, it had been decided that the prearranged location would be in a public, yet secluded location to attract as little attention as possible. Realizing his contact would be nervous at having to meet in public, he concluded that a garden would lessen his anxiety. Finding a bench, he took a seat and waited.

Levi walked up quietly to the young, clean-shaven man sitting on a bench overlooking the fountain in the farthest corner of the garden. As he came closer, the man arose and introduced himself, "Hello, I am Benjamin Jasher and you must be *Señor* Suarez. Please be seated and let us discuss our problem." After both were comfortably seated, Jasher continued, "I was told our mutual friend was in need."

Singer was damp with fear. If this man was a spy sent by the Office of the Grand Inquisitor of Toledo, he was a dead man. If they had broken Ephraim, then his name would have been high on the list for investigation. He decided finally that he had really little choice; his only alternative was to leave his business and Catholic family and flee the country. Then, of course, his family would come under scrutiny and the erstwhile ministrations of the Office of the Inquisitor General.

"*Señor* Jasher, is your name Jewish? If it is, I doubt you could use it openly in Spain."

"You are quite correct, *Señor* Suarez, and that should lessen your suspicion that I am here to investigate you. My real name, as you may have surmised, is ancient Hebrew, though our Castilian friends here in Spain would hardly make the distinction; that being said, you and I are brothers in many ways. Let us say, for the sake of argument, that my assumed name is *Señor* Ximenez. You have a proposition for me from which we both stand to benefit, so please explain."

"I suppose I should trust you at this point, but discretion is called for. I have a Jewish name; do you know it?"

"I do. It is Levi Singer. Now, what do you know and how can I help my friend Ephraim ben Judah?"

Levi felt encouraged, yet the officers of the Inquisition could be insidiously subtle. Though his fear was palpable, he decided to proceed. "I was told by our mutual friend now imprisoned in a dungeon here in Toledo that, should he ever fall into the hands of the Inquisition, I was to seek you out and request your help."

"Yes, that was our arrangement. I suspect, however, that this is not the only reason why you have reached out to me."

"No, *Señor* Ximenez, I fear my cowardice and anxiety of being exposed as a practicing Jew has motivated me to seek you out even though I should have reached out to you months ago, though I doubt seriously you could have done much up until now."

A slight knowing smile registered on Jasher's face. Men were predictable and their plights anticipated. "Your fear, *Señor* Suarez, was warranted. No doubt had you not taken precautions and been highly circumspect in your inquiries, you would occupy a cell next to your friend, Ephraim ben Judah, then the inquisitors would have been one step closer to ferreting out your entire secret circle of the kabbalah."

Singer visibly flinched when he heard that Jasher had divined his real fear, the discovery of his secret group. Levi ruefully smiled and said, "Very well, *Señor* Ximenez. What I know is this: our friend, Ephraim ben Judah, is to be publicly executed in a few weeks in the city square. The fact that I and the rest of my kabbalah group have not yet been arrested would seem to indicate that our friend has not yet denounced us, but there is a breaking point for any man and on the day of his execution, moments away from the fiery faggots, he may decide to bargain for his life."

"Yes, he would not be the first to do so, but our friend is stubborn and has endured pain and persecution before while living in Italy. The tortures he now endures may be more painful, but the trials are similar."

Levi cast his eyes down and confessed, "I would like to hope that I could endure as he has, but I lack his courage and would have long given up my friends to avoid the torture that he must have received."

Jasher shrugged as if the fear of cowardice held little interest and bore nothing on current affairs. He would not be the first to judge. "How may I help?"

A hopeful look appeared. "Ephraim must be abducted in route to the execution site in the square and spirited away to somewhere safe. Otherwise, he may succumb to the right to confession that he will be asked to publicly announce one last time. Can this be arranged?"

Knowing that he would be dangerously exposing his operation to abduct someone in full view of the public, Jasher cautiously played for time. As he thought over the request, he asked delicately, "*Señor* Suarez, are you aware of my means of payment? Some might think it eccentric, but I never take money; I trade in favors and sometimes barters."

Nodding, Levi explained, "I am aware and our friend instructed me exactly what you would need, though I can't see that it would have much value for someone in your line of work. It was obtained in a most unusual way." From the inside pocket of his overcoat, Levi pulled out a leather bound book that appeared to be a diary. Wiping the sweat from his brow, he cursed the weight of the jacket, but the alternative would have been to expose the diary and that, apparently, was his only means of barter. He carefully handed it over to Jasher.

Jasher opened up the book and began to read. After a few minutes, he said, "It is a rutter for a passage through to New Spain in the Americas. A most unusual document; is there more?" The rutter was a detailed navigational diary of the journey by sea from one point on the globe to another.

Levi nodded his head and instructed, "Turn to the last page."

As he flipped through to the end of the diary and scanned the pages, Jasher began to purse his lips. Then there it was: a mathematical equation and an explanation of the symbols. At first he had trouble understanding its value and relevance to the diary then all at once it occurred to him and it left him astonished and incredulous at the same time. The formula related to solar days of a lunar orbit. "This can't be what I think it is." He looked back over to Singer for his concurrence.

"*Señor* Ximenez, I am no mathematician, but Ephraim said you would know and appreciate its significance. Was he right?"

"Yes, but how did he obtain the journal and the formula on the last page?"

"As to the formula, you must remember that Ephraim is a master kabbalist mystic and his normal means to achieve this heightened state of suggestiveness is mathematic in nature; he focuses on symbols and numbers."

"Yes, I am quite familiar with kabbalism and his method of achieving light and understanding. The kabbalist practitioner creates a self-induced dream state that makes him highly suggestible to a spiritual plane of consciousness. In this state he receives enlightenment."

"Correct. During this dream state, he was shown an algebraic formula and I suspect he subsequently made note of it and later wrote it down near the end of the diary. As to the journal, he said while in this dream state, he was told a messenger would give him a book as a gift. Moreover, he was told where he was to meet the messenger and what the man would have for him. He followed the directions of the dream and after having entered a garden across the city he was given the diary from a visitor that he swore was more angel than man." Suarez appeared apologetic, expecting Jasher to scoff or appear skeptical at the notion of such a visitation, but when none was forthcoming, Levi shook his head disbelievingly and commented, "The man instructed him to guard it safely until the day he would need it in exchange for a favor from you. That was the way he put it. Was he wrong, *Señor* Ximenez?"

With a smile and knowing that he had received many such visits, Jasher said, "No, he was not." He made a quick analysis of all that had been discussed then informed Levi, "From this point forward, you and I will not meet again. I and my men will plan and rescue Ephraim ben Judah from his scheduled execution at the hands of the Holy Inquisition and the *auto-da-fé*.

For the first time in months, Levi Singer felt a surge of hope, but he had to ask: "*Señor* Jasher, how can you be so sure of your success?"

"Because, *Señor* Singer, the Archbishop of Barcelona owes me a favor and I intend to collect."

Jasher knew without being told, that simply appearing off the street and petitioning to see the Archbishop was outside of normal protocol. But, he did not intend to give the man an opportunity to avoid a meeting. Arriving at the outer office of the archdiocese, he saw the secretary available and decided to announce his arrival.

The private secretary, Father Benito Lopez, heard the approach of another visitor and looked up from the archdiocese correspondence in time to size up a man approaching his desk. As he did not recognize him, he concluded that he must be a stranger and definitely not on the Archbishop's calendar for the day. "Good morning *Señor*, I am Father Lopez. May I be of service?" Whoever the man was, he intended to send him away and have him return another day.

"Father Lopez, I am Benjamin Ximenez, an old friend of His Eminence the Archbishop, and wish to pay him a visit this morning."

The secretary went through an elaborate routine of looking over the calendar and the Archbishop's schedule. He turned a few pages and moved paperwork around on the desk, but in the end it was all for show and Jasher knew what he was about to say. He decided to pre-empt whatever rebuttal the secretary was about to offer with a statement so urgent that it would be sure to at least motivate the secretary to move out of his seat long enough to inquire from within the inner office.

"Father, I have just arrived from Bargas, the hometown of the Archbishop, and I have alarming news regarding his mother, who as he is aware, has been seriously ill for some time." He had not, in truth, arrived from Bargas, but this was a predetermined code that would be used in the event that Jasher had ever needed to see him. "Please inform him that I am here to deliver a message from his sister."

Father Lopez, who also had an ill mother, was immediately concerned over the matter and wasted no further time or discussion whether the stranger should gain an audience this morning. "Wait just a moment, *Señor* Ximenez. I will see if His Eminence can be disturbed." Turning to Jasher, he whispered, "I hope it is not too serious."

Jasher tried on his most convincing bleak face and decided it was sufficient to reassure the priest of the validity of the troubling news. Inwardly, of course, he smiled for the ruse had never failed him before when dealing with overprotective personal secretaries. Father Lopez quietly knocked and entered the office. A moment later, the secretary followed closely by Archbishop Luis Sans y Códol emerged from the office, a slight frown of grim concern creased on his face.

"Benjamin, it is good to see you. It was so kind of you to bring me word of my dear mother. Please enter my office and you can tell me all you know and please omit nothing."

"Of course, Excellency." As he walked by the secretary, he was careful to keep up the appearance of one who has sadly brought bad tidings. With reluctant steps, he seemed to trudge gloomily through the door, closing the door quietly behind him.

The secretary, of course, was consumed with concern over the bad news that Jasher's arrival might portend for the Archbishop. He made a mental note to visit his own devoted mother before the week was out.

Once inside with the door firmly shut and the charade now over, both men could relax and smile. The Archbishop gazed across the desk at his visitor and shook his head in disbelief. "Benjamin, it has been over fourteen years since last we talked and you have not aged a minute. You must tell me your secret," he joked. Though of course, he was not really joking, he was simply perplexed. He had only to look in a mirror at his own face to confirm the passage of time. *And time is winning the battle.*

Jasher smiled indulgently and shrugged his shoulders as if to say, *well, what can I do?* He returned the banter with, "It seems to be out of my control. As you are aware, Excellency, the passage of time is relative and different for all of us." This statement was closer to the truth, but it was a concept beyond that of the Archbishop, so Jasher refrained from elaborating.

The prelate cleared his throat and proceeded. "But the subject of time was really not the point of your visit any more than my mother's condition. The esteemed lady is still hale and hearty and will undoubtedly outlive both of us, though perhaps in your case, I suppose not."

"I too, hope, she outlives us both." Jasher was sincere, though the reality, he knew was far from the truth. "But, you are quite right, of course, there was another reason for my visit other than a reunion of old friends. I have just come from Toledo and was made aware that there was a pressing matter that required my attention."

The Archbishop leaned back in his chair then shifted to become more comfortable. The pain in his back had only gotten worse lately, making it even the more difficult to find a good position to sit. He was determined, though, to not allow Jasher to see his discomfort and weakness. It had been some time since their last meeting and he had known that eventually this day would come. Favors had been extended and promises were made and now it was time to pay the piper. "What can I do for you, Benjamin?"

"A close associate of mine languishes in the dungeon of the Toledo arm of the Grand Inquisition. Given the nature of our unique friendship, Excellency, naturally I thought you should be made aware of it."

"What is his crime?"

"The usual, heresy, I suspect, though we both know how broad an accusation of that nature can be. What is especially troublesome is that he is a leading citizen of the city, a doctor of medicine no less."

"And Jewish, I suppose?"

Jasher said nothing, merely smiled and nodded.

The prelate was hardly surprised. "It would appear a Crypto-Jew was caught in the act."

"Perhaps, or the man may simply have been trying to practice his religion in the privacy of his own home. No one would have been infected by his heresy."

"How was he caught? An informant?"

"His own wife, if that is to be believed."

"Don't tell me; the lady was from an old Spanish family and felt betrayed by his duplicitous nature?"

"So it would appear. I fear they had been experiencing marital difficulties for some time and this was simply a case of her being in the wrong place and for him at the wrong time. Clearly her emotions had simply gotten the better of her good judgment."

"It would not be the first time nor do I expect it to be the last. Would his name be Montezinos by any chance?"

"You have heard of him?"

With a rueful smile, he replied, "Word does get around in my world, you realize Benjamin."

"I was hoping it had; it saves me from having to bother you with so much detail." He paused to emphasize his official request. Now the dancing would begin. "Given his current desire to simply leave the country without further trouble to the community and Church, I was hoping you could intercede on his behalf, Excellency?"

With a smile, the Archbishop asked, "Benjamin is this your way of saying that the time has come for me to make good on my promise to you, even after so many years?" he asked in jest, though the levity of his remark never reached his eyes.

"I would think after so many years of being your sponsor in high places that you would want to square our arrangement with a slight accommodation."

Nodding skeptically, he asked, "This Montezinos... is he truly a Crypto-Jew?"

"Excellency, we all have secrets, but that does not change the nature of our souls. He is a good man and I wish him to live much longer than the Inquisition will permit him. He has already endured four months of ongoing rigorous questioning. I think he has served his time and a stern message has been sent to the populace at large."

The prelate steepled his fingers and meditated a moment as if in prayer. "I am doubtful that would be sufficient. He is, after all, a leading citizen. Perhaps a message should be sent that the Church cannot tolerate such duplicitous behavior in our society even at the highest levels."

"That would be one way of looking at it. However, let us turn this same line of reasoning around so that, instead of subjecting the community to a particularly brutal death, we simply allow him to escape."

The prelate was momentarily taken back at the suggestion. "Escape? How can that be a solution? Please explain."

"Such a spectacle sends more than a message of fear to the citizenry. It can also produce anger, something I am sure the Church will prefer to avoid. Consider this. A man of his reputation and influence would no doubt have many other leading citizens caught in the web of his treachery, and upon his public death, he could easily become a martyr to their hopeless cause which might encourage others to join in their conspiracy. The backlash will cause more trouble than if he were simply allowed to slip away into the night. In time, he will be forgotten and his conspirators will be lacking their leader and martyr. In all truth, they will probably pack up their tents and melt away into the deserts of Morocco, now frustrated at being leaderless and directionless. If you remove the potential for anger, you avoid spreading his dogma."

The Archbishop seemed to seriously examine this option then finally nodding his head he replied, "I am inclined to give your offer room for serious thought." Now stalling, the prelate commented, "Benjamin, for one who appears so young, you think like a man who has done something like this before many times, but we know that cannot be so. Or could it?"

Jasher smiled and replied, "Excellency, you are a reasonable, upright man. I am sure you would have eventually come to the same conclusion I have. I merely helped you along the moral high-road, the one well-traveled by all men of maturity and experience. It would be the just thing to do."

The priest was not yet ready to concede the point, but was close. "How are your friends in high places? Do you still have as many as you once had?"

"Enough to say without hesitation that whatever can be given in friendship also can be regrettably withdrawn when that friendship has become strained. But, knowing you as I do, I am sure that it need not come to that, Excellency."

The priest grunted and displayed a cynical smile. "Since we are already along this moral high-road, as you put it, perhaps you can help me a little farther along. How do I go about allowing him to (how did you describe it?), "slip away into the night," you said?"

Smiling, Jasher elaborated, "No doubt my man, Montezinos, will be transported through the streets of Toledo on his way to meet the scheduled public burning. He will be accompanied, of course, by the chief inquisitor priest. While I am expediting the escape, the priest could be persuaded by you to look the other way at the right moment."

The Archbishop smiled and said, "And just how am I to persuade him. He is, after all, a servant of the Office of the Chief Inquisitor of Toledo, Archbishop Sandoval."

"I have done some investigating on my own. This priest, Father Ignacio Castro, is well past middle age and he is somewhat of a pedantic, lacking in any political finesse. In other words, he has gone as far as he is going to go in the Church. I am sure that he feels, as do most of us, that there is much more he would like to contribute, but unfortunately he is lacking in a proper sponsor to help him along. I propose you provide him the nudge he needs."

"How much of a "nudge" are we talking about here?"

"I am sure the poor man feels that his management opportunities have passed him by, though he yearns to provide a greater service to such a grand cause. Do you not have an opening in your archdiocese for a bishop?"

A look of surprise surfaced on his face and to his extreme discomfort he realized his back was aching even worse than before, if that could be believed. He winced in pain has he sputtered, "A bishop? You are reaching, Benjamin."

Now Benjamin would have to sell a man he had never met. "Father Castro has a fine reputation and many years of dedicated service. The man feels absolutely despondent over his recent failure with Montezinos and so will be highly motivated to serve you in the archdiocese with unflagging dedication. He is no fool; undoubtedly, he will know that an accommodation has been extended. Therefore, he will realize to whom he is indebted, and over time that loyalty will become a great asset to the archdiocese. I do not think it would be much of a stretch to recommend him for a bishopric position. But, don't take my word for it, Excellency. Do your own investigation. I am sure you will come to the same conclusions that I have."

The prelate was in obvious pain from his back and Jasher noticed his discomfort. "Father, I could not help but notice your pain. I know of a reputable expert in back problems that could reset your bones to relieve much of your distress. I have observed this process myself and the results have been nothing short of amazing."

"Is that so?" He was clearly embarrassed at showing his weakness.

"Please allow me to send him over to you."

The Archbishop would have allowed the Devil himself entrance to his chamber if he could just help relieve the misery. "Very well, send him over. I will notify my secretary." He added facetiously, "He will not require a pass phrase to gain an audience."

With a smile, Jasher replied, "Always happy to help, Your Excellency."

Archbishop Códol reluctantly returned to the original matter. "This business with the priest; is this the only way for me to square my indebtedness to you, Benjamin?"

"This is just one friend making an accommodation to another, Excellency. Besides, it is the just thing to do."

He was silent for a moment then murmured; "Only time will tell." He paused and with an indulgent grin added, "But, I will embrace this moral high-road of which you speak and take your word for it. I will have it set up by the end of the week. The priest will look the other way and you may perform the escape of your man Montezinos. But, Benjamin, he must leave Spain. If he comes back, I will walk him to the stake myself."

"I will point that out to him when I next see him." Jasher arose and bowed slightly then with complete sincerity added, "As always, it has been a pleasure to see you, Excellency."

His Excellency decided that he never intended to see Benjamin Jasher again. He shook his head wryly and thought: *No doubt the man will outlive me anyway.*

CHAPTER 6

THE ESCAPE

His Eminence, the Archbishop of Barcelona, Luis Sans y Códol, sat pensively in his office chamber awaiting the arrival of a Dominican priest from Toledo. Since they were of the same order, it would be a rather simple process to have him transferred to Barcelona. But that was not exactly part of the dilemma that bedeviled him at the moment. Summoning the priest to Barcelona was less problematic than convincing him to be a party to Jasher's plan and that would require an incentive, which he was willing to provide. However, it could ruffle a few feathers and might raise unwanted questions as to the management of his office should it ever be whispered in the wrong circles.

The Archbishop had not forgotten Jasher's influence at the Vatican many years earlier. A few of his colleagues, including some Cardinals, were in their current positions there through Jasher's artful intervention and, to hear them talk, each owed Jasher several favors. And one of those Cardinals had stepped in at a key juncture in Códol's life and had provided him, then a long-time Bishop, a strong recommendation at a time when he suspected he would have ended his years in that subordinate office. And, as Jasher had pointed out, what can be given can be taken away just as easily. Códol was of the mind to believe him; at least he intended to give Jasher the benefit of the doubt since his own career depended on it. The Archbishop had to hand it to him, though. Given his notoriety among those of the cloth at the Vatican,

Jasher had developed quite a talent for politics. Thus, he was not anxious to test Jasher's influence among his colleagues so he had reluctantly agreed to extend an accommodation to Father Castro.

The Archbishop had found a comfortable position in his chair from which he would conduct the interview. Thanks to Jasher's physician he had sent over a few days ago, his back felt wonderful; in fact, he had not felt this fine in many years. *How does he do it? He seems to know something about everything and always has a contact on retainer. For such a young man, he certainly does get around.*

A few moments passed and an older, middle aged priest nearing fifty with graying hair entered the audience room and presented himself before the Archbishop. In obeisance, he humbly kneeled then offered an introduction, "Excellency, I am Father Castro, how may I be of service?" The good Dominican Father had no idea why he had been summoned, but he had wasted little time making his travel arrangements once the request had been presented him.

"Father Castro, how is the weather in Toledo? I understand the winter was stormier than usual this year."

The Dominican was not gifted politically. He was more of a plodder and suspected that is what had made him ideal for his current posting as an inquisitor. He was therefore somewhat surprised when the Archbishop began speaking with a familiarity that was both unexpected as well as singularly gratifying. "You are quite right Excellency, the weather has been harder than normal, but it appears that here in Barcelona it remains as calm and clear as I once remembered it to be."

"You know, of course, that I hail from a small town near Toledo called Bargas and it has been far too long since I have visited my old parish. Perhaps next year I will have the opportunity."

The small talk continued for a while longer between both priests, but finally during a pause in their conversation, the prelate began to arrive at the point. "Father Castro, I have heard wonderful things of you. Please tell me about yourself."

Castro cleared his throat and now began to explain his service and experience to the Church and after a few minutes, he confessed, "Well, there is little to tell except that my current labors have required I toil for the Grand Inquisitor of Toledo, Archbishop Sandoval." He cleared his throat and with due humility, he pointed out, "My successes have produced some gratifying results, I suppose."

The Archbishop shook his head in chastisement. "Father, you are far too modest. I have heard your efforts have produced marvelous results for the Archbishop. Your attention to detail and dedication to the truth has been highly instrumental in bringing even the most hardened heretics to confess. Please, you must tell me of your latest conquest. Omit nothing."

The Dominican priest became a little subdued, his enthusiasm having now been deflated at having to confess his recent failure. Clearing his throat, he replied hesitantly, "Excellency, I regret my sterling record of achievement has been finally bested by a Jewish heretic, a *Converso* that has refused to confess despite all encouragement that I employed."

"Yes, I have heard of this Doctor Antonio Montezinos."

With a start, Father Castro was surprised that the prelate had become aware of his failure. He stammered a reply. "Your Excellency, I feel so ashamed to have allowed Montezinos to escape his chance for repentance." Shaking his head despondently, he related, "I felt that I was so close to reaching him, but Archbishop Sandoval, in his wisdom, has decided to terminate the interrogations. Now, his sins still crimson, the man must face his judgement of the *auto-da-fé* unrepentant."

With compassion, the Archbishop pointed out, "You should not feel badly for your efforts. There are those who simply refuse the mercy and condescension of our Savior, but what has impressed me the most were the unfailing, dogged efforts to reach this heretic and provide him mercy. It speaks volumes of your charity towards your fellow man. Moreover, your reputation for perseverance in the face of so much opposition has reached the ears of my archdiocese. It is felt we would all benefit by having your presence in our service here in Barcelona."

Father Castro was frankly surprised but elated by this sudden turn of events. Knowing he had failed at extracting a confession from Montezinos, he felt his service would end in a lowly parish in some backwater. *But, now what is His Eminence suggesting?*

He stammered, "Of course, I would be happy to serve in any way I could."

Archbishop Códol became silent as though he was pondering a matter of great importance. In reality, he carefully reasoned how to properly bait the hook.

After a few moments he replied, "At it occurs, there is a posting for a bishop in my archdiocese for someone of your dedication and humility, and clearly you are a man of exceptional talents." He paused, as if to qualify his accolades then proceeded, "But, what I do not yet know is your degree of recognition and commitment to a higher cause when a dilemma is placed before you."

A bishopric position? That is well beyond anything I had ever imagined. He tried desperately to appear confident, yet humble when he asked, "Please, how may I be of help to allay your reservations, Your Eminence?"

The Archbishop nodded his head in approval and stated, "This heretic you have, Montezinos, would serve the greater good if he would simply depart from Spain. Some unrepentant *Conversos* should burn and send a strict message that the Church cannot tolerate such deception. After all, Mother Church must occasionally send a warning to all ravening wolves that would harm our flocks from within. On the other hand, such persons may by their example encourage such deviant behavior to others and become martyrs to their unjust cause. Having followed the case closely, I have come to the conclusion that this Jew will follow the role as martyr. Our best intentions may later come back to haunt us and leave us worse off than if we had just made the man disappear."

"Of course, I see your point completely, Your Excellency, but I fail to see how this can be accomplished now that the Inquisitor General has been made aware of my failure to extract a confession. As you are aware, the *auto-da-fé* now demands justice be served."

"Father Castro, we have a clear dilemma here that I feel only you could remove for all of us, including Mother Church. With your help, perhaps there is a way that could be found to deny this man the martyrdom he persistently seeks." The Archbishop seemed to be pondering the quandary, and having come to a conclusion confided, "If he were to be abducted before the execution, would you be willing to look the other way and allow his escape to prevent the dishonor this man would surely bring upon the Church?"

Castro looked blandly at the Archbishop, afraid to respond. Yet, this was the dilemma he had alluded to earlier, the choice he would have to make for the greater good, a higher purpose, and a nobler cause. With a frown, he asked himself, *who was this Antonio Montezinos, after all, who would dare to bring so much shame and disrespect to the Church?*

Nodding his head, he replied, "Of course, Your Eminence, I see quite clearly your concern and I would have no issue with what you ask."

"Thank you, my Son. Once this shameful business is behind us all, I will dispatch a message to Rome lauding your recent action and prior successes then request your immediate posting to the diocese in Cartagena as its newest bishop."

The priest was elated, but a sudden thought came to him and so pointed out, "What of the workmen who will accompany the prisoner? Surely, they will make note of the abduction and take notice of my lack of interest in stopping the act. They may even attempt to resist this abduction themselves."

As if already taken this matter into account, the Archbishop replied, "Father, these workmen are little more than barbarians who do the work that no one else will do. We pull them from those same prisons in which they did languish then ask them to perform a service there for the good of the Church." Shaking his head, the prelate confided, "But they are the dregs of our society and if their lives must be forfeit for the greater good, then their sacrifice will serve a greater purpose in death. Should they lose their lives in their service to our cause, it will be sanctified toward their heavenly reward hereafter. Please do not concern yourself over such mundane matters. When the time comes, just hang back out of the way and allow these abductors to relieve us of a heavy, unwelcome burden."

Still, there was doubt. "As you know, Your Excellency, I report to the Inquisitor General, Archbishop Sandoval. Will he not ask questions?"

The prelate appeared unconcerned and confided, "The Archbishop of Toledo is a sick man. Should he have the strength to object, I am sure he could be persuaded that this abduction was in the best interest of the Church. Do not be concerned; these are matters that I will address should they arise."

As thick clouds scudded across the dark September sky in central Spain, starlight was scarce and the moonlight could only partially bless the expected sanctification to come that night. The supreme moment of truth had arrived for Antonio Montezinos; it was the evening of the *auto-da-fé*. Three men from the castle of the archdiocese accompanied the condemned man through the streets of Toledo: two were workmen driving the cart wherein sat Montezinos, and the third, a priest that walked by the side, his eyes cast in sympathy for the captive who still refused his opportunity to repent.

The cart driver, Diego, had looked up at the overcast conditions and commented over his shoulder to the other workman, "Ricardo, the rain might put a damper on the festivities."

Ricardo, hanging to the back of the cart, had laughed and derided his companion for such foolish talk. "You should not be concerned, Diego. After all, this is a night of celebration as another heretic will soon burn in Hell."

"You are very right, Ricardo. And to be present at the blessed moment when the screaming begins for the tormented sinner is more than either of us could have ever hoped for."

"Agreed, but I should not want to be Antonio Montezinos as the fire approaches his feet."

"Nor I, my friend, but he did have his chance to repent." He spat in the mud. "May he burn in Hell forever."

The workmen had happily thrown the broken form of Antonio Montezinos into the back of the prison cart to be paraded through the city, part of a public spectacle reserved for those heretics who refused to confess sins and receive absolution. In spite of the proffered posting to the Barcelona Archdiocese, Father Castro was still disappointed. Even after four horrific months of incarceration and repeated persuasion on the torture rack, Montezinos still maintained his silence. Notwithstanding, despite his continued defiance of offered mercy, the Dominican priest knew there had to be a part of the man who desired forgiveness for his heresy. The priest was not worried so much as determined to ensure that Mother Church was not to be held accountable for doing less than was necessary to reclaim a lost soul from eternal damnation.

In a last effort to absolve Montezinos, Castro continued his litany of petition to the prisoner. Walking step for step next to the cage, he warned, "My Son, now that you are so near to death, you must confess to receive absolution for your heretic ways. Allow the merciful blood of Christ to wash away your sins and cleanse your soul. The salvation of your soul demands it."

Antonio remained silent. Even now, when Montezinos knew he was so close to losing his last opportunity to repent, Father Castro could see he would be unable to appeal to the prisoner. Wearily, the priest shook his head in sympathy and for the last time turned away from the tortured man.

As the procession wound its way slowly through the streets of Toledo on the way to the square where the execution was to occur, Montezinos received a constant barrage of jeers and vituperation from the citizens. Moreover, the street rabble had become creative. In addition to spitting upon him, they managed to throw every rotten, noisome vegetable, even dead rats, in his direction. Antonio Montezinos, though weary from his incarceration and knowing his end was near, still maintained his silence and merely looked on as the frenzied crowd of Toledo busied themselves with this final act of abuse.

As the wagon slowly turned the final corner, the unruly crowd thinned then disappeared. A larger crowd was a block ahead and could be easily heard in anticipation of the public burning. The public burning had attracted many of the proud nobility as well as the common citizens who had come to view the soul of a famous heretic burn physically before he was condemned to burn spiritually in torment for eternity. As the cart approached the square, a workman was standing nearby the combustible wood for the bonfire. He carried a lit torch that would be applied to the pyre once the condemned man had been tied to a cross. Once the signal had been given from Castro then the show could begin.

This would have been the usual procedure, but on this day the workman was not who he appeared to be. When he saw the horse cart in view, he turned away from the restless throng of onlookers and, to their utter amazement, he lit the pyre prematurely. Within a few minutes of the blaze, there was an explosion, then several more followed by a fireworks display that few had ever before witnessed. None of the spectators were injured, but all were surprised as well as overcome with an astonishment so intense they remained mesmerized throughout the spectacle and would remember the moment for the rest of their lives.

As the crowd was thus occupied and the pyrotechnic show was at its most intense, Jasher and his men slipped out from the shadows of a nearby alley then ran up to the cart that contained ben Judah. The driver, Diego was completely agape by the fire and light show, thus he was scarcely aware when his horse was stopped by a man in a mask. As the driver gazed stupidly at the light show in the square, one of the rescue team pulled him off the cart and hit him on the back of the head; another pulled his cohort, Ricardo, from the back of the wagon who also received a blow to the head for his trouble. Once both workmen had been incapacitated then Jasher removed the key from the prone form of Ricardo, and inserting it into the lock, the gate began to swing open. Quickly, Jasher and another of his men leapt into the cart and carefully removed the prisoner and tenderly placed him in the back of a covered wagon heading the opposite direction. Within minutes the assailants had all cleared the street and fanned out in different directions to avoid causing undue notice during their retreat.

The last assailant still held the horse and gazing down at the driver who had just awoken from his blow to the head he said, "Diego, you saw nothing but the light show then you were hit from behind. Try to remember that and mention it to your friend when you are both questioned. It will save your lives." With that, he too melted into the crowd that was still being entertained by the show.

During the whole scene that included both the fireworks and the abduction, the Dominican Father Castro had moved back into the shadows to avoid stumbling in the way of the rescue. He watched silently while all but one man had stolen away into the late evening darkness.

The priest's eyes fell upon the last man. "So, it is you."

Jasher walked slowly up to the priest and bowed slightly then asked politely, "Father Castro, do you understand your part in our performance this evening?"

"I do. Moreover, I have heard tell of a man who walks among the powerful within the Church and who makes deals. I suspect that would be you." Glancing over at the injured jailers, he commented, "I am glad that no harm came to the workmen aside from a little knot on their heads and face. I assume that was for their benefit?"

"It was, as it was also for the workman who was replaced in the town square. They will all have a few lumps to show the Grand Inquisitor should he ask how it was they could have been so easily overcome and allowed the abduction to occur. But, then we both know how simple that was to arrange, don't we Father?" The insinuation was clear.

"Too easily, I fear." Castro changed the subject slightly. "How is it you know of *Señor* Montezinos or should I say Ephraim ben Judah?"

Jasher realized that he was not dealing with a fool and perhaps his promotion to Bishop in Cartagena was well founded after all. "I owed him a favor and the Archbishop Códol of Barcelona and I have mutual friends with whom we owe favors and who owe us favors even as you and I now do."

The priest sighed inwardly at the truth of this statement, and nodding his head in understanding said, "Yes, and I fear your heresy may be as great as that of ben Judah."

"I assure you Father Castro, that if I were of your faith, you would consider my beliefs much worse. Perhaps we should just leave it at that." A pause then, "Go with God, Father." Jasher turned and walked quietly down the street then melted into the shadows of a darkening night.

As Father Castro watched the man retreat between two buildings, he offered a quiet prayer for his soul.

CHAPTER 7

REST AND RECOVERY

Much to his surprise, a month after his abduction Ephraim ben Judah discovered he was now a guest of Benjamin Jasher at his home on the western side of the island of Cyprus. It had taken him that long to recover sufficiently to express his relief as well as his thanks to Jasher's timely intercession in his rescue from the *auto-da-fé*. Benjamin had seen he was cared for by the finest Moorish doctor that could be found in Morocco, and Ephraim's healing, though slow, was encouraging. Jasher had been assured that his friend would make a complete recovery.

Jasher walked quietly into the room where his friend had been convalescing and noting he was alert asked, "Ephraim, how are you feeling?"

Ben Judah glanced tiredly in the direction of Jasher's voice. "Benjamin, I don't know how to express my thanks." With a smile, he asked, "How did you arrange my removal? Sadly, I was too bruised and beaten at that moment to appreciate your delicate touch."

"It was a simple matter, really, if you know the right person."

"And it just so happened that this was the case?"

"As it turned out, yes. The Archbishop of Barcelona seemed anxious to assist in your release. He sends you his love and a fervent desire you never return to Spain."

Ephraim winced from pain as he attempted to laugh at Jasher's wit. He decided to let it go; there would be time later for the laughter once the dreams of horror had abated. He seemed to remember another matter. "I understand there was quite a light show performed in my honor. How did you manage that?"

"You might recall that I mentioned a Chinese gentleman from Canton I had helped into Portugal a few years ago."

"I do indeed. The gentleman had incurred a number of powerful enemies in his native country and was searching for a new home and a place to safely hide. I assume he must have had something to barter."

"Nearly everyone does. As it turned out, the Portuguese were quite interested in his understanding of explosives and were persuaded to look the other way at his heathen customs and allowed him sanctuary. As a result of their now enlightened views toward Chinese, at present they own an armaments program that will soon rival if not exceed that of any nation in Europe."

"So, your Chinese friend was disposed to return the favor."

"He owed me a favor that I collected in the form of Chinese fireworks. He deeply approved my form of compensation and was highly amused in the manner in which I applied it. The explosives were quite remarkable and sufficient to offer me a needed distraction at a critical moment in our little performance in Toledo."

"However you managed it, I thank you for the effort. A few more minutes in the streets of Toledo and I would have discovered, no doubt, how the Catholic Hell would have felt."

Jasher smiled at the man's understated wit. "Actually, it was Levi Singer who brought your plight to my attention. He was persuasive and you know how much I value returned favors."

"Indeed I do. Will the nautical diary be of much value to you?"

"I am confident that it will. As to the mathematical formula you wrote on the last page, how did you derive it? You realize it is the formula for obtaining the longitude for a specific point on a map given the solar days of a lunar orbit?"

Ephraim nodded his head. "I saw it in a dream and when I awoke, I wrote it down. Also, in the dream, I was told to receive a man, a messenger no less, who had obtained a special rutter for navigating through the New World. No explanation was provided for what its use might be; he simply delivered it to me with little comment. I noted the formula on the final page of the diary because it seemed relevant."

"What else did he tell you?"

"What makes you think there was more?"

"Intuition?"

Ephraim averted his eyes for a moment then after consideration he met Jasher's gaze and simply nodded then added, "Yes, there was more to it than a simple delivery of an item."

"There usually is."

"He told me I would be a witness to the evil cruelty and hatred of those who would persecute my people. It was the Creator's will that I remain silent and reveal nothing of my beliefs or the whereabouts of those within my circle of friends. What is this all about?"

To Jasher, given the man's trials, it was a fair question, but the answer would only bring more questions, the answers to which Ephraim was not yet ready to understand. He replied reluctantly, "I cannot begin to explain the mind of the Creator. Only to reassure you that in time, with patience, you will attain the wisdom to accept what you have experienced and that answer will be for you alone. I suspect you are already well on the road to attaining that enlightenment for yourself and my answers for such matters are not meant for you, but for me only."

Ephraim decided not to press for more; he had an answer. But he did have another question, one that had bothered him throughout his ordeal. "What is evil? Is it merely the absence of good?"

Jasher had pondered this question much of his life. He was always left yearning for better answers than he had acquired over the years. Slowly, he commented, "Perhaps the evil in this life can best be understood if we attach a purpose to it. Once, a wise man told me that evil is the crucible of all righteousness."

Nodding at the obscure reference, Ephraim did follow the logic, but as always, the answer only led to more questions. "So, evil is necessary? That would seem to be your position."

Jasher considered his friend's conjecture, but replied with a proviso, "Only to the extent that there would be no purpose to this life without an opposition in all things. But, where does that leave us? That evil must exist? That we must have this choice? I can only confirm that somehow evil serves to work out the will of the Creator. I have had much time in my long life to observe the truth of this."

Ephraim gazed at the youthful contours of the face of his friend and smiling said, "And just how long have you had to develop these astounding conclusions?"

Jasher skillfully deflected the question. "Who says I have them worked out?" A knowing smile had crossed his face.

Ephraim nodded his head and wondered, not for the first time since his release, if Jasher, too, carried a similar mission to be a testifier. "Benjamin, why did you befriend me all those years ago in Italy?"

"Until your recent ordeal, I was never sure when would be the best time and opportunity to reveal that information to you. I suppose you are now ready to hear it."

Ephraim found a more comfortable position and shifted slightly on the bed. "So, there was a reason. I had always suspected; it just seemed right, I suppose, that we should have met."

Nodding, Jasher commented, "Few encounters are truly coincidental." He glanced out the window, noting the blueness of the ocean then turning he said, "A long time ago, I had an opportunity to develop a short friendship with a remarkable man who was a doctor like you. Before we parted for the last time, he promised he would look after a relative of mine and take care of him and his family for as long as he was alive. In return, I promised to befriend and to look after his descendants and I have done so."

"How could you know I was his descendent?"

"His name was Manasseh ben Judah and I just knew."

Ephraim let it go then changed the subject. "Benjamin, before I was incarcerated, I saw a reflection of myself in the mirror. It was me, but it wasn't me. The man in the reflection was older and greyer; he seemed more guarded and subdued as though he had gone through a grim and dangerous test, but had survived the ordeal. At that moment, I blinked my eyes as if I was dreaming and when I looked back, my usual reflection was there. What do you make of that?"

Jasher paused and slightly pursed his lips as though pondering the response. Then he replied, "For everyone it is different. There are moments in our lives when we enter a dark tunnel and only a pinhole of light ahead through the dark can be perceived. That light we see at the end is hope. Eventually, we exit, but we are different, changed sometimes for the good, but always we emerge differently from how we entered." On a shelf in the corner was a hand-held mirror, exquisitely cut with a true reflection.

Jasher walked over to the alcove and returned with the mirror in hand. He held it out to Ephraim who cautiously accepted it then placed it before his face. Within the reflection looked back the man he had seen months earlier in his own mirror before his incarceration. He flinched slightly then slowly nodded his head. "It is him and it is me."

"You must decide soon what you intend to do with the rest of your life, Ephraim. You may stay here as long as you wish, but things are changed with you now, are they not?"

The former prisoner of the Inquisition felt sick for his loss. "My life will never be the same. I have no wife, no children, no home and nowhere to go. Everything and everyone I once knew have been taken away from me. Benjamin, they nearly broke me. That man in the mirror is the new me and I must learn to adapt to a life for which I never expected."

"Perhaps the new life you must seek is to begin somewhere within you, waiting to emerge. There are still a few things I can teach you if you are still of a mind to learn and are unafraid to dream of something better. Are you ready to dream again, Ephraim?"

Ephraim was still bruised from his trials in Spain, so with a crooked smile, he asked, "So, you are a believer in dreams, Benjamin?"

"I am a believer in hearing the truth, from wherever and however it comes."

Remembering such thoughts of his own from a previous life, Ephraim pointed out, "Then you would find Spain an uncomfortable place to live, my friend."

Jasher laughed aloud, "Which is why, my friend, I will never call Spain my home."

In appreciation of that sentiment, Jasher arose and walked over to the balcony then threw open the door overlooking the great Mediterranean Sea. A panorama of greenish-blue water could be seen to the far horizon then a gentle salty breeze wafted through the windows from a blue cloudless sky, catching Ephraim ben Judah, the former Prisoner of Toledo, with a soft evening caress. The sun was setting on another glorious day.

Looking down at the mirror he still held, Ephraim experimented with a smile. When he found the right look, the reflected face now seemed younger and less troubled, but wiser and definitely not beaten. With a nod, he thought, *I suppose it is all right to dream again.*

PART 3

THE NEW WORLD

Time and memory are true artists; they
remold reality nearer to the heart's desire.

----- *John Dewey, American*
philosopher and psychologist

Popol Vuh (modern K'iche') is a corpus of mytho-historical narratives
of the Post Classic K'iche' kingdom in Guatemala's western
highlands. The title translates as "Book of the Community",
"Book of Counsel", or more exactly as "Book of the People".
Popol Vuh's prominent attributes are its creation myth, its dilu-
vian (Great Flood) suggestion, its epic tales of the Hero Twins
Hunahpú and Xbalanqué, and its genealogies. The myth begins
with the exploits of deities described with human attributes and
concludes with a royal genealogy, perhaps as an assertion of
rule by divine right.

As with other texts, for example the Chilam Balam, a great
deal of Popol Vuh's significance lies in the scarcity of earlier
accounts dealing with Mesoamerican mythologies. Popol Vuh's

fortunate survival is attributable to the Spanish 18th century Dominican friar Francisco Ximénez.

Though some variation has been tested by Tedlock and Christenson, editions of the Popol Vuh typically indicate the following historical accounts: the creation of animals and humans; lineage of principal figures in K'iche' mythology; human migrations and K'iche' prominence over other tribes; evolution of distinct languages. The feathered serpent lord institutes elaborate rituals, cities are founded, and significant architectural structures emerge to which fortifications are later added. Finally, intertribal strife ensues. The final anthropological wars correlate to the terminal classic period (roughly 790 - 1000 CE). The document states the lineages of several tribal rulers leading up to the Spanish conquest. (https://en.wikipedia.org/wiki/Popol_Vuh)

Prologue, Lamanai, 277 BCE

Aaron walked slowly up the hill to the temple site where he had buried the plates nearly fifty years earlier. Actually, slow was the only way he got around these days, he reflected cynically. He was the headman or *cacique* of Lamanai and had been for nearly forty years now. It was time to pass the burden of knowledge to his son who would assume this role and he fervently hoped this rite of passage would signal his eventual demise. At least he hoped it would. Growing old had not set well with him and he only wanted to die comfortable in the knowledge that the secret would soon be in the hands of his eldest son. If this was the only comfort he could glean these days, then he would take it.

He looked back over his shoulder at his son, Ammon, and grunted his displeasure. "Son, please try to keep up. I have little time remaining to live and I do want to pass this last bit of advice and counsel on to you before I depart this life."

"Father, of course, I will hurry." Ammon, nearing age forty with a family of his own, was already old by most standards and could see little point in whatever else his father may have to leave him by way of counsel. Besides, his father had been dying for the past five years now, or so he had maintained; assuming you could keep up with him long enough to appreciate his tone of finality. He loved and revered the man, of course;

everyone did, which was why the King of Tikal had granted his descendants to be the headmen of Lamanai in perpetuity. Of late, he had grown more taciturn and stubborn and most, especially his family would be more than happy to have him buried, but still he persevered. So up the hill they climbed, the older man convinced his time in mortality was growing short and the younger man, safe in the knowledge that soon he would inherit control of the village.

It was late afternoon and night was beginning to chase the day. Soon the nocturnal creatures would begin to prowl and forage and raise their chatter and howls to the stars and moon. Aaron wanted this task to be completed before full night had creeped in on them, but timing was everything. The last thing he needed was an audience; only his son was to know this secret he had been keeping for fifty years. Thus, there was haste in his step and his son would just have to keep up. Ahead, he recognized the temple. Only he was privy to the reasons why this particular edifice had been kept and maintained so fastidiously over the years. Only he knew why he had given it the name of the Star of Jasher and would forever be known as such.

"My son, we are here."

"So I see. It is the Star of Jasher, the temple which you have named after the dipper star that does point to the east."

"Partially correct, but what you do not know is that in reality I named it for a man who is to return to our land one day from the east and recover an item that lies within the very walls of this temple."

Ammon's eyes went up at that revelation. "And all these years I thought you had named if after a star in the heavens."

"That is what everyone in the area has been led to believe," he added sagely. He put his hands upon his hips and nodded his appreciation of the site that had been chosen so long ago. It had always seemed to be just the right location at the top of the hill. It could be seen from every vantage point along the river and from the village, yet far enough away from the center of the community that it did not appear too obvious to most travelers moving along the main pathways through the area. Then, of course, there was the majesty of the building itself which had been originally consecrated to the one true God, the Creator.

A frown of impatience crossed Ammon's face; His father was beginning to digress again. Ammon cleared his throat and was about to point out that the onset of night would make his demonstration all the more difficult unless he hurried. Suddenly his father walked up the stair step a few meters, bent over and unseated a stone that had not been completely set into the building. He turned around and sat on the stairway then looking at his son he began to speak.

"Ammon, reach in there and pull out a leather bag that has been buried deeply into the wall. It is in the shadows now, but I assure you that it is there."

Now curious and eager to see what his father had declared was in the niche, Ammon reached in and felt a leather hide covering something metallic. Using both hands, he leaned in and pulled out the bag then turned and rested it on the stairway.

"Open it," his father directed.

Ammon pulled open the bag, reached inside and felt something hard, but yielding, so he pulled out the object. The metal reflected the waning light of the day and there was a slight glare and shimmer from the artifact as he sat it down on the stair steps. In awe, he asked, "What is it, Father?"

Aaron ignored the question, only replied, "You must listen carefully to all I say and you must tell this story to your son before your death so that he may relate it to his. As I have explained on many occasions, my origins are not from the area of Lamanai, but much farther west and before you is an abridged record of the history of my people. Through their own care-lessness, they were destroyed many years ago when I was about nearing the same age as you are now. The plates are made of brass, not gold, and are a composite of metals which can be found in abundance in my native coun-try. As you can see, the sheen on the plates indicates a process of exquisite workmanship."

"Did you forge them father?"

"No, I merely took the existing pristine plates and made an abridgement of the larger history I found nearby located inside a place of worship."

Ammon touched the plates, rubbing his hand across the symbols engraved within the metal. After a moment, he whispered, "Then who did forge the plates?"

With pride, his father explained, "In life he would have been known as Seth, son of our first parents, Adam and Eve. An ancient people, my ancestors received the plates either from Seth or by way of Jasher, a wise man who is the greatest of all historians. I was never told which one; I suppose it does not matter. At that time, my people wrote many records on plates and left them in a large depository beneath a synagogue in my native land. It was my task to write a short abridgement of the recorded history of my people found therein."

Ammon shook his head in amazement. After a moment, he asked, "Where is this depository located?"

"Far from here and you must never speak of it again. The source location of the plates is a knowledge you need never be concerned about. It is enough to know that they came from my homeland to the west."

As Ammon was growing up, his father had been gregarious, even comical at times and kept his family sometimes laughing and at other times fascinated with unusual tales of his younger days. He reflected, however, that over the past few years, his father had grown more withdrawn and taciturn, less open and more introspective. He suspected he now understood the reasons for the change. What he was now explaining was unlike anything he had ever heard his father speak of before. As he related each point of fact that he wanted him to remember, Ammon could detect a tone of gravity that was absent from the usual timbre of optimism in his voice.

"Father, I understand that you have written of your ancestors, our village of Lamanai has done the same, but to what end was *your* history written?"

"They relate in detail the cause of the destruction of my people by a society of men who lived in the shadows of my government and turned our people against one another for their own selfish interests. My anger and hatred of these men run deeply for I was a first-hand witness of their influence and its devastating effects."

"What did they want, aside from the wealth and influence that all men want?"

"For some men, power is used as a means to enrich themselves at the expense of others, but for these, power was all they wanted and their aim was to subdue all men and remove the very rights of choice which the Creator has ensured we all should have. The destruction of whole societies was simply the by-product of their efforts to achieve this aim. The genocide of my people gave them not one moment's pause of the moral implications of their actions."

"If not for wealth and influence, to what end would they want this power?"

"The end they sought was the removal of our right for choice and they could only maintain their absolute power over time at the expense of this right. Their contempt for our ability to rule ourselves was so complete that they were unwilling to allow us the choice of personal rule and self-determination. It was almost as if their society was trying to prove a point that we were incapable of ruling ourselves, that we would need them always to show us the way of rule."

"Could you not rebel? Even our king in Tikal allows us many freedoms to move about and decide upon trade and where we would live."

Aaron shook his head sadly and commented, "There was no rebellion without complete retaliation. They would have us blindly move about and acknowledge their superiority without as much as a cry of dissention. Where ever they ruled, it was absolute."

"What happened to them after your people disappeared?"

"Over the years I have talked discreetly with those who have wandered into our city here in Lamanai and others nearby. So far as I was able to discover, their lands have become infested with a disease of the mind and many have fled before them. Before, pagan idolatry consisted of benign, helpful gods of the land, the air and water, but these have been replaced by those of war, destruction and death and they pay more than simple lip service to them."

Ammon nodded his head in understanding and made the connection also. "As you know, in my travels, I too have noticed this change. Those who live in those regions to the west now openly offer human sacrifices to their gods. I have heard of whole villages being gathered up and taken back to their temples to satisfy the blood lusts of their idols."

Aaron agreed and pointed out, "These are the means by which the people have been manipulated to believe that they are no longer capable of making their own choices and so require the need for pagan gods to make the choices for them. Of course, these gods are no more than surrogates for the men behind them. This tells me this same society is in full control of events in the country to the west and soon we will feel it here at home."

"Surely this could not happen in our own land, Father. For generations many headmen up and down the river have reported to the King at Tikal and our traditions have survived. How would this society break our control?"

"The key to their power is the encouragement of ignorance and dissemination of fear. With enough of this pressure over time, our citizens would be more than willing to turn their ordered lives over to others who would claim to make the difficult decisions of life and death for them. In return, their society would provide limited peace, but with a high price."

Ammon pondered all that had been explained then asked, "Father, how was it you were able to escape when so many perished?"

"My son, there is a time in every person's life where everything is separated into what was before and what came afterwards. For me, it was the abridgement of the records. Before, I was a warrior, a taker of lives, but I was someone who fought for his people to preserve their liberties. Then, I was hunted as a wild beast by hunters who could not be reasoned with and they absolutely would not stop the hunt until either they were dead or I. It changes you."

"They were after the records?"

"They were sent by the same shadow society that had corrupted and destroyed my people and still infest the land with their disease. My abridgement contains a history of their influence and if they knew of the whereabouts of these records you see before you, they would burn this whole village to the ground to recover them."

"But why? They are just records."

"The records represent proof of their existence and their influence and one day their brotherhood will have to answer for their crimes and this record will help indict them. Without it, their punishment would be far less than they deserve."

"And that would be so bad?"

With passion, Aaron said, "They deserve the full measure of punishment that the Creator has set aside for them. You have never had to live under the fear for the loss of your liberties as I have nor have had to fight to the death to preserve them. Pray you never have to."

It was a somber moment between father and son. A message had just been passed between the two that in time would become a rite of passage between the village headman and his descendants who would follow.

Ammon looked at the plates and again rubbed his hand lightly over the surface of the symbols his father had created at the expense of so much loss of life and blood. "Why did you want me to see the plates, Father?"

"After I die, and it will be soon, it will be up to you to safeguard the records and ensure that no one discovers them or they fall into the wrong hands. Before you die, you must bring your son here, show him the records and pass along everything I have told you to him and this must be done through each generation. You will carry many responsibilities over the remainder of your lifetime, but I can assure you that none will be greater than this one. The safety and well-being of our city and our families will depend upon it. This burden will be yours and then to your son then his."

"For how long, Father?"

Aaron had also asked himself the same question. He had been waiting many years for the answer, but none had been forthcoming save one: "Until Jasher arrives to collect them."

Nodding, Ammon asked, "Who is this man, Father?"

The sun was setting; the light nearly gone from the day. Aaron sat on the step of the temple and gazed out across the verdant jungle and a large expanse of ocean towards the east. Blinking his tired eyes, he replied softly, "He is our brother."

CHAPTER 1

FLORENCE, 1413

*T*he House of *Medici was an Italian banking family, political dynasty and later a royal house that first began to gather prominence under Cosimo de' Medici in the Republic of Florence during the first half of the 15th century. The family originated in the Mugello region of the Tuscan countryside, gradually rising until they were able to fund the Medici Bank which became the largest in Europe during the latter half of the 15th century. Though officially they remained citizens rather than monarchs, their fortune insured the Medici gain political power in Florence.*

Their wealth and influence initially derived from the textile trade guided by the guild of the Arte della Lana. As did other signore families, they dominated their city's government and were finally able to bring Florence under their family's power. On the positive side, they did manage to create an environment where art and humanism could flourish. They, along with other families of Italy, such as the Visconti and Sforza of Milan, the Este of Ferrara, and the Gonzaga of Mantua, fostered and inspired the birth of the Italian Renaissance.

The Medici family produced three Popes of the Roman Catholic Church, Pope Leo X (1513–1521), Pope Clement VII (1523–1534), and Pope Leo XI (1605), two regent queens of France, Catherine de' Medici (1547–1559) and Marie de' Medici (1600–1610). In 1531, the family became hereditary Dukes of Florence. In 1569, the duchy was elevated to a grand duchy after territorial expansion. Until the death of Gian Gastone de' Medici, they ruled the Grand Duchy of Tuscany from its inception until 1737. Under the earlier grand dukes of the Medici family, the grand duchy of Florence witnessed degrees of economic growth, but by the time of Cosimo III de' Medici, whose financial irresponsibility and lack of concern for the citizens of Florence had become so detrimental, the duchy had become fiscally bankrupt.

At the height of its influence, The Medici Bank was considered the most prosperous and respected institutions in all of Europe. From this base, they acquired political power initially in Florence and later in wider Italy and Europe. They introduced a notable contribution to the profession of accounting with the improvement of the general ledger system through the development of the double-entry bookkeeping system for tracking credits and debits. (https://en.wikipedia.org/wiki/House_of_Medici)

Cain had always preferred being a king-maker to that of a king. History had seldom been aware of the man behind the great ones; kings and emperors came and went, but the king-maker always remained in power and Cain intended to keep it that way. He had often lamented that it had been a shame that he had had to relocate his base of operations from Syria to Turkey. The invading hordes of the Mongols had been unreasonably stupid; their leaders had refused an alliance. In time, they would be dealt with, but for now he was making the most of his current involvement with the followers of Allah, and that empire was now well under his control. It had been rumored, but never substantiated, that in the thirteenth century he had been known as Ertugrul, father of Osman I, the founder of the Ottoman Empire. Though this had been the truth, he went to great efforts to ensure history knew little about him or his influence in the establishment of that empire.

As of late, he had decided to shift his center of influence from the Middle-East to Europe, specifically to Florence, Italy, where, with his considerable resources, he had wanted to establish a banking house. There were still a few issues that had needed to be addressed before this could happen, so he had sought the counsel of prominent bankers of the area, specifically two in particular, Alberto Bardi and Cosimo de Medici, though for different reasons.

The Bardi Banking House had strong ties to many European cities and so Cain had shrewdly established a meeting time with the head of the House, Alberto Bardi. Unfortunately, as it turned out for Bardi, he had roundly rebuffed Cain and he swore he would have him run out of Florence. But, Cain was neither offended nor disappointed by the setback, and so he wished him well. Cain had concluded that perhaps in time his son, Bucini, would be more approachable, but not until his father was out of the way, of course.

Realizing that most of the more prominent bankers of the region would have a similar attitude to that of the Bardi, Cain decided to approach the Medici Banking House. Cosimo Medici was not yet a local mover and shaker within the Florentine community, but all reports indicated that he had the ambitions to become one. Cain reasoned he would be hungry to forge a relationship, which to Cain meant little more than a financial alliance in which the Medici House would act as a front for his base of operations. Because of his ruthless potential to be more than just a local banker, Cain had naturally felt Medici could be manipulated as he had used others before him. In due time Cosimo had been asked to visit Cain at his villa, and of course, the man had arrived sumptuously attired for the auspicious occasion. Though his outward arrogance would have been annoying on many, he seemed to wear it as comfortably as a well broken in pair of boots. Upon arrival he had been escorted into Cain's inner office for the meeting and Don Caino, as Cain was now calling himself, arose and bowed.

As both were being seated, Cain sized him up quickly and hoped that the man's intelligence was equal to his hauteur. "*Signore* Medici, welcome to my home and thank you for coming. Please be comfortable. My servant will bring us a local wine that I am told has promise."

Medici found a chair and settled in. "*Signore* Don Caino, thank you for your gracious invitation. On behalf of the banking community of Florence, you, too, are quite welcome."

Cain signaled a servant to serve the wine and they both waited as the drinks were poured. Cain had an amazingly large fireplace, an old affectation of his that he never seemed to discard. As they sipped their wine Medici watched the fire with one eye and with the other he had begun to size up his host. Medici was curious where this discussion would take them and thus was the first to break the silence. "*Signore* Caino, if it would not be too impertinent to ask, from where do you hail? Your surname is Italian, but highly unique and would seldom be used. Your appearance is darker than most, though on you it sits most handsomely, if I might be permitted the observation. You are new to Florence and many will be curious of your origin, so I would like to be the first to set any rumors to rest."

"You are quite correct, *Signore*, I am not Italian, but Syrian and my birth name would be unpronounceable, I assure you, so I have adopted the Italian surname of Caino. But, what is in a name anyway? A man should be known by his accomplishments and reputation, not by his name. Would you not agree?"

"Perhaps in Syria, *Signore* Caino, but in Florence a name is everything."

Cain gave the impression of grudging agreement. "So I have heard, and for that reason I have sought you out over the other prestigious financial houses in the region."

"And of what use could I be for you?" His tone was neutral, noncommittal.

"You represent the banking family of Medici. At the present time, you are small, but I intend to help you grow into the largest in Europe. I have substantial resources at my disposal with which I am prepared to invest in your House. By the time I have consummated my labors here in Florence your family will be more than just mere citizens, but have the power of monarchs."

Cain's guest slowly smiled but commented warily, "Now you have my interest, *Signore* Caino. But how do I repay such generosity?"

"There is much for you to learn, but if you allow me to guide you, both of us will benefit. I wish only to be the counselor behind the great man."

Cosimo looked around the room with its elegant chandelier and ostentatious furnishings. "A modest, self-effacing man? I should like to truly meet one with your trappings, *Signore.*"

Cain shrugged and lightly smiled. "There is nothing wrong with being comfortable and modest. Perhaps that is something that can be learned. I can assure you, I am an exceptional teacher."

"And under certain circumstances, I can assure you, *Signore*, that I am open for lessons of any sort." He took another sip from the wine glass and said, "Please continue."

Cain leaned forward slightly in his chair and remarked, "Your bank is poised to become the most influential in Europe. With my counsel to guide your direction, I plan to introduce new practices of banking heretofore unknown. I can guarantee your House will become a power for centuries, but only if things are done my way."

Medici was uncertain whether the man was all mouth and no substance and he intended to find out. He asked bluntly, "How much do you intend to invest, *Signore*, if I may be so bold as to ask?"

"Five million gold florins."

Medici tried desperately to rein back his excitement. For a few moments he watched the dance of flames in the fireplace then turning back to Cain, he quietly, but firmly responded, "Impossible. No one has that much money in all of Europe."

Cain's response was firm. "But, as I have pointed out, *Signore* Medici, I am not from Europe. I assure you I have it and more can be made available when the time and circumstance arrive."

Medici was skeptical, but probed a little deeper. "You must excuse me, *Signore*, but from where do your resources and this investment come? Mine, as you know, are from textiles."

Cain smiled and modestly replied, "Among other things, they come primarily from shipping along the Barbary Coast."

Medici was scandalized by the implication. "The Barbary Coast is a place for pirates and cutthroats."

"As I have pointed out, *Signore* Medici, there is much for you to learn and the first lesson of acquisition of wealth is this: there are no rules for acquisition unless you make them yourself. I made them in that part of the world and plan to continue doing so. I wish now to make them here, but I will need your help to facilitate that process."

Medici cleared his throat and said, "*Signore*, you should know, that there is keen competition among my fellow bankers in Florence. In truth, there are a few, specifically of the House of Albizzi, who are quite powerful and have publicly announced to either banish me or destroy my bank. My life may even be in jeopardy, especially if the growth of my bank suddenly begins to threaten them."

"*Signore*, how would you like to be the one in control and making the threats, pulling the strings of popes, monarchs and kings?"

Medici was hard pressed to hold back a smile. The man was making promises that he found hard to believe let alone seriously consider. He decided that it would do no harm to humor him. "Of course, *Signore* Caino, and if such power could be conferred to me, you would have my unwavering loyalty and support."

"As long as we are partners, you need never fear such men. He, who controls the purse strings, controls the men in power."

Medici was frankly astonished at Cain's bold talk, but if he was truly who he said he was, he would know soon enough. He pointed out, "*Signore* Caino, for now, all of this is little more than off-handed, idle talk. If you have the money, then we can move from mere speculation to a serious discussion. Have your factor meet with mine tomorrow and once your investment is safely within my bank, then we can recommence our conversation."

"A wise precaution, *Signore* Medici. My servant will see you out and please have a pleasant evening."

As Medici walked out of the room, Cain smiled slightly at the prospect of a new world to conquer and this pretentious banker would be the first step in that direction.

The assassin, Omar Alamut, dropped quietly down from the tiled roof of the estate belonging to Maso Albizzi. He was a small, lithe man in his mid-thirties who Cain had used on a number of occasions over the past decade. For over one hundred years, assassins had been trained in Cain's personal fortresses in the mountains of Persia then later Syria, and of all such men Omar had been the best in the stable. Before leaving for Italy, Cain had selected a half dozen of such professionals to accompany him.

Once in the courtyard, Omar had blended into the shadows, evading the cautious eyes of the castle guards. He had donned a black hood, shirt and trousers; his feet clad with moccasin-like boots, strong but quiet like the man himself. He lithely climbed the stone outer walls and finding an unlocked window, he quietly opened it a slight crack then slithered snake-like though the cranny and tumbled softly to the tiled floor. He followed a candle-lit hallway until he came upon a room with a large roaring fireplace. Turning into the room, he moved quietly forward then came upon two men and a woman deep in conversation and seated near the hearth. He approached them from the back, and with a practiced stealth he calmly removed a razor-sharp blade he carried under the sash tied around his waist. Now creeping in from the shadows he moved directly behind the elderly man and cupped his mouth with his left hand and jerked his head to the left, exposing his jugular.

The assassin, with a slightly amused voice, calmly gazed at the other two and said, "You will make no noise and alert no one or the *signore* dies. It is your choice, so decide now."

Maso Albizzi struggled for a moment, but quieted once it was obvious he was not going anywhere and a razor was at this throat. It did not stop him, however, from experiencing real fear for the first time in his life.

As he held the older man, the assassin cast an impassive gaze in the direction of the two younger adults. He asked, "So, what is it to be, a quiet conversation or your father bleeding all over the furniture and floor?"

Rinaldo, Maso's son, struggled to keep the bile from rising up from his gorge, but after glancing over to his sister, Lucrezia, who was in mild shock and deathly quiet, he decided to placate the intruder with calm words. "Of course sir, you have our attention, but please do not hurt our father."

"That will depend upon you." He playfully moved the blade around the old man's throat. His eyes met their ashen faces and announced. "Are you acquainted with a banker by the name of Cosimo de Medici?"

Rinaldo reluctantly nodded his head and replied, "Yes, we are."

Lucrezia, the woman, pleaded, "Please sir, put the knife away."

"Not so fast, I am not finished with my inquiries." Placing the blade in his left hand, he slowly removed his veil and smiled at the woman, appreciating her beauty and made it obvious his interests. Her hand came up slowly to her mouth to hide the fear that his feral grin had produced. Lucrezia sat deathly still.

Now all business, the intruder again had the blade at the old man's throat. He continued. "I have it on good authority that you have falsely circulated rumors in Florence that Medici is a man who cannot be trusted. These calumnies must cease. Also, Cosimo feels that his business as well as his life may be in jeopardy by your family. These efforts will, too, cease."

"Yes of, course," replied Rinaldo, "but there must be some mistake. No such lies or threats have come from our House."

The blade moved quickly down the right cheek bone of the old man, leaving blood to trickle upon his vest and jacket. The assassin replied smoothly, "Why would my employer lie? Are you insinuating that he is a liar and a man who cannot be trusted to tell the truth?"

A silent sob could be heard from behind the hand of Lucrezia who was trying hard to stifle a scream, knowing that such an outburst would result in her father's death. Rinaldo was also visibly shaken at the total lack of concern of the darkened man with the blade at his father's throat. It was then he noticed a scar running along his left cheek bone. It would be hard to believe anyone could approach him that close and live.

Rinaldo cleared his throat and tried to remove the quiver from his voice. "Very well. He is a competitor of our banking services in Florence and on occasions there have been harsh words exchanged that have led to bad feelings. I truly apologize for those indiscretions and they will not recur."

"They must never recur publicly or privately, Rinaldo. If I hear of such future slander on your part, I will return and finish the job on your father, and just for my personal amusement, I will start in on your sister. Is every-thing clearly understood?"

Rinaldo gripped the arm of his chair and nodded; so did Lucrezia.

"Sorry, I did not hear your responses?"

With fear in their eyes, both intoned a shaky *yes*. Rinaldo knew beyond a doubt that this was not a bluff. It was happening now and it would happen again in the future, only worse.

The assassin yanked on the head of Maso and whispered, "What about you old man? Do you think you can keep your lying tongue from wagging of the Medici family around Florence?"

Maso was frightened, but now relieved that a reprieve had been granted on his life. He nodded his head in the affirmative.

"I want to hear it old man." He let go of Maso and uncapped his hand from the man's mouth, but the blade stayed at his throat.

"Yes, and you have nothing more to be concerned about," he whispered.

"I am not the one you have to convince, old man. Just remember, no more rumors, calumnies or libelous threats. Otherwise, I will make a surprise visit to your daughter one night." His eyes danced at the possibility and his glance in Lucrezia's direction was not lost on the men. After a moment, he said, "You three will remain quietly in your seats for the next half hour. Do not attempt to have your guards pursue me; they will not catch me, only anger me and you already have some idea what I am capable of when I am reason-able. Do not make me show you how I am when I am irrational."

That said he turned around and melted back into the shadows to leave them to their fears and private thoughts.

After a few somber minutes of reflection, Maso found a cloth and began cleaning his neck and clothes. The blood was still dribbling and so he held it in place; he looked angrily at his son. "You young fool. I told you to cease this nonsense long after it had gotten so tiresome that even that fool the mayor was tired of hearing it."

Rinaldo was furious, but careful not to offend Maso who was still tech-nically in control of the family business and fortune. He had about decided it was time to procure his own assassin and have the old man gutted like a pig. At the very least his sister could push the old goat down the stairway and break his damn neck. "You know the games we play in Florence, Father. They were never meant to be taken so seriously, at least not to the extent we would have such a man pay us a night time visit and threaten us."

There was fire in Lucrezia's eyes as she said, "That may be so, but it ends tonight. I do not wish to have that man calling on me again, so Brother, you will keep your mouth shut and conduct business, not threaten your competition."

The three sat somberly watching the fire for the next thirty minutes then quietly got up and went to bed. It was a long, sleepless night.

The visit to the House of Albizzi was not the only visit that night by Cain's illusive assassins. Five other Houses were also on the chat list and each of them had a similar meeting with identical results. Cain watched as his six assassins filed back into his receiving room the next morning and when lined up, as was usual, he had only one command: "Report."

Their reports were short and the news encouraging. Cain ordered, "Until further notice, each of you has a full time job to follow and surveil the members of those Houses. Any deviation from their routines that would cause Cosimo or me undue agitation will be met with the harshest consequences. Does each of you understand?"

After each had affirmed, one-by-one he filed by his master, and bending low, kissed his ring, arose and left the room, all save one. Cain nodded his acceptance at their obeisance and when the last one had bowed and was about to leave, he motioned to his chief assassin. "Omar, please remain, there is one final matter that requires a more deliberate message be sent."

The assassin remained standing, awaiting further orders.

"There is a banking family here in Florence by the name of Bardi. The head of the bank is Alberto. The father has proved to be unwilling to be a part of my operation and might eventually block our expansion. His son, Bucini, seems to be sufficiently motivated and intelligent enough to realize when it is time to forsake the old guard and embrace change. His father is in the way and must be removed to allow the son free rein to move forward. I would like you to pay a visit to Alberto and expedite his early retirement.

Before he exits this world, I want to know everything about Bucini and his family. I will leave the details of his demise in your capable hands."

"It shall be done, My Lord." Omar smiled. *Who said a job had to be boring?*

It was two nights later when Alberto Bardi was laying comfortably in his bed. It had been a long day but he had finally negotiated a profitable deal with the Count of Urbino. The count was expanding his territories around the area of the Marche, just east of Florence and required a large line of credit to fortify his position. Of course, as was the custom, the House of Bardi reserved the right to dictate the particulars of land acquisitions, and fortunately, the negotiations had proven to be mutually beneficial. He felt exhilarated, but he realized that at his age he should be thinking of retiring to his villa north of Florence and leave such complicated financial deals to his son. He shook his head ruefully at the idea of allowing Bucini control of the bank; he was competent enough, and of course ambitious, but just not quite ready to assume complete control. He closed his eyes and within a few minutes he was fast asleep. His slumber was disturbed by a slight whisper.

"*Signore* Bardi, it is time to awake." A gentle push and the old man became alert then alarmed. The problem was he was unaccountably having trouble breathing. His arms were pinned and someone had his nose and mouth blocked, cutting off all oxygen. He began to buck in fright, then another whisper to his ear, "*Signore*, I will let you breathe again but only if you provide me answers to my questions."

A vigorous nod from the old man and blessed air re-entered his nose. A sigh of relief emanated from his mouth as he began to breath normally again. "What do you want?" He asked fearfully.

With a titter, the voice persisted, "What everyone wants, I suppose: to be educated and entertained. After that, what else is there? But, I digress." A pause then the man in the dark found a more comfortable position on the bed then directed, "You will begin telling me all there is to know about your son and his family. You will enlighten me with your personal observations as well as criticisms of his management of the business. You are an old man, so I realize there may a moment in which you will wander off the true path of the teacher and become dotty. When that occurs, I will regrettably reapply my hand and you will lose air, but never fear, I am a patient man and as long as you prove useful, you will be allowed to breath. Do you understand?"

"Yes."

"Then *Signore* Bardi, you may begin to teach your lesson."

Alberto Bardi began to teach. He edified and enlightened and then he began to illuminate and produce erudite observations; he waxed eloquently for nearly fifteen minutes and when the assassin Omar had gotten as much out of the old man as he thought he could, he patted the old man's cheeks in appreciation.

"Was that what you wanted?" Bardi whispered, now hoping this unwanted guest would soon depart.

"You were brilliant, *Signore*. You have a true gift of education. Rarely have I heard a better lesson taught. You may have truly missed your calling in life."

Relief spread over Bardi's brow and he asked once more, "Now you will leave me in peace?"

"Of course, *Signore* Bardi, but only until after I have been properly entertained." He placed his hand over the mouth and nose of the old man once again and this time he held it firmly in place as Bardi bucked and rolled from side to side. Finally, out of air, the old man simply deflated. Omar left his hand in place another few minutes just to make sure. Finally, after the evening entertainment was over, Omar arose and slipped out the window into the shadows of the night.

Cain had always, even from the beginning, procured the best advisers money and influence could buy. Invariably, the men within his inner circle all had certain traits in common, not the least of which was complete loyalty to Cain and his brotherhood. To retain such men was no simple challenge. They all had to be so well compensated that they would be beyond recruitment from rival groups; in other words, they would belong to Cain for life. But beyond this, Cain had always had a knack for attracting a certain type of man: brilliant, aloof and unaffiliated, and, of course, ruthlessly objective. They were beyond mundane matters of ethics, morality and religion. Indeed, they could best be described as amoral, devoid of conscience. And, of course, eventually they all wore his mark of allegiance, a cut along the left cheek bone.

Each of the six members of the Inner Council of the Clan of the Scar hailed from discrete parts of Cain's considerable empire and each, of course, directed all financial and political affairs for each region under his control. After relocating to Florence, Cain quickly deduced that the future influence of his Society would center in Europe. Looking around the seated group, he recognized that the linchpin of its growth and influence would depend upon one man capable of overseeing it all and holding it all together, including all other spheres of influence. He had decided the Frenchman, Jean Gottesmann, had the most promise and eventually had appointed him chairman of the yearly conclave in Florence. Urbane socially and brilliant in financial matters, it would be he who would ensure the tentacles of the Clan of the Scar would move slowly, but thoroughly behind the monarchs, rulers and popes to ensure the destiny of the Clan's future would be successful.

Cain despised men who mistook idle talk for intelligence and all seated around the austere meeting table were well aware of it. Not on a few occasions had each learned the hard truths of that fact. All except the Frenchman who learned without the trial and error; he seemed to understand Cain's moods and agenda intuitively. For that reason, he had become the spokesman for the group. Cain's only comment to begin the meeting was: "Report." He looked over at Gottesmann who was ready to begin.

"Mr. Cain, as you are aware, we are now poised to become the preeminent banking establishment of Europe and much of Asia. Owing to your due diligence, there are no others here in Tuscany who will stand between us and accomplishing our aims for European expansion. At this moment we have financial advisers in place not only in each of the major capitols, but also at the Vatican. Soon, neither their wars nor socio-economic progress will be possible without first coming to our bank for the needed resources to begin their efforts."

Cain nodded in agreement, but commented, "I am confident we are off to a fine start, but have you come to any conclusions as to how we might best not only expand our political interests but to ensure that there is a sustaining source of wealth to maintain our banking establishment over time."

"Mr. Cain, as you have mentioned on many occasions, war is good business, and as advisers of your inner circle, we have come to the conclusion that continuous wars, if properly controlled, could be the best means to ensure our long-term prosperity."

"How would you propose to do this?"

"Our monarchs we place in power must neither be nationalistic nor willful. They have to see that their goals and ours are inseparable. In spite of our resources, if they are not pliable and refuse to be leveraged, then we will have difficulty controlling the outcomes. I am sure that you have had issues in the past when some men, after having assumed control, have invariably decided to change the agenda and forget their allegiances. For lack of a better phrase, they forgot who put them there."

"Too many times, I fear."

"Quite right. I merely point out, that a long-term examination must be taken into account before the right man is placed in a position of power."

Cain nodded, but pointed out, "The problem, as you are all aware, is the hereditary exchange of power here in Europe. We can control this only to a point, but in the end the inherent weakness of this process cannot be ruled out. A son will not always agree to carry on the plans of his fathers."

After a pause, Gottesmann commented, "Perhaps, going forward, each should be led to believe his current regime will only be successful unless they continue to put our agenda in the fore front. The more they tamper with our plans, the less likely they will receive the support they will need to maintain their kingdom should they be invaded. This must be orally stressed at the outset of their reign. Our advisers to their thrones must be willing to remind them of this should the monarchs appear to waiver."

"Very well. Make it so." Cain had to admit, Jean was as ruthless as he. "Now, has anyone given any serious thought as to how we might acquire and have access to more hard currency over time?"

Clearing his throat, Jean moved on to the next point. "As you are aware, there are fewer and fewer places from which gold and silver can be successfully extracted. Unless we can find a new land containing the available ore and dominate it, we will eventually lose control of the market."

Cain looked around the room and asked, "What of the Western World?"

Carefully, Jean pointed out, "Mr. Cain, lately you have alluded to what you call the Western World, but as you know there have been few who have been willing to venture out that far. Our reports indicate that Marco Polo had limited his travels to the Near East into Asia and even then had followed the known coast lines. No one is certain that such a land as you describe even exists to the West."

Cain took a moment to fix his gaze upon every man around the table. Finally, he affirmed, "I assure you all that it does and we must position ourselves to be the financial bank for any kingdom willing to send expeditions in that direction."

Jean Gottesmann met his gaze and with curiosity asked, "If I might ask, what do you suppose they will find?"

"The key to our future."

CHAPTER 2

INCIDENT AT TENOCHTITLAN, 1520

*T*enochtitlan was the *capital of the Mexican civilization of the Mexica people (Aztec) founded in 1325. The state religion of the Mexica civilization awaited the fulfillment of an ancient prophecy: the wandering tribes would find the destined site for a great city whose location would be signaled by an eagle eating a snake perched atop a cactus.*

The Aztecs saw this vision on what was then a small swampy island in the middle of Lake Texcoco, a vision that is now immortalized in Mexico's coat of arms and on the Mexican flag. Not deterred by the unfavorable terrain located high in the central plateau of Mexico, they set about building their city, using the chinampa system (misnamed as "floating gardens") for agriculture and to dry and expand the island.

A thriving culture developed, and the Mexica civilization came to dominate other tribes around central Mexico. The small natural island was continually enlarged as Tenochtitlan grew to become the largest and most powerful city in Mesoamerica. Commercial routes were developed that brought goods from places as far as the Gulf of Mexico, the Pacific Ocean and perhaps even the Inca Empire.

*After a flood from Lake Texcoco, the city was rebuilt under
the rule of Ahuitzotl in a style that made it one of the grand-
est ever in Mesoamerica. Spanish conquistador Hernán Cortés
arrived in Tenochtitlan on November 8, 1519. At the time of
his arrival, with an estimated population between 200,000 and
300,000, many scholars believe Tenochtitlan to have been among
the largest cities in the world. Compared with European cities,
only Paris, Venice and Constantinople might have rivaled it in
size. It was five times the size of the London of Henry VIII. In a
letter to the Spanish king, Cortés wrote that Tenochtitlan was as
large as Seville or Córdoba. Cortes' men were in awe at the sight
of the splendid city and many wondered if they were dreaming.*

*Although some popular sources put the number as high as
350,000, the most common estimates of the population are of
around 200,000 persons. One of the few comprehensive academic surveys of Mesoamerican city and town sizes arrived at a
population of 212,500 living on 13.5 km2 (5.2 sq. mi.). It is also
said that at one time, Moctezuma II had rule over an empire
of almost five million persons in central and southern Mexico
because he had extended his rule to surrounding territories to
gain tribute and prisoners to sacrifice to the Aztec gods. (https://
en.wikipedia.org/wiki/Tenochtitlan)*

It was early morning and Moctezuma II looked out over the balcony
of his estate perched high above the city of Tenochtitlan. The sun had just
crested the volcanic peaks to the east and the rays had begun to shimmer over
the waters of Lake Texcoco. Turning to his soothsayer, he inquired, "Tototl,
tomorrow is the festival of Toxcatl. What do the stars say of the portents for
the yearly celebration?"

The medicine man, Tototl, had been a part of the royal inner court for
much of his fifty-two years. In previous times, the portents would have looked
favorable. But, that had been before the coming of the Spaniards. "Sire, the
war god must be appeased. If he becomes displeased, we will suffer greatly
and be destroyed." Since this god also represented darkness and despair, the

priest was more than a little concerned that if King Moctezuma vacillated to the Spaniards on this point, he would have a public uprising.

From his balcony view, to the north, Moctezuma could clearly see the temple built to the war god. He wondered if the Spaniard's god of war was more powerful than that of his people; he decided he did not want to put it to the test. He had a dilemma, one that had continued to resurface nearly every week that the white men from the East had come to occupy their city. Perhaps occupation was the wrong word, but they could hardly be described as guests any longer and they had made it abundantly clear that they were not going anywhere either. Cortés had even had the effrontery to name himself Governor and had begun to dictate state policy. The Aztecs, also known as the Mexica, had started to murmur that King Moctezuma was no longer in control, that he was a failed monarch. He rubbed a tired hand across an anxious face; he had not slept well lately. *They just do not understand the pressures that I am under.*

"I am aware that the war god must be appeased," he replied testily to his adviser. He began to pace the floor then finally out of frustration he grasped a ceramic urn dedicated to the god Centeotl and flung it across the chamber. It hit the wall and shattered with a resounding crash that reverberated across the room.

"Sire that was the god of maize. Not a particularly nice god to anger what with our harvests now at an all-time low."

"I am aware of the importance of Centeotl, but if we do not resolve this matter with the Spanish and soon, we will have worse problems than angering our gods. There may not be any of us left to worship them."

"All the more reason we must celebrate the festival to the god of war and appease him. Without his help, the Spanish will definitely destroy us. Sire, we have been preparing for this event all year and the people expect you to appear and make proper obeisance. They fear the Spaniards and without a show of control over our own destinies, they will depose you."

"Depose me? Are you mad? I am descended from the gods and I am the only earthly link to our sun god. Without me to intercede in their behalf, the Mexica will be destroyed and will enter an endless night!" He began to pace again then hurled out a threat. "Perhaps I should sacrifice you to the god of war. I am tired of hearing the rumors that I am a fallen leader!"

"What is your decision, Lord?"

"About what?!" he fumed.

"The festival."

"Well, obviously we must move forward on it. Tell the priests to prepare for the festival. We will celebrate the holy day on the morrow."

"And our *guests*?"

"I will talk to the deputy governor that Cortés left in command of the city and will secure his "permission" to have our celebration. Please remind me once again why they have been given so much control?"

"They represent the god Quetzalcoatl and he cannot be defeated in war. We must obey, but at the same time, we cannot abandon our rituals. Perhaps the Spaniards will grow tired of living here and move on to the south?"

"Perhaps you and the priests could make that a priority request tomorrow at the festival," he shot back.

"Of course, Sire. Shall I send for the deputy governor?"

Moctezuma threw up his hands in frustration and replied, "Of course, what else can be done?"

La Malinche, known among the Spaniards as Marina, walked into the audience room with Father Gerónimo de Aguilar. For the moment, they were an interpreter team the Spanish needed to communicate with Moctezuma. Aguilar spoke Spanish and Mayan and she spoke Mayan and *Nahuatl*, the lingua franca of the Aztec. It was a little awkward, of course, but the alternative could have been much worse. They were followed closely into the room by a Spanish detail led by Deputy Governor Pedro de Alvarado.

What few Spaniards understood was Marina's everlasting distrust and hatred of the Aztecs. She especially despised Moctezuma in particular, who she saw as a weak leader at best and completely undeserving of the obeisance that her adopted people, the Tlaxcaltecans, had been forced to endure. From an historian's perspective, it was suspected that she had more to do with his downfall than had any other person. At least those apologists for the Mayan people would like to think so, and of course, being in the role of interpreter for the Spanish did place her in a unique position of influence. Her voiced concerns may have been responsible for the drastic steps that precipitated the tragic events on the day of the Aztec celebration.

Moctezuma, unfortunately, knew almost nothing of her background except she was a peasant woman from a conquered people. They were forced to work together, but it was obvious Moctezuma found the experience almost as distasteful as she did. Steeling himself for the compulsory greeting, he attempted a short, but near sincere welcome. "Ah, La Malinche. How are you today my dear?"

She loathed the man and so skipped the amenities and got to the point. "We were summoned. What do you want?"

Moctezuma flinched at the obvious rebuff and bit back a scathing remark regarding her rude behavior. With more effort than he thought possible, he held his temper. After greeting them, he resumed his place upon his throne. He needed a show of strength and there was no better way to remind them who was in control than to sit resplendently upon an outward show of his office and power. "I have a favor to ask of the Deputy Governor, our esteemed guest. Our annual celebration of the festival of Toxcatl is upon us and we respectfully ask permission to pay obeisance to our god."

The Spanish Commander of the garrison, Deputy Governor Alvarado, began a conversation with Moctezuma through the interpreters. "When is the celebration planned?"

"Tomorrow morning. The Deputy Governor is, of course, invited to attend and observe our prayers."

"What does this ritual consist of?"

"Dancing, singing, chanting and such."

"Who will be in attendance?"

"A few of our priests and, of course, the people of the city."

"Sounds like a perfect excuse for a riot." It was one of the officers from the detail, Lieutenant Manuel Cisneros who had interjected a tone of caution. "If we allow this and we lose control then we will be unable to contain it."

The Deputy Governor turned to Cisneros and asked, "Are you saying we should deny them permission?"

"They are heathen idol-worshippers. My advice is to tell them no."

There was still so little he understood about these people. He was not yet convinced to decline their request. "What do you think Marina?"

She inwardly smiled at the dilemma. Immediately she saw it as her chance to take her revenge upon Moctezuma for the destruction of her family members by Aztec warriors who had carried them off to be sacrifices for their gods. "I would advise to allow them to have their festival, but make sure they are well guarded. Speaking from experience, they do tend to become very wound up after they drink peyote tea and if that should occur, they will quickly become unmanageable. But, you can always quell any disturbance." She smiled smugly, "After all, Governor, you have superior weaponry, do you not? They would be no match for you if they got out of control."

Deputy Governor Alvarado favored caution, but thinking it over he decided to allow them the festival. He turned back to Cisneros and directed, "Have your men arrive in full armor, well-armed, but keep them restrained. The last thing Cortés told me was to avoid any decision that could not be recalled." What he did not mention to them was Cortés' follow-up comment: *"The populace is willing to work with us as long as we continue the charade of benign governance. We will win their hearts and eventually they will end up under our fists."*

Looking at Marina, Alvarado nodded his head in agreement then he looked back at Moctezuma and said through his interpreters, "Very well, you may have your festival, but no weapons, no blood sacrifices and no people killed. You must maintain control or we will. Do you agree?"

Marina turned to Moctezuma and provided him with a slightly different interpretation. "Sire, they say your people can celebrate the festival and the soldiers will observe. Does that meet with your approval?"

"Of course, Malinche and as always it has been a pleasure to talk with our honored guests."

Moctezuma's polite façade did not fool Marina. She turned to the Spaniards and commented, "We should go now and allow the emperor and his priests enough time to prepare for the festival." What she really wanted was time to weave an intricate plot to ensnare not only Moctezuma but the Spaniards as well.

After they had gone, the soothsayer turned to Moctezuma and asked, "Do you trust her?"

"No, not for a moment and if I could separate her from the Spaniards for five minutes, I would cut her throat and toss her off the temple myself."

"Accidents could be arranged, Sire."

"Not yet. Let us wait until during the festival. Who knows but a stray arrow might find its way into her conniving face."

Deputy Governor Alvarado was deep in conversation with Lieutenant Cisneros. Marina and Father Aguilar were also present to provide much needed advice on what could be really expected from the celebration.

"Governor, we have the manpower to quell a small disturbance if the savages misbehave and incite a public protest, but if their celebration turns into an excuse to throw us out of the city, it will be a blood bath. Their sheer numbers would eventually overrun us no matter how well we come armed. We should prepare for the worst with a maximum show of strength."

"By that you mean use our weapons?"

"Is there any other way? If it means them or us, I would prefer that we be the ones to walk away to fight another day."

Alvarado woefully nodded his head in acceptance of their situation. He was already regretting his decision. Looking toward the woman he said, "Marina, we have been here only a short while and have not seen a high festival of this nature before. Is it likely to turn ugly?"

"Anything is possible with these people. However, though they have a warrior mentality, it is unlikely the celebration will turn riotous. They will be too busy paying obeisance to their gods." What she failed to tell the Spaniards · was that the people would be paying homage to their god of war and darkness and it was highly probable it would turn confrontational. If she had notified them of this, it is doubtful that Alvarado would have permitted the festival in the first place. And that would have disrupted her plan. She continued to explain, "The priests will enter the temple, all the while dancing to the beat of drums. They will exit with their sacred relics and lay them before the altars and begin chanting. Then there will be more dancing and swaying."

"How long will it last?"

"I have never witnessed a celebration ceremony that lasted more than an hour." More half-truths; she was becoming very skillful at misleading the Spaniards.

It was a warm day, but because the city was located at a high altitude in the mountains, it seldom grew hot. Usually an afternoon shower cooled down whatever chance the heat had of gaining an advantage. Looking up at the position of the sun, Commander Alvarado calculated that it had been well over two hours since the celebration had begun. He glanced toward the distant peaks and noted a cloud moving in on their position from the west. He and his men were wearing full armor, complete with shields and breastplates and it was becoming uncomfortable. He commented to no one in particular, "Thank God, perhaps the shower will cool things down a bit."

Lieutenant Cisneros, overhearing the remark, wiped the sweat from his brow, and concurred with Alvarado. "Yes, a little rain would feel good about now, but the armor was a prudent precaution. If anything happens we will be heavily outnumbered. I can endure a little discomfort if it means we maintain the military advantage."

A large crowd had turned out for the celebration. It had been largely dancing, and as had been predicted, there was much chanting by the priests. Then drums began to beat and after several minutes the Aztec priests disappeared into the temple then reappeared and they also joined in with the dancing and swaying to the music. Their headdresses were all unique, each wearing the colors and symbols of the major gods of the Aztec religion. The celebration occurred directly in front of the Great Temple, and just when it seemed that the festival had begun to wind down, the priests raced into the temple and emerged with gold relics. They moved through the crowd toward the soldiers and began to offer them as gifts with outstretched arms, heads bowed.

Alvarado felt a needle of panic. "Marina, what is happening?" he asked.

A small cynical smile played upon her face. "They are bestowing treasure upon you and the soldiers and asking you to take the treasures and leave."

The greed of the soldiers was apparent. Never in their experience had they ever seen such an overwhelming quantity of gold and silver on display. Ignoring the orders of their officers, a few dropped their weapons to reach out and take ownership of the offered treasure. In an effort to be the first to reach the gold that was still being brought out by the armload, a few even began scuffling and pushing amongst themselves. Others, having seen their comrades enjoying the spectacle and feel of the treasure, also began to discard their weapons of war in an effort to manage the fortune in gold being placed at their fingertips. Most of these men were not soldiers, but mercenaries. They had come to the New World with Cortés for the gold, not for the Crown and now that they had found it, they were not giving it up. After a few minutes, it was clear that all order had disappeared among the Spaniards.

It was at that moment Marina took the opportunity to scream, "Captain, group your men. We are under attack!"

The history of the Mexicas' records the following incident:

Seeing the Spaniards pull their swords and begin to take a defensive position, the chief priests sounded an alert. Immediately, Aztec warriors began to emerge from the temple armed with knives and spears. As one they began to scream their intention to attack and remove the soldiers from their temple site. One of the warriors ran up and impaled the nearest soldier to the side of the temple meanwhile others launched their javelins into the remainder. If not for their armor, many Spaniards would have gone down in the first assault.

Alvarado screamed, "Form ranks and attack!" Of course, by now all military order had ceased to exist; it was everyone for himself. Lieutenant Cisneros took a rear guard and began to close all the exits to the temple site and when all the gates had been closed, nearly a thousand civilians had been contained. Once they had closed off the line of retreat, the Spaniards turned on the people now trapped within the temple grounds and then the slaughter began. They slowly entered the Sacred Patio carrying swords and metal shields. Immediately, they surrounded those priests who still danced, then rushed to the large raised dais where the drummers were still playing and there they attacked the men and began cutting off their arms. Then one native was attacked and his head was slashed off with such a force that it flew off, slamming into the oncoming ranks of the angry warriors.

At that moment, the Spaniards ran amok and attacked all the people, men, women and children, warriors or not, stabbing them, spearing them, wounding them with their swords. They struck some from behind, who fell instantly to the ground with their entrails hanging out of their bodies. The soldiers, now near berserk with a killing frenzy, began to chase the people about the forecourt of the temple, cutting off the heads of some and stomping the heads of others into pieces. While some soldiers rested on their swords regathering their strength, others tracked down the temple priests and bludgeoned them in the shoulders then began tearing the arms from their bodies. They struck some in the thighs and some in the calves. They slashed others in the abdomen and their entrails fell to the earth, tripping many as they attempted to flee the massacre. A few civilians attempted to run to the barricaded gates, but it was in vain; the soldiers caught up with them and spilled their bowels as they ran. Several women, in their haste to avoid the swinging arcs of the swords, seemed to entangle their feet with their own entrails. Though eager to flee, they found nowhere to go.

Alvarado, also caught up in the killing frenzy, saw some trying to escape over fences, but he ordered several soldiers to murder them at the gates as they ran. A few Aztecs managed to climb the walls, but they could not save themselves as each that attempted it was immediately hacked down by the ever swinging blades. Other citizens entered the communal house, where they were safe for a while and others even found temporary sanctuary among the dead victims and pretended to be dead. But if they stood up again, the Spaniards would see them and the murder would continue.

The Spaniards searched everywhere, even searching the communal houses to kill those who were hiding. Finally, the spectacle was winding down but it had been so gruesome, so beyond imagination, in an effort to relieve the tension, many soldiers could do nothing more than to lean on their swords and laugh.

The blood of the warriors ran like water as they fled, forming pools that widened even as the smell of blood and entrails fouled the air. When the people outside the Sacred Patio learned of the massacre, they began to shout, "Captains, Mexicas, come here quickly! Come here with all arms, spears, and shields! Our captains have been murdered! Our warriors have been slain! Oh, Mexica captains, our warriors have been annihilated!"

Then a roar from the vicinity around the Great Temple could be heard. The natives screamed and wailed as they beat their palms against their lips. As if planned in advance, quickly the Aztec captains assembled and carried their spears and shields. A coordinated offensive attack began and then the Spaniards finally knew they were in a fight to the death. The Mexicas attacked the Spaniards with arrows and even javelins, including small yellow cane javelins used for hunting birds. They furiously hurled their javelins at the soldiers, but to no avail. They had armor and shields and all around them lay a thick layer of yellow canes spread out in front of them at their feet. In spite of the furious Aztec counter-attack, the Spanish soldiers prevailed. When it was over, the Spanish gathered all the gold and treasure that lay about the forecourt of the temple, reformed their columns then quietly left the scene of death behind them. Their day done, they marched victoriously back to the military garrison in the middle of the city. (https://en.wikipedia.org/wiki/Massacre_in_the_Great_Temple)

Along the path the Spaniards marched, the people parted. Their Mexica eyes were glassy and some burned with anger, but within all there was a debilitating, numbing fear that had left them helpless with an impotent dread they had never before known. Until this debacle, their warriors had been invincible in the field. To all, it was inconceivable that they could have ever experienced defeat. The Aztecs had been the bane and scourge upon the land for so long that it was impossible to envision a greater force existed than did they. That realization and knowledge would change their lives forever.

CHAPTER 3

NIGHT OF SORROWS, 1520

The massacre at the Grand Temple two weeks earlier had not galvanized Moctezuma II into decisive action; in fact, just the opposite had occurred. Today, he paced distractedly about the throne room and when he was not so inclined, he simply sat moodily upon his throne, an all too common occurrence while he agonized over a solution to his current dilemma. He had spent most of the time alone, seldom listening to his advisers who always counselled the same thing: surround the Spaniards at their garrison and burn them out. His dithering had wasted so much time, that Cortés had since arrived back into the city, fresh with new recruits from the battle he had won against a Spanish force sent by his commander in Cuba to terminate his command. Unknown to Cortés, however, Moctezuma was privy to that information and was contemplating a plan of action which would involve extorting the Spanish leader. He could see no other way out of the problem. He wanted them to leave, but had no idea how to extricate them form his city without another bloody confrontation.

His Chief Adviser, Tototl, arrived into his audience room and informed him, "Sire, the Spanish commander Cortés is here and wishes to have a word with you.

This news had greatly surprised the leader. "Why would he come here and willingly put his head into my hands? Surely, after the massacre he must know that I hold him solely responsible for the excessive behavior of his soldiers."

"I would have no way of knowing, Sire. Perhaps he came to work out a compromise or an accommodation."

"Do you think so?" There was hope in his voice. Now bolstered by the thought that he could somehow manipulate Cortés to his advantage for a change, he willing allowed them leave to enter and with a majestic sweep of his hands, hc said, "Send them in." Then his hope turned to ashes. Angrily, he asked, "Oh, I suppose that Mayan tramp Marina is with him?"

"Yes, Excellency, as always."

"I wish there was a way to talk directly to the man. The woman has to be spewing venom in his ear and weaving a web of deceit. That is the only explanation for what happened at the temple site. It was a misunderstanding that got out of control and she was behind it. I am sure of it."

The adviser gazed upon his king with thinly veiled contempt. He felt Moctezuma was either too stupid or too self-consumed to see what was happening. He prayed to the gods another would step forward to assume the reins of control, because King Moctezuma had clearly lost them. His response, though humble, lacked any of its previous depth. "Of course, Sire, I will send them right in."

The self-proclaimed Governor General of New Spain, Hernan Cortés, strode in with a few officers, including his ever-present translators. Presently, he stood before the monarch and bowed slightly then addressing him directly said, "Moctezuma, I send you greetings from my king in Cuba who looks forward to a continued peace and mutual cooperation between our people."

"Captain, thank you for your visit. I, too, look forward to a continued alliance of friendship between us. Nevertheless, as you are aware, the massacre at the temple a few weeks ago has left my people doubtful as to whether a long term relationship can be re-forged. I would like to know what you are doing about the incident. My priests tell me your soldiers made off with gold and our sacred relics. You may keep the gold, but the artifacts must be returned. Moreover, I demand that your soldiers be punished publicly for their butchery of my people."

A serene smile of false-friendship played over Marina's lips as she made the translation. *I will have you on your knees, you butcher,* and she silently cursed the man. She turned to Cortés and translated, "He says it will be impossible to re-establish peace until the murderers of his people are publicly executed. Moreover, he considers the theft of the gold and sacred relics to be of religious value and you will return them all."

"And if we do not agree?"

Moctezuma replied, "Captain, my spies tell me that your reunion with your fellow Spanish soldiers to the east was not a friendly one. In truth, it would appear that a battle ensued, or a mutiny, if you will. You clearly won the battle, which is evidenced by the fact that you stand before me now, but I think it is only a matter of time before your leader in Cuba sends another expedition, a larger one next time, and you will be executed. You will do as I suggest or I will offer you up to the next army that your king sends to capture you."

Marina felt it to her benefit to translate Moctezuma's reply accurately.

"And suppose I refuse?"

Moctezuma was in a dilemma. He desperately wanted peace with this man. The Spanish soldiers were far too powerful and he realized now that to accept them as guests into his city had been a colossal error of judgment, but if he did not make a show of force and stand up to them now, the mood of his people indicated they would probably revolt. If he offered resistance to the Spanish rule, either Cortés or the next man they send would probably raze his city to the ground. At length, he made what he felt was the only rational decision now available to him. Cortés had left him little choice in the matter. He concluded that he must capture Cortés now then offer him as a hostage to the next Spanish army. He could always broker a peace for his people with the next commander.

His message to Cortés was final. "You will do as I say or you will be bound and detained in my castle."

His ultimatum was translated, but Marina added, "Captain, the Mexica will no longer tolerate our presence in their city. Moctezuma is a fallen king and will soon be deposed or killed outright. Once they have finished with him, we will be next. I suggest you make whatever use you have of him now because his days are numbered."

"What do you suggest?"

"Perhaps he could be used as a hostage to delay their intentions."

Nodding, Cortés turned to his officers and quietly commanded, "Seize him. He will remain our hostage until we are safely out of the city."

Lieutenant Cisneros quickly moved forward and grabbed the monarch by the forearm and threw him from the throne and had him bound. Meanwhile, his soldiers spread out and moved through the palace killing every guard and servant they encountered. Though most of the advisers were found and killed, a few, including Tototl, managed to escape to raise a cry of panic throughout the city. When Moctezuma was turned over, now bound and on his knees, the first face he saw was that of Marina, a smug smile of victory and contempt etched across her face.

Night was beginning to fall. The last of the sun's rays bounced off the gold inlay of the Grand Temple. It would have been beautiful, thought Moctezuma, but all was now doomed. He was not a visionary man, but at this moment he experienced an epiphany of the future: his kingdom was gone and his people dying a dreadful, burning death from a plague brought to them by the bearded white men from the east.

A Spanish priest would later comment in 1521:

As the Indians did not know the remedy of the disease, they died in heaps, like bedbugs. In many places it happened that everyone in a house died and, as it was impossible to bury the great number of dead, they pulled down the houses over them so that their homes become their tombs. On Cortés's return, he found the Aztec army's chain of command in ruins. The soldiers who still lived were weak from the disease. Cortés then easily defeated the Aztecs and entered Tenochtitlan. The Spaniards said that they could not walk through the streets without stepping on the bodies of smallpox victims.

After having seen his king roughly thrown to the floor by the Spanish soldier, Tototl had immediately realized that the woman had somehow orchestrated these events. He wasted no time in clearing out of the throne room just ahead of the next Spanish killing spree that swept throughout the castle. Upon reaching the street, he immediately began to spread the news among the people, and within the hour from all parts of Tenochtitlan, an angry throng of Mexica assembled in front of the palace walls and demanded to see their king.

Moctezuma was thrust outside on the balcony of his throne room, his hands untied. He now knew that all was lost whether he allowed the soldiers safe passage from his city or not. Below him was assembled a multitude of his people, angry and shouting. Behind him was a Spanish sword at his back. *Surely, my people will see that there was no alternative but to surrender to their demands. We must obey or die.* "What would you have me tell them," he intoned quietly then glancing over his shoulder to the woman translator.

From behind him came the purring, taunting voice of Marina. "Tell them the truth, Oh Exalted One. Inform them that the Spaniards are stronger than your warriors and their one god is more powerful than all your gods together. Do it!" The tip of the sword grazed his spine, drawing blood that trickled down his back. There was little doubt that it would be used unless he cooperated.

From his balcony overlooking the square below, he looked out over the masses of his once-adoring people; they who would loudly acclaim him a god divinely descended from gods. And now, he was reduced to this public spectacle. There was little left for him to do except obey and try to convince his people of the futility of fighting them. "My people, you have all seen what these bearded white men from the east are capable of doing. Their god is mightier than any of our own. It was foretold many years ago they would arrive and they have and now we in our time must obey them or be destroyed."

The crowd began to stir in agitated anger. Many shouted, "They are just men and can be killed! Away with them and take back our city and remove our shame!"

Moctezuma sadly shook his head in denial. Now raising his voice, he loudly proclaimed, "I say no. We must make peace with them or lose our kingdom. If we kill Cortés and those in the garrison, more will follow and there will never be an end to our suffering. I beseech you to listen to reason!"

Suddenly from below, several within the aggravated crowd picked up stones and began flinging them in his direction. Moctezuma could not retreat from the balcony, because to do so, the officers of Cortés were waiting to finish him off. He could only raise his arm to protect his face. From within their midst stood a mighty warrior, irate with the man he had always revered, but now he saw as a coward and so unfit to rule. Cuauhtémoc, nephew to the King, raised his bow and let loose and arrow directly at the chest of his king, piercing his heart and Moctezuma, the last of the great Aztec emperors, was no more.

Cortés and his contingent had found the family of Moctezuma cowering in the back corner of the castle that overlooked the east patio. Realizing they were likely to be attacked by the furious mob as they made their retreat back to the garrison, the Spaniards trussed up each member and used them as human shields. As they left the castle grounds and made their way carefully back to their quarters, the hostages were all between them and the massacre to come. Whatever tenuous hold Cortes had held over the Aztecs was over. There was now only one solution: escape the city or die trying.

On the night of July 1, 1520, the army of Cortés left the military compound and headed east toward the Tlacopan causeway. Scouts had discovered the road was unguarded, and though realizing it could be a trap, the Spaniards nonetheless made their way out of the garrison. Under the cover of a rainstorm, the Spaniards proceeded, seemingly unnoticed, winding their way through the still sleeping city. Before reaching the causeway, however, they were detected by Aztec soldiers known as the Eagle Warriors, who sounded the alarm. Immediately, all warriors under Cuauhtémoc took to the streets to pre-arranged locations and lay in wait for the retreating Spaniards.

Cortés, along with his interpreters, was at the forefront of his army of nearly one thousand Spaniards as well as an equal number of native allies. All, save their allies, were heavily armed with shields, breastplates and armor and they should have had a clear advantage in the field, assuming they had been familiar with the terrain and if the weather had cooperated, but unfortunately they had neither. As the men rounded a bend in the road, a long row of houses stood on both sides, deserted and waiting. Cortés called his officers forward to decide upon a plan of action. Until now, it had been simple: leave the garrison and head eastward over the causeway. The fact that they had not yet met any resistance did not alleviate his anxiety, but had only worsened it.

Rain fell heavily down upon the breastplate of Captain Cortés. His usual confident nature had been severely dampened at the prospect of what might lay ahead. All his best intentions of a peaceful takeover of the Aztecs had come to naught and now he was left with this desperate retreat to safer territory. He turned wearily to his first lieutenant and asked, "Lieutenant Cisneros, what is your assessment of our situation? You know the city far better than do any of us."

Cisneros, a brave man, but not keen on dying decided that the time had come for a swifter retreat than they had planned. "Sir, this boulevard is over a mile long to the causeway. Once we reach that objective, we still have another mile before we obtain the other side. If we are to be attacked, it will be now. I suggest we double-time our pace and prepare for an ambush."

"Are you saying we are about to be attacked?"

"Yes, it will be now or never. If we are slowed or halted, they can bottle us up and pick us off at their leisure from all sides; there will be no line of retreat. And because of the houses lining the street, we will not be able to gather as a group and offer any tactical resistance."

"You do not think they will meet us head-on?"

"No sir. They know nothing of our tactics and so far as I am aware, they have none. They will harry us every step of the way. Once we begin, we should stop for nothing, not even to pick up or help our wounded comrades, but keep running. We must break through; stopping is suicide."

Cortés examined his options and came to a decision, but owing to the seriousness of the situation, he turned to the woman and asked, "Marina, what are your thoughts?"

She looked down the long avenue; she knew it well. "Your officer is correct. It will be now. Stop for nothing and no one."

"Lieutenant, take my interpreters back to the middle of the ranks and assign your best men as personal guards to surround them. Cisneros, I expect both to be alive when we arrive at the other side of the causeway. You are solely responsible." He turned to his Sub-commander Alvarado and said,

"Pass the word to all platoon leaders that we are to move up on my command, double-time paced."

"It will be done, Sir."

Five minutes later, Cortés raised his sword and motioned all men to pick up the pace down the long boulevard leading out of the city of Tenochtitlan. The Aztec warriors must have been anticipating the tactic, because as soon as the Spaniards began moving swiftly forward, a volley of arrows and javelins began hitting the men from all sides from doorways, rooftops and nearby buildings. Because of the mud in the street, the Spaniards were not making good time and the front squad had only made the problem worse by churning up the mud with their boots. Those in the rear were met by a street of muddy, viscous goo as well as fallen men, bleeding out and halting their headlong retreat in many places. While some were held fast by the tacky, clinging mud, others slipped and fell, and when either occurred they were immediately rushed from the shadows by warriors carrying knives and clubs. The Spaniard's native allies, on the outer ranks and lacking armor, were being butchered as cattle. The soldiers were able to inflict grievous wounds on the enemy, but it was clear they were receiving the worst of the ordeal. Finally, the warriors discovered that by striking exclusively from ambush, they could avoid any direct confrontation, though of course, that did not deter those warriors who lived for the bloodletting. The arrows from the shadows continued as the Spanish army under Cortés struggled slowly down the road to the causeway.

If anything, the causeway was even more treacherous. As Cortés and the few remaining native allies reached the footbridge the fighting became savage. Because of the stone and shell of the road, their footing had improved, but they were hopelessly outnumbered and exposed with water on both sides of their escape. Suddenly, hundreds of canoes appeared from the dark alongside them and began to harry them as they stumbled and fell from the relentless onslaught of the arrows. For the soldiers, this was a new experience; there was no defense and no sure line of retreat. They died in the mud, unable to defend themselves. Then, halfway across the causeway, the rain began to pour down upon them in buckets. Now weighed down by gold and equipment, some of the soldiers lost their footing, fell into the lake, and drowned.

Cortés gave a command to have the cavalry brought up to the front ranks to offer his leading contingent the best chance of survival. Many Spanish soldiers were unprepared for the approaching horses of their comrades and were either trampled over or thrown off the causeway. Moreover, he directed that his interpreters be brought forward, and now with many of his group severely wounded or dying, the Spanish army desperately pressed ahead. Finally, though his point group had been severely decimated by the onslaught of the Aztec attack, he ultimately reached the mainland at the village of Tacuba on the other side of the causeway. The remainder of the expedition was left to fend for itself in the treacherous crossing.

Little by little, that which remained of the great Spanish Expeditionary Army trickled into the village. Seeing the wounded survivors straggle into Tacuba, Cortés and his horsemen turned back to the causeway and there they encountered Pedro de Alvarado. He found his deputy commander unhorsed and badly wounded and in the company of a handful of Spaniards and Tlaxcaltecas, their native allies. Cortés signaled Alvarado to join him in a nearby hut.

The rain had abated, leaving the air clear and cool. Cortés was happy to be alive, but concerned for his men. He asked his sub commander, "Pedro, do you have a sense of the condition of the army?"

His sub commander, bedraggled and bloody, blinked in disbelief then slightly shook his head and whispered, "It is gone, Sir."

"Gone; how can that be?" Cortés was incredulous. Now bewildered at the state of affairs, he peered out into the night and said to no one in particular, "We were nearly a thousand strong." Then another thought caught his mind. "What of the gold and treasures?"

"As you had requested, mostly intact, excluding that which the soldiers took with them to the bottom of the lake. Their armor was too heavy and they sunk like cannonballs. All of the native metallic records and historical parchments survived, though I can't see why we even bothered with those."

Cortés was quick to point out, "We might be able to use them as barter for future concessions. The Aztecs take stock in keeping such things; they might become useful later on." The Captain seemed to pause, now exhausted by his trial. "Where are Lieutenant Cisneros and the rear guard? Surely he survived."

Alvarado hesitated then bowing his head, he crossed himself. He shed tears as he related, "Cisneros and his rear guards were cut off from the main group then surrounded. He and most of his men were captured alive."

"Then he is not dead?"

Marina, who was nearby and hearing the Mayan translation, replied, "Sir, the Mexica Aztecs will take him and his men back to the Grand Temple and offer them up as sacrifices to their gods. They will die badly."

Cortés looked around desolately. With tears in his eyes, he realized the extent of the debacle. He screamed, "This is not the end! I swear it before God!"

Although they were all wounded and exhausted, only the strongest and most skilled of the men, including Cortés and Alvarado, had managed to fight their way out of Tenochtitlan. All of the artillery had been lost, as had most of the horses. The sources are not in agreement as to the total number of casualties suffered by the expedition, but Cortés himself maintained that 154 Spaniards were lost along with over 2,000 native allies. Thoan Cano, another eyewitness to the event, said that 1170 Spaniards died, but this number probably exceeds the total number of Spaniards who took part in the expedition. Francisco Lopez de Gómara, who was not himself an eyewitness, estimated that 450 Spaniards and 4,000 native allies died. Some records state the Spaniards suffered 860 soldiers killed, which included those from the later Battle of Otumba.

But, whatever the numbers involved were, the casualties were high; it was a slaughter. The native allies, the Tlaxcaltecas, lost a thousand. The noncombatants attached to the expedition suffered terribly, 72 casualties, including five Spanish women. The few women who survived included La Malinche the interpreter, Doña Luisa, and María Estrada. The event was later known as La

Noche Triste ("The Night of Sorrows") on account of the sorrow that Cortés and his surviving followers felt and expressed at the loss of life and treasure incurred in the escape from Tenochtitlan.

Further battles awaited the Spaniards and their allies as they fought their way around the north end of Lake Zumpango. Two weeks later, at the Battle of Otumba, not far from Teotihuacan, they turned to fight the pursuing Aztec warriors, and because he slew the Aztec commander, Cortés claimed a decisive victory. Nevertheless, despite the questionable victory, the Spaniards were forced to flee Otumba and they took refuge in Tlaxcala, to the east of Tenochtitlan. There Cortés signed a treaty with the Tlaxcaltecas that if they would help the Spaniards conquer the Mexica, their greatest enemy, eventually he would offer to them the control over the Aztec city. It was there in Tlaxcala that Cortés plotted the siege of Tenochtitlan and the eventual destruction of the Aztec Empire.

Moctezuma, following his death, was then succeeded by his brother Cuitláhuac, who died shortly thereafter during a small-pox epidemic. He was succeeded by his adolescent nephew, Cuauhtémoc who surrendered to Hernán Cortés along with the surviving pipiltin (nobles) in 1521. Cuauhtémoc continued to hold his position under the Spanish, keeping the title of tlatoani, but he was no longer the sovereign ruler. In 1525, now fearing that Cuauhtémoc might lead an insurrection in his absence, Cortés took him and several other indigenous nobles on his expedition to Honduras. When the expedition was stopped in the Mayan capital of Acalan, Cortés had Cuauhtémoc executed for allegedly conspiring to kill him and the other Spaniards. Cuauhtemoc is today honored as the embodiment of indigenist nationalism in Mexico, being the only Aztec emperor who survived the conquest by the Spanish Empire and its native allies. (https://en.wikipedia.org/wiki/La_Noche_Triste)

CHAPTER 4

DISCOVERED RECORDS, 1541

D on Caino, as Cain was calling himself among the Italians of Florence, had been speaking to the unofficial Ambassador from the Court of Carlos I of Spain, Julio Diaz de Castillo. As he glared at the hapless official, his loud, acerbic comments to the man reflected his displeasure. He shouted, "I don't care what Cortés wants, he will do as he is told or he will be replaced."

Castillo struggled to remain calm. Don Caino was His Majesty's greatest patron and the ambassador had been instructed to tread carefully when dealing with him. He pleaded, "But Don Caino, you must realize that Cortés has many admirers at home and devoted followers in New Spain. Many of the court surrounding King Carlos agree that the Governor should be honored and receive the title of Viceroy of that land."

"Viceroy? I think not. It would be fine if he were to receive a lesser title. He is, after all, entitled to something after his years of service to us. But, his refusal to turn over to me the records he took from those Aztec savages in New Spain will not be forgiven or forgotten. He is a rogue out of control and I want him heeled like a dog."

"But, surely you could petition the Pope to return the records to you?"

"Surely you are joking! First of all, I don't petition the Pope, he petitions me. Second of all, I suspect those records were squirreled away in some dingy corner of the Vatican and not even he would know where to look."

"Then is not the problem solved?"

"Don't be so dim-witted! The problem is not solved until I say it is. If those records appear unexpectedly someday, I do not wish to hear about what they contain from some scullery maid who had been gossiping in the local market."

The Florentine Ambassador to the court of Spain, Bernardo Antonio de' Medici, waited nervously in an ante room outside the door of the senior partner and major shareholder of the family bank. Castillo's cringing voice could be heard clearly through the closed door and the discussion was alarming.

"Don Caino, please accept my apologies on behalf of my King. Of course his highness will turn over to you whatever you feel you are entitled to."

Cain pounded his fist on the desk and shouted, "Castillo, I don't want apologies, I want what is mine. I want my money paid back, along with my *quinto* of the gold recovered from those savages. Also, I want assurances."

This was new. Castillo gulped air, trying to calm himself. "Assurances, Don Caino?"

"Yes, damn you, assurances that from this point forward you turn over to me whatever records are found in New Spain." He waived the ambassador over to a table on which sat parchments as well as metallic plates. "Do you see those artifacts?" He shouted.

"Yes, Don Caino, of course."

"I instructed King Carlos that his hair-brained explorer Cortés was to bring me back any artifacts he might find in the New World. Do you know where I found those?" he indicated with a wave of his hand the items on the table.

"I am sorry, I do not."

"On my last visit to your miserable country, I saw them decorating the dining hall of the Duke of Aliaga. He was kind enough to sell them to me, especially after I threatened to have him thrown from a turret of his own castle. Do you know where he got them?"

The ambassador withered under Cain's glare and whispered, "No, I do not."

"He maintained that Hernán Cortés sold them to him directly and had assured him that the great explorer could provide more for the asking. I told

Carlos, your king, I wanted those records and now I hear they are being sold in the town market to the highest bidder. What does Carlos intend to do about this?"

"Yes, of course Don Caino, you may be assured this matter will be addressed and this behavior will not recur." He cleared his throat and delicately petitioned, "The King wishes another advance for the next expedition and hopes you would be willing to extend the funding."

Cain fumed, but realized that cutting off the Spaniards would not help him close in on his goal. If he were to control the purse strings of Europe, he would need hard currency and without it the rulers would go elsewhere for favors. "Very well, but if I hear that someone else has hauled off any more records for their personal amusement or if they end up as a decoration in some duke's dining hall, I will cut your king off from any more advances for future expeditions. Then he can see how far his next expedition can sail to the Americas in row boats." He glared at the ambassador and stated, "Before you leave for Spain tomorrow, come back around and pick up my list of demands to Carlos. My secretary will have them ready for you. Now, get out."

Castillo reached for his cap then turned to go, always happy and relieved to be clear of Don Caino's presence. On his way out the door, he noticed Lorenzo de Medici was waiting in the foyer and did not envy the man's position. No doubt the result of his patron's angry outbursts, he appeared deeply concerned. Perhaps he should be. They had met briefly a few years earlier, but he thought it best not to make any comment to the man. He wanted to avoid the appearance of loitering in Don Caino's foyer, so he sidled by Medici as quickly as possible.

Lorenzo de Medici reflected that this would be his first meeting with the powerful Don Caino; he normally dealt only with the Don's advisers. He cautiously walked into the room now vacated by the ambassador from the court of King Carlos I of Spain. He looked over to the desk and expected to find his patron, but instead he noted he was deep in study, examining an ancient metallic artifact on a table against the far wall.

Looking up, Cain smiled and beckoned Medici to enter the room. "I am truly sorry, Lorenzo, for the noise created by the argument, but the Spaniards are difficult to work with." Cain looked him over and commented, "I was told that I could work with you."

"Of course. I quite understand, Don Caino."

Cain resumed his perusal of the items before him. After a moment, he looked up and directed, "Lorenzo, please join me at the table. There is something I want to show you."

Medici dutifully walked over to the table on which lay not only ancient parchments, but brass tablets. "They are marvelous," whispered Lorenzo.

"Feel free to touch and handle them, Lorenzo. They are of ancient origin and were found in the Americas and I want you to become expertly familiar with them."

Lorenzo reached out and cautiously examined the parchment. There were not only writings upon it, but colorful designs of suns, moons and stars as well as animals such as jaguars and quetzal birds. Also on the parchment were depictions of men of war, some dark and others light-skinned, and both seemed to be in the act of doing battle with the other. Spears and weapons of war could be clearly seen as the figures appeared to be holding them in a menacing way.

"Don Caino, I have never seen anything like this." Having an eye for art and sculpture, Lorenzo could appreciate their importance. "If this is truly ancient then it would be priceless."

"I assure you that it is and because of its age it must be preserved." Turning now to the plates, he said, "Lorenzo, now look at the plates and give me your assessment of them." Cain noted his immediate interest, but wanting to assess the man's intelligence, he remained silent.

Medici took hold of the plates that were held together in a binder. Each plate appeared to be a metallic page with symbols written upon them. Having spent some time in Egypt, he had become familiar with the look of ancient writings that had been discovered on papyri and had been kept in tight wooden boxes to preserve them. He had petitioned to the sultan of Egypt a request that he be permitted to examine the scrolls and write several of the glyphs for future reference and his request had been granted. As he looked upon the writings contained upon the records before him, he was impressed by the similarities to the ancient Egyptian characters he had noted years earlier.

"Don Caino, the symbols on the plates appear to be similar to ancient Egyptian, though not quite. You say these were found among the Aztecs?" His question was filled with disbelief.

"They were. Though I doubt seriously they were written by them. Cortés brought them back from his first voyage to New Spain. What do you make of the quality of the plates?"

"I am no metallurgist, but I am familiar with the feel and composition of certain metals. The metal must be malleable enough such that the characters can be engraved, but the feel and look is what impresses me the most. It is not gold; the feel and heft are all wrong. I can only presume it to be brass, but of a high quality I have never before seen. And if it is then this would account for its luster as well as its preserved look despite its age."

Cain was relieved that he had found such a man of science and art as Lorenzo de Medici among a family of dolts and dullards. It is a good thing I am running their family bank, he thought, or they surely would have dumped it into the ground long ago. Inasmuch as they can keep their knowledge of me secret and abide by my agenda, they will continue to prosper in spite of their ineptitude.

Cain continued to explain. "Cortés had reported that the temples of the Aztecs were encrusted with gold and silver, so there has to be rich deposits of those ores nearby and I intend to have as much as possible to line the coffers of our banks in Florence." But, obtaining these artifacts before anyone else is the real priority, he concluded desperately. Only by keeping these records away from the prying eyes of Jasher and others can I be sure that history vindicates my actions.

"Well, Lorenzo, you are quite right on both accounts. The plates are high-quality brass and the symbols are what some might identify as reformed-Egyptian. An Iraqi alchemist by the name of Abu Talib first began deciphering such Egyptian writings he called hieroglyphs. Some of his translations might have been in error, but his efforts were on the right track."

Lorenzo nodded his head in appreciation. "You are quite right, Don Caino." Lorenzo looked down again at the plates and their inscriptions, then after a moment commented, "It is a pity that the famous library at Alexandria was destroyed during the fourth century by Romans. If not for its destruction, we would undoubtedly have more records to which we could compare with those found in the New World."

"Yes, it is a pity." What Lorenzo did not know and never would was that the famous library in Alexandria had been burned down by the Romans on his orders. The rulers had refused to allow him access to their archives, so he had invaded Egypt and had overseen the destruction. He had ordered everything in the building put to the torch.

"Don Caino, this has been most enlightening, but how can I be of service to you?" As Cain was the most favored patron of the Medici family, he was honored to have finally been able to meet the man. It was rumored that he was very old, yet his appearance indicated a young, though middle-aged man. Clearly the rumors were exaggerated as rumors tended to be. Regardless, his family owed their wealth and influence throughout Florence and Europe through the patronage of this man. He intended to serve him the best he could, but was still unsure why he had been asked to make the visit this day.

As if reading his mind, Cain said, "Lorenzo, I have a special labor for you to perform on behalf of your family interests as well as mine, which I can assure you are identical. Over the next few decades, Florence will become the richest, most influential city in Europe. The Medici bank will underwrite every expedition to the New World by the European monarchs and as their wealth increases, so will ours. Within a few years, we will be able to influence history in a way no one has ever dreamed before. We will buy thrones and those who sit upon them and popes who can and will control the populace through their dogma. I am poised to be in that position and the banks of Florence will control our destiny. All it takes is a few men of will who know what I want and are prepared to help me achieve it. I think you are one of those men."

Lorenzo was flattered that his patron thought so highly of him and from that point forward committed himself to live up to Cain's expectations. "And what is that labor, *Signore*?"

"My goals in the New World are two-fold: first, to extract as much wealth in the form of ore and hard currency as possible and bring it back to Florence; the second, the recovery of all ancient records and have them brought back to me for my personal examination. Your job is to examine each article of cargo coming from the New World and ensure the ancient artifacts they bring back are delivered directly to my doorstep. Having now examined the records, would you be able to recognize those items if you were to see them amidst the incoming cargo from the Americas?"

Lorenzo never hesitated; he knew just what his patron was looking for. "Of course, Don Caino. You may depend upon me."

Nodding in excitement, Cain continued, "Lorenzo, you are to be my personal ambassador to the court of King Carlos I of Spain. You will work directly with my factor to ensure my accounts are correct and all shipments of artifacts are in order and accounted for."

Lorenzo de Medici was overwhelmed by this great honor and humbly responded, "Very well, Don Caino. When would you prefer I leave?"

"You will leave tomorrow and travel in state with the ambassador from Spain with a letter of introduction and a detailed list of your duties. I do not want any misunderstandings on the part of King Carlos and his advisers. This will be done my way or he will have to seek elsewhere for his adventure money. Please return in the morning and my secretary will have these letters written and stamped with my personal seal."

The streets of Valladolid, Spain were heavily laden with people hurrying to see the procession of His Majesty King Carlos I of Spain. January 2nd was a yearly celebration that filled every Spaniard with well-deserved national pride. 1492 had been the year the Emir Muhammed XII had surrendered the Emirate of Granada to Queen Isabella I of Castile, completing the Christian *Reconquista* of the peninsula. Thus, for most, the date was a festive occasion and attracted Spaniards all over the country that came to express their gratitude for the King who would continue to protect their nation from foreign control and heathen, non-Christian influence.

There was one, however, who had come to express a differing opinion. Hernán Cortés was born in Medellín, Spain, to a family of lesser nobility and no one was more aware of this lack than he. Though he tried with difficulty over a lifetime to convince the upper nobility that he was worthy to be accepted into their ranks, each attempt was met with failure. He and his daughter, Catalina, had arrived and were stationed along the parade route, now standing within the throng of spectators.

His daughter was well aware of her father's bitter feelings towards the Crown; he never tired of discussing it. "Father, you must try to contain your anger. It will do your cause little good if you end up in a dungeon tied to the wall."

"Catalina, I have been unappreciated since the day I set sail for the New World and Cuba. I was stagnating under the ever present shadow of that disgraceful bootlick Diego Velázquez. He was never going to allow me to realize my dreams."

"Father, you have told me many times that you had received an *encomienda* in Cuba and even recognition as a magistrate on the island. How can you continue to say that you were unappreciated?"

"The fief I was given was hardly more than a grove of banana trees and a dozen lazy black slaves. As to being a magistrate, it was a flea-bitten village that was under water most of the year!"

Catalina shook her head in despair. How was she going to keep her father from being jailed? He meant to cause a public scene and unless she could convince him otherwise, the King's Royal Guards would surely strike him dead. Her only recourse would be to placate him, but she had tried it all before without much success. "*Papá*, please re-petition the King for another audience. He is a reasonable man and I am sure that he will listen. But, causing a public scene is not the way to get his attention."

Cortés became subdued, but self-pity and then anger replaced whatever marginal restraint he had. "Catalina, you know very well I should have been made Viceroy of the New World, not given some meaningless sinecure, hardly a title with no authority and little or no legacy for my descendants."

"Of course, *Papá*, the position of Viceroy would sit better upon you than any other, but the title of Marquisate of the Valley of Oaxaca brought you an important fiefdom and all of us now bask in that legacy."

"Perhaps, but without my leadership and experience as Viceroy, within a few years the whole of the New World will fall into anarchy. Don't they know that?"

"Of course, *Papá*, but you must give them time!"

"Time? You are a foolish girl! I have run out of time! I am up to my armpits in lawsuits from Spanish civilians because of my debts and supposed abuse of power. Everyone spits upon me now and unless I gain redress from the king, all is lost."

About the time he loudly voiced this last charge, the royal procession had wound its way around the street corner and was quickly approaching the location of Cortés and his daughter. Catalina easily recognized the crazed look in the eyes of her father and realized he was about to do something foolish, probably to throw himself in front of the horses. She reached out to grab his shirt and missed.

Realizing this might be the only opportunity he would have to attain access to the king and being desperate to be rescued from his current dilemma, Cortés ran out in front of the carriage and grabbed the reins of the animals. When he had them stopped, he forced his way past the guards and mounted the footstep a few feet from the Emperor's face. Cortés cried, "My King and Emperor, I beseech you to listen!"

King Carlos was outraged by the man's impertinence and pretended to not know him. "Who are you?" he shouted over the crowd.

Cortés was now angrier and more mortified than he had ever been in his whole life. He shouted back, "I am a man who has given you more provinces than your ancestors left you cities! You have an obligation to redress my wrongs!"

The Emperor was appalled at the man's audacity and shouted to his guards, "Seize that man and take him away!"

The Royal Guard grabbed Cortés and threw him to the ground then bound him as a common criminal. As he was led off, his daughter Catalina buried her head in her hands and cried in desperation. Her father was quite insane.

King Carlos I of Spain, also known as Emperor Charles V of the Holy Roman Empire, was seated on his throne surrounded by a special council of advisers known as The Council of the Indies; officially, the Royal and Supreme Council of the Indies. At the time it was the most important administrative organ of the Spanish Empire for the Americas and Asia. From the outset, it was placed as a section under the jurisdiction of the Council of Castile and it had legislative, executive and judicial functions. Moreover, The Crown of Castile had officially incorporated the American and Asian territories into its domains by a papal bull issued by no less than Pope Alexander VI.

In addition to the council, present were Diego Velázquez de Cuellar, Governor of Cuba and Antonio Mendoza y Pacheco, current Viceroy of New Spain. By special request, an invitation had also been extended to Lorenzo de Medici, special envoy from the Bank of Medici of Florence, Italy, and their primary patron and benefactor, Don Caino. The topic under discussion was over how they were to deal with Hernán Cortés, who of late, had become more of a liability than an asset to the Crown.

Velázquez had been an outspoken critic of Cortés for over twenty years. While in Cuba in 1519, and against his direct orders as governor, Cortés had gathered a small army of mercenaries and had sailed west. The fact that his expedition had opened up the entire region to exploration and plunder, bringing back untold treasure to Spain at a time when the nation was still recovering from centuries of Moorish rule, was the only reason he was not hung for treason. A year later, Velasquez had sent a small army to New Spain to terminate his command forcefully. This army was ambushed by Cortés after they landed in force on the mainland with the result that the captured soldiers were all folded into Cortés' army, thereby augmenting his reserves for the conquest of the Aztecs. Even after twenty years, Velázquez still seethed with impotent hatred. He was of the opinion something drastic should be done about him.

"You were fortunate, Sire, that you were not injured by that man's attack on your person in full view of the public on the day of our celebration. Your Excellency, it is time we put paid to this business of Hernán Cortés. He now openly assaults royalty in the streets with his demented notion of becoming Emperor of New Spain."

"Only Viceroy, Diego," commented Antonio Mendoza with a rueful tone.

"Viceroy today, Emperor tomorrow. The man knows no shame and has never understood his place."

King Carlos shook his head in consternation. "Very well, Don Diego. That will be enough! This bickering between old rivals is pointless and is getting us nowhere." He had released Cortés from the castle dungeon, but could not squeeze a promise from him to desist from more public scenes. He needed a solution, but one that made sense given the man's popularity. However, he had no intention of venting the frustration of this council in full view of Don Caino's personal envoy, Lorenzo de Medici. They would hear the emissary now and dismiss him as soon as possible.

Clearing his throat, King Carlos announced, "I am sure our esteemed envoy from Florence representing the Medici Bank will have no objection if we hear Don Caino's petition for our continued support. Lorenzo, if you please?"

Lorenzo Medici was unaccustomed to be in the presence of such exalted heads of state. In Florence, he had mingled with dukes and other lesser nobility of semi-royalty and those who aspired to be, but nothing could have prepared him for this occasion. "Thank you, Your Excellency. I will try to brief."

King Carlos smiled condescendingly then replied, "Of course, Lorenzo. We all are highly interested to hear from our esteemed patron from Florence, Don Caino."

Lorenzo stood and noting his lips dry, attempted to move his tongue about without causing too much attention. Clearing his throat, he began, "Excellency, our patron, Don Caino, is well aware of the exploits and remarkable handling of our mutual interests in the New World by Hernán Cortés. He has done an amazing job and we feel as recognition for his years of dedicated service to us, he be allowed to use his exemplary management skills towards the needs of the Throne of Spain closer to home. It is our hope that he never be allowed a return trip to the New World. Let his retainers and descendants manage his holdings there and permit him to live out his later years as a true hero accessible to the Spanish people at home. Perhaps he could be persuaded to assist the Crown in pushing back the resurging Ottoman threat to Spain here at home."

The members of the court nodded their heads in mutual approval of the suggestion. He was, after all, a popular figure here in Spain. If accepted, this idea could permit them the control over the man that had been lacking when he was in the field managing the savages and conquistadors. Indeed, Cortés had expressed his disdain for following their directives and, in truth, had followed his own ambitions before putting the desires of the Crown first. He would always be a "loose cannon" as long as he felt he was beyond their reach.

King Carlos beamed a smile and replied, "I think I can speak for the council and say without hesitation that such a notion has found our favor and will be carried into effect immediately. A splendid idea! Did our esteemed patron have any other matters he wished to bring up before the council?"

Lorenzo was gratified that the first issue was so well received. Though Don Caino had made it a point of priority, the second matter, however, he was not as confident of its reception. It was, after all, over a personal matter that only Don Caino would have a concern. Reluctantly, he concluded, *it is up to me to ensure they fully understand what is at stake here.*

"It has come to the notice of our patron that many records of the history of the indigenous people of the Americas have been discovered. As a patron of the arts and as one who has taken a keen interest in preserving history, wherever it may be, Don Caino feels that the acquisition and preservation of such ancient relics are of equal importance to the precious ore and treasures being mined and returned to the Crown. He will, of course, take personal ownership of them and remove any responsibility on your part to maintain them."

Every member of the council knew exactly to what Lorenzo was referring; all except the King. A puzzled look came over Carlos' face and, looking about the room, he asked, "Ancient records? Of whom, the Aztec savages?"

Antonio Mendoza, the Viceroy of New Spain, cleared his throat and delicately pointed out, "Excellency, we have all seen them, but few are being loaded with the other cargo that is shipped back to Spain."

"What is happening to them, Don Antonio?"

"Some are being burned; others have been melted down into gold bricks. It depends upon who finds them first. My conquistadors and Spanish overseers have had to physically restrain many of the Catholic fathers who view them as blasphemous and have destroyed many on sight. Some of us have acquired them or taken a few back home with us home to Spain as oddities."

"So, unless they have some obvious worth, they have not been given any priority handling."

"That would appear to be the case, Excellency."

King Carlos turned his attention back to Lorenzo de Medici. "Lorenzo, I take it that our patron from Florence finds these relics to have value beyond their obvious outward worth?"

"That is correct, Excellency."

"Does he have a specific plan in mind to acquire and track them?"

"He does. May I present this letter for your immediate review? It throws light on our current discussion." Lorenzo approached the King and handed over the list of suggestions, though if truth be known, they were more along the lines of demands. He hoped the King would not find the language of the letter too peremptory or offensive. As the perusal of the letter and its discussion continued, Lorenzo found a seat.

The King looked over the list, nodded his head then had his secretary pass the letter around the table where the council was seated. After all had read the letter, and a brief discussion had followed, King Carlos said, "It appears Lorenzo that you are to play a grander role in our council than we had first thought. Very well, your patron will have his records and you will be his secretary in such matters. You will liaise with our factor who will oversee to the accounting of all cargo. Once a relic has been identified, it will be turned over to you. What is done with the item after you take it will be between you and our patron. Does that sound about right?"

Lorenzo, now being addressed again, had arisen to his feet. "It does, Your Highness. And thank you for your timely intervention into this important matter."

"I have read the letter and understand the message, but sometimes the tone of these matters does not come through clearly via correspondence." With a pause, the King asked, "Having a familiarity with our patron that we lack, what is your true opinion of the degree of importance of this issue?"

Medici shuffled his feet then placing his hands behind his back to avoid obvious agitation, he stated, "Don Caino wishes to convey to each of you that any more discoveries of this nature are to have the highest degree of importance and handling." Here was the part he dreaded the most. "Moreover, and I quote him on this: "If you bungle this matter, you will soon understand what it feels like to have a coffer full of gold, but no way to protect it."

Deadly silence filled the hall as each pondered what it could mean to lose a patron like Don Caino. The threat could mean different things for everyone, but at the end of the day, what it would really signal was the end of the growing Spanish Empire and back to being ruled by outsiders, probably the Ottomans. Carlos I, King of Spain and Emperor of the Holy Roman Empire, nodded his head in understanding as did the other members of the council. They had decided to obey.

CHAPTER 5

THE BANQUET, 1619

Over the next seventy years, in order to better oversee his interests in the New World, Cain had begun to spend at least half of his time in Spain, and so had purchased an estate outside Seville. When in Spain, he was now addressed as Don Caín, and though no one could ever remember exactly how he had come to deserve that appellation of respect, he was nonetheless in possession of it. Few could identify him, which was how he had always intended that it should be. The fewer persons who could recognize him, the easier it would be to avoid any discussion of his true identity as a subject of speculation. He had taken to growing his beard longer, adding a touch of grey by occasionally using plant dyes. He knew it would not last forever, but in the meantime it had suited his needs.

His being a recluse may have been to his advantage in the past, but lately he had needed a more personal touch in order to better manage his holdings, which thanks to his investments in the New World, had become substantial. Moreover, he had realized that if he wanted to have things done right, he had needed to be more directly involved. Save for his inner circle of advisers, he now eschewed the use of front men to manage his business. It was more personally satisfying anyway, he reasoned. After all, he could not be an effective businessman if he used others to carry his messages which often as not involved intimidation and veiled threats. Of course, he could be charming when the need arose, and lately it had arisen more than he had expected. Spanish society was outward in appearance and this required the use of social contacts to ensure efficiency of his ventures.

He had accepted an invitation to attend a dinner engagement at the country home of one of the more prominent citizens of the Seville area, Alfonso Diego de Zuñiga, the Duke of Béjar and his wife Teresa. As always, either when entertaining or being invited to a social event, he was careful to ensure that an unattached, but attractive woman accompanied him. The lady that evening was the Duchess of Alcalá, Ana Ribera, a wealthy widow of three years. It was all for show, really. His love interests were non-existent and had been for many years now, but the society game demanded the appearance of normalcy even if the reality was something else quite different. Doña Ribera, the lady he was escorting that evening, was deep in discussion with the Duke and his wife when an unexpected table topic of conversation arose. Cain had been trying hard that evening to remain engaged despite Alfonso's sincere efforts to bore him to distraction.

The Duke was telling what he considered an amusing anecdote of a conquistador officer who had served in the New World and had to restrain some Catholic priests one day from burning a native chief and his family. "The officer and his detachment had been out patrolling the general area around Pachuca as well as overseeing the progress of nearby silver mining interests. As they pulled into the encampment, a roaring fire could be seen nearby and it was clear from the noise a disturbance was well underway. The soldiers dismounted their horses and proceeded to the source of the commotion and once they arrived they then discovered a scene of pure tumult. Half a dozen Dominican priests along with several Catholic *mestizos* had tied up the local *cacique* and his family and they were in the process of roasting them along with some old relics."

"Relics, you say? Come again?" Up until then Cain had only been half-listening to his host. It was, after all a common enough story, the type that had been oft repeated up and down the length of the Iberian Peninsula of Spain, but the mention of relics had finally gotten Cain's attention.

The Duke had worried that the table topics had become too tiresome for his guest. Up until the mention of relics, Don Caín had paid little attention to any of the discussions. "Yes, I was about to say that the priests had observed the local chief entering a nearby structure and decided to follow the *cacique* inside and investigate. They found the old man in the act of prayer as he read from an ancient set of metallic records, if you can believe that." Alfonso looked to Cain trying to fathom his now intense interest.

"Go on," he intoned, though it sounded more like a threat.

"Yes, Alfonso, please continue." It was the duchess, Cain's escort.

The mood was now unexpectedly strained and any mirth was definitely out of the story, so the Duke decided to conclude his anecdote. He cleared his throat slightly and offered a hesitant comment, "Well, there is little more to tell. The priests dragged the old man out of the structure along with his records. The priests, assisted by some local Catholic *mestizo* workers, tied up the old man and his family. The soldiers had just arrived to see the chief being questioned about the records, but he refused to talk about them."

"What do you suppose the priests wanted to know?" asked his wife, Teresa.

"I was told by the officer that they were looking for more records, but the chief refused to cooperate, so the priests had his whole family brought before the bonfire and one by one, they were all thrown into the pyre as the old man looked on, still refusing to talk."

"And the old man? I suppose they threw him in the fire along with his family," Cain commented without much interest.

The Duke smiled briefly, anxious now to offer the punch line. "Exactly, though, according to the officer, the priests hung him upside down and dangled him over the fire from a nearby tree limb." Then he could contain his mirth no more and burst out laughing. "His hair caught on fire then the priests threw oil over him, all the while dancing and chanting. The officer commented that he could not tell which sight was more ridiculous, the *cacique* in agony screaming from the burning flames or the Catholic priests jumping and chanting around the fire."

The Duchess of Alcalá was clearly scandalized by the image that the Duke had painted. Bleakly she managed to ask, "What was so humorous about the sight?"

Cain remained ambivalent; he had seen much worse. He replied, "Clearly, my Dear, the soldiers could not decide which was more ludicrous, the burning *cacique* hanging from a limb or the dancing priests. They decided the whole scene was beyond their comprehension. Laughter was all they could manage in the face of the unimaginable." What none of them realized was that Cain was not interested in the fate of the old man and his family. His only concern at this point was the final disposition of the records.

Cain threw a casual glance at the Duke and asked, "And what happened to the records, if I may ask?"

"Well, the parchments were burned, but the officer was able to save the metallic artifacts. So, at the end of his tour in the New World, he brought them back home."

"How was he able to slip them past the port authority without the items being confiscated?"

The Duke shrugged his shoulder and with an indulgent smile declared, "There are many ways to move around the port authorities if you have enough money to convince them to look the other way. You know how it is, Old Man," he laughed with well-bred humor as one man of the world to another.

"Indeed I do. Would you know who might now have those relics?" Cain suspected he already knew, but was keen to keep the excitement and anger out of his voice.

"I am," replied the Duke genially. "Would you care to see them?"

"I know I would," replied the Duchess of Alcalá. "I have heard of such relics, of course, but I have never seen any nor have I met anyone who owned any."

"Dear, don't you have them stored in the basement somewhere?" asked Teresa, the Duke's wife.

The Duke seemed quite pleased by the prospect of displaying his newest acquisition so he replied enthusiastically, "Of course, all please follow me to the basement."

Cain's eyes had grown flinty as he attempted to work out how to separate the records from their current owner. Obviously, the man had no idea what he had and was treating the relics as if they were some child's toy or a trinket which some housewife could pick up at a market half-price sale. If what he said was true, then there was a severe gap in his security at the port authority and it needed to be closed as soon as possible. But, for the moment, he had to gain possession of those records.

Once in the basement, the Duke began to light candles and after several had been lit, he escorted his wife and the two guests to a corner in which a table was located. Upon the table was a blanket covering something that was rectangular, and from the impression, probably metallic. With a flourish he pulled off the covering and presented his prize of which he was clearly proud. "*Voila!*" he proclaimed self-importantly, now anxious to see the reaction of his wife and guests. He need not have worried; they were all equally impressed, one more so than had the other two.

Duchess Ana inquired, "May I touch it?"

"Of course," replied the Duke as if bestowing a great honor. He was clearly enjoying the display of his collection.

"Is it gold?" she asked.

Cain spoke for the Duke. "No," he replied. "It is brass."

"How can you be so sure?" asked the Duke. He was a little deflated. The previous owner had insisted it was of gold.

"You could have it tested, but I assure you the metallic value is nearly worthless. It has a high golden sheen, but that is simply a result of the high degree of zinc in the alloy. Look Duke, I have already acquired several similar pieces at my home in Italy and I have been approached by a fine arts committee to start a museum in Florence. By adding this piece to my collection, I would have a sufficient selection to cause enough interest to establish a fine display. Would you consider selling it to me?"

The Duke thought it over and replied, "I have already been approached by a few art aficionados here in Spain and I will admit that it might be tempting, but I do not need the money and I would like to gather more pieces from the same source and start a private collection."

"And that is your final word on the matter?"

"Alfonso, my love, if the relics have no value, why not sell them?" It was his wife, always the pragmatic one.

The Duke ignored his wife. Looking smugly at Cain, he said, "It is, my friend. I am sorry, but the piece is not for sale nor is the name of my source at the port authority."

Cain's smile was engaging, but its geniality never touched his eyes. As he had business to attend to, Cain was anxious now to have the evening over. "Very well, my friend, I quite understand." Now looking around the room then back to his hosts, he said, "The hour is late and I must have the duchess back home before her father sends out the palace guards looking for her." At that, all four broke up in laughter and The Duke and his wife saw Cain and his escort to the door.

Waving to the departing couple, the Duke turned to his wife and commented, "I had heard that Don Caín was a bit of a cold fish, but his conversation was engaging tonight, all rumors and gossip to the contrary."

His wife was not so easily fooled as her husband, "Perhaps so, Husband, but I don't think he took well to your turning down his offer. I think you should reconsider."

"Nonsense, besides why should others own such oddities and not me?"

Nodding, she shivered slightly at the night air. As they went back inside, she glanced upwards at the dark roof, full of shadows. She made a mental note to have the guards doubled that night.

When the assassin came to the outer wall of the estate, the new day was still dark; obscure shadows hung low over and around the chimneys and turrets. It was a time when most if not all would be either asleep or drowsy from a long night of vigilance. His clothing was black and close-fitting and he wore darkened boots made of soft, but durable leather. A mask covered his face save for two slits over his eyes. A black cowl completed his early morning attire that he would use later to navigate surreptitiously through a darkened house. He ran noiselessly up to the soaring walls and stopped just short of its stones. He felt the texture and with a practiced tug of his wrist, he reached inside a waist band of his trousers and pulled out a cloth-covered hook with a thin silk rope attached to it. With a deft flick of his wrist he threw the hook upwards and when it caught on the stone ledge, he lithely began pulling himself upward and over the wall. Once on the other side, he moved quietly through the shadows of the courtyard to gain access to the rear of the estate. He noticed all windows on the ground floor were shuttered, but the second floor balcony was open and accessible. Again, he used the silk rope to gain access then once over the top, he disappeared inside a darkened hallway.

He searched the upstairs rooms until he found one of the master bedrooms wherein lay the Duchess of Béjar. A smile etched his face as he contemplated the job. Cain had assured him that tonight's assignment was going to be more appealing than the usual midnight slash-and-flee-out-the- window job. He quietly walked over to the side of the bed and carefully placed his hand over the mouth of Teresa. Being a light sleeper, she immediately awoke, but he was prepared for that. When she attempted to arise, he carefully whispered into her ear, "Duchess, please remain quiet and still. We are going on a treasure hunt and your husband is going to lead me to the treasure." He slowly pulled her up out of the bed and brandished a knife in full view so that she could see he was armed and ready to use it.

"It's those damn relics, isn't it?" Her voice did not betray any fear, only resigned acceptance.

"Indeed it is, Duchess. Please show me to the Duke's room and we can proceed onward with our little hunt." She felt the point of the knife stick lightly into her back, so there was no hesitation as she led the way into the next room with a lit candle to guide their way.

Once into the room, the assassin whispered gently into her ear, "Very well, Duchess, now go over to your slumbering hubby and tenderly wake him as you would a small child."

She nodded her head in understanding. Now kneeling next to the bed, she gently gave him a shake, but being a heavy sleeper, it required several attempts to fully rouse him, but once awake he sat bolt upright in the bed against the head-board. As his eyes became accustomed to the still darkness of the early morning, he recognized his wife, but next to her stood a man dressed in dark clothing.

"Sit on the bed, Doña Teresa, next to your loving husband." After she was seated, the assassin began to explain what was to be done, all the time holding the knife next to Teresa's neck. "Duke, you will fetch either a satchel or saddle pack from your wardrobe then the three of us are going downstairs to the basement."

"What is this all about?"

With an exasperated shake of her head, his wife hissed, "It's those relics, you fool. What do you think?"

The Duke was honestly perplexed. "The relics, what would you want with those? They have no value."

"My patron feels otherwise."

"It's Don Caín, Alfonso. I told you to sell him the worthless things."

"Don Alfonso, you should have listened to your wife," chided the stranger with a concealed smile. "Please, you are wasting time. Now find a satchel big enough to cover the records."

"And if I refuse?"

The assassin seemed to consider his reply then stated casually, "I will cut your wife in places that she will be unable to hide."

"Alfonso," whispered Teresa fiercely, "find a satchel or use your night shirt. I don't much give a damn, but don't test this man."

"She is very wise, Don Alfonso. Do not test me in this matter."

The Duke walked over to his wardrobe and pulled out a bag of just the right size, and now disgusted with the whole business he said, "Follow me down to the basement."

Alfonso led the small procession followed by his wife with a knife to her back. Teresa insisted on carrying the candle stick, preferring to insure sufficient light in the event her club-footed husband stumbled and she ended up with a knife stuck in her spine. She was definitely not happy.

Upon entering the basement, the assassin directed, "Alright, Don Alfonso, please place all the records carefully in your satchel. My patron will want the artifact intact, without nicks or scars, so please take care to insure it remains in a pristine state. I would not want it damaged as I might have to take out payment for repairs on your lovely wife." He squeezed Teresa's shoulder and she gave a sharp yip of surprise.

Alfonso did as he was told, and when the task was completed, the dark stranger said, "Duke, there is only one more item of business that must be conducted before I depart and as I am sure you are both anticipating my departure, I will be brief with my request. My patron would like to know who at the port authority in Cádiz was responsible for acquiring and selling you the artifact, so you will oblige me by sharing his name." He squeezed the Doña's shoulder again, this time a little harder and he was rewarded again by a sharp yelp of fear.

"Alfredo Mendoza, the Chief Port Officer."

"Thank you Don Alfonso. Your cooperation has been appreciated. Nowadays, so few realize the importance of honest cooperation." He removed two short silk ropes from his pockets then said, "Now you will both be seated on the floor, your backs to one another then place your hands behind your backs." As he was tying them up together with the cords, he commented, "My patron wanted to leave you both a message. He says: you will both forget about the incident as well as the man who made the visit and the man who sent him; unless, of course, you would prefer a return visit, in which event he will gut you both like hogs and burn down your house." So that both could see his eyes, he removed his veil, and knowing the wife to be the practical one, he asked, "So, what is it to be, Doña Teresa?"

The Duke was about to speak up, but she elbowed him in the back and gritting her teeth she hissed, "Shut up, Alfonso." Then, with more decorum, she responded, "Yes, whoever you are, we understand and tell your *patrón* we will forget everything."

As he nodded his acceptance, a smirk played across the assassin's face. Before leaving, he checked the ropes and ensured both were as comfortable as possible in their back-to-back positions. On his way out, he walked over to the Duke and with a quick movement of his hand he cut his right cheek along the jaw line, hardly more than a nick, but it would leave a slight scar. With a smile, he whispered, "And that Don Alfonso is to make sure you never forget." He turned to his wife and patted her cheek and said mildly, "Please remind him, Doña Teresa. I have a feeling he is not the sensible one of the family."

The assassin left the candlestick next to the couple and exited the basement with the satchel on his back. The last thing he heard on the way out was the loud remonstrations of Doña Teresa and the story she intended to tell of the midnight prowler who broke in and stole the silver then tied them up for sport. Don Alfonso, the Duke of Béjar, felt the slow dribble of blood from his cheek and realized he had little to add to the conversation. For the next few hours, she did most of the talking, much of it quite loud.

On a clear, star-filled evening a week after the assassin had delivered the satchel to Don Caín, he was again asked to pay another visit, this time to the customs house that was located a block from the main pier in Cádiz. The Chief Port Officer, however, did not fare as well as the Duke of Béjar. He was found the next morning with his throat cut and a sign around his neck that declared: I took a bribe. This took care of the security gap on the European side, but there was still the Cuban connection that required Caín's special and immediate attention. A visit was long overdue to the new monarch of Spain who had misunderstood Caín's agenda.

CHAPTER 6
THE COURT OF PHILIP IV, 1622

Cain was muttering under his breath. It was the same complaint he had encountered since the Great Flood: the short life span of those around him. Now, once again, he was forced to break in a new monarch, this time it would be King Philip IV of Spain. Because of the secrecy upon which he insisted, his true identity was largely unknown outside of his inner circle, which was the way he had wanted to keep it. The downside was that he would have to officially introduce himself on at least one occasion and this one was it. And, of course, Cain hated to be kept waiting like some petitioning peasant in the street.

The court secretary walked out into the hall way where Cain was seated and beckoned him to enter. "Don Caín, you may now enter the presence of His Majesty the King of Spain."

He experimented with a stock phrase of pleasure and gratitude, but decided that today was not the day to try something insincere. Once he had approached the King, he merely bowed and restrained his natural impatience. Upon the throne sat His Majesty King Phillip IV, only recently coronated to the throne of Spain. He was surrounded by his court advisers and personal secretary. It was rumored that the new king was indecisive and had a slight tendency to overly defer to others to make the hard decisions for him. If rumors were true, then Cain intended to exploit that weakness.

Cain was the first to speak. "Excellency, it gives me great pleasure to meet the man responsible for the maintenance of such a large empire."

"Thank you Don Caín. My predecessors, as I am sure you are aware, were highly competent at expanding our overseas holdings, but their maintenance as well as future expansion will require substantial resources. Of course, this is where you continue to be such an integral part in helping us achieve our goals."

"Of course, Excellency. Please explain your concerns." This polite dancing was growing tiresome, but the game had to played, at least for now. As was usual, both he and the king would have personal petitions and agendas to address.

"Don, my advisers have informed me that our territories in the eastern Pacific may require significant infusion of funds to maintain our colonies in the Philippines. Reports are coming back that the holdings of the Crown are coming more and more under fire from Japanese and Chinese pirates. Moreover, there are signs that England is showing an interest in our spheres of influence guaranteed to us by the Pope. Soon we may have to deal with them and I would rather we be prepared in the event that day arrives sooner than later."

Cain was also aware of the state of affairs and concurred. "Yes, my reports also indicate that the English are starting to take a keen interest in our colonies in the Americas, both in the Caribbean as well as the Pacific. There is much potential in those areas for trade and, of course, plunder. Any disruption would cause a serious problem to my banks as well as to Your Majesty's Crown."

The King nodded, happy that the interests of the Crown and that of Don Caín would be mutual. "Since the English feel they are under no obligation to adhere to the guidelines set by our wise pontiff in Rome, should they decide to invade our trade routes, it will be up to us to ensure that they are well met. As you know, our invasion of the British Isles instigated by my grandfather in 1588 did not fare well. The fleet was essentially destroyed during those campaigns and it has taken us decades to recover. Again, much thanks to your support, Don Caín, for assisting us in that recovery process."

Cain was sympathetic, especially since he continued to benefit by such setbacks. "Yes, those storms were devastating, but who can control or predict the weather? As to our current concerns, the Pope, Ferdinand II, will likely expect your continued support, along with other nations, to sustain his bid to reunify Europe under the flag of the Holy Roman Empire. Moreover, in the midst of our conflicts at home, I think we are both in accord that preventive maintenance is required for our Pacific assets. May I suggest a new borrowing concept I have developed for this type of need. It will allow you to use or withdraw funds up to a credit limit that I will work out with your factor. The amount of available credit decreases and increases as funds are borrowed and then repaid and, if you wish, this credit line may be used repeatedly. This method will give you maximum flexibility with regard to needed capital for your ventures."

The King was impressed, but asked with a suspicious smile, "I can see how that would benefit the Crown, but what is your end of the deal?"

"You are quite correct, Excellency. Flexibility and access to capital on demand comes with a price. Of course, the interest rates will be higher and in addition to my usual fees of a fifth of all gold and silver, the *quinto*."

The King was under extreme pressure to maintain his overseas investments and saw little choice in the matter. Don Caín was offering an answer to an oft-delivered prayer. He turned to his secretary and said, "Very well. Make it so."

"Thank you, Your Majesty." Cain paused knowing that the next matter was what he had truly in mind from the jump. "There is another issue that I feel should be discussed and I hope to enlist your help with the problem."

"Please proceed, Don Caín."

"As you are aware, Excellency, our brave conquistadors and dedicated fathers of the Church have had much success in New Spain bringing the civilized truth to savage cultures and they should be commended for their duty. In the course of their labors they began to discover ancient artifacts and some records with a written history of those same civilizations. Though the artifacts upon which the records have been written represent little worth monetarily, understanding the language and history of the people might be a key to our future success as we deal with them going forward."

The King was a little perplexed and asked, "I was unaware that such histories had been uncovered. How long have you been aware of their existence?"

Here Cain had to be highly circumspect or he might reveal key information regarding the true nature of his identify. "Their discovery began to surface at the time of the early conquest of the New World under Governor Cortés. My banking House in Florence became aware of their social and military value and from that time forward, as these artifacts were brought back to Spain, we began to collect and translate them for future use."

"What have you discovered about these records?"

"Very little, Your Majesty, but the more we have acquired, the closer we have come to unlocking the key to their language in the hope that perhaps they would point us to locations of other caches of their treasures and mines."

"Fascinating, but how is this now a matter of my concern?"

"It has come to my attention that lately several of these records have entered the ports of Spain, but instead of being remanded to the custody of my House, as was agreed by your great-grandfather, they have instead been sold to private parties as oddities and decorations for their homes. I have been a witness to those sightings myself."

The King, clearly appalled and outraged at the accusation, asked, "Are you saying that our port authorities are selling property of the Crown as so much crockery in the market?"

"Your highness, I suspect that the collusion goes even deeper. It is quite probable that such behavior is not only condoned but encouraged at the final inspection docks in Cuba before the cargo even leaves for Spain."

The King was silent for a long moment. At length he asked, "If what you say is true then the confiscation and sale of these artifacts might be a small part of a larger effort to defraud the Crown and rob treasure that should rightfully belong to our sovereign nation."

"This was my thought also, Your Highness." Cain paused, allowing King Philp to fall into his trap.

After a moment, the King seemed to mull over the matter then asked, "What should be done?"

Cain smiled inwardly at how easily the king had been manipulated. "With your permission, Sire, I would like to conduct my own investigation into this serious matter by travelling to Cuba and establish an office there. I am prepared to remain as long as it is necessary to halt any future leakage of our precious cargo. I am sure you would agree that too many have died and sacrificed so much, only to allow our resources to end up in the wrong hands."

"I quite agree, Don Caín. What would you need to expedite this process?"

"I would need a letter giving me complete authority over the offices of the Governor in Cuba as well the Viceroy in New Spain. Moreover, I would need power to enforce my decisions with military control if necessary."

The King turned to his advisers and asked, "Do you all concur?"

More than a few advisers smiled knowingly at Cain. Each had owed his current position of trust through Cain's careful patronage in the court of Spain. "We do Your Highness." It was unanimous.

"Very well." He turned to his secretary and directed, "Please coordinate your efforts with Don Caín and write a letter providing him the powers he has asked for. Have it ready for my signature and seal. His request is to receive the highest consideration in this matter."

For Cain, the meeting had gone according to plan. "Thank you, Sire. I will stay in New Spain as long as it is necessary to address this issue." He was pleased at the prospect of returning to that part of the world. As a result of the division of the land mass centuries earlier, his last efforts to gain a foothold there had not fared well. *Save for the coming of that damned comet, the land would have been mine much sooner. This time it will be different,* he silently avowed.

CHAPTER 7

A NEW MISSION, ENGLAND 1621

In 1905 a young patent clerk in Zurich by the name of Albert Einstein published a paper that proposed that light was made up of tiny particles that traveled at the speed of light. That paper eventually earned him a Nobel Prize in Physics. Later, in 1926, the chemist Gilbert Lewis gave this small particle of light a name, calling it a photon, which he found to be massless and with no electric charge, thus it also exhibited the characteristic of a wave. After numerous experiments, it was discovered that light consisted of not only discrete particles with mass, but also waves, causing scientists to conclude that the phenomena represented a wave-particle duality. Further experiments into this duality resulted in an unexpected conclusion: if the photons are observed they behave as particles and if they are not observed they act as waves, the implications of which cannot be underestimated. In essence, the act of a visual, personal measurement determines whether the photon is a particle with mass; thus, when unobserved and not being measured, the photon acts as a wave, now massless. So, we have nothing that becomes something by the mere act of a personal observation.

In 1987 a team of Japanese physicists from Hitachi laboratories proved scientifically that electrons exhibit this same wave-particle duality. Electrons, of course, are incredibly small and it was thought that the larger particles of an atom such as a proton or neutron would act according to normal, expected laws of physics. In the early 1990s, however, a German research group proved the impossible: atoms also travel as a wave at the speed of light and arrive as a particle. They posed a simple, but mind-blowing question: What causes them to make this change in state from a massless wave to a particle with mass? After several laboratory experiments, they concluded that the means that turns the atom from a non-physical wave to a solid point of matter is your mind. Another way of viewing it is: the act of observation by a thinking being brings matter into physical existence. This suggests that all the building blocks of our reality are brought into existence by simply observing them. According to this "wave function collapse" phenomena until the event is observed, all outcomes are possible. (https://en.wikipedia.org/wiki/Photon)

Benjamin Jasher had been in England for nearly four years and had enjoyed his stay in spite of the weather and the infernal stench of the cities. Of particular interest was the English fascination with politics and literature. He had seen several Shakespearean plays, and although he had never met the man (he had died a few years earlier), Jasher had met his secret literary contributor Lord Francis Bacon, a man with a keen, scientific intellect. Bacon was of the opinion that the English were still centuries behind the Arab world in medicine and science, but, in time, he felt their stubborn persistence would win out over national pride and a reluctance to learn from others. Moreover, after a lengthy discussion regarding literature and science with him, Jasher had come away with the impression that Bacon may have been more than a mere patron of the arts; he may have been a major contributor and Shakespeare was merely his front man.

Jasher was especially impressed with the English countryside. After so many years living in a dry, warm Mediterranean climate, the cool dampness of England seemed a welcome reprieve to his senses. On a crisp early autumn day, he was on an extended walk along a winding pathway through the country near Kent when, just off the side of the road, a light appeared between two large ash trees. Now curious, Jasher stared in wonder as an old acquaintance stepped out of the light.

As the man exited, the light quickly diminished then disappeared behind him. As he drew closer, Jasher recalled that though he recognized him, it had been several centuries since the last meeting. His first thought was that on some level he must have something in common with Joseph for, in the interim, neither had seemed to have aged. He had planned to extend a formal greeting of welcome in the usual manner as before with a bow, but as he did so he became aware that there was something peculiar about his old friend. This time he sensed that their meeting would be somehow different and it wasn't long in being evident for Joseph appeared to be *more there,* if that could describe him. He now understood to what Ephraim ben Judah had been referring when confronted with his messenger in Toledo.

Joseph smiled in greeting and extended his hand in friendship and brotherhood. He then embraced Jasher as kinsmen all over the world had been doing since time immemorial. "My Brother Jasher, it gives me great pleasure to finally greet you in a manner befitting brothers!" he exclaimed happily.

"Joseph, my old friend and brother!" was all he managed to say.

As Joseph had scrupulously abstained from any physical touch in all previous encounters, Jasher was both pleased and surprised, not to mention curious, because up until now the messenger had always been highly circumspect in his manner, never allowing any physical contact.

Joseph looked him over and with a knowing smile declared, "As you can see and feel, things are different with me now. The process is far too complicated to explain to you on this occasion and it would be forbidden for me to do so in any event, so let us just say that I have moved on to a higher order of existence and can now touch and feel you, and as you have noted, I do indeed have more substance."

"Your clothing has also changed, I see." His white robe was gone, but his clothing was still all white. He was now wearing a white suit, white shirt, cravat and boots. The style and cut of the suit, however, was unfamiliar, though pleasing in appearance.

"Where I come from, white will always be the appropriate color. As to the style, my current wardrobe would seem more acceptable, given the times." He paused for a moment then declared, "We need to talk. May I accompany you on your stroll?"

"Of course," replied Jasher, now eager to converse with his old friend after so many years.

He noted that Joseph seemed to be in a pensive frame of mind, simply content to walk down the path in no particular hurry, almost as if he were encouraging Jasher to ask questions of him. With a smile, Jasher looked around at the forest and took notice of the early fall colors and the vast variety of plants and trees in all nature's majesty then a thought followed by a question occurred to him.

"Joseph, we have known one another many years now and there is one question that has puzzled me and I hope you can help satisfy my curiosity."

"I will if it is permitted, though I suspect by now that there is very little I can withhold from you."

To Jasher, this seemed an odd remark. He then tried to phrase his question so that he would not appear obtuse or unclear. He despaired that he might fumble it about so instead blurted, "How is it that you move about in that light portal?"

Joseph could have given him a simple, direct answer, but instead wanted to teach and he sensed that Jasher had reached a point in his development where experience and wisdom had melded together sufficiently for the response to be of use to him.

"Look up through the trees at the sun in all its glory. What do you see?"

"I see sunlight."

"Yes, quite true. However, there is one other thing that you have not yet noticed, but is nonetheless there and have never considered."

"What is that?"

"Time. For your information, the sun is 93 million miles from the earth and the sunlight you see this moment in time required slightly over eight minutes to reach you so that you could make that astounding observation. If you do your math, you will quickly conclude that light travels at the incredible speed of 186,000 miles per second."

A frown then a look of surprise gradually suffused his face. "That is a staggering speed and well beyond my normal sense of reckoning."

"The moment has now arrived when you must expand your normal process of thought. In a literal sense, our minds make the time that it takes the light to reach us a physical reality."

Through the overhead trees, Jasher gazed up toward the sun once again then commented, "If light has speed and generates heat, would it not also be physical in nature? I feel the heat of the light, of course, but I can't see it in the sense of a discrete mass."

Joseph smiled then went on. "Around three hundred years from now, some highly intelligent men will discover that light is composed of solid particles and they will call these *photons*. These *photons* are very unusual because sometimes they can be a wave."

"I have observed a wave-like shimmer of heat in the summertime, especially in the desert, but I don't think you refer to that phenomena."

"No, the waves to which I refer are invisible to the naked eye and so sometimes the photons exist in that state. Sometimes these photons can be solid and in that state they exist as extremely tiny particles and have mass, but why do they change from one state to the other? Does a photon have the free-will to make a choice to be solid or wave-like? Clearly not, so how is it accomplished? The answer is simple, but a bit amazing. Our perception of it changes its state of being. If that is so and I assure you it is, what does that tell you about the human mind as it relates to light, time and physical reality?" He gave Jasher time to think it over.

Jasher was a few minutes digesting the information, but his look of surprise was evident as he reached his own conclusion. Nevertheless, he stated it a bit tentatively, "That we have the potential to control the nature of light depending upon how we wish to view it?"

"Yes, and if that is true then what else can be controlled?"

Jasher took a few moments to make the next logical leap, but when he did his eyes grew large with the complete magnitude of his logic. He looked over to Joseph and with a smile uttered incredulously, "Are you telling me that my mind can also control time?" His head was reeling from the possibilities. Shaking his head, he commented, "My mentors Pacioli and da Vinci never prepared me for anything such as this."

Joseph smiled and proceeded with his explanation. "Our perception of time is what makes it real for us. Now we move to the concept of faith, which is the power to observe and comprehend precepts and reality as they truly exist and manipulate them for a desired purpose. The will of my faith controls how I make the connection with these small particles of light and move them about. Thus, my portal, as you have noticed, is hardly more than light particles that travel at tremendous speeds until time dilates, essentially stops, then I exit to my destination where and when I need to leave the portal. Later I regather the light then re-enter my light portal to take me when and where I need to go from there and my mind does the rest. Of course, I should also point out, that my body is not mortal as yours and therefore better equipped to endure this process of transportation at the speed of light."

Though he quickly recovered, the look on his face revealed that Jasher was astonished by this explanation. Since the gist of what he had heard was so uniquely novel, a number of questions seemed to assail his mind at once, but before asking more, it occurred to him that he had enough information to offer an astounding conclusion, "So essentially, light, physical matter, and time are interrelated and all can be potentially controlled with the mind, assuming one has sufficient faith to initiate the process."

Joseph's smile and a nod gave him the reassurance he needed to comprehend, what now was obvious and always had been. Jasher thought, *faith is not only the key to understanding the truth of all things, but is the means to reach out and connect with all things in nature, whether the past, present or future.* Some distant memory seemed to flood back to his mind as though it had happened only yesterday and he grappled with its relevance to the current conversation, but knew there must be one.

"Joseph, who helped me back in Babylon when I was asked to go out to the desert to meet with Mahonri? The voice in my dream sounded so familiar and yet I know it was not you."

Joseph appeared slightly amused by the question. "You have already made the connection in your mind; I can see it on your face. You simply have yet to accept the reality of it. Allow your faith to manifest the truth for you."

Jasher rocked back on his feet and opened his mouth, hesitant at first, then with more conviction he confided, "It was me." A thought, (perhaps a message?), seemed to escape from his mind; it slipped seamlessly outward and beyond.

"In view of what you have just learned regarding the connection between thought and time, is it so difficult to accept you might have received a message from your future-self as regards to that mission?"

"If that is true, then when will I send the message?"

"I suspect you just did."

A slight frown crossed his face; that response was unexpected. "But, how....?"

"Those may have been your thoughts, but we all share a common reality and time line, and assuming that you apply your faith for the right reasons, to a certain extent that time line can be controlled." He let Jasher dwell on that truth for a moment then added, "So, when I said that there was little I could now keep from you, I was stating another one of the basic principles of faith, which is a willingness to be taught the truth and comprehend it then apply that understanding towards the will of the Creator. Your life experiences and accumulated wisdom make it possible for you now to comprehend eternal principles and accomplish acts of faith that are beyond what most persons can understand and perform. Once you have reached that point of development, the truth can no longer be withheld from you; it will flow naturally as a mountain spring. My Brother, never forget your potential; it is limitless and eternal."

Joseph placed his arm amiably about Jasher's shoulder and excitedly confided, "Now we must talk of your new assignment!"

Actually, Jasher wanted to find a quiet place to ponder the truths that he had just discovered about himself, but Joseph's enthusiasm was contagious and he seemed anxious to move on. As it turned out, there was much time later to ponder and reflect over what he had learned. A voyage was up ahead, though he was uncertain how he knew that, but it felt true.

"Of course," he responded excitedly and added, "It has been many years since last I received an oral assignment. As you know, I have been collecting records around the continent and delivering them to special locations. I am sure you are aware that the mountain depository no longer exists on this continent, but was part of the last shifting of the earth."

With compassion, Joseph confided, "I know you buried your family nearby, but soon you will have the opportunity to revisit the valley, your home."

A feeling of unease had risen unbidden to Jasher as he attempted to describe his current state of mind. "Joseph, for the past few months, I have sensed that my time is nearing a close and simultaneously events are moving well beyond their usual ebb and flow. Perhaps our discussion of time has made that reality all the more immediate."

"Your observation was correct. The work from this point forward is about to take incredible leaps." With emphasis, he added, "Your next assignment will require all your exceptional talents for organization and management as well as your knowledge of languages and customs."

Jasher nodded his head and stated with some conviction, "It will be a voyage, and a long one, I believe." Stating it aloud, it seemed more real. He nodded as though receiving a confirmation.

"See what I mean? I think you have moved beyond mere intuition." Joseph gazed about the beauty of the countryside and understood why Jasher had chosen this location for a temporary home. He would be sorry to interrupt his sojourn here. "You are to relocate to Morocco to a location just opposite the peninsula of Spain. There you will plan and supervise an expedition to the New World and travel directly to an area along the latitude 20 degrees North, near a large bay on the peninsula of New Spain. Once you have arrived at the bay, you will travel up a river some forty miles to a village known in the area as Lamanai."

Jasher recalled an unusual item he had received a few years back as payment from a friend he had rescued from the Holy Inquisition. *Was it just mere coincidence?* He asked himself.

"I suspect this mission may have something to do with the rutter I acquired in Spain, does it not?"

Joseph indicated his agreement with a knowing grin. "While in life, I detected very few coincidences when I went about the Creator's errand; I suspect it is now the same for you. At Lamanai, there is a native temple that was constructed centuries earlier and within the temple contains a record of a civilization that existed in the New World. It is an abridgement of many records and it speaks of a people that the influence of the Clan corrupted and eventually plunged them into a civil war that nearly destroyed them. The remnants of that group were scattered about the land and their descendants now inhabit the entire continent. You will cross the ocean to the Americas and remove the records from Lamanai, now located in New Spain, in time to be known as Mexico. Once you have retrieved them then you must guard them in a safe location until the day arrives when you will carry them to the mountain depository and consign them there, along with the other records, you have accumulated." He watched Jasher for a reaction and seeing none he finished, "Is everything understood?"

Jasher nodded his head and remembered a promise that a friend had made to him many centuries earlier. "So, it would appear that I am finally to recover one of Mahonri's records. I am saddened that his people were nearly destroyed, but it will be a pleasure to retrieve and review the records then eventually deliver them to the mountain." Jasher thought for a moment and asked, "How long will I be required to wait until depositing these new records in the cavern vault?"

"The Americas will one day undergo an incredible movement of exploration and you will be there on hand when that day arrives."

"That land is now a vast, unexplored wilderness. Only recently have settlements been established along the Atlantic Coast and England is beginning to see them as her holdings. I suspect eventually she may go to war against the Spanish and French to protect her interests."

"That hold on the Americas will not last. Remember the promise that was made regarding the New World to Mahonri. That land is hallowed and the spirit of freedom is strong there and cannot be denied for long. Those English colonists will have the assistance of the Creator and His influence will be upon the land to ensure they have a chance to exercise their agency in peace even as your ancient ancestors. Eventually, a manifest destiny of discovery will lead them ever westward across the continent to your valley. When that occurs, you will await the right moment for a mode of transportation that will allow you a safe and speedy passage to the mountain."

"I take it then that I won't be using a donkey any longer?" he replied with a grin.

"Given your number of records, that would be impractical. The Creator has made other arrangements."

Jasher wasn't sure what to make of that last statement but decided an explanation would not yet be needed. Instead, he asked, "It has been many years since my last visit home. Will I still recognize it?"

"It is now located in the far western area of the continent in a place that will one day be known as California. As that journey brings you closer to the valley, you will begin to once again feel that irresistible pull that it has always had upon you. Though there may have been many changes in the landscape surrounding the area, you will nonetheless recognize it and there you will deposit all your records in the cavern. Moreover, there will be others who will be prepared to assist you in this endeavor."

Jasher accepted the explanation and turned the conversation back to his current mission. "There seems to be a sense of urgency to this new assignment to complete it now rather than at a future date when the political climate might be more amenable. As you are aware, all voyages to the New World are to dock in Cuba and report directly to the Office of the Governor of New Spain before proceeding onward. Otherwise, there is risk of being attacked and whatever records found in the open could be confiscated."

Joseph nodded his understanding then explained, "I am well aware of the challenges ahead. Cain has, in truth, been given *de facto* authority over the administration of New Spain and he will no doubt be aware of your activities in that area. He and his society have made it clear to all the European heads of state that any records found in the New World are to be brought back and guarded under the personal protection of the Society of Cain. The abridged record that you will recover would be of especial interest to him and doubtless it would be destroyed unless you take measures to remove it ahead of any future Spanish incursions or conquests into that area of the New World."

"So, it would appear that the agenda behind the conquest of the New World has the additional aim of retrieving or destroying the records that have been maintained by the inhabitants, my ancestors."

"From this point forward, you must assume that Cain will always have a dual purpose in leading and financing any expeditions and conquests. The financial benefits are obvious and clear to anyone who bothers to investigate his movements. The other purpose, however, will be the retrieval and destruction of records and this matter will be kept strictly *sub rosa* and restricted to his inner councils."

"One last question: How is it that Cain's society even existed in the New World and its influence managed to proliferate? I warned him away from the West just before the comet collided with the Earth and started the Great Continental Divisions, and to my knowledge he listened and obeyed."

Joseph sighed and reported, "He had an operative of the Clan placed in the Western provinces prior to the separation of the land masses, a man by the name of Sidon."

Jasher searched his memory and the name sounded familiar. "Is he the same Sidon who assassinated Rimush of Akkad as he sat on his throne? I heard rumors of his involvement, though since I could not substantiate them, I refrained from including his actions in my records."

"He is the same man. Later, in your ancient homeland, Cain had Sidon induct King Riphath and his son into the Clan of the Scar the year before your insurrection toppled that regime. After the land division, his descendants survived down through the centuries and carried on the purposes of Cain's society until even they were destroyed by the chaos they had created. Nevertheless, while they were in control, they were responsible for the destruction and downfall of every ancient civilization in the New World and that influence has been recorded."

"How was it these records of the Clan's involvement came under the eventual notice of Cain?"

"These discoveries were documented by the Christian priests and eventually rumors of the existence of those records have resurfaced during the Spanish conquests. Many of these ancient writings were destroyed by the Spanish priests as a means to undermine the native idolatry they discovered among the indigenous people and to send a message of the pre-eminence of Christianity. Other records were brought back as a curiosity and have now come to the attention of Cain."

"Knowing the priests as I do, I can see how Cain would prefer to take personal control of matters. The information contained on those recovered records would be beyond their comprehension and any handling of such affairs by the Church would not be definitive enough for him."

Summing up the new assignment, Joseph explained, "Cain has been behind every expedition to the New World for the last century now. He has made it abundantly clear that even if a native tribe cannot be conquered or converted to the dogma of the priests, he wants those records returned and they are to be a priority of every voyage." Joseph added for emphasis. "You are going there now to avoid the possibility of one of those special historical records falling into Cain's grasp.

CHAPTER 8

PILOT JOHN ARCHER, MOROCCO 1621

The English pilot had looked eastward at the oncoming storm and had decided that if the choice was between the storm and the Barbary pirates that had been pursuing them from the west, he would take the third choice and make for land southward toward Tunisia. Shaking his head at his bad luck, he would have preferred to try to outrun them, but his English vessel, the *Vanguard*, was in no condition to weather a storm on the high seas, especially one the size as the one bearing in on them from the east.

He glanced over to the captain and said, "Sir, we've no choice now. The corsairs we might have been able to outrun, but the storm is a gale. We have to put to port in Tunis."

"And lose our cargo to the pasha of Tunis? He's a bigger thief than those swine under Ward carrying the pirate flag. I think not, Mr. Archer. You had best grow a bigger set of testicles or I will throw you overboard myself and save Ward the trouble."

Archer shook his head in frustration. He had been fighting this hard-headed fool for the better part of the last two months. As long as the boat was in the water, custom demanded he make the decisions of life and death for the crew because only he had the skill and knowledge to return them safely home, but that tradition had never set well with Harkness. The Captain was a dark and burly Englishman with a bad temper who, over the course of his career, had always managed to bring back the rich cargos for the underwriters and owners of the shipping company, but it was usually at the expense of the crew and all on board was very much aware of his priorities.

A month earlier, they had run into a squall south of Corfu along the northern coast of Greece and Archer had decided to stay in port a few extra days until the weather had improved. A heated discussion had ensued between the Captain and Archer with the Captain overriding Archer's decision to stay in port. They had raced before the wind but the storm had caught them and they had had to turn around and head north into the Adriatic Sea to wait out the storm, which had cost them still more time. Though it had been Harkness who had decided to fight the storm outside of Corfu, he had blamed Archer for the delay and the bad blood still existed between them.

Now on their return trip, they had made a pickup of silks and spices from Greece and Sicily and were on their way back to the Straits when they ran into the freebooters near Malta. It had taken all of Archer's extensive skills to avoid the inevitable boarding of the corsairs but the pirates had been relentless. Now they were being pursued by Captain Ward, the most ruthless pirate in the Mediterranean who would likely kill all on board after they had plundered the treasure and cargo. Archer had argued that the ship was already heavy and could not outrun his pursuers; they would eventually be boarded by the hijackers. Now, with the storm approaching from the west, there was a risk of losing it all unless they found land and a port that could accommodate their ship.

"Captain Harkness, I am telling you that the moment that storm appeared, we were out of options."

The first mate, David Miller, and the helmsman had been listening to the conversation and both were well aware of the enmity that existed between the two men, but Miller was concerned for the safety of the crew and knew that was not a priority with Harkness. He offered a carefully worded opinion, "Captain, the pilot may be right. We should make a break for land while we still can. We really have no choice. Jack Ward is on our tail and the storm is before us." He added for emphasis, hoping the fool could read his meaning. "The men are not willing to take a chance with their lives."

"Miller you and the crew will do as you are told or I will have you all sacked the moment we land in Dover. We will drive towards the storm and lose the corsairs. Those swine are just as vulnerable as we."

"But, Captain," interjected Archer, "*The Vanguard* is too heavily laden. We can't maneuver her through the storm without risking our lives and the cargo."

"Archer, I am not losing the cargo and that is the end of it. We are going through the storm."

The next moment Captain Harkness lay face down on the deck, his head split open by a belaying pin that Miller was still grasping in his right hand. Blood was on the pin and was dripping down onto the captain's back. Miller looked up at Archer and asked, "Are you sure you can get us safely to land?"

"I can, but there is a good chance the cargo will be lost after we make port."

"Better the cargo than our lives." Miller glanced at the helmsman and said, "Nigel, here, lend a hand and help me with the Captain's body." The two crewmen grabbed Harkness by the arms and feet then both walked over to the rail and threw the body overboard into the sea. When the deed was done, Archer turned to the helmsman and ordered, "We turn south and port in Tunis. Better the pirates in Tunis than the ones on our tail." Pilot Archer had much time to regret his last comment to the first mate. In reality, there was little difference between the pirates who had been chasing them at sea and the one seated upon his throne in Tunis.

It was said that Jack Ward was beyond doubt the greatest scoundrel that ever sailed from England. He had been a privateer for Queen Elizabeth during her war with Spain in the late sixteenth century. After the end of the war, he became a pirate and with a few English crewmates had liberated a ship in 1603 and sailed it to Tunisia. It turns out Ward was as shrewd as he was ruthless. Realizing all of the rulers of the Ottoman Empire were Islamic, he made a canny decision and converted to Islam along with his crew. Immediately, he was accepted and protected by the various leaders of the Empire. In return for allowing him to plunder the southern Mediterranean, he bestowed gifts and treasure to the local pashas of the area. Needless to say, he had become a popular figure.

After the crew of the *Vanguard* had docked in Tunis, they were all rounded up by the local bandits of the pasha and thrown into holding cells until the privateer Jack Ward could make port. Eventually, the pirates made it to port just ahead of the oncoming storm. A few days later the negotiations began, though, truth be known, they were decidedly one-sided.

Pasha Murad, the *bey* of Tunis, looked over the Pilot of *The Vanguard* and began speaking to him through Jack Ward, the Englishman, who would act as interpreter. "Where is your captain?"

"He had an accident and fell overboard before we could dock," responded John Archer.

"An accident? Does that happen often around you Pilot Archer?"

"Fortunately, no, but the sea is a dangerous place." He looked contemptuously at Jack Ward. "You never know what dangers lurk about."

Murad smiled crookedly and said, "You realize, Pilot Archer, you will have to pay a port tax." The pasha glanced toward Ward and with a slight nod of his head he signaled for him to begin the bargaining.

Archer knew these two were only toying with him, but he sensed there might be a way to negotiate. He was tied up and longed to have a weapon in his hand, though, if nothing more than to wipe that silly grin off Jack Ward's face. "How much did you have in mind?"

"Everything you have, Pilot." The corsair was more than happy to answer for them both.

"Is that your final *offer*?" he responded sarcastically. "Would that gain us our lives and freedom?"

The Pasha smiled engagingly and said, "Of course, we are all civilized here, but the cost of running my city is very costly then there are the destitute to take care of. Unlike England, we are a poor country. That is my price and as long as you remain here, you will remain alive, but you may have to negotiate with Captain Ward for your release. I have made him an honorary member of my council and so he, too, must be satisfied."

Archer loathed having to negotiate with thieves, but there was little to lose by trying. He turned toward Ward who was still smirking, "Alright, Ward, you have my attention. What is your price, though I doubt there is much left for me to offer you after the port tax has been levied?"

"Well now, Pilot Archer, there is always something a man of your experience and understanding of the region can offer an old sea dog like me."

Archer knew what was coming next and feared it more than anything else, but he would not be the one to make the offer. It was, after all, the only thing left and the most important item he owned. "What could I have that would possibly be of interest to you?"

"Pilot, you are far too modest. I am surprised that you have not already laid it down at my feet. I want your rutter, of course."

A rutter was the navigator's greatest possession at sea. It was a detailed, usually daily account of how to sail to a given point of destination, but more important, how to return home. Such details as the magnetic courses between ports and capes, headlands, channels, noted soundings and depths, even the color of the water and the nature of the sea beds were recorded. This journal was especially important since longitude had yet to be discovered. Whereas latitude could be calculated using the position of the stars, there was still no way yet to calculate a given point on the globe with both latitude and longitude. For purposes of accurate navigation, seamen had to depend upon the details of the rutter, which were subject to human error. By the early seventeenth century, Spanish and Portuguese sailors were navigating the great oceans of the New World and Asia and the most important man on board was the pilot-major with his rutter. Once aboard and the journey underway, the pilot was the acknowledged leader, sole guide and final arbiter of the ship and its crew.

But now Archer's worst fear had been realized. To be beached and in enemy territory without a rutter was as bad as it could ever become. "And my crew? What of them?"

"My deal is with you and you alone. If they have something of value to barter then an arrangement could be made perhaps, but I already have experienced crewmen. What I never have enough of are galley slaves."

"Galley slaves? Ward, you know as well as I that is a death sentence."

Ward slowly shrugged his shoulders and smiled. "Perhaps that is true, Pilot, but many things can happen. Alive is still alive, whether a galley slave or not."

Archer was well aware of what was in store for his crew, but there was little he could do about it. Although the conditions working for the pashas were harsh, they were far better than those endured by galley slaves. Most Barbary galleys were at sea for around eighty to a hundred days a year, but when the slaves assigned to them were on land, they were forced to do hard manual labor. They remained alive, but with more opportunities for survival and possible escape.

Under freebooters like Ward, however, these slaves rarely got off the galley but lived there for years. During this time, rowers were shackled and chained where they sat, and were never allowed to leave. Sleeping (which was limited), eating, defecation and urination took place at the seat to which they were shackled. There were usually five or six rowers on each oar. Overseers would walk back and forth and would whip slaves considered not to be working hard enough. Needless to say, the mortality rate among galley slaves was extremely high, which is why Ward was always in need of them. Thus was life aboard a slaver, and Jack Ward had many such boats at his disposal.

Archer shuddered at the thought, but realized that he had little choice but to negotiate from whatever strength he had. "If I hand over my rutter, then what? You will just leave me here to languish under the tender care of Murad?"

Ward seemed to think that one over. "Ok, Pilot, I'm feeling generous today. You hand over the rutter willingly, and I'll take you as far as Ceuta in Morocco. After that, we are square and you are on your own." He smiled as though he had just proffered a great boon to a dying man in the desert.

"Ceuta?" He held his tongue knowing that he might be alive, but in Morocco near the Straits of Gibraltar, he was still well within the enemy reach. "We both know that the Spanish are still reeling from their defeat with the English and that puts me too close to their territory. My Spanish is not good enough to pass for a native; they will be all over me like flies on offal."

"But look on the bright side, Johnny. You will be alive and able to live among the Arabs who have not lost any love for the Spanish. Yes, Pilot, you will be beached and no one to help you, but at least you will have your life and your freedom, which is more than can be said for what awaits your crewmates."

"Damn you, Ward."

"Would you care to say goodbye to them?" Jack Ward let out an uproarious guffaw of laughter. When the Pasha asked him what had been so funny, Ward informed him and he too joined in on the gaiety.

"So, Pilot, what will it be, Ceuta or shall I fit you for an oar on one of my galleys?"

"When you put it that way, what other choice do I have?"

Ward shrugged and responded, "None that I would care for."

CHAPTER 9

CEUTA, 1623

*B*y the early *seventeenth century much of the Americas belonged to Spain. The trade routes were carefully patrolled, and unless first reporting to the Governor located in Cuba, no one entered the territory of New Spain and Central America without permission. Spain considered all this territory her possession and discouraged all other nations from intruding upon her conquered lands. It would be centuries later before the citizens of those regions had grown so weary of being exploited that they had turned on their Spanish masters in armed insurrections. But, by that time, there was scarcely anything left of the once rich treasures of the New World. Most of it had been carried back to the motherland to decorate the palaces and cathedrals of the noblemen and clergy, not to mention lining the pocketbooks and coffers of each. As most were either unsuccessful or had clandestine reasons for their attempts, history has recorded only minimal accounts of those who attempted to run this Spanish blockade.*

Jasher was going to the New World, the Americas as they were now called throughout most of Europe. Once he realized this mission had required a change of location from England, he relocated immediately following his last visit with the messenger Joseph. He then quietly began to plan a voyage unlike any other he had ever envisioned. And so, of late, he had called Morocco along the coast near Ceuta his home. Owing to its location near the Straits, the city had an unsurprisingly homogeneous population that had attracted Spanish and Portuguese citizens as well as the nearby Berbers.

It had taken several months to recruit the right crew. He needed experienced crewmen he not only trusted, but who were willing and able to make a journey of this magnitude. Thus, for his own peace of mind, he decided not only to test their mettle on recovery voyages throughout the Mediterranean, but additionally he intended to navigate these small voyages using the formula he had received for calculating the longitudinal point on a map. Over the course of several months and after successful recoveries of recorded artifacts spread out around Turkey, Greece and Israel, eventually he was satisfied and confident they could traverse the Atlantic and retrieve the records at Lamanai. The only person he lacked to seal his success was the right navigator.

As the Englishman made his way casually across the floor of the darkened inn, Jasher watched him with close interest. The man found a seat at a table against the back wall and began working slowly on the ale he had picked up at the bar. Jasher looked him over and concluded that in appearance he seemed commanding and confident enough, but was he as intelligent and cunning as his reputation purported? The only thing he really knew of him was that he had been a ship's master and pilot for seven years for the London Company of Barbary Merchants, the joint stock company that fitted fighting merchantmen class vessels to run the Ottoman Empire blockade and trade the Barbary Coast. A meeting had been set up by a close associate of Jasher who had owed him many favors over the years and Jasher had decided to collect on the man's debts. Over the years he had developed a network of contacts in this manner and this one had finally paid off in a way directly related to this important mission.

Jasher followed the Englishman over to his table, and with his back to the rest of the room, he sat down opposite him. He began with little preamble, "You are John Archer and I am Benjamin Jasher. Do you have time to talk some business?"

The Englishman was no stranger to secret meetings in the back of inns. Actually, he mused, lately most of his more appealing jobs had begun in this manner. He looked Jasher over and replied quietly, "As you can see, I am not terribly involved with anything except this ale." He took a few sips and nodded to Jasher that he should begin his pitch.

It was an auspicious beginning. Jasher had sized him up correctly: he was hardly a drunkard or a blow-hard and his bearing was one of quiet confidence borne out of experience, not a bottle. He decided to be direct and waste no more time talking around the subject. "I am looking for an experienced pilot-navigator willing to run the Spanish blockade in the New World." He would know quickly if this was his man.

Archer seemed scarcely intimidated by the thought of confronting the Spanish and appeared to give his response some careful thought. He replied, "Running a blockade would be unnecessary if your pilot had the right rutter. Since I don't relish the idea of being beached somewhere in the Caribbean, your rutter has to be authentic, and I might add, flawless."

Jasher delicately laid out the bait. "And if the pilot had the right rutter, could it be done?"

"It could be done, assuming the rutter could be trusted."

Up until now the Englishman had been scrutinizing Jasher to determine if he represented a serious means to extricate himself from his current dilemma. His English ship, *The Vanguard*, had been captured by Barbary pirates off the coast of Tunisia a few years earlier and most of his shipmates had ended up as galley slaves. He was able to buy his way out by handing over his personal rutter and now he was beached in Morocco with no way to return home. Whatever work he had been offered since, he had been forced to use another man's rutter and he was expected to return it to the ship's captain at the end of the voyage. The return trip invariably ended back up in Ceuta; he was never going home.

"The rutter I have acquired at great personal risk is unique. It contains, among other details, a manner of navigating a point on the globe, which can be calculated using both latitude and longitude."

The pilot slowly arched his eyes, smiled and said, "In that case, even a boatswain could do it, but I rather doubt you have such a rutter." But, in point of fact, he was very interested. The man sitting across the table from him had struck Archer as someone who was both cautious as well as well as serious.

Leaning forward, Jasher countered with, "And suppose I did? As navigator you would, of course, have full access to it along with the full descriptions of the shoals and reefs to avoid as well as the strength of nearby currents. At the conclusion of our journey, as partial payment, you would receive the journal and all the details you would need to navigate the Americas."

Archer was doubtful. "You would just turn it over? You realize that such a rutter in the right hands would in all likelihood break the Spanish choke hold over the rest of the world."

"I have no such ambitions; that would be a matter for you to examine."

"You understand that if we are caught in possession of such a rutter, we will all be executed?"

"I do understand, but if I have the right man to navigate my expedition to New Spain, it is unlikely we will be detained. Would you be that man? Can you captain and pilot the right vessel using such a diary?"

"Mr. Jasher, I would circumnavigate the globe to get back home. And with such a rutter, assuming it is real, I could pilot any ship anywhere."

"Mr. Archer, with the rutter I have you could do just that."

"Then I need to know everything about the voyage. Nothing can be withheld if I am to be successful. What are we looking for?"

Jasher smiled and replied, "We are looking for buried treasure, Pilot-Major John Archer. It lies upriver within the interior of New Spain along the 20th meridian North. We will find it inside a native temple located in an ancient, probably abandoned city surrounded by jungle."

"You seem to be quite sure of its location and description of the landing site," replied Archer skeptically.

"Your only concern will be to sail us there and back to your home in England. If you can agree to that, then I will show you the rutter and we can begin planning our expedition."

Archer said no more. He desperately wanted to examine the journal and hoped that it was everything Jasher had described. If it was then he would be a very rich man and could attain what every proper Englishman desired to achieve, a knighthood and a tie to the nobility. If he could deliver incredible riches to the Crown, then surely the good Queen would want to recognize him. *After all, Francis Drake had gained it, so why not he?*

CHAPTER 10

THE STOPOVER

They had been at sea for several weeks with a brig that Jasher had christened *The Miriam* and the transit across the Atlantic had been uneventful. Archer had suggested the use of a brig because it could be used as a small warship carrying twelve to fifteen cannon. He assured Jasher that its speed made the class popular among pirates as they were fast and maneuvered well for sailing. Their only downside was they tended to use a larger crew than did other ships their size. Nevertheless, a skilled brig captain could operate it with ease and elegance. A brig could for instance turn around almost on the spot, a trait that might provide them a quick exit should the need arise.

As to the rutter, Archer had to admit that Jasher had been as good as his word. The journal had proved to be highly accurate. Moreover, once Jasher had explained the mathematics and lunar positioning involved with calculating longitude, with careful planning, the navigator had been able to avoid any conflicts with Spanish patrol ships by circumventing the usual shipping lanes.

Most of the men on board had crewed with Jasher on earlier expeditions, and understandably Pilot Archer had occasionally asked them about the mysterious Mr. Jasher. To his surprise, the crew had been unable and even reluctant to share much information regarding their leader as well as any specific details about the current expedition into Spanish-held territory; they simply didn't know. If they commented at all, it was to extoll the man's virtues and planning skills, and even more significant to any crew, he had a reputation for returning his men home safely. Moreover, they had all crewed with him before in the Mediterranean and Jasher's expeditions had always been well prepared. The current undertaking might have been more potentially dangerous, but the crew was confident of a safe return.

Nevertheless, Jasher and Archer had a serious disagreement over an unscheduled stopover as they neared Puerto Rico. In his opinion, and Archer had voiced it most vocally, the brief layover was unnecessary and potentially dangerous as it might alert the Spanish to their presence in the area. In spite of the potential danger, Jasher had assured him the detour would be essential to the success of the mission, and though little more was said, Archer still felt they were pressing their luck. Jasher had gone below deck for a few minutes, but had returned. He had intended to continue the discussion for the stopover.

Pilot Archer had cooled down somewhat, and for the moment nearly placated, when Jasher reappeared and asked, "John, what do you know of Puerto Rico?"

"The only thing I need to know is that it's a strong-hold of the Spaniards and should be avoided at all costs."

"I disagree. Our stores are depleted."

"We can get them elsewhere."

"We need an interpreter."

"We can get one elsewhere."

"Not for what I need him for."

Archer stood his ground. "Thanks to my navigational skills, we have managed to keep clear of Spanish patrols, but you are seriously endangering the mission by docking in full view of the Spaniards."

"Then we must be clever. Which country in Europe is Spain not at war with?"

Archer thought a moment then carefully responded, "Holland?"

With a smile and a flip of his hands, he unrolled a flag. "It so happens that I have a flag of Spanish Netherlands in my possession. We shall display the colors of that country."

A smile crossed Archer's face. "So, we fly false colors into a Spanish harbor in Puerto Rico?"

"Exactly."

Archer thought a minute, but could not come up with a better alternative. "Well, Mr. Jasher, if you are so set upon docking in Puerto Rico, I don't suppose we have much choice. Do you speak Dutch? I know I don't."

"As a matter of fact, I do."

"That won't be enough you know. There will still be questions."

"Yes, but by the time they will have figured out who we really are, we will be long gone. I don't plan on staying longer than a day at the most. Moreover, I doubt that anyone will challenge us in Dutch."

"Make certain of it. The bluff will carry only so far for so long. What of our crew?"

"Most all speak Spanish, even better than do you. I would not allow them shore leave unless they spoke the local language. They know the mission, so chances are fine that we will leave with minimal scrutiny. They know how to behave themselves; this is not our first voyage together. Besides, you will be there to care over them, Master Pilot," he replied with an encouraging smile.

Archer was not easily appeased. He growled, "You can depend on it. If they make trouble, they will have to deal with me. I'm not risking my freedom over a bar fight."

An hour after docking in San Juan, Jasher cautiously asked the locals if they knew of anyone who spoke _Quechua_, the local dialect of the peninsula of New Spain. He was directed to a humble area about a mile outside of town. The day was warm and humid, now gravid with moisture being blown in from the Caribbean, but at least it was clear, if uncomfortable. As Jasher approached the village, he noticed a man of middle age sitting outside on his haunches in front of his hut; he was chewing on what appeared to be a tobacco leaf. Jasher had seen the leaf before in Morocco, but had never tried it. The man, however, seemed content to munch away, occasionally spitting out the dark juice it produced from the chewing.

He decided to use Spanish, though from looking at the man, there was a good chance he would have no idea what was being said. He had been told the Taino people lived in this direction, but decided to try his Spanish any-way. "Good afternoon, I am looking for someone who can speak *Quechua.*"

The man smiled, showing yellowed teeth, and nodding his head he point-ed to the hut across the pathway. "He over that way. He not like us in these parts."

"Thank you." Turning, he crossed the muddy path and walked up to a neat thatched hut at the foot of the hill. A vegetable garden was growing around the property, and from the looks of it, someone had a green thumb, though he supposed that in this climate, just about anything would grow. Nevertheless, what caught his eye, as he approached, were the flowers that had been tended with great care; doubtless a woman's touch. And no sooner had he thought this than a young woman in her mid-twenties rounded the hut with a small shovel in her hand. Not many up this way ever received European visitors so Jasher's presence startled her.

He experimented with a little Spanish by way of introduction, hoping she would understand. "I am sorry; I did not mean to alarm you."

Recovering quickly, she asked, "Who are you looking for, sir?"

"A man by the name of Manuel Gutierrez. Would you know of him?"

"Yes, he is my husband. What do you want of him?"

Just then, a man of average height, with lighter skin than had most of the area, jumped off the porch. Smiling, he walked carefully down the pathway in their direction. "I am Manuel. Who might you be? Clearly you are a stranger and a European, but not Spanish I believe."

"You are quite correct, Manuel. I am Benjamin Jasher and you come highly recommended by those in San Juan."

He laughed. "What do they say of me?"

"That you can be trusted and that you speak *Quechua,* the two qualifica-tions I am looking for in an interpreter."

"*Quechua,* why would you need that, if I may ask?"

"I am sailing to your homeland, Manuel, and only you can help me when I we arrive there."

His wife seemed disturbed. "Manuel, you must not leave me and the children!"

Manuel, a little embarrassed by her outburst, glanced toward his wife and said, "Hush Woman, I have not agreed to do anything. Where are your manners? What will he think of us?"

Now ashamed of her lapsed conduct, she replied, "You are right, of course, my Husband. Please forgive me, Sir. Please come inside. We are just sitting down for our noon-day meal."

"Thank you. I will eat with you if there is sufficient for all."

Manuel said, "Of course, sir. We are humble, but as you see, we can care for ourselves."

"I can. I noticed your garden and it is obvious that someone in the family knows much more than I do about gardening."

"It is my wife."

Jasher smiled appreciatively at the garden as they walked up the path. "Mrs. Gutierrez, I have tried gardening, but I never had the skill to grow anything properly. You, madam, are an expert." And such talk seemed to mollify the woman, for by the time Jasher had entered the home and sat down with them along with their two children, Elena, Manuel's wife was chatting happily with him.

A few minutes later and Jasher carefully changed the subject. "Manuel, do you work on the local tobacco plantations?"

"I do. As you can see it is very profitable if you happen to be the *patrón* around here. There is little that I do not know about planting and cultivating tobacco."

"How would you like to become a *patrón*, Manuel?"

Manuel smiled slightly, but with a cynicism grown from experience replied, "*Señor* Jasher, you are new to our area but even in Europe you must know that to be somebody you be born into it."

"Manuel, the only thing you must have is money and hard work to be someone. I can guarantee you the money; the hard work would be up to you."

Manuel pondered Jasher's declaration. Smiling, Manuel asked, "So, Mr. Jasher, you are departing soon for my homeland and wish an interpreter to be present and in return you intend to pay me sufficiently to attain patronage status?"

"If that is your wish."

Manuel looked at his wife whose brown eyes had grown huge at the mention of so much money. With a smile, turning back to Jasher, he replied, "My wife says yes."

"I thought she might. Women are more practical than we usually give them credit. Are you familiar with a village known as Lamanai?"

Manuel's eyes lit up and a smiled played across his face. "It is on a river about forty miles from the ocean. I had traded there on a few occasions in my youth before my new masters, the Spanish, decided it would be in my best interest to relocate to Puerto Rico. They said they would eventually return me, but as you see, it is twenty years later and they never have."

Jasher turned to Elena, and remembering how important it was to Miriam, his own wife, to be informed of everything so that she could be part of the decisions, he looked at her and said, "Elena, Manuel will be gone a few months at most. When he returns, and I stress *when* not if, he will be a rich man and will oversee my tobacco plantation."

"But, *Señor* Jasher, suppose he doesn't return to us?" she asked worriedly.

"Then you and the children will be well cared for." He reached into his pocket and pulled out a pouch full of enough gold coins to provide for her and the children for a year. The pouch disappeared within her apron. There were no further words of protest; she was the pragmatist of the family. Jasher never tired of remembering the small bits of wisdom his own wife had taught him about marriage life.

Manuel was impressed. "That is a lot of money, *Señor* Jasher. What are you looking for in Lamanai?"

With a quick smile, Jasher replied, "Buried treasure, Manuel."

As Jasher and Manuel were strolling slowly back to San Juan, with Jasher all the while explaining the details of the voyage, Pilot John Archer was standing in the middle of a Puerto Rican bar trying to break up what appeared to be the beginnings of a brawl.

Miguel, the bosun and first-mate, was looking at Archer, but pointing his finger at another man at the bar. "Look at him, John. He smiles because he knows I am right. He took my wife seven years ago in Ceuta and now he acts as if he doesn't know me. He thinks I am a fool!"

Archer cautioned, "Miguel, let it go. It's not even worth the effort to take a swing at him."

"I'm not talking about revenge, John. I want what's fair and when this *cabrón* took my wife away from me he jerked my heart right out of my chest." Miguel put on a good performance of someone losing his heart in that manner.

Archer turned to the other man at the bar and asked, "What's your name, friend?"

The man was reclining nonchalantly at the bar. "I am called Diego Fuentes."

"Have you ever lived in Ceuta?"

"I have lived in many places and I don't like being called a *cabrón*."

"Look, Diego, my friend here thinks you knew his wife. Any truth to that?"

With a leer on his face, Diego replied coarsely, "I have known many women. They cannot resist me, of course. Perhaps one of them belonged to him. But, once they have had me, they never want to return." He ended his boast with a laugh.

"I will kill you!" Miguel shouted.

"You could not kill an old woman, let alone me."

His shipmates all shouted and urged Miguel to get his revenge. The bosun, now enraged, lunged for the man at the bar, but Archer caught him by the shoulder, grabbed a bottle off a nearby table and hit him over the head. Miguel went down like a lead anchor. He hit the floor and rolled over on his back and lay there as Archer and his crew mates gathered around him, some protesting Asher's intervention.

The boatswain shouted, "What did you hit him for, Pilot?"

Another crewmate interjected, "The man at the bar has it coming!"

Archer angrily shot back in a whisper. "I don't care if he did. The last thing we need is to have the authorities on our backs asking us questions we can't answer."

"What do we do with Miguel?"

"You two pick up his arms and legs and carry him back to the ship. We are getting out of here as soon as Jasher returns."

"What about the cook? Is he done picking up the stores?"

"He will be by the time we return to *The Miriam*," replied Archer. Now, grab him and let's get out of here!"

After they had carted off the bosun through the door, Diego at the bar laughed out loud, "Good thing you hit him over the head, Englishman. You would have been feeding him to the sharks for bait after I got through with him." The bar erupted in laughter.

Archer was angry they had all seen through his accent. He walked up to the bar, toe-to-toe with Diego and said, "When I get back, *amigo*, I will turn him lose on you and if he can't finish the job, I will. Remember that." He turned around and stalked out the door of the tavern.

"*Adios, Inglés*. With a lazy smile and a smug salute, he replied, "I will be waiting."

CHAPTER 11

El Caminante, 1623

Among the Spaniards who knew his reputation for making an appearance at the least opportune moment, he was known simply as *"El Caminante"*, the Walker. It was definitely not an appellation of affection, but one of respect, and if you were unfortunate enough to incur his ire, which was normal, it was one of dread. Don Caín had arrived in Cuba two years earlier with a determination to intercept all confiscated documents relating to the history of the people of the New World and ostensibly to take the records back to Europe for study. Since the 1530s he had been receiving regular reports of sightings of metallic records and parchments in that part of the world and the rumors had eventually been circulated of recordings of cities and governments of these native civilizations that had been at war with one another. Since all this had been well documented by the Spaniards, he intended that these newly discovered records correctly reflect history in a manner conducive to the involvement of the Clan. He was curious as to how successful Sidon and his successors had been as well as concerned that any records relating to their activities should fall into the wrong hands. It had been many years since he had last confronted Jasher and he was keen to avoid being outflanked by any of his cunning efforts in the New World.

For over one hundred years the Governor of Cuba had been responsible for allowing ingress and egress of all cargo being transported along the shipping lanes within the Caribbean. This meant that nothing and no one was permitted into Central America or New Spain unless the visiting person first reported through that office and received an official stamp of passage; everyone else would be considered a threat to the Crown and indirectly to the Clan. Since Cain's society had underwritten every voyage the monarchs of Spain and Portugal had initiated since the days of Cortés, Cain's approval was now required for any new ventures. When he became aware that records were slipping through his net of control, he had arrived to put an immediate halt to any further leakage to parties unaffiliated with his Brotherhood.

The current Governor, Lorenzo Cabrera, cursed audibly as his adjutant, Rodrigo Lopez, handed him a brief of recent sightings of foreign ships being detected in Puerto Rico. Since Cain had arrived in Cuba, this weekly routine had become standard.

"Rodrigo, is this the entire list of new sightings?"

"They are, Governor."

"They had better be accurate this time. The last list did not contain two ships that had been sighted by Don Caín when he was in Puerto Rico."

"Excellency, that oversight can be explained. Those observations were made at different times of the week."

"I don't want excuses Rodrigo. The Don reamed me out on that one and the last thing I need is to have him on my back with a new shipment of cargo due in any day from Vera Cruz."

"I understand, Sir, but we never know when he is to make an appearance. One day he shows up in Puerto Rico, a few days later he is here in Cuba then the week after he is spotted in Vera Cruz."

"Yes, he calls his visits surprise inspections. He has a real knack for new phrases, Rodrigo. Did you ever notice that?" he asked sarcastically.

"As you say, Excellency." Rodrigo was sensibly non-committal. *El Caminante* had no sense of humor and words from a loose tongue had a way of ending up in the wrong ears.

Governor Cabrera walked quietly into his old office. It was now occupied by Don Caín and had been for the past two years, three months and two days. Cabrera was greatly perturbed his authority had been usurped so blatantly, and if truth be told, he was highly mortified and the shame could be seen clearly on his face as he made his daily rounds. He carried the latest ship sightings list and an unexpected ship had been noted in Puerto Rico and it had yet to appear in Cuba to receive passage stamps for a westward voyage. This misplaced ship appearing on the list would undoubtedly lead to questions for which he had no answers, further placing him in an awkward position for someone of his rank and stature, but he knew that Don Caín would insist upon seeing it.

It galled the Governor immensely to present himself humbly before this man for it was clear that Don Caín, *El Caminante*, was not Spanish and therefore unworthy of his obeisance. The letter of introduction from King Phillip of Spain had made it clear, however, that while he was in Cuba, Don Caín was titular head of all shipping authorizations in and out of New Spain and his authority superseded that of the Governor and the Viceroy. Cabrera may have still retained his title, but as long as *El Caminante* sat in his office, he knew he carried as much authority as a dead mule. And it was on this note of grudging humility that Lorenzo Cabrera requested an audience before the Don.

Cain was poring over the latest reports coming out of New Spain and he was highly vexed at the Viceroy of Mexico, Don Diego Carrillo, for being so lax in his reports of discovered records. There was an abundance of details regarding confiscated native treasure or the amount of ore being mined as a result of native slave labor, but scant information or descriptions of any recording artifacts. What was probable, though only tinged with rumor, was that when the Catholic priests were not busy burning the records, they were gathering them up and sending them back secretly to Spain or Rome.

It had been noted that on some occasions, the priests had even gone so far as to build over native temple sites with cathedrals and the records were left within. These methods might provide a temporary solution, but they were scarcely thorough enough to ensure Cain that his Brotherhood was safe from prying eyes or curious *conquistadores*. Moreover, he feared that at some future date, such records might be accidentally dug up and the records discovered in the debris. In any event, they would be brought forward as either a damning accusation or even coercion against him and the Clan. Besides, he preferred to deal with the problem in the present and avoid the risk that they might emerge unexpectedly in the future.

Aside from that, he was not above being curious as to how successful Sidon had been in the proliferation of his society among the people in the West. He was thus preoccupied with a few recently discovered records when the Governor entered his study and stood humbly before him.

Cain glanced up at the man standing before him and hardly cared a whit at his discomfort and embarrassment at having his authority usurped. "Report", was all he said.

Though Governor Cabrera was inwardly mortified at his now subservient role, he made a great effort to hide it. He cleared his throat and began respectfully, "Excellency, I have here the latest list of ship sightings from Puerto Rico. As the list indicates, our agents in Puerto Rico detected a ship flying the colors of the Spanish Netherlands, a brig carrying a name, *The Miriam*."

"*The Miriam?*" Cain tried to search his memory for the name, it being so familiar to him. Shaking his head in frustration, he realized it must be a name from his distant past, someone he should know but could not quite remember the face to go with it. After a moment, he shrugged inwardly then replied, "And then what?"

"It docked for provisions and a day later set sail westerly towards Cuba with a native Indian who spoke both Spanish and an Indian dialect. The ship never reached Havana. Though the brig was flying the colors of our allies, it was piloted by an Englishman."

"How do you know that the pilot was from England?"

"According to reports, he broke up what could have been a bar fight. He stepped in between two Spaniards, one that was a member of his crew, and laid a bottle over his head. He cursed in English and some of the patrons in the bar recognized the language."

"Very well, go on."

"Reports indicate that the crew was mostly Spaniards and Berbers from Morocco. Another man who was in charge and similar to the Englishman in appearance, was fluent in Spanish, but it was clear from his accent that he was not of Spanish birth."

Cain slowly leaned back in his chair and smiling enigmatically asked, "You mean he was like me?"

The response was careful and slow in coming. "That would seem to describe his report." The Governor cleared his throat nervously then said, "The report also mentioned that one of the crew was overheard to say this man's name was Jasher."

His pronunciation of the name may have been atrocious, but in Cain's mind, it left little doubt to who he was referring. His countenance changed from one of mild curiosity to outright anger. He abruptly stood and shouted, "Find my pilot and have him report to me as soon as possible!"

The Governor bowed and quickly departed, happy, as always, to be out of his presence. Nevertheless, he wondered what it was that had suddenly changed his interest. Governor Cabrera did not know who this Jasher was, but he was sure that he would prefer to be somewhere else when *El Caminante* found him.

Diego Gálvez was the captain-pilot of the Spanish fleet in the New World and the pilot-major of the fastest Spanish frigate in the Caribbean, *La Virgen*. Because of his vast understanding of the shipping lanes between Spain and the New World as well as his deft handling of ships, he was highly sought after and the best paid. In time Gálvez came under the careful scrutiny of Cain who sought out only the best. Understandably, Gálvez' unique talents, intelligence and cunning appealed to Cain, and within a few years, not only had he made the navigator his private pilot, but had initiated him into the Clan. He was set for life financially and thus was more than happy to confer his allegiance to Don Caín, thus when Diego was summoned, he responded quickly.

"Excellency, I understand you wish to speak with me. I am at your service." He stood where the Governor before had stood, but unlike the Governor, Cain amiably found him a chair next to him, thus allowing them both to speak frankly and openly, if not as equals then as close as Cain ever permitted.

"Thank you, Diego." Given Jasher's probable destination was the mainland of New Spain, Cain had tried to anticipate where Jasher might put ashore. "If you were a pilot trying to invade our shipping lanes in the New World, and had no intention to attack our cargo ships to commit robbery, but instead wanted to make a landing somewhere isolated to recover something and then to leave undetected, to where would you plot a course and how would you sail there?"

Diego Gálvez intently studied a nearby map of the Caribbean. After a moment he reasoned, "If the pilot were looking to avoid confrontation and his intention was to simply find something and take it back, then he would not dock in the usual bays and landings. If his party intended to trek overland and avoid our military outposts as well as our native allies, they would need to come in from the south—though the jungle is so dense I don't see how they would avoid it—but, given those conditions, he will land somewhere along the coast line here." He pointed to a place on the southeastern side of the Yucatán Peninsula that would one day be known as Belize, near Corozal Bay. "He would have to have an excellent rutter, though."

"Oh, why is that?" Cain inquired, now curious.

"The shoals are bad enough, but the reef is dangerous and extends about two leagues out into the bay. There would be no way to hide his ship. He would have to drop anchor in the middle of the bay and it would be exposed and easy to detect."

Knowing Jasher to be a meticulous planner, Cain suspected he did have such a journal. He looked again at the map and decided on his course of action.

"That is where he intends to go. Prepare the frigate and we will try to block them on their way out of the bay. I intend to board the ship and retrieve an article that he will be trying exceedingly hard to protect. If they try to pass, we will blow them out of the water." He smiled at the opportunity to renew his acquaintance with an old brother.

CHAPTER 12
LAMANAI, REVISITED, 1623

> *A people without the knowledge of*
> *their past history, origin and culture*
> *is like a tree without roots.*
>
> ----- *Marcus Garvey, Jamaican*
> *political leader and journalist*

*L*amanai was inhabited *as early as the 16th century BCE. Among the many important aspects of Post classic and early Spanish colonial period, Maya life at Lamanai is shown by the presence of significant numbers of copper artifacts. Copper indicates broader trade relations in the southern Maya lowlands and as a reflection of technological change, the history of metal artifacts used at Lamanai is an invaluable element in the reconstruction of Post classic and early historical dynamics. The archaeological contexts of copper objects recovered at Lamanai began with the appearance of metal at the site around 1150 ACE.*

Nearly all of the copper objects found at Lamanai are distinctly Mesoamerican in form and design and based on metallurgical analyses it appears that manufacturing technologies were distinctly Mesoamerican as well. The presence of production materials and miss-cast pieces along with the results of chemical compositional and micro structural analysis support the idea that the Mayans at Lamanai were engaged in the on-site production of copper objects by late pre-Columbian times (Spanish conquest era).

There were copper objects such as copper bells, elaborate rings, and button like ornaments recovered at Lamanai, beginning with the appearance of metal at the site by around 1150 ACE. The term "copper" is used to describe the metal found at the site, but all of the copper artifacts found at Lamanai were alloyed with other metals such as tin or arsenic and could technically be considered bronze. (https://en.wikipedia.org/wiki/Lamanai)

It was late in the afternoon and *The Miriam* was nearing Corozal Bay, off the western coast of Belize. John Archer and the bosun, Miguel, were deep in conversation, but it was almost loud enough to be considered as an argument.

The bosun was pointing his finger for emphasis at Archer and complained, "John, I still have a lump on the back of my head from that bottle you busted me with."

"Yes, and I would do it again," Archer shot back. "We were supposed to have a quiet drink after a long voyage, and what did you do? You accused another man of running off with your wife."

"He did run off with her!"

"Sounds to me like you are well rid of her."

"*Cabrón*, you dare say that about my Dolores?"

"That's a good name for her Miguel. She gave you nothing by pain."

Jasher had finally heard enough. "Ok, you two. No more! You can table this discussion for another time in private. I need you both alert and focused. Lamanai is close at hand and the last thing the crew needs to see is

TREASURE OF THE CLAN

the two senior crewmen brawling like drunken Portuguese bilge scrubbers!"
He looked at both sternly and said, "Enough I say." He looked at both and
asked, "Agreed?"

They both reluctantly nodded their agreement and Miguel playfully
punched Archer and said, "Ok, John a truce for now. But, when we're done
here, I'm going back to that bar and finish my business."

"And when that day arrives I'll have your back, Miguel." Archer smiled
and they both shook hands.

Jasher shook his head indulgently and commented, "On behalf of me and
the rest of the crew, I thank you both."

Miguel, now all smiles, asked Jasher, "Ok, boss, what's the plan?"

"John, what does the rutter say about the bay? We will need a close docking area, as close to the mouth of the river as possible."

"The rutter indicates a path through the shoals and reef exists, but it will
be a bit dicey to find it. Once in, we will have to follow the same path out, so
if we get blocked in, we are dead in the water."

The bosun commented, "We should drop anchor somewhere between
the mouth of the river and the opening through the reef to give us a better
chance of escape should we get unexpected visitors. As the pilot says, if we
are caught inside the reef with the exit blocked we won't be able to maneuver
out. We may have to choose between being ripped apart on the reef or blown
out of the water amidships as we cross the opening."

"Benjamin, the safest place would be just inside the reef, but close enough
to the main body of the bay to allow us a fast escape should we get uninvited
company."

"Is it possible any other ships would have the details of our rutter regarding the reefs?"

"Not a chance. The details of the rutter are very specific and these waters
have had few visitors."

"How do you know?"

"If anyone tried to maneuver through these waters without this rutter,
they would either run aground on the shoals or be ripped apart on the reef.

Benjamin, I don't know where this rutter came from or from whom, but he had intimate knowledge of this bay."

Jasher peered out over the deck to the far jungle. Nodding, he made a decision then turned to the pilot and said, "Mr. Archer, find us a way through the reef and a safe anchorage for us to fall back to. Make it so."

Archer sat at the helm and listened as the watchman rang the bell signaling the change of hour. He munched contentedly on fruit they had picked up in Puerto Rico and though a part of him was irritated at the unexpected layover for security reasons, he knew they had to pick up much needed stores. As they had docked, Jasher had stressed the need to lay up a good supply of fresh fruit to avoid scurvy. *Now, how would he know about that?* Archer had asked himself. Scurvy was the bane of every seaman having sailed on any long, extended voyage and he would know. He had seen boys return from such voyages without teeth or with eyesight so bad they were nearly blind as old men. Despite what appeared to be his lack of outward concern for security, Archer was beginning to understand that the loyalty and confidence the crew had in Jasher had been justified.

The day had dawned bright and clear, and of course, warm and humid. Pilot Archer had just returned from below decks from his cabin to check the rutter when a crewman shouted from the bowsprit lookout above him, "Land, I see land."

Of course, Archer had gradually become aware of the tell-tale signs of a shore line, such as sea birds, for the past few days now, and this morning they had even spotted small fishing boats being rowed by local fishermen. The natives had seemed friendly enough and had even waved, but kept to themselves, as though their business was more pressing than entertaining men on a foreign ship.

This was where the details of the rutter would truly pay dividends. That information told Archer that there would be coral reefs that would extend well out into the bay and that they would have to set down anchor well away from shore. Hence, he had navigated *The Miriam* steadily closer until he reached the point where he could safely have the sails withdrawn and the anchor dropped.

Archer had been so busy with the intricate process of anchorage that he had failed to notice when Jasher had emerged from below decks.

Because he had never before gone so far and to such lengths to gather a record, Benjamin was wondering where this latest adventure would take him. As he was looking out intently at the distant outline of verdant jungle, he congratulated himself that he had chosen the right man to pilot *The Miriam*. As Archer supervised the final operations prior to dropping anchor, the men had jumped to obey his orders and complete the tasks that would permit disembarkation. Jasher could feel the heightened activity around him and it was obvious that the man had proven himself to be unusually skilled and knowledgeable. Moreover, the crewmen were equally responsive to his commands.

Jasher had ordered two rowing boats to be lowered from the port side that would accommodate their expedition inland. A few minutes later, he and a dozen men, including his interpreter Manuel, then descended the side and lithely boarded the two boats. As he and the men readied themselves to follow a river that snaked slowly up into the hinterland of a dense jungle in the New World, Pilot-Major John Archer remained with the brig along with most of the crew to perform any repairs.

Before climbing over the side for the descent to the long boat, Jasher said, "John, if it looks as if the ship is going to be bottled up within the reef, you move out into the bay and leave us and return later for a pick up. Do not endanger the ship unnecessarily. It is our only way home."

"Understood. How long do you expect your expedition to last?"

He looked toward the river and replied, "If everything goes well, we should be back this time the day after tomorrow. He swung over the side and grabbed the netting then lowered himself into the boat. Looking up he said, "John, as soon as you see us return, weigh anchor and have *The Miriam* prepared for a fast departure."

Pilot Archer was quick to reply, "Aye, sir, I am well ahead of you."

Once they had entered the mouth of the river, a foreboding came over Jasher. It was nothing specific, just a concern that the records would soon again be in the open once he had reacquired them.

Jasher signaled the rowers to pull the longboat toward the far shore of the river. The air was gravid with humidity, the heat oppressive and the total effect of the two gave him reason to second-guess his decision to regrow a beard he had not sported for many centuries. Though it was not long yet, the scruffiness was enough to remind him why he had often cut it over the years. He was not sure why he had decided to allow it to grow out again except that it had seemed the right thing to do.

After a few hours on the river, a crewmate muttered, "A lot of crocodiles in the water around here. Big ones, too."

Manuel, their interpreter, pointed out, "The word Lamanai is ancient and refers to the crocodiles that infest these waters and land here about. The early people of the area considered them a symbol of royalty, but the name probably related to a person of royalty who assumed the symbol of the crocodile to distinguish him from other rulers."

"Still, not a nice place to fall overboard," commented another member of the crew.

Jasher turned to Manuel and asked, "Manuel, you mentioned that you lived here in the area many years ago. Is your home nearby?"

"Actually, *Señor* Jasher, we will be arriving near my village soon; it is just around the next bend in the river. I was hoping perhaps we could make a stop and visit my parents. I hate to be a burden, but it has been many years since I have seen them."

"Of course, Manuel. We could all use a rest."

"Thank you." His attention returned to the river bend ahead. Once relief had washed over the man, anticipation began to set in. The last sight he remembered of his village was looking back at his parents waving their goodbyes on the tiny dock. He was silent for a moment then, as if imparting wisdom learned the hard way, reluctantly he began to share feelings he had kept bottled up far too long.

"As a youth, you have so much of your life before you and do not often realize that some things left unsaid cannot be reversed. I regret never having told my parents how much I had appreciated their love and influence upon my life. At the time I said farewell to them, I had no idea that it might be so final. But, I think they knew."

Jasher envied his friend's moment of personal epiphany. For Manuel, he had come to realize that time was finite so each of us must make the most of today because tomorrow may never come. By comparison, his own life experience was twisted and warped, outside the normal view of everyone else; everyone except Cain. *How strange, to finally realize that I have more in common with Cain than anyone I have ever known.*

Jasher, having been moved by Manuel's words, counselled, "Being parents, I am sure they knew your love for them. After all, who would know you better than would they?"

"Perhaps you are correct, *Señor* Jasher, but it does not relieve my guilt for having been remiss in telling them more often."

"Then you will soon have a chance to make up for that."

Manuel smiled at the thought. As they rounded the bend in the river, he asked, "*Señor* Jasher, do you have a family?"

The inevitable question always arose it seemed. It was another reminder of how incredibly unique his life experiences were to all but one. To avoid confusing answers that would have only led to more questions that he could not answer, he had developed a stock answer over the years. "I lost them all to a disease many years ago. Since then I have been on my own." *It was not exactly a lie,* he thought. *Death is the greatest of all diseases.*

"I am sorry to hear of your loss. It is a sad thing for a man to be alone."

Jasher nodded his agreement. "You are wise beyond your years, my friend."

Manuel smiled at the complement. Looking at the bend in the river, he noted, "Unless the river has changed its course, I think we are nearing my village. That should be it up ahead." He pointed at a clearing as several villagers began to descend to the dock.

"They seem to be expecting us." It was a comment from one of the crew from the other longboat.

Manuel pointed out, "They have been aware of our presence for some time now, probably since we entered the mouth of the river. There is little movement along this river without someone taking notice then passing it along." Manuel noted a tremor of anxiety from the crew at this new discovery.

"Do not be alarmed. They are just curious and will welcome you as long as you come in peace."

Jasher looked around at his men and said, "Manuel is correct. We are here in peace, and as long as we conduct ourselves peacefully, they will welcome us as friends."

"How do you know?" another crewman asked.

"Deception is the last thing they will expect from a stranger who they consider to be an honored guest. It is the same nearly everywhere."

"Not in Spain," the same crewmate muttered then spit into the river.

Jasher, remembering his experiences not so many years before, sadly replied, "No, not everywhere. But, perhaps someday that will change."

After docking the boats, the crew and Jasher, led by Manuel, walked carefully up the path to be welcomed by a small crowd. Two villagers, an elderly man and woman, emerged from the group, and ran up to Manuel and all three embraced. Words that had not been said for over fifteen years were now being expressed, but mostly it was just the being together. A family had been reunited again after many years and now was the time to celebrate their feelings; the talking would come later. Jasher caught Manuel's silent thanks and smiled. A family together after years of absence was special and he was glad he could accommodate Manuel this short stopover.

Jasher and his crew were quietly surrounded and led through an opening into the jungle. As the procession began to wind its way along a path, all the villagers had emerged along the walkway to greet them as they passed. Some sang, others clapped hands and still others threw flowers of welcome, but all smiled. A few minutes later, they arrived before the hut of the village elder that greeted all the visitors and bade them sit. According to Manuel, he wanted to hear of their voyage. All had a seat while Manuel conversed with the elder, simultaneously translating the conversation to the Europeans.

The Elder began. "Manuel, you have returned to us. You must now tell us your story that it may become part of our village history."

Manuel began to relate the events subsequent to his departure from the village. When he arrived at telling of his wife and children all burst out in applause and laughter. Tears were visible on the cheeks of his parents when he told of his home in Puerto Rico and their grandchildren. When he was finished, all clapped hands while others sang, but smiles were on all the faces, including that of Jasher and his crew.

After the excitement had quieted, the village elder turned to Jasher and brought up the matter that was on the minds of all. "I am Kiché Mopan. Manuel has told us that you have come to our land for a purpose and that you are not merely explorers. Please explain; perhaps we can help."

Jasher began by introducing himself. "I am Jasher. Friends, my crew and I have travelled from afar to your land to retrieve a record of the history of your ancestors who once lived upon this land many generations ago." He paused to ensure all understand the scope of their mission.

Those who were in attendance began to whisper their comments. Finally, the chief elder raised his hand to quell the noise. He pointed out, "Our own village keeps an account that is added from time to time. The visit of our brother Manuel will be noted as soon as he departs. This record of which you speak, can you describe it?"

"It will be made of metal and the writings upon it will be of ancient origin. They were written by a man who arrived in your land and buried it in Lamanai many generations ago."

When word of Lamanai was mentioned, many nodded their heads as though unsurprised by the Jasher's revelation. The Elder explained, "The ancient city of Lamanai is considered sacred to us here in the area. Many of us can trace our lineage from those who live there still. It is not surprising that you seek this record in their midst."

"Is there one among the village that we can talk to on this matter?"

"You should see the village Elder by the name of Atlatl. I know him well and he will help you in your quest for the records you seek."

"Thank you. Is there one among your people who could accompany us up river to introduce us to the chief elder of Lamanai?"

The Elder smiled and replied, "I would be happy to greet my old friend again on your behalf. I will send runners up ahead to announce our arrival."

"Thank you, Kiché Mopan. That would be most appreciated."

Jasher and the crew spent the next few hours exchanging information and tasting the local cuisine of the village. It had been an interesting morning, but the crew and Jasher were both anxious to move farther upriver to Lamanai and collect the records. Jasher did not vocalize his concerns, but felt their visit with those up ahead would have to be brief. Time seemed to be running out.

Cain paced impatiently across the quarterdeck behind his pilot, Diego Gálvez. This had the effect of making his pilot more anxious than was usual. Normally, when Cain accompanied him on a voyage, he awaited below in his quarters, ascending to the deck only when necessary. But, and though Diego was reluctant to express his observation on the matter, everything about this voyage was unusual.

Up ahead, Cain could just make out the mast of a brig. The sails had been withdrawn and now the ship was at anchor in the bay and was waiting. *But, waiting for what and who,* he asked himself. It had to be Jasher, and if it was then he was out there to recover some records. There could be no other explanation.

"Diego, can we maneuver any closer?"

"I would not recommend it, Don Caín. The shoals are bad here and the reef extends well out into the bay. Whoever navigated the ship that deeply into the harbor has an exceptional navigational chart. I would like very much to see that rutter for myself."

"You will Diego. I shall deliver it to you as soon as my business with the captain of that ship has been consummated." Cain hated being out of control of the situation, but knowing he had the most skilled pilot in the New World, he would have to yield to his pilot's superior experience in such matters. "What is your recommendation, Diego?"

"We move in as close as possible, but wait for them to exit the bay. Then we catch them in the open seas. We should wait for them to come to us."

Cain shook his head. "No, I want whatever Jasher has discovered in the jungle. When he returns I will take a long boat out and pay him a visit. You will await me in the bay outside the reef."

"I would counsel against such a decision. He may decide to hold you hostage; if you are aboard, I will not be able to fire against the ship. It would be too risky."

"I, too, have thought of that, but taking a hostage is not his style. He will try to out-think me as he has done in the past. I want to see his face up close when it is obvious that I have him beaten."

"That is a dangerous game, Don Caín."

"But one that he and I have been playing since well before you were born, Diego."

Diego gazed upon his *patrón*, still agitated with excitement. He looked scarcely forty years of age and yet on several occasions he had mentioned details of places and events that only a much older man could have known about. It was a mystery, but it would have been impolite to ask the man his age. He sensed he would not have been forthcoming with the truth in any event.

Off to the right, Jasher noticed a small landing and a clearing, which indicated that even though the jungle appeared deserted of men, there was a good chance they were about to meet some. It was fortunate that Kiché Mopan, the village elder, had sent runners ahead to announce their arrival. He noted that it was quite probable that the trip up the river had already been observed for the past few miles and their course reported farther ahead. This was to be the culminating moment of their voyage and he did not want any unforeseen misapprehensions among the people of Lamanai. The Elder and Manuel continued to exchange information as the party rowed peacefully up to the docking area.

So as to appear as non-threatening as possible should they meet any local natives, Jasher had instructed his men to leave all weapons on *The Miriam*. Though many of the men felt naked and helpless without them, Jasher had convinced them that the success of the mission depended upon an appearance of peace. Besides, he had reminded them, the natives would undoubtedly outnumber them anyway, so if the people along the river were prepared for hostility, he wanted to reassure them his party was not there to engage them in open conflict. Both Manuel and Kiché Mopan had assured him Lamanai was just up ahead and their party would be received peacefully.

As if to confirm this, as the boats drew near the clearing, two men stepped out of the dense bush and seemed to await their arrival and while the boats drew nearer, they walked out closer as if to greet them. They were dressed about the head and legs with bright ornamental feathers of local fowls and, as one would expect to find in a tropical humid climate, their loincloths were brief; moreover, they wore sandals on their feet, also multi-hued. It seemed clear that they had dressed up for the occasion for, as the European men stepped off the boats, they were met with welcome friendly faces.

Making note of the reception and warm smiles of his hosts, Jasher was relieved that he had made the right decision regarding the weapons. Apparently, the runners sent on up ahead by Kiché Mopan as well as others up and down the river had alerted the villagers that foreign men had been spotted and were deemed to be friendly and had no hostile intentions. Kiché Mopan made the preliminary introductions and asked permission to enter their village.

Now looking at the natives while pointing towards the Europeans, Manuel declared, "These men have come in peace from a long distance and wish to extend a hand of friendship." He then signaled toward Jasher and declared, "This man wishes to speak with your village elder on a matter of great importance. Could you take us to him, please?"

In ceremony fashion, and all the while smiling, the men of Lamanai turned and led them though a jungle alcove that had been slashed away and neatly trimmed. They then passed through to an opening that gave way to a scene of numerous thatched huts made of much of the surrounding material of the jungle, namely ferns, fronds and bamboo-like tresses that had been lashed securely by overhanging lianas of nearby trees. The women and children appeared, along with the remainder of the men, their curiosity outweighing any initial fear or qualms, but all came forward in quiet deference to the occasion. A few of the native men began whispering among themselves, and noting their open curiosity and oral speculations, the interpreter, Manuel, explained in *Quechua* to the natives the purpose for the visit. After receiving an answer, the interpreter turned to Jasher and his men and explained in Spanish that the native men had agreed to fetch the man they sought.

While in the village, Manuel proved to be a good interpreter and continued to render a faithful translation.

Now eager to assist, the men of the village indicated that Jasher and his party should follow them through the bush. After a few minutes' walk, the Europeans were led to a small, unpretentious hut near the center of the village. One of the native men peered inside and beckoned an old man from within to come out and greet strangers who had come from afar to speak with him.

"*Cacique*, the man you have been expecting is looking for you," he announced.

From within could be heard a faint voice reply, "Make him comfortable and I will be right out." A panting followed by a slurred comment: "A few more days and I will have to be carried about." After a moment, he mumbled, "Behold, the old man who becomes an infant." Then they heard a rustling of clothes being slowly arrayed over an old frame.

Jasher smiled when he heard the translation. He motioned his men to be seated upon the ground; as was custom, women and children appeared and provided food and drink. Presently, the village elder, attired in ceremonial clothing, appeared and wearily sat down opposite Jasher. He was old and wrinkled, wizened as if used to eating sparingly, but his eyes sparkled wisdom with the knowing eyes of age.

Jasher took this moment to address his men, including the interpreter, Manuel, in Spanish; moreover, he indicated to Manuel that it should be translated to the villagers as well. "Gentlemen, you are about to witness and hear things that will stretch your understanding of what is conceivable, even possible. In most ancient societies the customs, even religion, are kept alive by carefully maintained stories passed down from one generation to the next. Do not underestimate the truth of these tales for they are as important to the people who tell them as the rain and sun they need to cultivate crops or the medicinal herbs they use to maintain their health. It has been my experience, as you open your mind to new possibilities, you will discover that all these elements are interwoven. Listen carefully to what is discussed here today and you will learn much about the eternal nature of our lives and how we are all inextricably linked together for a common purpose."

The old man smiled and assented to what Jasher had just declared then added in his language, "Well said for someone who appears to be so young." Looking a little closer at Jasher, he commented, "Or are you really as young as you appear?" It was clear his eye-sight had diminished over the years; as a result, he peered quizzically at Jasher then shrugged.

After a moment, the Elder proceeded to explain to Jasher. "Our people have lived along the shore of this river for many generations. There is a legend among us that one day a white man, bearded as you, would arrive from a far eastern land declaring to be our brother and he would come to collect an ancient relic of our people. His name would be Jasher. Are you he who would make this claim?"

As he heard mention of Jasher's name, Manuel appeared momentarily stunned then proceeded to translate his words to the Europeans around the circle. A few audibly gasped; others shook their heads in disbelief that surely they had misunderstood what had just been translated. After a moment, they all gaped at one another with wonder then all eyes fell upon Benjamin.

Jasher smiled, bowed and declared, "I am Jasher and yes, I am your brother. It is good to be among my family again."

Merely nodding his head, the old man smiled and seemed to need no translation. He continued his story as if recalling an extraordinary tale. "I am Atlatl. My fathers before me all told the same story and each looked forward to the day when you would arrive. I am happy that it has occurred in my life-time." With a note of chastisement, he added, "Though if you had delayed your visit much longer, you would probably be talking with my son instead of me." With that he and the villagers all laughed at his wit.

The occasion often determines the degree of humor in any situation. When Jasher heard the translation, he too, laughed, but because he felt he was not just among friends, but family, he laughed with an unabashed, unrestrained emotion he had not known in many centuries. The old man nodded his head to acknowledge the laughter his wit had produced. Gazing at Jasher, he commented boldly, "My Brother, you should laugh more. It suits you."

Nodding his head, he had to agree. "You are quite correct, Brother. It gives me great pleasure to be again among my kinsmen."

"Yes, family is the most important tie of all."

On a less optimistic note Jasher commented, "I fear your days in this pristine paradise are numbered, Atlatl. There will be many who will come after me that will not consider you and your people to be brothers as I do."

Now a more somber shadow fell across the old man's brow. "Yes, we have also heard of them. They bring diseases and weapons of war, but worst of all they bring their greed. Our brothers to the west have all fallen prey to them and are now enslaved or dying out. Yes, our time will come, I fear." He seemed to reflect on this and then commented, "But, we have been kept alive, free and healthy all these years and I think it is because of you." He paused a moment as if to collect his thoughts then thoughtfully added, "Once you have what you have come to collect then we will be no more. It is sad, but we were never meant to live forever in our jungle home."

Atlatl shook off this despondent epiphany of the future. He was now more direct. "The location of what you seek has always been passed down throughout the generations of our village from one elder to the next, from father to son, and this secret we have kept to ourselves. You will follow me." With that being said, he slowly arose and signaled all the men to follow him down a carefully manicured path behind his hut. Since this information was new to the rest of the village, their curiosity was as heightened as that of the men of Jasher's party, including Kiché Mopan from Manuel's village.

The crewmen had all heard rumors of the Aztec and Maya temples, but never had they seen one. In the distance could be heard the chatter of spider monkeys at play in a nearby ficus tree then a brightly hued quetzal bird flew past them and gracefully landed on a stone building nearly five stories in height. It perched high atop the nearby temple then hearing the approach of men, it quickly flew away. Jasher and his party were carefully led to the front of the building by the village elder and a few others to support him if he should falter. The Europeans drew closer and marveled at the majesty of the architecture and the skill it must have taken to build it.

The temple was intricately carved with bas relief inscriptions ornamenting the surface around all sides. Beginning at the bottom and ascending all the way to the pinnacle was a stairway constructed into the building and on both sides ascending were delicately carved animals; on the reverse side of the temple, one could see pictures of the sun, moon and the stars carefully chiseled on the stairway. Additionally, on both sides of the stairway could be clearly seen the sculpted likeness in high-relief of the great bearded god, Quetzalcoatl to the Aztecs and Toltecs or Kukulkan to the Mayans. The whole building was made of limestone from nearby quarries, but how the heavy stones could have been excavated then later hauled to the site up a hill was a mystery. The temple was at once beautiful and enigmatic.

Upon reaching the temple, Atlatl turned to the Europeans and declared to Benjamin, "Our legends tell us that the temple you see before you was dedicated to the one true God, the Creator of all. Though no one seems to remember how it occurred, over time it had acquired an actual name, The Star of Jasher. So, Brother, your coming has always been a part of our village culture."

Jasher was speechless, but managed to respond, "I am honored, Atlatl." *Somehow I suppose I have Joseph to thank for that.*

Turning back to the temple, the old man pointed to a stepping stone in the stairway, which appeared on closer inspection to be loose and manageable. He signaled a few men to remove the stone and beneath it could be seen a leather satchel now battered, old with age and mildew. He turned to Jasher and declared, "In there is what you have come for, I believe."

"Do you know what it is?" Jasher knew, of course, but he wanted to see if the Village Elder was aware of the secret he had been keeping for so long.

"It is a record of our brothers who had lived in a faraway kingdom to the west, or so I was told by my father many years ago. It was written by a man by the name of Aaron." This information, once revealed to the crowd, created quite a stir of conversation.

Jasher, nodding as if satisfied, reached inside and withdrew the satchel. He then placed the old covering on the ground and gently pulled out the brass plated records. A sigh of astonishment emanated from the crowd looking on.

As Jasher began to relate his impressions, the interpreter proceeded to explain everything.

"Gentlemen, the artifact you see before you is not of gold, but of the highest quality of brass to be found anywhere. Inside contains an abridgement written over two thousand years ago taken from a larger and much older record stored somewhere on this continent. The material on which the record was kept is hardly worth much, but the information contained thereon is priceless. Our mission to this point is complete."

The old man bent down low to touch the plates. As he did so, his hand trembled slightly as he ran his fingers over the ancient engraved glyphs. It had been over forty years since he had last seen them. On the day his father had shown them to him he had been a young man with his whole life ahead of him. Shortly thereafter, as those before him, the elder man had passed away, leaving Atlatl to carry on the tradition. Seeing the ancient relic again suddenly brought back a flood of memories of all that had happened from that moment until now. Blinking his eyes at the lustrous metallic object, he could finally appreciate its symbolic nature and its tie to the life cycle and struggle of his village and the people to whom he had been entrusted. Sadly, he turned his gaze back to Jasher and asked, "So, you have what you have come for. Will you now be leaving us, Brother?"

Jasher noted the daylight was ebbing and felt a tremor of presentiment that their departure should be soon. Jasher nodded his head and added, "We must begin our return early tomorrow morning and we must move quickly to our ship and depart this land for I believe that now that the records have been discovered, there will be those ready to take them away from us."

The old man nodded as if expecting to hear as much. He added, "There is a legend among my people of a man, like you, who entered our village with these plates many generations ago and hid them up. His name was Aaron. Once he had done this he quickly left for there were those following him and surely would have killed him. He was a great warrior and a few days later this man returned, but those who had pursued him did not for he had killed them all in the jungle. Aaron, the great warrior, stayed on in our village until he died an old man. I am a direct descendent of him and my son may be the last of his line for I now fear that our village may soon be no more." The old man glanced toward his son then blinked back tears of sorrow.

Jasher, with a look of compassion, assured him, "Atlatl, The Creator of us all has preserved your line. Yes, your village may soon cease to exist, but your blood line will live on. I promise you that it will. They will yet be a great people with a special destiny."

After a moment, the old man nodded his head. He murmured, "Then I will die content."

CHAPTER 13

THE ESCAPE

*Always bear in mind that your own resolution
to succeed is more important than any other.*

----- *Abraham Lincoln*

Pilot-Major John Archer was beside himself with nervous worry and he was now pacing up and down the decks muttering under his breath. Half an hour earlier, one of the mates had spotted two Spanish frigates approaching from the eastern end of the bay and unless he could move *The Miriam* out of the harbor quickly they would be flanked and unable to make an escape in any direction. He silently cursed Jasher and his boundless confidence in the mission. Shaking his head, he recalled that, against his counsel, Jasher had insisted on taking aboard provisions and finding an interpreter in Puerto Rico. This was an open invitation for a spy to report their whereabouts back to the wrong company and the result was two frigates aggressively moving to block any exit through the harbor.

Archer had no intention of being boarded, captured and beached on some faraway Spanish colony, or worse, put to the oars on some slaver. He inwardly shuddered as he recollected that he knew of too many who had been left to languish away their lives on some deserted island for serving on the wrong ship at the wrong time and he intended to avoid that fate at any cost. He scanned the horizon toward land and thought he saw movement, so he called up to the mate in the lookout and ordered him to scan westward. With a shout, the mate had spotted the shore party making their way slowly back to the ship. *It is going to be close,* thought Archer, *and if we can't slip past the frigates maneuvering to intercept us, The Miriam is likely to be blown apart; they are much faster and their guns more powerful and they have more of them.*

With agonizing slowness, Jasher's group finally arrived and all scurried up the rigging on the port side then hauled up the rowing boats. Archer angrily stalked up to Jasher and declared, "It's too late. Two Spanish frigates are squatting in the harbor and we are well within range of their cannon. I suggest we try to offer up some defense."

Much to Archer's surprise and growing anger, Jasher looked over the situation calmly and counselled, "Do not turn our cannon in their direction. We shall remain in a non-aggressive position and wait to see what they will do."

His anger now reaching a boil, Archer could do little more than to sputter, "I will tell you exactly what they are going to do. They will blow us out of the water with little effort and lose very little sleep over the results!"

Jasher disagreed and pointed out, "I have a feeling they may want to talk before taking any direct action. In the meantime, I suggest you plot an escape route for us in the event we may have to make a quick retreat out of the harbor." Without waiting for Archer's reply, Jasher turned and went below decks to secure the brass records in his cabin.

Archer bit back a scathing remark, muttering under his breath; he, too, went below decks to consult his rutter. A few minutes later he returned and informed the helmsmen of a slight directional change due northeastward then signaled the men to ready *The Miriam* for a quick departure. In a few minutes they had slowly slipped past the reef and into the harbor, but now well within range of the enemy cannon. There they waited, outflanked and outgunned, just as he had feared.

Five minutes later a longboat descended from the Spanish frigate *La Virgen* and seven men boarded the launch, one of who was Cain. As he sat and waited patiently on the prow, six others took to the oars and slowly moved the boat forward toward *The Miriam*, now safely away from the reef. As the scull drew nearer, Jasher and Archer could clearly see a man near the front, rather dark in complexion, with a neatly trimmed beard that did not quite cover the left side of his jaw. Though it had been many years since their last encounter, Jasher easily recognized his old adversary who, as the launch drew ever closer, was even then wearing a victory smile.

When the boat arrived astern, Cain's eyes looked upward at the awaiting crew and as his gaze fell arrogantly upon Jasher then Archer, he asked politely, "Gentlemen, may I come aboard?" A small smile etched his face. "I assure you that it will be to your benefit."

Jasher walked up beside Archer and glancing downward replied, "Only you Cain. Your men stay in the boat." Rigging was thrown over the starboard side to allow him access to the deck.

Without taking offense, he replied, "Of course, Brother. And, may I say, it is good to see you again." He reached up and began pulling himself up along the rigging until he could easily swing over the side. His eyes glinted impishly and a mirthful, indulgent expression never left his face.

Jasher easily recognized the look. It was one he had seen many times over the years when Cain fully expected to have his way. It was his manner to show his victory as though it were a foregone conclusion. Jasher studied the man and decided that what they had to say would be better said in private in his cabin. "Cain, follow me below to my quarters and we can discuss our dilemma privately."

"As you wish, Brother," he replied casually. As they descended, Jasher could hear him complain, "I do wish we could have met under more comfortable circumstances. The below cabins are far too close to the bilge." He cast a *moue* of distaste in the direction of the odor.

"Cain, please spare me your airs of civility. They are wasted on me."

"No need to be rude, Brother." The mirthful levity never left his voice.

After they entered the room, Jasher shut the door behind him and came right to the point. "Alright, Cain, you have my attention. Your ships are blocking our exit from the harbor and I demand you let us pass!"

Cain walked about the room casually, glancing here and there, in no obvious hurry as though he were a bored cat playing with a small mouse. "Where are the records, Brother?" he asked patiently. "I know you have them. It is unlikely you would have come all this distance only to have a peek at my latest acquisition." He added matter-of-factly, "I think I shall call it Mexico though no one really knows the etymology of the term, though I suppose that *Mexica*, the name of the Aztec savages, probably comes closer to describing it. But, it has a nice ring to it, though, don't you agree? Mexico?"

"And if I refuse to turn them over to you?"

"My frigates will blow this scow out of the water!" he bellowed, now tired of the banter.

"You know our rules of engagement, Cain."

"Yes, how well I do know those inane, damnable rules!" he spat with all the pent-up hatred and venom of one who has been frustrated on more than one occasion. He pointed an accusing finger in Jasher's direction. "They allow you all the advantage in this tiresome game we have been playing for so long."

"The rules are there to ensure a fair judgment."

Cain was in no mood for a lecture on the subject of equity. "It is favoritism, not fairness! When I am in the position of a victory I should be allowed to savor it completely," he angrily added.

"Cain, there is no victory here for you today. You are too late. I have recovered the records and have them safely on board the ship so you are not to interfere any further. You should focus your scheming efforts on the cringing, avaricious priests and kings you have at your behest. They are more than happy to oblige your whims and wishes."

"Yes, they are at my behest and they will remain that way. There is much to pillage and exploit from this land and I will have it all, including the treasure to build my kingdom and the records to ensure that history will vindicate my actions."

"Then, I suggest you get busy at it and leave me to pass through the harbor with my boat and men unmolested."

Shaking his head, Cain replied emphatically, "No, not this time, Jasher. The boat is mine and everything in it, including the men. There is no mountain vault here to provide you a convenient retreat. I will remove the records and set you adrift in a launch then blow up *The Miriam.*" With a look of false sympathy, he commented, "A pity the ship you named after your dearly departed wife will have to find a new home at the bottom of the bay." The idea appealed to him so much that a small smile drifted casually across his face.

Jasher knew he was trapped. His bluff was simply not working because technically Cain could remove them at his whim; they were out in the open. The only location that was off-limits was the mountain depository where the records were on consecrated, hallowed ground. With all his desire, he knew that the history he had recovered from Lamanai was necessary and it was up to him to ensure that it was properly safeguarded. He reached out in his mind and knew there had to be a way out of this dilemma. A notion seemed to turn over and he willed the idea to take force then he felt a thought slip out and away. He was aware that something fundamental had changed, almost as though the idea had slid from his mind as a seed before the wind and had found fertile ground upon which to gain nourishment and grow.

"I repeat, Cain. You are too late. Go topside and see for yourself."

"What do you mean?" Suddenly, he heard the voices of his men shouting for him to return. Cain abruptly understood that events had indeed changed. With a sudden cry of "no!" he ran through the cabin and up the flight of stairs with Jasher close behind him. What Cain saw was hardly unknown in those waters, but the coincidence of the timing, though fortunate for Jasher, was galling for Cain. A fog so thick had rolled in that he could scarcely make out the bow of *The Miriam.* The two war frigates were nowhere to be seen; the ships had simply been swallowed up in the low-hanging cloud.

As the two ran up to the railing, they passed Pilot Archer who would have been relieved at the sight of so much fog had it not rolled up as suddenly as it had. He, as had all the crew, remained more than surprised; they were flummoxed. As Archer groped for an explanation that would fit the bewildering scene, Jasher glanced his way and ordered, "John get the ship and the men ready. We are leaving now."

Archer looked around at the dampening fog and asked, "How?"

"Move out. It will clear."

The pilot then turned to the crew and began giving orders to set sail.

Jasher, now trying hard to keep the smile from his face, turned to Cain and pointed out, "Cain, as I see it, you have two choices. You can remain aboard with us as my guest and watch as we ply our way through the fog past your ships and out of the bay; I would be happy to drop you off in Puerto Rico. Or, you can take your chances and row back through the fog. Perhaps your captain will hear your call. Or perhaps not?"

Looking out across the dense fog cloud and noting its insidious tentacles of mist, Cain sensed a defeat he had not felt in many years. His victory celebration now deflated, he turned around to Jasher and muttered, "I would rather face the fog than to be with you one more moment than is necessary." He headed for the rigging, but suddenly turned and declared, "If I see you on the high seas, I will turn this scow into cordwood and kindling. Goodbye, Brother." Venomous sarcasm was all he could manage. With Cain, it seemed fitting.

Without another word, Cain threw himself over the side and clambered down the rigging spider-like to his frightened men still awaiting him in the longboat. As he dropped into the boat, he turned to the men and muttered, "Take me back to the ship." His command was obeyed in short order. As the men rowed out, each prayed desperately he was rowing northward into the swirling mist back to their ship. Cain looked up at Jasher with the deadly silence of hatred until the encroaching fog had suddenly consumed them. Finally, the rowers heard the cries of shipmates and cautiously rowed in that direction until all could board La Virgen. They would languish there impotently until the next day awaiting the mist to dissipate. Cain descended to his cabin and refused to come up until the weather was clear.

The rutter had again proved to be quite useful and as Archer had seen the fog rolling in, he had studied the diary with minute detail. Before the slowly drifting mist could reach them, he had turned the ship around and had positioned them in a northeasterly direction that would make them non-threatening to the frigates yet take them out of the bay away from them both. Besides, he realized that as long as Cain was aboard, the Spanish ships would not fire upon them. Once Cain and his launch had cleared the bow and had disappeared into the fog, he had the seamen pull up anchor and they quietly slipped out of danger. With eerie, tattering movements, the fog cleared ahead of *The Miriam* and the brig piloted by John Archer carefully pulled out of the bay. Within a mile the fog had mysteriously dissipated and the sky cleared. Once out onto the open sea, they caught an unexpected breeze and Archer had the crew open up the sails. With a steady tailwind, they made good time back to Puerto Rico.

In San Juan, the crew replenished stores and relaxed in preparation for the long voyage north and across the Atlantic. Miguel, the bosun renewed his acquaintance with Diego, the man he had known from Ceuta, and got some measure of revenge for the alleged insult he had received during their first meeting in the bar. And Archer did have his back.

It was also time to bid farewell to the interpreter, Manuel. Jasher had been true to his word and had bought a tobacco plantation then had placed his interpreter in complete control as chief foreman. Manuel, now the newest *patrón* in San Juan, walked with him out of the office of the banker then down to the end of the dock. The two men shook the other's hand and both said their good-byes with an *abrazo*, or embrace common to Hispanic friends.

"*Señor* Jasher, it was a pleasure to work with you. When can I expect to see you again?"

"Not for many years, I suspect. I have made arrangements with the local banker to oversee the financial concerns, so now you will have all you need to make it successful. May I suggest that at some point you consider as a business plan the diversion of our interests away from that of tobacco? In time, perhaps in the days of your grandsons, you will focus only on the production of sugar."

"Sugar? I have heard of it, but have never seen its manufacture. There is abundant sugar cane in the area, though. Do you foresee a time when sugar will become more important than tobacco?"

"Perhaps not more important, but certainly more rewarding. Think about it."

"I will." Manuel seemed to remember something he had witnessed and heard in the jungle during their mission. "Near my home at Lamanai, if what you said to the old *cacique*, Atlatl, was true, then you and I are also brothers?"

He looked at Manuel fondly and replied, "From the moment we met, Manuel, we have been brothers. Our family is ancient."

Manuel smiled at that and commented, "It is a shame that the Spaniards do not think so." As a fond afterthought he added, "*Adíos, mi Hermano.*"

"*Adíos*, Manuel." He turned and Jasher watched him walk down the dock alone then into the crowd to whatever pre-ordained destiny awaited him. He silently blessed the man and all those who would call him Brother; all except one anyway.

After Jasher had boarded *The Miriam* he met John on the quarterdeck and announced, "Master Pilot Archer, let us be off. England awaits us!"

Archer smiled and had to admit that Jasher was the most confident man he had ever met. There were still many leagues left to travel before they were outside of hostile waters, but he had to admit, the man's optimism was reassuring. Without a pause he answered, "Aye, sir, it will be a pleasure!"

It was a fine day for a long voyage home.

EPILOGUE, CYPRUS 2025

Benjamin Jasher was gazing thoughtfully at a Monet painting. A heightened air of suspense had settled heavily upon the two professors Bedford and Levinson as they settled comfortably into Spanish leather chairs and awaited the new developments that Jasher had decided to share. Turning toward the two men, he announced, "Gentlemen, it has come to my attention that a terrible tragedy has occurred and I felt that you both should be aware of it. It may require that we must adjust our time schedule. He sat down reluctantly on a nearby chair and leaned forward slightly and looking directly at the television mounted on the wall before them he said, "Television, ON. BBC International News." Immediately, the television responded. A news broadcast was in progress and all three men heard and witnessed the details of the tragedy over Crete in autostereoscopic 3-D clarity:

"This is Amanda Russell reporting live from Heraklion on the island of Crete. It has just been confirmed that this afternoon a jet airliner, an Airbus A320 flying out of Athens, Greece, experienced engine trouble a few miles off the island of Crete. Preliminary investigations have indicated that the plane exploded with a complete loss of life on board. Sources from Thomas-Reuters News Agency have confirmed that many of the passengers on that flight to the country of Cyprus were representatives of that agency. Had the accident not occurred, they and the remainder of the crew and passengers would have landed that afternoon

on Cyprus. There the news media passengers had scheduled a news conference with the international fugitive from the law, Benjamin Jasher. It has been confirmed that the Israeli fugitive Jasher would have provided the news media with a statement of his intentions, but as a result of the tragedy over Crete, that conference has been postponed indefinitely. Authorities on Crete have reported that it is too early to determine the cause of the explosion, but engine failure has been suspected. Coastal rescue officers are now sweeping the area around the region, but they hold out little hope of finding any survivors."

Isaac Levinson was the first to say anything. With a strained voice he asked, "Did we cause this tragedy, Jasher?"

"No, it was Cain. Now we must reconsider our strategy. How soon can we finish the final editing of *The Abridgment?*"

Both professors glanced at one another and nodded in silent agreement. Bedford declared, "Essentially, we have completed most of the translation; only slight editing remains. I would say another few days, a week at the most."

Isaac asked, "What options are still open for us?"

With a desperation that comes when all other options have run dry save one, Jasher replied, "There were only two venues that would have afforded us a degree of security and friendly support. I would have preferred to remain here on Cyprus, but if we remain here, there is a good chance now that we will never be permitted to make our full announcement to the world."

"What has changed?" asked Bedford, now concerned.

"It is quite likely we may have to flee to Israel for sanctuary. Cain's influence will be able to reach out as far as Cyprus and have us forcibly removed. When that occurs, we will likely be turned over to him, thus we will need to prepare an emergency exit plan from my estate. We must hurry. Since the records have been in the open, time has always been our enemy and Cain will not forget us or give us time to rest."

THE END

Preview, the Book of Jasher, Part 4

Fort Worth Town Marshall Jim Davis was sitting across the desk from his Deputy Tim Garner. Both were deep in concentration as they bent over the checker board in front of them. The deputy pondered his next move. Then suddenly, the Marshall grabbed a nearby newspaper and swatted at a couple of flies that had made the mistake of landing within his reach. Having killed them both with one swat, he hooted his victory, which further irritated the other man as he was about to make his move. The two had been playing another lively game of checkers for the past hour and the Marshall had his deputy dead to rights again; he was already gloating over his expected victory.

"Timmy Boy, you might as well give up, I've got you cornered and there's no place to run. That makes three games in a row. You and the flies just don't stand a chance today."

Tim Garner didn't like being called "Timmy Boy" and the Marshall knew it. Garner knew he was a better man, even on his worst day, than the Marshall who sat across the desk from him. He looked around the room, now distractedly, wishing mightily he was not in a subordinate position to Davis, but for now he would have to wait and bide his time. The elections were coming up soon and Deputy Garner planned to run against him and win. Then all this nonsense, the way the town was being run, would cease. The Marshall's voice was coarse, his eyes were rheumy and the aroma wafting from his body was ripe, all of which had begun to work on Garner's nerves. The heat had made the office oppressive and Tim suddenly felt confined, almost caged. The Deputy decided he needed a walk.

"I hear you, Jim. I think I'll go out and make the rounds."

Marshall Davis, now with a condescending grin of victory over his face, suggested, "Timmy, how 'bout you first start with the stock yards then end up in "Hell's Half Acre"? I'll meet you over there in a half hour."

Fort Worth was a cow-town and the Marshall was making reference to a strip not far from the stockyards comprising the largest collection of saloons, dance halls, and bawdy houses south of Dodge City, Kansas.

While Davis cleared the desk of the checker pieces, Garner grabbed his shotgun and hat then headed for the door. As the deputy opened the door on Main Street and looked out, a warm wind greeted him along with an unhealthy dose of trail dust. He blinked his eyes at the glare then noticed the barkeep of the Broken Saddle Saloon limping up the street in his direction. Close behind him could be seen a panicky rush of men streaming out in every direction coming from the direction of Hell's Half Acre. He turned to the Marshall and quietly commented, "Looks like trouble, Jim. Better grab your shotgun." Of course, both men were already wearing Colt Peacemakers in their holsters, but since nearly everyone these days carried one, the shotgun was the primary means of persuasion.

It was noon-day and the sun was already hot, the dust already kicking up dickens every time a man on horseback or leading a team from a wagon moved through the dingy street. Now with men running through the grit and stirring it up, the irritation was especially bad. Up ahead, Ellis Richards, proprietor of the Broken Saddle, could be seen half-running, half-limping down the street, waving his one good arm. He had shattered a knee-cap and lost an arm during the war. With what was left, the way he moved around was a sight to see, especially when he became agitated as he was now.

"Deputy Garner, there's a gun battle 'bout to happen in my saloon! You and the Marshall need to get a move on if you want to stop the massacre that I know's acomin'."

Marshall Davis had just reached the front door of the office when he heard the last remark from Richards. "Settle down Ellis, what's goin' on down there?"

"It's those Texas Rangers again, Marshall! They came into my saloon lookin' for trouble and tried to face off against some strangers who blew in from Missouri."

"From Missouri, did you say?"

"Well, they was tellin' stories 'bout how they was mixed up in the war up there; I guess that's where they're from."

Davis and Garner looked at one other and shook their heads. Davis grumbled, "Damn those Rangers. I wish the Governor would rehire 'em back and take 'em off my hands."

All three men set off quickly down the street hoping they could get there in time to break up whatever was about to happen in the saloon. They were half a block away from the doorway when they heard an explosion, probably a shotgun then the rapid fire of Colt handguns sounding off closely behind. The three men glanced quickly at one another; the Marshal cursed roundly under his breath. They picked up their pace, but by the time they reached the batwings to the saloon, the damage was done and the carnage was over.

Twenty minutes earlier, Samuel Jasher, Crow Daughdrell, and six ex-Rangers, John Lender, Hugh McClellan, Alex Rainer, Harvey Blackstone, Albert Nelson, and Matthew Dale all walked through the entrance to the Broken Saddle Saloon. The Rangers each wore rawhide chaps and silver spurs that clinked and spun as they stomped importantly across the wooden floor. As usual, Lender and Blackstone were complaining about the heat and dust and wishing they were somewhere farther east where it rained more often. Using their hands, they all dusted off the best they could and made their way casually inside then found seats near the bar. A few other patrons made note of their entry but said nothing. Nonetheless, respecting the Rangers' reputation for disturbances, they all kept a careful eye on them.

Nelson yelled at the bartender, "Ellis, bring us all a round of beers. We're in a celebratin' mood."

Ellis cleared his throat and asked, "Is that a Injun I see with you? You know I won't serve him, Albert."

Ellis was referring, of course, to Crow Daughdrell, a Paiute Indian that Sam Jasher had recruited in East Texas. He had joined the group and would act as tracker as well as guide for the upcoming trip to the West.

Albert Nelson looked balefully at the barkeep and barked, "You'll serve him now Ellis or I'll blow off your other kneecap so instead of gimpin' 'round on one leg, you'll have two crippled legs to keep company with your missin' arm."

Ellis got the message, said no more and brought the eight men drinks. He was careful not to meet their eyes as he served them. It was a fool who looked a wildcat in the eyes and he intended no more disrespect.

The five men standing at the bar had been in loud conversation when The Rangers and their group had entered the saloon, but had quieted to see what would transpire after the newcomers had been seated and their drinks served. When it appeared nothing more would happen, they resumed a discussion loudly enough for all to hear. The five men, Michael Parr, Hence Privin, John Maupin, Charles Higbee and Dock Corley all hailed from the state of Missouri and to hear them tell it, they had served proudly with William Quantrill during the War, which they referred to fondly as "the cause." They had already had a few beers, and more than a couple shots of whiskey, and were waxing eloquent with stories of glory and battle. Charles Higbee resumed his tale unaware that the ex-Rangers were listening attentively to every word he was saying.

"So, our patrol had been ridin' with "Bloody" Bill Anderson and Quantrill that day when we came into the town of Gallatin. After talkin' with a few of the locals, "Bloody" Bill decided there was far too many Yankee sympathizers in this Missouri town that mornin' and decided it was a good day to send 'em a message, Raider-style. Quantrill gave us the go-ahead so we fanned out through the town and pulled all the townspeople out of the stores and nearby houses and then pushed 'em all up against the side of the wall of the mercantile store. There must've been 'bout thirty people in all. All the men in town had already been conscripted and were fightin' somewheres back east, so all that was left was mostly old men, women and children. One old man actually had a baby in his arms and was on his knees beggin' for mercy." Higbee seemed to pause as if perplexed by this memory.

The expressions on the other men at the bar, however, were not of consternation but of anticipation of a punch-line of a potentially hilarious joke. Dock Corley, now smiling and knowing from personal experience of what was to come, encouraged him by saying, "Charley, I'll bet ol' "Bloody" Bill was laughin' out loud. Did he pull the trigger hisself on the old man?"

Now laughing, Charley replied, "You know he did, Dock. He walked right up to the old geezer, but instead of puttin' the barrel to him, he stuck it up to the eye of the baby, all the time the baby was cryin' and Bill was just laughin' to beat the devil. Bill pulled the trigger and the baby's head blew apart then the very same bullet went out the back of the baby's head and entered the old man's face right through his right eyeball. Bill turns around and says, "Boys, I got me a two-fer-one." Then we all let loose on the rest of 'em. It was a bad day for those Yankee-lovers in Gallatin that day."

The other men at the bar guffawed laughter at Charley's understated wit. Mike Parr, between gales of laughter, added, "That was a good one, Charley, but ya' know, that was just another day on the range. We've all done the same thing."

After the laughter died down a bit, a voice came from behind, "I'll just bet you have." It was John Lender, unofficial leader of the ex-Rangers.

All six ex-Rangers slowly stood up, the other two, Samuel Jasher and Crow Daughdrell, however, remained in their chairs. The two men still seated glanced worriedly at one another, both realizing they had walked into the middle of a reprise of the Civil War. All six ex-Rangers had fought the war for the South in the 1st Texas Infantry Regiment. Their battle campaigns had made them oblivious of fear; they all held the unanimous opinion that death no longer held any concern for them. They just didn't give a damn.

Samuel whispered to the Indian, "Crow, don't make any sudden moves, but get your gun ready."

Sam's shotgun was under the table and the moment the men stood up, Sam had pulled back the hammers on his shotgun and slowly pointed it toward the front of the bar. He dared not move it to the top of the table for fear of starting what he sincerely hoped would not occur. The other patrons, including the barkeep, had already decided that the inevitable was about to happen and they wanted to be somewhere else when it did. They all ran for the door and out to the street as fast as their feet could take them.

The five men at the bar slowly turned and took notice of the six men who had just sidled up next to them. They grinned oafishly as the saloon emptied of everyone except those thirteen men. All five of the Missourians slowly pulled back dusters they were wearing and exposed Colt .45 pistols ready to draw.

Bill W. Sanford is the author of the *Book of Jasher* series, in which he explores possible reasons why there are so few existing records for so many important historical events.

Sanford received his bachelor's degree from the University of Texas at Austin. He spent fourteen years as a schoolteacher. Sanford currently lives with his wife of twenty-four years in Grand Prairie, Texas.

Made in the USA
Lexington, KY
03 October 2018